The ~~Delicious~~
D...

JENNIFER HAYWARD

Llyfrgelloedd Caerdydd
www.caerdydd.gov.uk/llyfrgelloedd
Cardiff Libraries
www.cardiff.gov.uk/libraries

OMILLS

ACC. No: 05089119

First Published in Great Britain 2017
By Mills & Boon, an imprint of HarperCollins*Publishers*
1 London Bridge Street, London, SE1 9GF

THE DELICIOUS DE CAMPOS © 2017 Harlequin Books S. A.

The Divorce Party, An Exquisite Challenge and *The Truth About De Campo* were first published in Great Britain by Harlequin (UK) Limited.

The Divorce Party © 2013 Jennifer Drogell
An Exquisite Challenge © 2014 Jennifer Drogell
The Truth About De Campo © 2014 Jennifer Drogell

ISBN: 978-0-263-92978-2

05-0917

Our policy is to use papers that are natural, renewable and recyclable products and made from wood grown in sustainable forests.The logging and manufacturing processes conform to the legal environmental regulations of the country of origin.

Printed and bound in Spain
by CPI, Barcelona

Jennifer Hayward has been a fan of romance and adventure since filching her sister's Harlequin Presents novels to escape her teenage angst.

Jennifer penned her first romance at nineteen. When it was rejected, she bristled at her mother's suggestion that she needed more life experience. She went on to complete a journalism degree, before settling into a career in public relations. Years of working alongside powerful, charismatic CEOs and travelling the world provided perfect fodder for creating the arrogant alpha males she loves to write about.

A suitable amount of life experience under her belt, she sat down and conjured up the sexiest, most delicious Italian wine magnate she could imagine, had him make his biggest mistake and gave him a wife on the run. That story, THE DIVORCE PARTY, won her Harlequin's *So You Think You Can Write* contest and a book contract. Turns out Mother knew best.

A native of Canada's gorgeous east coast, Jennifer now lives in Toronto with her Viking husband and their young Viking-in-training. She considers the meetings of her ten-year-old book club, comprising some of the most amazing women she's ever met, as sacrosanct dates in her calendar. And some day they will have their monthly meeting at her fantasy beach house, waves lapping at their feet, wine glasses in hand.

You can find Jennifer on Facebook and Twitter.

THE DIVORCE PARTY

BY
JENNIFER HAYWARD

For my husband, Johan,
who gave me the chance to fly.

And Sharon Kendrick, Connie Flynn and Linda Style
for being the most amazing mentors a writer could have.

CHAPTER ONE

IT WAS GOING to be bad.

Lilly Anderson winced and put a hand to her pounding head. If she held herself in just that position, with the pressure building in her head like the vicious storms that picked up intensity across the plains of the midwest, it might not become a full-on migraine.

Might not.

Except staying in the dim confines of Riccardo's Rolls-Royce, driven by his long-time driver Tony, wasn't an option tonight. She was late for her own divorce party. Excessively late for the one thing that would give her what she wanted above all else. Her freedom from her husband.

"Oh, my God."

Her twin sister Alex made a sound low in her throat. "How can they print this stuff?"

"What?"

"Nothing."

"Alex, read it to me."

"It's Jay Kaiken's column. You don't want me to."

"Read it."

"Okay, but I warned you." She cleared her throat. "In what's expected to be the most scandalous, juiciest, talked-about water cooler event of the season, billionaire wine magnate Riccardo De Campo and former Iowa farmgirl-turned-sports-physiotherapist Lilly De Campo host their divorce party tonight. I once suggested they were the only passionately in love couple left in New York. But apparently even that fairytale doesn't actually exist. Rumors of heartthrob Riccardo's infidelity surfaced and this once solid marriage ended up in the toilet. So it's with mixed feelings that I bid this partnership adieu tonight. I have the invite and will bring you all the salacious details."

She crumpled up the tabloid and threw it on the floor. "He's such an SOB."

Lilly closed her eyes, a fresh wave of nausea rolling over her. No matter how many times she'd envisioned this moment, this freedom from Riccardo, she had never envisioned this. Nor the insanely mixed feelings she had right about now.

"Sorry, Lil. I shouldn't have started on those."

"You're a PR person, Alex. You're addicted."

"Still, I suck. I'm really sorry."

Lilly smoothed her fuchsia silk dress over her knees. It was elegant enough—and in Riccardo's most hated color, which was an added bonus—but it felt as if it was clinging in all the wrong places. A glance in the mirror before they'd left had told her she was paper-white, with dark bags under her hazel eyes. Haunted. In fact the only thing that *was* right was her hair, blowdried to glossy, straight perfection by her savior of a stylist.

It was a problem—this not feeling together. She felt she was already at a disadvantage. Facing Riccardo without her mask, without all her defences in place, was never a good way to start.

"You look a little too good," Alex murmured. "I think you should have put something frumpier on. And maybe messed your hair up a bit."

Lilly took the compliment and felt a bit better. Her sister was, if nothing else, the bluntest person she'd ever met. "Now, why would I do that?"

"Because Riccardo is like a banned substance for you,"

her sister said drily. "And your marriage almost destroyed you. Be ugly, Lilly, it's the easiest way."

Lilly smiled, then winced as her head did another inside-out throb. "He's finally agreed to give me the divorce. You should be doing a happy dance."

"If I thought he was giving in I might be. Has he given you the papers yet?"

"I'm hoping he'll do that tonight."

Alex scowled. "It's not like him to do this. He's up to something."

Her heart dropped about a thousand feet. "Maybe he's decided it's time to replace me."

"One can only hope."

A stab of pain lanced through her. She should be elated Riccardo had finally seen the light. Seen that there was no way they could ever reconcile after everything that had happened. So why had his decree that they finally end this with an official public announcement hit her with the force of an eighteen-wheeler? She certainly hadn't been pining away the past twelve months, hoping his refusal to divorce her meant he still loved her. And there was no way she'd harbored any silly notions that he was going to come climbing through her window and carry her back home, like in some Hollywood movie, with a promise to do everything differently.

That would have been stupid and naive.

She squared her shoulders. He likely did have another prospect in mind. Everything Riccardo did was a means to an end.

"If I ever want to be free to pursue a real relationship with Harry I need Riccardo's signature on that piece of paper."

"Oh, come on, Lil." Her sister's beautiful face twisted in a grimace. "Harry Taylor might be a decorated cardiothoracic surgeon, Doctors Without Borders and all that lovely stuff, but *really?* He's dull as dishwater. You might as well marry him and move back to Mason Hill."

"He's also handsome, smart and sweet," Lilly defended tartly, not needing to tell her sister there wasn't a hope in hell of her moving back to the miserable existence they'd escaped at eighteen. "I'm lucky to have him."

Alex waved a hand at her. "You can't tell me after Riccardo he doesn't seem like some watered-down version— like grape juice instead of Cabernet."

"You just told me Riccardo was bad news for me."

"So is Harry Taylor. He'll bore you to death."

Lilly had to steel herself not to laugh out loud, because that just would have hurt too much. "I'm through with men who make my heart pound and my palms go sweaty. It's self-destructive for me."

"The particular one you picked might have been... What time were we supposed to have been there, by the way?"

Lilly checked her watch. "A half-hour ago."

Alex gave her a wicked smile. "Riccardo's going to love that."

She squirmed in her seat. She was always late. No matter how hard she tried. Because it was just in her nature to try and squeeze too much into the day, and also because her multi-million-dollar athletes kept waltzing in half an hour late. But Riccardo had never seemed to care what the reason was. He wanted what he wanted when he wanted it. And that was all.

Alex's expression shifted. "I talked to David today."

Lilly froze. Alex talking to their brother back in Iowa only meant one thing. "How's Lisbeth?"

Alex frowned. "He said she had a really bad week. The doctor is saying she needs that experimental treatment within the next few months if it's going to do any good."

Dammit. Lilly twisted her hands together in her lap, feeling that familiar blanket of hopelessness settle over her. Her youngest sister Lisbeth had leukemia. She'd been told three months ago she was out of remission, and her doctor was advocating a ground-breaking new treatment as the one thing that might give her a fighting chance. But the treatment cost a fortune.

"I can't ask Riccardo for the money, Alex. I know it's crazy, but I can't give him that kind of power over me."

"I know." Alex put her hand over hers and squeezed. "We'll figure it out. There has to be a way."

Lilly pursed her lips. "I'm going to go back to the bank tomorrow. Maybe they'll let me do it in installments."

There had to be a way. Lisbeth *had* to get that treatment. Tonight, however, she had to focus on survival.

Her hands shook in her lap and her head throbbed like a jackhammer as they turned down a leafy, prestigious street toward the De Campo townhouse. She had taken one look at the beautiful old limestone mansion and fallen in love. Riccardo had taken one look at her face and bought it for her. "You love it," he'd said, not even blinking at the thirty-five-million-dollar price tag. "We'll buy it."

They swung to a halt in front of the home she'd run out of with only a suitcase twelve months ago, when she'd finally had the guts to leave him. It was the first time she'd been back and it occurred to her she was truly crazy making that time tonight. Divorce parties might be in vogue, but did she really want to detonate her and Riccardo's relationship in front of all the people who'd made her life miserable?

She didn't have a choice. She scooted over as Tony came around to open the door. Riccardo had been adamant. *"We need to end this standoff,"* he'd said. *"We need to make the state of our relationship official. Be there, Lilly, or this isn't happening."*

She forced herself to grasp Tony's hand. But her legs didn't seem to recognize the need to function as she stepped out of the car on trembling limbs that wanted to cave beneath her. The long, snakelike line of limousines made her suck in a breath. The memory of Riccardo sweeping her out of this car the night of their first anniversary and carrying her upstairs made it catch in her throat. He had made love to her with an intensity that night that had promised he would love her forever.

The images of the beginning and the end collided together in an almost blinding reminder of how quickly things could turn bad.

How hearts could be shattered.

"We can still turn around," her sister said quietly, coming to stand by her side. "If Riccardo really wants this divorce he'll come to you."

No, he wouldn't. Lilly shook her head. "I need to do this."

Do this and you won't ever have to live in a world you don't belong in again.

She walked woodenly up the front path alongside Alex. A dark-haired young man in a catering uniform opened the door and ushered them inside.

"How weird to have someone invite you into your own home," Alex whispered.

"It's not my home anymore."

But everything about it was. She couldn't help but stare up at the one-of-a-kind Italian cut-glass chandelier that was the centerpiece of the entryway. She and Riccardo had chosen it together on their honeymoon in the little town of Murano, famous for its glass. They had hand-picked a crystal to have their initials carved into, which had been placed on the bottom row. Riccardo had insisted on adding two entwined hearts beside their initials.

"It symbolizes us," he'd said. "We're no longer two separate people—we are one."

She lurched on her high heels, feeling whatever composure she'd had disintegrate. The urge to run far away from here as fast as she could was so overwhelming she could barely keep her feet planted on the floor.

"Lilly…" Alex murmured worriedly, her gaze on her face.

"I'm okay." She forced herself to smile at the young man offering to show them up the staircase to the ballroom. "We know the way."

She climbed the gleaming wooden staircase alongside Alex, her heartbeat accelerating with every step she took. By the time they'd reached the top of the stairs and turned toward the glimmering ballroom it was in her mouth.

You can do this. You've done this hundreds of times before.

Except Riccardo had been by her side then. A rock in a world that had never been hers. And tonight was the beginning of LAR—Life After Riccardo.

She paused at the entrance, taking in the glittering colors and jewels of the beautifully dressed crowd, set off by the muted glow of a dozen priceless antique chandeliers that dated back to the English Regency period. A jazz band played in the corner of the room, but the buzz of a hundred conversations rose above it.

Her back stiffened. She hated jazz. Was Riccardo trying to make a statement? To illustrate to her how he'd moved on?

Alex grabbed her arm and propelled her forward. "You need a drink."

Or ten, Lilly thought grimly as dozens of curious gazes turned on them and a buzz ran through the crowd. She switched herself on to autopilot—the only way she knew how to function in a situation like this—and started walking.

She lifted her chin when she saw Jay Kaiken and kept walking. As they moved toward the bar at the back of the room the strangest thing happened. Like the parting of the Red Sea, the crowd moved aside, dividing down the center of the room. On her left she recognized friends and acquaintances who had chosen to keep in touch with her rather than Riccardo after their separation. On her right she saw Riccardo's business associates, his brother, cousins and political contacts.

"It's like our wedding all over again," she breathed, remembering how she'd walked into that beautiful old Catholic cathedral on the Upper East Side to find her family and friends on one side—the neatly dressed, less-than-glamorous Iowa farm contingent alongside her girlfriends and schoolmates—and Riccardo's much larger, understatedly elegant clan on the other—all ancient bloodlines and aristocratic heritage.

As if their marriage was to be divided from the beginning.

Maybe that should have been her first clue.

She held her head high and kept walking. A tingle went down her spine. Her skin went cold. Riccardo was in the room. Watching her. She could feel it.

Turning her head, she found him—like a homing pigeon seeking its target. He looked furious. Seething. She swallowed hard, a flock of butterflies racing through her stomach. Riccardo spoke four languages—English, Spanish, German and his native Italian. But he did not have to utter a single word from those sensuous, dangerous lips for her to understand the emotion radiating from his eyes.

Hell. She touched her face in a nervous gesture that drew his gaze. Only Riccardo had ever been able to pull off that passionate intensity while still calling himself a twentieth-century man.

"Don't let him intimidate you," Alex murmured. "This is your divorce party, remember? Own it."

Easier in theory than in practice. Particularly so when Riccardo relieved a waiter of two glasses of champagne and strode toward them, with a look of intent on his face that shook her to her core. She absorbed this new Riccardo. He looked as indecently gorgeous as ever in a black tux that set off his dark good looks. But it was the hard edge to him that was different. The strongly carved lines of his face seemed to have deepened, harshened. He'd shaved off the thick, dark waves that had used to fall over his forehead in favor of a short buzz cut that made him look tougher, even more dangerously attractive if that was possible. And the ruthless expession on his face, the glitter in those dark eyes, had never been used on her quite like that before.

Her tongue cleaved to the roof of her mouth, her pulse picking up into a rapid, insistent rhythm that had her nails digging into her palms. Why, after everything they'd gone through, was he still the only man who could simply look at her and make her shake in her shoes?

Alex nudged her. "Dangerous controlled substance, remember?"

Lilly squared her shoulders and pulled in a deep breath as Riccardo stopped in front of them. He leaned down and brushed a kiss against her cheek. "Late and wearing pink. One would think you're deliberately trying to antagonize me, Lilly."

Her pulse sped into overdrive. "Maybe I'm celebrating my new-found freedom."

"Ah, but you don't have it yet," he countered, moving his lips to the other cheek. "And you aren't putting me in the kind of mood to grant it to you."

Lilly was aware of all the eyes on them as he pulled back and stung her face with a reprimanding look that made her feel like a fifth-grader. "Don't play games with me, Riccardo," she said quietly. "I will turn around and walk out of here so fast you won't know what hit you."

His dark eyes glinted. His mouth tipped up at the corners. "You've already done that, *tesoro,* and now you're back."

Something exploded in her head. She was about to tell him exactly what she thought of his ultimatum, but he was bending down and kissing Alex.

"*Buonasera.* I trust you're well?"

"Never better," Alex muttered.

"Do you think I might have a word with my wife alone?"

Wife. He'd said the word with such supreme confidence—a statement of fact that hung on the air between them like a challenge. A tremor went down Lilly's spine.

"Whatever you have to say you can say it in front of my sister."

"Not *this.*" His gaze bored into hers. "Unless you want every gossip columnist in New York reporting on our conversation, I suggest we do it in private."

Considering it was only in the last few months Lilly's name had finally *disappeared* from those columns, she conceded that might be a good idea. "Fine."

Riccardo turned to Alex. "Gabe is getting you a drink at the bar."

Alex rolled her eyes. "Determined to force a confrontation between all the members of the De Campo and Anderson families tonight?"

"You're only antagonistic toward the people who evoke strong emotions in you," Riccardo taunted. "Try not to rip him in two, will you?"

"You think that's a good idea?" Lilly murmured, more to distract herself from the warm pressure of Riccardo's big hand splayed against her back as he directed her from the room than out of concern for her sister, who could hold her own.

"They love baiting each other. It'll be the highlight of their evening."

She struggled to keep up with his long strides as he walked her up the stairs to the third floor, where the bedrooms were, nodding at the security guard stationed there. "Why are we coming up here?" she murmured, flushing at the guard's interested gaze. "Why don't we just talk in your study?"

He kept walking past the guest bedrooms toward the

master suite. "I won't risk being overheard. We'll talk on the patio off our bedroom."

"*Your* bedroom," Lilly corrected. "And I don't think—"

"*Basta,* Lilly." He glared at her. "I'm your husband, not some guy trying to come on to you."

Lilly clamped her mouth shut and followed him through the double doors of the master suite. She would not, whatever she did, look at the huge canopy bed they had shared. The scene of more erotically charged encounters than she cared to remember.

Their marriage bed. The place where she and Riccardo had always been able to communicate.

He pushed open the French doors to the large patio. The rose bushes he'd had planted for her along the edge had already started to bloom, emitting the gorgeous perfume she'd always loved.

Ugh. She shoved her sentimentality down with a determined effort and spun to face him.

"So?" she prompted, hostility edging her words. "What is it you have to say?"

His gaze darkened. "You're not too big for me to put you over my knee, *tesoro.* Push me a little harder and I will."

Lilly's cheeks burned at that very seductive image. To her horror, her mind took her there—took her to a vision of Riccardo holding her over his muscular thighs, her naked behind squirming as he brought his hand down in a stinging reprimand.

Dear God.

A satisfied expression crossed his face. "Unnerving, isn't it, that we only have to speak to each other in a certain way and that happens?"

"*Damn you,* Riccardo." She planted her feet wide and faced him head-on. "For over a year I've been trying to get you to give me a divorce and you've flatly denied it. Then you call me out of the blue with this crazy idea of making it official with a party, and now you're playing cat and mouse with me. What the hell are you playing at?"

He crossed his arms over his chest and leaned back against the railing. "Maybe if you'd agreed to see me I wouldn't have resorted to this."

"Nothing good ever comes of us being together. You know that."

His eyes glimmered as they swept over her. "That's a big fat lie and you know it."

She wrapped her arms around herself. "Sex is not a good basis for a marriage."

"We had more than sex, Lilly." His deep voice softened, taking on those velvet undertones that could make her melt in a nanosecond. "We had way, way more than that."

"It wasn't enough! Do you know how happy I've been this past year?"

He paled beneath his deep tan. "*We* were happy once."

She hugged her arms tighter around herself and fought the ache in her chest that threatened to consume her. "We're better off apart and you know it."

"I will never agree to that."

She lifted her chin. "I want a divorce. And if you won't give it to me I'll have my lawyer fight you until you do."

His mouth flattened. "I will drag it out for years."

"Why?" She pushed her hair out of her face and gave him a desperate look. "We're done. We've hurt each other enough for a lifetime. We need to move on with our lives."

He jammed his hands into his pockets. The fierce, fighting expression in his eyes was one she knew all too well. But he said nothing. Silence sceamed between them until she thought she'd jump out of her skin.

"All right."

She stared at him. "All right what?"

"I will give you the divorce. On one condition."

She knew she should leave now—get the hell out of here as fast as she could. But she couldn't force her feet to move.

"I need you to remain my wife for six more months."

Her jaw dropped open. "Wh-what?"

"My father feels I need to present a more grounded image to the board before they make their decision on a CEO." He lifted his shoulders and twisted his lips in a cynical smile. "They apparently still haven't bought my reformed image."

Lilly came crashing back to earth with the force of a meteorite bent on destruction. Any illusions she'd harbored—and she realized now she *had* harbored a few—about Riccardo not wanting to divorce her because he still loved her vanished at the point of impact. Something hot and bright burned the back of her eyes.

"That's ridiculous," she managed huskily. "You left racing three years ago."

He shrugged. "It is what it is. I can't change their perception."

Lilly almost choked on the irony of it. Everything Riccardo had ever done when they were together had been to dispel the image of himself as a reckless young racecar driver who hadn't been committed to the family business.

She shook her head. "Our *marriage* fell apart because of your obsession with your job. Your single-minded fixation on becoming CEO."

"One of any number of issues our marriage had," he corrected grimly. "Be that as it may, my father wants us back togther. He thinks the media coverage will go a long way toward stabilizing my image with the board, and he's made it a condition in my having his support."

His father wanted her back in his life? She'd always believed Antonio De Campo had thought her far beneath his son, with her poor upbringing, but he had been too polite to say it.

"My father thinks you're a good influence on me." He gave a wry half-smile that softened those newly hardened features of his. "He's quite likely right about that."

"This is crazy." Lillly shook her head and paced to the opposite end of the patio. "We aren't even *capable* of pretending we're a happily married couple."

"You have a short memory, Lilly."

His soft reprimand drew her gaze to his face.

"Six months. That's all I'm asking."

"I want a divorce," she repeated, raising her voice as this insane conversation kept plowing forward. "What makes you think I would ever consider helping you?"

He tilted his head to one side. "What are you afraid of? That we have way more unfinished business than you care to admit?"

She squared her shoulders. "We are over, Riccardo. And this is not a good idea."

"It's a great idea. Six months buys you your freedom."

"What other conditions has your father imposed?" she asked helplessly. "Are you to stop driving fast cars and dating international supermodels?"

He scowled. "Not one of those rumors are true. There's been no one since you."

She stiffened. "We all know there's truth to the tabloids."

"Not one, Lilly."

"*Riccardo,*" she said desperately. "No."

He stalked over, invading her space. "What is it, *tesoro?* Got plans with Harry Taylor?"

How did he know about Harry? They'd been so low-key as to be socially non-existent. "Yes," she snapped. "I'd like to move on, and maybe you should do the same."

He lifted his hand and took her chin in his fingers. "You forget we made a vow, *amore mio.* 'For richer and poorer, in sickness and in health...'"

"That was before you broke it."

A dangerous glimmer entered his eyes. "I never slept with Chelsea Tate. We've had this conversation."

"We are never going to agree on *that*," she bit out, throwing his words back at him. "Nor could we ever fake any real affection for each other. It would be laughable."

"Oh, but I think we could," he murmured, lowering his head to hers. "Even the thought of me spanking you turns you on."

She pulled out of his grip. "Riccardo—"

He slid a hand into her hair and brought her back. "You went there, Lilly. And so did I."

"No, I—"

He smothered her reply with a kiss Lilly felt down to her toes, deep and sensuous. He didn't bother with the pre-liminaries. He simply took—kissing her exactly the way he knew she liked it, using every weapon at his disposal. Lilly curled her fingers into his shirt, intending to push him away, but she didn't quite seem to be able to do it.

He pulled her closer, anchored her against him. "Ric—" she murmured as he changed angles and came back to her.

"Shut up, Lilly," he commanded, sliding his fingers up her bare arms and closing his mouth over hers.

This time his kiss was softer, more persuasive than con-trolling, pleasurable rather than punishing. And something fell apart inside her. It had been too long since he'd kissed her like this, too long since she'd been in his arms, and God help her...of all the things they had *not* been good at, it hadn't been this.

"Dammit." She grabbed a handful of shirt to steady herself. "This is not fair."

He slid a hand down over the curve of her hip and brought her body into full contact with his. The feel of his hard body against her made her shiver, remembering everything.

"Nothing was ever fair between us. It was like a wild rollercoaster ride we couldn't get enough of."

He shifted her between the hard muscles of his thighs and brought his mouth down on hers again with a look of pure intent. His rigid, pulsing arousal pressed against her, making Lilly ache all over.

No, an inner voice warned. But all that came out was a groan.

He dragged her even closer, a satisfied growl escaping his throat. "Open your mouth, Lil."

Caught up in the pure, hot sexual power he had over her, she obeyed. She didn't think about the one hundred and fifty people downstairs, or even what a huge mistake this was. She just wanted this kiss, this magic, the hot intimacy of his tongue tangling with hers.

Oh. She melted into him as her knees threatened to give way. It was like someone offering an alcoholic a double shot after months of abstinence. Pure hedonism. And she wrapped herself in it.

A flash of light exploded around them. She stumbled backward, disoriented, blinking into the bright light that kept coming and coming.

Riccardo cursed and pulled her away from the railing. "*Dio.* How did they get here?"

"A photographer?" Lilly asked dazedly.

He nodded.

She touched her fingers to her mouth, still burning from his kiss. Riccardo had security everywhere. It didn't make sense that a photographer would be able to get up here. "You planned that," she said flatly. "You set that up for your father's benefit."

"I set this party up for my father's benefit," he agreed darkly. "For the board's benefit. Not that photo."

She pressed her palms to her temples. She didn't want to be back here. She couldn't go on walking around like a half-alive person, going through the motions but never really feeling anything. She needed this divorce.

His face tightened. "What? Afraid the good doctor won't understand a six-month hiatus?"

She shook her head. "The answer is no. No, no and no."

He straighened his shirt and raked a hand through his hair. "We'll make the announcement at ten."

She turned her back on him and started for the door.

"I'll give you the house."

She stopped in her tracks.

"You've never wanted anything from me, but I know you love this house. I'll sign it over to you at the end of the six months."

Lilly opened her mouth to tell him where he could put his offer, but the words died in her mouth. The house would pay for Lisbeth's treatment. Fifty times over.

"Tempting, isn't it? Your dream house…without me in it?"

She counted to five before she turned around. As if any amount of money would be enough to convince her that revisitng their ruin of a marriage was worth it.

But she was desperate. And she didn't have the luxury of time.

She lifted her gaze to his. "I will think about it."

"Ten o'clock, Lilly." His smile didn't quite reach his eyes. "Think of yourself as Cinderella, only your deadline isn't midnight—it's ten. And I'm the devil you know."

CHAPTER TWO

LILLY SPENT THE intervening hours coming up with a million different reasons why she would be crazy to agree to Riccardo's proposal. He was once again using her in his single-minded pursuit of the De Campo CEO job. He didn't really want her—he wanted Lilly De Campo the figurehead, his perfect society wife who could smile and say intelligent things to the very intelligent people they met. And, dammit, her life was finally back on track! She had built up her practice, she had started to do the things she loved again, and she had a life.

Whether or not she was just going through the motions was irrelevant. She had been moving on.

Until that kiss tonight.

She touched her fingers to her mouth and tightness seized her chest. How could she kiss Riccardo like that when the same from Harry inspired only lukewarm affection?

"Which do you prefer, Lilly? Snakeskin or alligator?"

She gave the trendy young shoe designer who had cornered her and Alex a blank look. "Sorry?"

"I was asking if you prefer snakeskin or alligator... If I'd known you were doing this tonight I would have begged you to wear *my* shoes."

If *she'd* known she was doing this tonight she would be halfway across the Atlantic!

"Snakeskin, definitely," she murmured.

The other woman nodded and continued her relentless discussion of fashion.

She *would* be crazy to go back to Riccardo. But what choice did she have? The idea that the bank would lend her the money—more than she'd make in ten years of work—was laughable. Even in installments. Her parents were barely getting by on the farm, and although Alex had a great job with one of the city's top PR firms they would never, collectively, be able to scrape up that kind of money.

She had the power to help Lisbeth. Her stomach seemed to go into freefall at the thought of what that might entail. The question was, could she?

Alex gave her an *I need to talk to you* look and politely whisked her away from the designer. "People keep stealing you away," she hissed, dragging Lilly toward the windows. "What *did* he say to you?"

Lilly stared at her sister's flashing blue gaze—the only thing that differentiated them as twins. Her eyes were a mirror image of their sister Lisbeth's. And suddenly her guilt for never having been there for her younger sister made her next move crystal-clear.

She forced herself to smile. Riccardo had made it clear no one was to know about their deal. Not even family. There was too much of a chance for someone to say the wrong thing at the wrong time to the wrong person. The press would blow it wide open.

"We had a really good talk, Alex. I—"

The music stopped. She spun around to find Riccardo standing at the front of the room, his gaze trained on her. She swallowed hard as he nodded for her to join him.

Judgement time.

She steeled herself and raised a trembling hand to push her hair out of her face. "I'll explain afterward," she whispered to her sister. Then she walked to Riccardo's side.

Her presence there said everything.

A satisfied gleam lit her husband's eyes. He raised a hand to quiet the room. The elegantly dressed crowd fell silent as every eye moved to them and hushed anticipation blanketed the air. The first marriage in the history of the De Campo family to disintegrate. A golden couple at that.

She was distracted by a waitress, who presented a bottle for Riccardo's inspection. "The 1972 Chianti."

A 1972 Chianti? The same wine as on their wedding? Her gaze flew to her husband's, which was impaling hers with a burning darkness that seared her soul. He was really doing *this* to her?

What kind of a game was he playing?

The waitress passed each of them a glass of the ruby-red wine. Its deep, rich color was hypnotizing, reminding Lilly of the emotional blood the two of them had spilled. Her hands shook so much around the crystal she was terrified the wine was going to end up down the front of her dress.

Riccardo turned to face their guests, with a controlled, purposeful ease to his movements. "Lilly and I would like to thank you all for coming. You are our closest family, friends and acquaintances and we wanted you to be the first to share in our news."

He paused. The room grew so silent you could have heard a pin drop. Lilly's fingers tightened around the glass, her heart pounding in tandem with her head.

"Sometimes it takes a momentous occasion to bring true feelings to the surface." Riccardo returned his gaze to her face. "For Lilly and I, it took contemplating divorce to realize how much in love we still are."

A gasp rang out. Alex gaped at her from the front row, where she stood with Gabe.

Riccardo cast his gaze over the crowd. "Lilly and I are reconciling."

A shocked buzz filled the room—the sound of a hundred conversations starting at once. Flashbulbs exploded in her face. Hearing the words spoken out loud made her knees go weak. But she kept her gaze trained on her husband's and forced what might have passed for a smile to her lips.

Now her acting role began.

Riccardo tilted his glass toward her. "To new beginnings."

Lilly lifted the glass to her mouth and drank. Her lashes fluttered down over her cheeks as the heady, intoxicating flavor of the Chianti transported her back to the day when her life had seemed poised at the beginning of a rainbow that stretched forever.

The day she had married Riccardo.

And at that moment she knew her mistake for what it was. She had never been, and never would be, in control of her feelings for her husband. Six months wasn't just going to be self-destructive. There was going to be collateral damage.

Riccardo poured himself a two-finger measure of Scotch and sank down in the chair by the window, his gaze on his wife, who lay sleeping in their bed. She had swayed on her feet after the toast, her hands moving to her head in a warning sign that one of those migraines that had always terrified him was about to take her out. He was fairly sure she would have hit the deck had he not slid a subtle arm around her waist and hustled her from the room.

He had left Gabe in charge of winding up the evening and, although Alex had flatly refused to leave her sister, had overridden her and sent her home with his brother. There was still some of Lilly's migraine medication in their medicine cabinet and the key to these attacks, he knew, was to get it into her as soon as possible and put her to bed. Which he'd done—right after she'd been violently ill in their bathroom.

He took a sip of the smoky single malt blend and moved his gaze over her face. It was ghostly white and pinched even in sleep, and for a moment guilt rose up in him. He had dangled the one thing she loved more than anything else in front of her when he knew she wanted nothing to do with him. But then again, he thought, his lips twisting, she hadn't given him any warning when she'd walked out on him. When she'd called it quits on their marriage and left without even having the guts to face him.

A fury long dormant raged to life inside him, pulsing like an untamed beast. Who *did* that? Who took a perfectly good marriage with a few of the usual speed bumps and just quit? Who thought so little of what she had that it was easier to turn into an ice queen and refuse him than to talk it out?

The woman who'd turned into a stranger before his very eyes. The woman who'd taken a lover—a world-renowned cardiothoracic surgeon so highly decorated for his work that he made Riccardo look like the most heartless of corporate raiders. That was who.

His fingers tightened around the glass, drawing his gaze to the fiery amber liquid. No, he wouldn't feel any regret. His wife might have looked at him with those accusing, pain-soaked cat's eyes of hers and begged him to let her go home. But he was through giving her time and space to come to her senses. She was back in his bed, where she belonged, and she was staying there.

Not for six months.

For good.

He lifted the glass to his lips and let the Scotch burn a path down his throat. It had been that conversation he'd overheard that had set him off. Not his father's bullish suggestion that he repair his marriage in order to present the kind of image the De Campo board was looking for in a CEO.

The trash-talking locker room chatter he'd heard on his way out of the gym after a squash game with Gabe had amused him at first. There were things guys said in a locker room that were never repeated outside of them. He had smiled, remembering the crude conversations he and his fellow drivers had had after their races, when all the tension was gone, and then started packing up his stuff. But the conversation had turned to injuries and rehabilitation and he'd heard Lilly's name.

He'd pulled the zipper shut on his bag and had frozen in place as the three men he'd figured must be professional athletes from their height and brawn, went on.

"She's the best there is," one of them had said. "Fixed my bum leg in a month."

"Seriously hot," added one of the others. "I bet you'd like to have more than her hands on you."

He'd been halfway across the room before Gabe had intercepted him and shoved him bodily out the door.

"Not worth it," his brother had muttered. "She's your estranged wife, remember?"

But it had been too much. *Troppo.* It was time Lilly remembered who she was. Who she belonged to.

He skimmed his gaze over her still form. If anything, she had grown more beautiful since that day he'd bumped into her in that SoHo bar. She'd reminded him of a young colt, tripping over those long legs of hers, over *him,* as he'd stopped to put his wallet back in his pocket. She'd apologized, biting her lip in that trademark gesture of hers, and everything about her—her beautiful shoulder-length glossy brown hair, her big hazel eyes and her air of extreme innocence—had knocked him sideways. He wasn't used to women without artifice. And it had made him want to possess her like no other.

He hadn't let her leave the bar until he'd had her reluctantly given number. Then he'd pursued her, called her every day for a week, until she'd agreed to go out with him.

Finding out she was a virgin had been the end for him. He'd put a ring on her finger the week after.

She shifted restlessly onto her back and rubbed her hand against her face. Her vulnerability hit him like a punch to the chest. Lilly was different from any other woman he'd met. She hadn't been attracted to his power or money. In fact it had made her distinctly uncomfortable, given her poor upbringing. But he'd pushed his agenda through anyway, like the big, forceful bull of a man he was. Because that was what a De Campo did. Took what he wanted. Success at all costs.

Lilly fought her way out of the drug-induced fog that held her under, reaching desperately for the glass of water she kept on the nightstand. But her hand grasped only air, and this didn't feel like her bed. It felt bigger, softer, familiar and yet...

It was her old bed.

She bolted upright.

"Here—drink," a husky, fatigue-deepened male voice urged, pressing a glass to her lips.

A strong arm slid around her waist. She blinked and opened her eyes and stared straight into the worried dark-as-night gaze of her husband.

Oh, God. She was in bed with Riccardo.

She pushed the glass away and pulled, panicked, at the sheets.

"Lilly." He placed firm hands on her shoulders and held her down. "Drink for *God's* sake. Those pills are always rough on you."

She shook her head and reached for the side of the bed, but a series of wheezing coughs racked her body. She reached desperately for the glass and drank greedily. Her thirst quenched, she pushed the glass away. "What time is it?"

"One a.m."

A dull, deep throb at the front of her head made her sit back against the pillows. "I want to go home."

"You are home," he said quietly. "Stay in the bed, Lilly. You're in no shape to be going anywhere."

It was then that she realized he was still fully dressed. Hazy memories filled her head. Him holding her hair out of her face while she vomited. Him carrying her to bed. Her cheeks heated with mortification. *She needed to get out of here.*

"My home is my apartment." She swung her legs over the side of the bed, wincing as the movement made her head throb. *Her legs were bare.* And she was drowning in one of Riccardo's white T-shirts. "Did you *undress* me?" she demanded, flicking him an accusing look.

An amused glitter flashed in his eyes. "That's the way it's usually done, *tesoro,* but I stopped at the underwear. I prefer to dispense of that when you're fully conscious."

Her face felt as if it was on fire. She scanned the floor desperately for her things. "Give me my goddamned clothes, Riccardo."

His expression hardened. "Are you forgetting our deal? You live here now. You're mine for six months."

"*Tu sei pazzo,*" she spat at him. "I might have agreed to your crazy plan, but in no way, shape or form will your hands ever be on me again."

"*Tu sei pazzo?*" he murmured appreciatively. "I do believe your Italian's coming along. And, yes, I am crazy when it comes to you." He gently pushed against her shoulders and sent her back into the soft pillows. "Tomorrow we go over the ground rules. Tonight you rest."

"You are such a bully," she muttered wrathfully, too weak to defy him. "I have an early clinic tomorrow."

"I'll drive you there. You still have some clothes in the spare room you can wear."

He'd kept them? She'd left in such a hurry she'd taken only what would fit in a suitcase. Left all the beautiful gowns and jewelry behind.

"Yes, I kept them," he murmured, a bitter smile curving his lips. "Unlike you, I didn't give up on this marriage."

She closed her eyes. "You have no idea what you're talking about, Riccardo."

"Maybe you can enlighten me over the next six months, then. You never did grace me with an explanation."

Her gaze met his with blazing fury. "You never wanted to hear what I had to say."

The belligerent tilt of his chin matched hers. "Maybe now I do."

And maybe there was a blue-cheese moon out there tonight.

A jagged pain whizzed through her head. She winced and held a hand to her temple.

"*Hell*, Lilly," he bit out, waving a hand at her. "We're done arguing. Close your eyes and go to sleep."

She tried to fight it, but nature was having none of it. He tucked the covers up to her chin, then everything went black.

CHAPTER THREE

SEVEN HOURS OF sleep, one migraine-hangover-filled morning, three patients and one trip to the bank later, Lilly retreated to her office like a maimed fighter who'd escaped to her corner.

Coffee, she decided, setting her briefcase down. It was time to reintroduce the other banned substance in her life. Maybe it would help lift the paralysis that had gripped her since she'd woken up in her old bed this morning, dazed and confused at what had transpired.

She had agreed to become Mrs. Lilly De Campo again. The one thing she'd said she'd never do.

Worse, she'd let her husband see how deep her feelings ran. Distracted, she raised a hand to her hair and pushed it out of her face. The power Riccardo still held over her was disconcerting.

And *that* was the understatement of the year. She pressed her lips together, picked up her purse and let Katy, the receptionist at the small clinic she shared with another physiotherapist in SoHo, know she'd be in the café across the street. Scanning the menu board, she thought, *To hell with it,* and ordered the largest, creamiest latte they had, which would certainly knock her brain back into working order, and sat down to drink it in the window facing Broadway.

It helped. But with her escape hatch rapidly closing it was a case of avoiding the unavoidable. Her only alternative to accepting Riccardo's deal had been to secure the money at the bank. And she was pretty sure the bank manager would have laughed at her request if she hadn't officially reinstated her position as Mrs. Lilly De Campo by having it splashed across the morning papers.

She'd been getting to her feet when he'd given her a curious look and said, "Your husband is also a client, Mrs. De Campo. We'd be happy to draw up the papers with *him*."

She had given him a withering look. "No, thank you, Mr. Brooks. This is a personal matter."

He was an opportunist, she conceded, scraping the froth off the sides of her mug. Like almost everyone else in this city. Unfortunately Harry Taylor had also seen the news, if his multiple calls to her cell phone were any indication. A stomach-churning glance at her phone revealed she now had a message from him too. The latte seemed to curdle inside her. She'd been waiting, hoping there was some other solution that would allow her to call things off with Riccardo.

And who are you trying to fool? a voice inside her ridiculed. Their reconciliation was the subject of intense public speculation this morning. There was no getting out of it. And how could she when it was Lisbeth's only chance at survival?

She squirmed on the stool. What *was* she going to say to Harry? *I'm so sorry, Harry. I've gotten back together with the man who destroyed me?* Or, *I'm sorry for saying I wanted you when really I want my sexy, controlling somewhat ex-husband, who kissed me within an inch of my life last night and made me want more.*

Ugh. There was no good way to put it that wouldn't end up making her look like a horrible, horrible woman.

The café door chimed. She looked up to see the *other* person she was trying to avoid waltzing through the door.

"You really didn't think you could hide, did you?" Alex

asked grimly, tossing an order at the barista and plopping herself down on the stool beside her.

Lilly pushed her empty mug away. "I'm not avoiding you. I had a jam-packed morning."

Alex's eyebrows rose. "I'm your twin, remember? I can sense inner turmoil."

"I'm fine. Just a little groggy from the medication."

"Good." Her sister threw the words at her with a determined tilt of her chin. "So you can tell me what the hell's going on. Your autocratic husband ordered me out of the house before I could see if you'd actually lost your senses."

Lilly pulled in a breath. "It was like Riccardo said. It took a tough conversation for us to realize our feelings for each other."

Alex sat back in her chair and crossed her arms. "*Do not* try to spin me, Lilly. I know you too well. You walked in there last night intent on a divorce. What happened?"

"We talked…we came to some realizations…"

"Like what?" Alex waved her hand in the air. "Like the last hellish year of your marriage was just an apparition? Like he didn't almost annihilate you?"

"It takes two to tango," Lilly murmured. "Riccardo wasn't the only guilty party in our marriage."

"Only the majority holder." Her sister screwed up her face. "What about Harry? Last night you were telling me he's the one."

"I didn't say that. I said I wanted the opportunity to truly pursue things with him." She bit her lip, realizing how confused that sounded. *Dammit, she needed to make this believable. For Lisbeth's sake.*

"You know I've never really stopped loving Riccardo," she said quietly. And the fact that saying it didn't seem like too much of a stretch shook her to her core. "I want to give it another shot."

Alex's mouth tightened. "You left him to save yourself. And I for one don't relish being the one to pick up the pieces again when he reverts to being his domineering, controlling self."

"He's changed," Lilly lied.

"Men like him don't change. They come out of the womb like that."

Her mouth curved. "Probably true."

"What about his infidelity? Are you prepared to put up with that again?"

Everything around her faded, blurred into the series of carefully manufactured images she had created to keep herself in one piece. Control. Because to imagine Riccardo in bed with another woman—to imagine the man who'd promised to love her for life doing that to her—would damage her beyond repair.

"It won't happen again."

"How do you know?"

"Because he promised me."

In actual fact Riccardo had denied the whole thing. He'd put it down to the vicious money-making tactics of the tabloids. But Lilly had seen the photos. And photos didn't lie.

Her teeth clamped down on her bottom lip. The effort it took not to blurt out what was actually going on was immense. "You have to trust me," she forced out huskily. "I'm doing the right thing."

Her sister gave her a long, hard look. "You promise if things start to get bad you'll end it? You'll walk away?"

"I promise. And, Alex—this means we can get Lisbeth's treatment."

A light went on in her sister's cornflower-blue eyes. "Lilly Anderson, you promise me right now you are *not* doing this because of Lisbeth. I do *not* need two sisters in critical condition."

"I wouldn't do that," Lilly said firmly. "It's just a very wonderful outcome of this decision."

But she would. She would do anything it took to make Lisbeth well.

* * *

Riccardo came to pick her up at six. "You still don't look good," he said bluntly as she slid into his beast of a car.

She shrugged and pulled her seatbelt on. "You know what my migraines are like. It takes me a few days to get over one."

He put the car in gear and pulled out into traffic, the low-slung powerful machine reminding her of the man himself. Smooth, dangerous.

He flicked her a glance. "I'd forgotten just how bad they get."

She wondered if he'd done what she had. Used any method available to wipe her head clean of him—finding it impossible on so many levels.

Don't fool yourself, Lil. Riccardo wasn't the type to pine for anyone. Especially the woman who'd walked out on him.

Which begged the question: why hadn't he had other women over the past year? If she was to believe the highly sexed man she'd married was capable of celibacy, the question was why had he chosen it? Riccardo loved women. He lived for the contrast. Hard versus soft. Rational versus emotional. And with his superstar racing background they were like a feast that had been put on this earth for him to enjoy in endless supply.

She had fooled herself that she could be the only one for him.

She twisted her hands together in her lap and stared sightlessly out the window. They drove in a tense silence until he passed her street.

"What about my apartment? I need to get my stuff."

"I sent Mrs. Collins over to pick it up."

Her jaw dropped. He'd had Magda go through her stuff? Sift through the very fiber of her personal life?

"Stop the car."

He frowned over at her. "Lilly, it was—"

"Stop the car."

He swore under his breath and pulled to the curb. "It was the efficient way to get it done."

"Efficient?" she demanded, her voice shaking with anger. "You violated my privacy. My God, how did you even get in to my apartment?"

"I was the one who had the locks installed for you. You're overreacting, Lilly."

She clenched her hands in her lap for fear she might slap his handsome face. He'd pretended to be worried about the dismal state of the locks on her front door and had insisted on having them changed and a deadbolt added. She'd been grateful at the time, because in New York a solid set of locks was never a bad idea. But really it had just been another of his attempts to control her.

"You did that so you could spy on me," she hissed, pressing her head back against the seat. "How could I be so stu—"

"Stop." His eyes blazed into hers. His bronzed skin was pulled taut across his cheekbones. "You know I have security on you. You are still my wife and, like it or not, there are people out there who itch to get their hands on you. But I have never, *ever* spied on you."

"You knew about Harry."

"I *saw* you with Harry. You were eating at Nevaros the same night I was."

"You didn't introduce yourself."

"And say what? *How do you find my wife in bed? What would you rate her out of ten?*"

Her breath caught in her throat. "This is not going to work."

"You agreed to the bargain. You're my wife for the next six months. Deal with it."

She closed her eyes and pressed her palms against her thighs, forcing herself to take deep breaths. If she was to survive the next six months without having to go into emotional rehab she was going to have to learn to control her emotions.

She turned her gaze on him—defiant hazel on arrogant black. "Ground rule number one. You don't *ever* go into my apartment again without my permission and you do *not* enable someone to go through my personal possessions."

He nodded. *"Bene."*

Shocked at how easily he'd acquiesced, she kept going. "I want to go to my apartment now."

"Why?"

"Because I doubt Mrs. Collins packed my book. Or brought my two violets with her. And there's a few things I don't want hanging around."

"Like the sex toys you use with Harry?" he taunted.

"Why, yes. Harry knows how to keep things interesting."

He froze.

Her fingers curled around the door handle.

In a lightning-fast movement his hand slammed down on top of hers. "You know what a comment like that does to a guy like me, Lilly. Are you looking for me to up the ante? Because I can assure you Taylor doesn't make you scream like I do."

Lilly slunk back in her seat, her heart hammering in her chest.

He lifted his hand away from hers and returned it to the wheel. "Choose your fights carefully, *tesoro*. You know how many times you've won."

Never. She never won against Riccardo because he was too strong, too smart, and he knew her too well ever to let it happen.

They didn't speak during their brief stopover at her apartment, nor on the drive to the house.

Magda enveloped her in a warm hug when they walked through the door and told them dinner was ready when they were. Lilly went upstairs to change.

Riccardo was waiting for her in the small, private dining room when she came down. Magda had closed the doors to the terrace as the chill of the early May evening set in, and lit candles on the table in the warm dark-floored room with its elegant white wainscoting and glowing sconces. For a moment she stood standing in the entranceway, a sharp little pain tugging at her insides. She had been so desperate for her husband's attention in the latter days of their marriage that all she had dreamed about was coming home to a meal like this with him.

She took him in as he opened a bottle of wine, his muscular forearms flexing in the candlelight as he worked the cork out of the bottle. He hadn't bothered to change, but had taken off his suit jacket and tie and rolled his shirtsleeves up. In charcoal-gray trousers and white shirt he looked better than any man had a right to look. They molded his leanly muscular body into a work of art. She sank her teeth into her bottom lip. Women actually stopped in the street to stare at her husband. He was just *that* good-looking. In the beginning she hadn't minded, because she'd known she had him and they didn't.

In the end it had been crucifying.

Her gaze slid up to his face. He was watching her, the bottle in his hands, his dark eyes seeming to reach inside of her and read her every emotion. She shifted her weight to the other foot and stood her ground. Six-foot-four and broad-shouldered, he made the room seem stiflingly small.

He'd always been vastly intimidating. Except when he'd been naked beneath her. Those times *she* had been in control—her thighs straddling all that golden muscular flesh, his taut, powerful body beneath her tense, begging her for the release that had always bordered on the spiritual with them.

A glint entered his dark eyes. Her lashes swept down over hers. *What in God's name was she doing?*

"Rule number two, *cara*," he murmured. "No looking at me like that unless you intend to follow through with it."

Wildfire raced to her cheeks. *Dammit.* She walked jerkily across to him and took the glass of wine he'd poured.

Magda came in with their salads, her round face beaming. "How nice to see the two of you sitting down to a meal together."

"Yes, what a novelty," Lilly agreed. "I hardly remember how to converse."

Magda gave her a wary look, told them the casserole was in the oven and left.

"You will curb your tongue when others are around," Riccardo said curtly when the housekeeper was safely out of earshot. "Our deal depends on us being discreet."

"You liked it in the bedroom," she taunted.

"Right on the money, *tesoro,*" he agreed, showing his teeth. "Knock yourself out."

She shrugged. "Since we won't be sharing a bedroom, I'll pass."

He took a sip of his wine, then lowered the glass with a slow, deliberate movement. "Here I am, speaking *your* native language, and still you don't get it."

"Get what?"

"We need to make this authentic, Lilly. We *will* be sharing a bedroom."

Her stomach dissolved into a ball of nerves. There was absolutely no way, with all the rooms in this house, that she was sharing *that* bedroom with *him*.

"Magda is completely trustworthy. There is no need to—"

"This isn't up for debate." He leaned back against the sideboard and crossed his arms over his chest. "Eyes are everywhere. People traipse through this house on a daily basis."

Lilly gave him a desperate look. "But I—"

"Rule number three." He kept going like a train, steamrollering right over her. "You will accompany me to all the social engagements I'm committed to over the next six months, and if I need to travel you'll do that too."

"I have patients who count on me, Riccardo. I can't just pick up and travel at will."

He shrugged. "Then you work around it. Our first engagement, by the way, is Saturday. It's a charitable thing for breast cancer."

She bit back the primal urge to scream that was surging against the back of her throat. She had a career, for God's sake. Responsibilities. And no wardrobe for a charity event. She was at least ten pounds heavier than she'd been when she'd been with Riccardo. None of her gowns upstairs would fit, and nothing she'd been wearing in her low-key life since then would be appropriate.

"Oh," he added, almost as an afterthought. "It's a fashion thing. They called today to ask if you'd model a gown when they heard our news."

She felt the blood drain from her face. "On a stage?"

"That's usually how they would do it, isn't it?"

The thought of modeling a gown in front of all those people with her new, curvier figure sent a sharp response tumbling out of her. "No."

He frowned. "What do you mean, no? It's for a good cause."

"Then *you* get up there and do it."

His gaze darkened. "Are you going to fight me on everything?"

"When you ask me to get up on a stage and parade myself around in front of a bunch of people when you know I hate that stuff, *yes*."

He tipped his head to one side. "You're a beautiful woman, Lilly. I never understood why you were so insecure."

And he never would. He had no clue how deep her insecurities ran. The demons she'd finally put to rest. And that was the way she preferred to keep it. Weakness left you vulnerable. Exposed. Open for people to pick at and slowly destroy you.

"I won't do it."

"You will," he returned grimly. "Ground rule number four. You will have no further contact with Harry Taylor."

The man she still hadn't had the guts to call back yet. "I have to talk to him. He's been trying to call me and he sounds—"

"Trying?" He lifted a brow. "I see your old patterns of avoidance haven't changed."

"Go to hell," she muttered. "You sandbagged me with this last night. I need a chance to explain it to him."

"One conversation, Lilly. And if I find out you've seen him after that—if I find out you've even chatted with him in the hallway—our agreement will be null and void."

It was fine for *him* to cheat in the public eye but when it came to her the same rules didn't apply!

He flicked a hand at her. "It's not like it should be a tough call, ending things. Or have you become such a tease you can kiss a man like you did me last night and still go back for more?"

She shook her head. "You're such a bastard sometimes."

A savage smile curled his lips. "You like it when I'm a son-of-a-bitch, *amore mio*. It excites you."

She turned her back on him before she said something she'd regret. She'd loved that about him in the beginning. That he'd called the shots and all she'd had to do was sit back and enjoy the ride. For a girl who'd been taking care of herself most of her life it had been a relief. An escape from the hand-to-mouth existence that had seen her work two jobs to put herself through college and graduate school to supplement the scholarship she'd won.

What she hadn't been prepared for was the flashy, no-end-to-the-riches lifestyle he'd dropped her into with no preparation, no defences for a girl from Iowa who'd never really grown into the hard-edged, sink-or-swim Manhattan way of life.

It had been her downfall. Her inability to cope.

"Ground rule number five," he continued softly. "You and I are going to be the old Riccardo and Lilly. The perfect couple. We're going to act madly in love, there will be no other men, and when you get weak and can't stand it anymore you'll come to me." He paused and flashed a superior smile. "I give you a week, max."

She spun around to face him, her gaze clashing with his. "I'm not the same person I was, Riccardo. You won't find me groveling at your feet for attention. And you won't walk all over me like you did before. You treat me as an equal or I'll leave and blow this deal to smithereens."

He lifted his elegant shoulders, as if he found her little outburst amusing. "But you want this house. Badly... I saw it in your eyes last night."

For a reason entirely other than what you think.

"Are you finished?" she asked quietly. "Because I suddenly seem to have lost my appetite. I'm going to go make sense of my stuff upstairs."

His gaze narrowed on her face. "Don't make yourself into a martyr. I've had enough of that to last a lifetime."

She lifted her chin. "Martyrs die for their cause. When this is over I'll be free of you. Eternally happy is more like it."

Lilly took her time unpacking her things, her arms curiously heavy as she hung her delicate pieces on hangers in the huge walk-in closet. Every item she unpacked was an effort, and her stomach was growing tighter with each piece she added with her usual military precision. Sweaters with sweaters, blouses with blouses, pants with pants. It was as if her old life was reappearing in front of her hanger by hanger, row by row.

And there was nothing she could do to stop it.

She'd said she'd never come back. What the hell was she doing?

She plunged on, doggedly working until everything was in its place. Then, when she was sure Riccardo was working in his study—which he undoubtedly would be until midnight—she slipped downstairs and made herself a snack. She wasn't remotely hungry, but skipping meals was a warning signal for her. She put some cheese and crackers on a plate, poured herself a glass of wine and took it to bed.

She had finished her snack and read about half a chapter of her supposedly scintillating book when her husband walked through the door. *It was only just past eleven. What was he doing?*

"You're coming to bed?"

A mocking smile twisted his mouth. "That's what it looks like, no?"

She shifted uncomfortably. "You usually work later than this."

"Maybe having my beautiful bride back in my bed is a draw."

Heat flared in her cheeks at the sarcasm in his voice. "As if," she muttered under her breath.

"What?"

"Nothing."

He flicked her a glance. "Mumbling is rude, Lilly. If you have something to say, say it."

She stuck her nose in her book. She didn't have to play this game. Except it was impossible not to sneak a glance at his bronzed, muscled chest as he whipped his shirt off. In keeping with his new harsher haircut, his body seemed even harder than before. As if someone had taken a chisel and worked away the remaining minute amounts of excess flesh until all that was left was smooth, hard, defined muscle, tapering down to that six pack she loved.

Hell. She buried her face back in her book. The rasp of his zipper and the sound of his pants hitting the floor had her desperately reading the same sentence over and over. His boxers flew across the room and landed in the hamper. Her breath seized in her throat. *She would not—would not—look.*

She took a deep breath as he sauntered into the bathroom and shut the door. Her passing out moment last night had meant she hadn't seen any of *that.* Her hectic pulse indicated she hadn't gotten any more immune to the show in the past twelve months.

This was just *so* not good it was laughable. No wonder she hadn't come near him in months. Because *this* happened.

She'd made it through a miraculous two pages when her husband emerged from the bathroom, the smell of his spicy aftershave filling her nostrils. A flash of skin in her peripheral vision revealed he hadn't lost his predisposition for sleeping in the nude.

She took another of those steadying breaths as he walked around the bed to his side, but all that did was overwhelm her with the cologne some manufacturer had for sure pumped full of every pheromone in the book. The bed dipped as the owner of the pheromones whipped the sheets back and got in. She made a grab for the material, feeling far too exposed in her short silk nightie, but not before her husband swept his eyes over her in a mocking perusal. She gritted her teeth and pulled the sheets up high over her chest.

Her husband's rich, deep laughter made her grit her teeth even harder. "I saw it all last night, Lil, and I have to say I like the changes. You look like a properly voluptuous Italian woman now. Your breasts are fabulous—and those hips..." He sat back against the headboard, a wicked smile pulling at the corner of his lips. "Without a doubt my favorite spot on a woman's body. That curve near the hipbone you can slide your hand over, and—"

"*Stop.*" She flashed him a murderous look. "I may be

living with you for six months but these—these types of conversations are *not* happening."

He lifted his shoulders and pursed his lips. "This is the point where you'd usually freeze me out anyway."

She flinched. "It was always about sex. Sometimes I actually wanted to communicate."

"That's where men and women differ," he drawled. "When we're stressed we crave sex. It's the way *we* communicate."

"It was the *only* way you communicated. Too bad it wasn't conducive to working out our problems."

His face hardened. "You didn't want to work them out. You checked out, Lilly. You wanted us to fail."

"I wanted us to *work*." She blinked back the emotion stinging her eyes. "But we were light years apart. And we always have been. We were just too stupid to realize it."

He reached over and grabbed the book, tossing it on his bedside table. "You haven't read a thing since I walked into this room, *cara*. You're so busy trying to deny what's between us that you can't see a foot in front of you. That isn't light years apart—that's total avoidance."

"The easier way," she flashed. "Because we both know how it ends."

She took satisfaction in the frustrated flash of his eyes before she turned away from him and doused the light, curling up as far away from him as she could in the big king-sized bed. It was still impossible to ignore his presence. His warmth, his still, even breathing was everywhere around her.

She curled her fingers into the sheets and focused on keeping it together, shocked by the need, the almost physical ache for him to reach out and comfort her in the way he always had. When Riccardo had made love to her she had always known where his heart was. The problem had been when the cold light of day had dawned and their problems hadn't gone away.

She squeezed her eyes shut. Tomorrow she had to tell Harry it was over between them. It should have been a horrible thing to have to do. But with Riccardo back in her life, bearing down on her like a massive all-consuming storm, she knew her relationship with Harry was doomed.

There had only ever been one man who'd had her heart. Too bad he hadn't been worthy of it.

CHAPTER FOUR

RICCARDO WOKE UP Saturday morning with the need to hit something. To flatten something. Anything that got rid of the tension sitting low in his belly after he'd been jarred awake by some fool's motorcycle racing down the street.

Eternally happy. His wife's words echoed through his head, made worse by the paper-white state of her face when she'd returned home last night after ending things with Taylor.

He wanted to put a fist through the doctor's face.

He rolled over to glare at her, but there was only an imprint in the pillow where her head had been. Lilly? Out of bed before him? She liked to sleep more than any human being he knew.

He flicked a glance at the clock on the bedside table, his eyes widening as he read the neon green numbers. *Eight-thirty.* That couldn't be right. Sure, he was tired, because his wife was driving him crazy, but eight-thirty? A glance at his watch confirmed it was true.

Swinging his legs over the side of the bed, he struggled to clear the foreign-feeling fuzz in his head. He'd plowed through a mountain of work last night before coming to bed. To avoid the urge to come up here and make his wife eat her words. To pleasure her until she screamed and forgot Harry Taylor even existed.

A chainsaw would do it.

He picked up his mobile and called Gabe. There was a half-dead oak on their Westchester property that was a serious safety hazard. He'd been meaning to ask the landscapers to take it down, but suddenly the thought of a physical, mind-blanking task appealed to him greatly.

"Matteo got in last night," Gabe said. "I'll bring him and we can have some beer afterward."

"As long as you don't let him anywhere near the saw."

His youngest brother, who ran De Campo's European operations, and their father were in town for the annual board meetings. Which was probably another reason his gut was out of order. Whatever his father said in those meetings would make or break his chances of becoming CEO. And it had better go in his favor.

"We'll make him the look-out," Gabe said drily. "See you in forty-five."

Riccardo showered, put on an old pair of jeans and a T-shirt, and went to procure a travel cup of coffee in the kitchen. Lilly wasn't in there, or in the library she loved.

He was wondering if she'd made another run for it when she rushed into the front entryway just as his brothers arrived, a black look on her face, a curse on her breath.

"Matteo!" she exclaimed, her frown disappearing as his youngest brother stepped forward and scooped her up into a hug. "I had no idea you were in town."

Matteo gave her a squeeze and set her down. "If that means you two are busy making up for lost time, I'm good with that."

A flare of color speared Lilly's cheeks. She and Riccardo's youngest brother were close—or had been until their separation. Matteo was the more philosophical and expressive of the three brothers. Women naturally gravitated to him. Used his shoulder to cry on far too much, in Riccardo's opinion.

"It's so good you're here," Lilly said, pulling back and flashing his brother a warm smile. She gave Riccardo's boots and jeans a brief glance, her gaze staying well away from his glowering face, then looked back at Matteo. "Maybe I'll see you when you're back?"

Riccardo's shoulders shot to his ears. Where did she get off, giving his brother a smile like that when she hadn't offered him one in days?

He glanced at her purse and sunglasses. "You're going out?"

"I need to buy a dress for tonight."

"You have hundreds upstairs."

Her mouth tightened. "They don't fit."

He couldn't understand how at least *one* of those dresses didn't fit. Yes, she'd put on a few pounds since they'd been together, but they were undoubtedly in all the right places. *Women.* He lifted his shoulders. "You do still have the credit card?"

She flashed him a sweetly apologetic look. "Cut it into a million little pieces… But I have my own."

The urge to put her over his knee glowed like a red neon sign in front of him. Gritting his teeth, he dug in his pocket and fished the keys to his Jag out. He handed them to her. "Take the car. We'll go in Gabe's."

Her fingers curled around the keys, a hesitant look crossing her face. She loved driving that car. He knew it as surely as he knew where to kiss her to make her crazy. At the base of that beautiful long neck of hers, and most definitely between—

"Okay, thanks." She gave Gabe a kiss on the cheek and left, the car keys jangling from her fingers. Fury swept through him, raging through his veins. She might not think she had to put on a show for his brothers, but by God she was going to start acting the part—or she had a serious lesson coming her way.

Gabe gave him an amused look. "Glad to see you have everything under control."

"I can't believe you gave her the Jag," Matteo added,

leading the way outside. "She looked like she might drive it into a wall just for the fun of it."

Riccardo muttered something under his breath and took the front seat of the Maserati beside Gabe.

"She looks fantastic, though," Matteo said, sliding into the back. "Being away from you agrees with her."

"We all know you're in love with my wife," Riccardo shot back. "Why don't you spend your time finding one for yourself rather than drooling over mine?"

"Lilly needs someone in her corner with you as a *coniuge*," his brother returned, unperturbed. "You haven't exactly been husband of the year material."

Riccardo turned in his seat as Gabe backed out of the driveway. "What, exactly, does *that* mean?"

"You work fourteen-, sixteen-hour days and you treat Lilly as an afterthought," Matteo said belligerently. "I can't believe she put up with two years of it."

Riccardo was halfway into the backseat when Gabe threw up his hand. "*Sit the hell down. I'm* going to drive into a wall if you keep this up."

Riccardo sat back, pulling in a deep breath. "Keep your mouth shut until you know all the facts."

"You never talk so how would I know them?"

"Try living with the Ice Queen."

"She wasn't always like that," Matty murmured. "Maybe you should ask yourself what happened."

"Maybe you should mind your own business."

That set the tone for the forty-five-minute drive north of the city to Westchester. Riccardo kept his gaze on the scenery while Gabe and Matty caught up. Suburban New York blurred into a continuous stream of exclusive green bedroom communities. But if the scenery was tranquil, his mood was not.

What did they think? He was going to make the De Campo name a player in the North American restaurant business by being home for dinner at six every night?

That he was going to claim his birthright by being any less driven and focused than his father Antonio? He rubbed his hand across his unshaven jaw and shook his head.

"You never wanted to hear what I had to say," Lilly had lashed out at him the other night. "I'm through groveling at your feet, begging for your attention…"

Dio. Was he really that bad?

There'd been a time when he'd been much more laid-back. When he'd been driving a racecar for one of Italy's top teams and all he'd been focused on was winning. The shockingly alive feeling of driving a car at one-hundred-eighty miles an hour finally free of his father's iron grip. He had eaten up life with the appetite of a man determined to savor every minute.

And every beautiful woman who came along with it— like the froth on top of his espresso.

But Lilly had not been one of those easy-to-attain women who had chased him from track to track. Lilly had been the ultimate challenge. The one woman he could never have enough of. Her sharp wit, her loving nature— before she'd turned cold—and her bewitching sensuality had made her the hottest woman he'd ever touched. He had been consumed with the need to possess her, body and soul. And it had almost made him make the biggest mistake of his life.

He shifted in his seat. The sheer stupidity of what he'd almost done was something that would haunt him forever. He had kissed Chelsea Tate with the intent of taking her to bed at the absolute lowest point of his marriage. When Lilly wouldn't talk to him and he'd felt so alienated in his own home he hadn't been thinking straight. He'd wanted to prove he didn't need her, that he didn't love her so much that it was sending him straight to hell. But all it had done was backfire on him when he'd kissed Chelsea and realized Lilly was the only woman for him.

A bitter taste that had nothing to do with the espresso he

was consuming filled his mouth. Lilly, on the other hand, seemed to have moved on as easily as if she was shifting to the next course at dinner.

His fingers dug into the flimsy paper cup. If he had to sleep in that bed with her one more night with her freezing him out—warning him away from those sweet, soft curves that were his and his alone—he wasn't going to be responsible for his actions.

The tension in the car spilled out into the brisk morning as they parked in front of the Westchester house and stepped from the car. Riccardo took a big breath of the clean, woodsy air and felt the tension seep away as the soul-restoring properties of his home on the lake kicked in. He'd fallen in love with the beautiful rolling countryside on his first visit here, to a business associate's home on the Hudson River. When this estate had come up for sale he'd snapped it up as an escape for him and Lilly. But he'd been so busy they'd rarely ever made it out here.

Another promise to her he hadn't kept.

To hell with Matty.

Locating the chainsaw, he applied his frustration to the tree and they managed to take the huge old American white oak down without hitting the house—which was a good thing, since it had to be ninety feet tall and at least three feet in diameter.

Afterward they sat beside the huge old tree, now sprawled in front of them, drinking cold beer out of the can. As different as they all were—Gabe, the intense, serious one, obsessed with the craft of winemaking, who'd known what he'd wanted to do from the time he'd been a little boy; Riccardo, the rebel oldest son; Matty, the in-touch-with-his-feminine side youngest—they were as close as three brothers could be. Even scattered around the globe, with Gabe spending most of his time in Napa Valley, where their vineyards were located and Matty in Tuscany, where he oversaw the company's European operations.

Maybe it was because their mother Francesca, who had come from one of Europe's oldest families, hadn't been the nurturing type. Maybe that was what had bonded the three of them so tightly. Because they were all each other had alongside Antonio's domination. It was sink or swim in the De Campo family, and they had learned to survive—together.

Gabe set down his beer and looked at Riccardo. "Any idea where Antonio's head's at?"

He shook his head. They called their father Antonio because he was not only their father, he was the dominant, larger-than-life figure who had transformed the small, moderately successful De Campo vineyard his grandfather had passed along to him into a force to be reckoned with in the global wine industry.

Gabe shrugged. "Everybody knows it's going to be you. You've been the *de facto* head of the company since Antonio started scaling back."

Riccardo searched his brother's face for any sign that the logical heir to the De Campo empire harbored any bitterness toward him after his father's decision to put Riccardo in control of the company when he'd fallen ill—despite the fact that Gabe had been the obvious choice with Riccardo off racing. But his brother's face was matter-of-fact. As if he'd long ago given up fighting his father's predisposition for his eldest son.

Riccardo took a long swig of his beer. "It's impossible to predict what Antonio will do."

Particularly when teaching his eldest son a lesson seemed to be a greater priority than doing what was right. Antonio had never forgiven Riccardo for wasting his Harvard education on a racing career. No matter how good a driver he'd been—he'd been on track to win his first championship title when his father had fallen ill—Antonio had never forgiven him for his decision. He'd seen racing as a frivolous, ego-boosting activity that pandered to his son's ego and was disrespectful to the family—to everything Antonio had raised him to be. He hadn't talked to his eldest son for years, and had only relented when Riccardo had returned to take the reins of De Campo.

Now Antonio was letting Riccardo sweat his guts out in purgatory.

Rolling to his feet, he reached for the chainsaw. "Let's get this done."

He worked his way from one end of the tree to the other, with his brothers hauling and stacking the pieces. His muscles relaxed and his head cleared. He was nothing if not a man who knew how to solve a problem. His wife might think this was the way it was going to be, but she had it all wrong. This icy détente was ending. And it was ending tonight.

Lilly adjusted the plunging bodice of the lavender gown for the millionth time and asked herself why in the world she'd allowed the owner of Sam's to convince her this gown was *it*.

She felt conspicuous and exposed. Okay, sexy and desirable too. But maybe it was *too much*. And the last thing she wanted to do was attract any more attention than she and Riccardo already would tonight. Their first appearance as a reunited couple since their divorce party was going to cause enough waves.

And as for when she came to model Antonia Abelli's gown… All eyes would be on her, searching for and exposing her flaws. And they were going to have a field-day with her. With her less than perfect body, she could only imagine what they'd say.

Her stomach rose to her throat. Her fitting with the designer had been humiliating. The eclectic woman, whose romantic designs she'd always loved, had circled around her, frowning at the tight fit of the chosen dress. "We'll have to let some seams out," she'd muttered. "But it'll work."

Lilly had left, cheeks burning, wanting to tell her to make someone else wear the dress—someone it fit! The only problem with that was this was the *new* Lilly. The Lilly who wasn't going to care. The Lilly who was going to go out with Riccardo tonight, act like the perfect wife and not let anyone see how it got to her. She was older and wiser now—she'd gained perspective in the past year. She could handle this. And Lisbeth was all that mattered.

She heard Riccardo turn the water off in the shower. "Shoes," she murmured, ignoring the anticipatory surge of her pulse. And then she'd be ready.

She searched through a shelf full of shoes: slingbacks and stilettos in every shade of the rainbow. Her husband had walked in after his day with his brothers, taken one wary look at the pile of couture creations stacked on the floor for Magda to give away, and had said only, "Ready to leave in fifteen?"

"Aha!" She located her silver slingbacks on the top shelf. At least her shoes fit. They were her absolute weakness and, oh, did she love the strappy soft leather of these, which molded to her feet and felt like heaven...

She sat down on the bed and pulled them on. They made her legs seem a mile long, and if there was anything she needed tonight it was that. The fact she couldn't walk in them was of little consequence. Anything that increased her confidence level was worth it.

Her fingers clumsily refused to obey her as she struggled to thread the thin strap through the tiny loop. The fashion show was one thing. How she and Riccardo were going to fool all those people they knew and make them think they were still in love when they were in the middle of the War of the Roses was another matter entirely.

She managed to get one shoe done up, then started on the other, enduring the same frustrating process. Maybe

what she needed were glasses, because the strap didn't
seem to want to—

"Dammit."

"Need help?"

Riccardo's rich, sexy drawl sent the strap pinging out of
her hand completely. "No, thanks," she murmured, snatch-
ing it up again and yanking it desperately through the loop.
This time the pin slid right into the hole and stayed. Thank
goodness. She didn't need a naked Riccardo any closer than
he was right now because—

Hell. The blood had rushed to her head, bent over like
that, but now, sitting up, her gaze moved over her husband
leaning against the doorway of the bathroom and it seemed
to congeal right there, pounding in her ears. *Not naked.*
He'd wrapped a towel around his waist, but that was almost
worse, because far, far too much mouthwatering muscled,
bronzed flesh was still on display. Everything she hadn't
let herself look at the other night.

She gulped in a desperate breath as that six-pack she'd
loved to tell him turned her on stared her in the face. Her
gaze moved lower, over the grooves in his abdomen only
the most defined men had, skipped the next part, because
really she couldn't go there, and ended up at his gorgeous
thighs and calves. Riccardo had the best legs of any man
she'd ever encountered. Muscled, strong and perfectly
shaped. *Heavenly.*

*No looking at me like that unless you intend to follow
through with it.*

She stood abruptly, teetering on the high shoes. "We
should go. We're late already, and if we're going to get
through traffic—" *He was so not listening to her.* His long-
lashed dark gaze was conducting a thorough inspection
of her physical assets that had begun with her face, swept
down over the plunging neckline of her dress, over the flare
of her hips in the clinging gown to her lavender-tipped feet.

Heat rushed to her face as his gaze lingered. Riccardo had always had a thing for feet.

Her feet in particular.

He turned, walked to the dresser and pulled something out of a drawer. Her heart-rate increased as he walked back toward her, a purposeful look on his face.

"We need to go," she repeated in a strangled voice. "We're already late."

He stopped in front of her, took her by the shoulders and turned her around.

"You need a necklace," he murmured, lifting her hair aside. "What are you worried about, Lilly? That I might tear this dress off you and end this détente?"

It wasn't as if he hadn't done it before… She shivered as he slid the necklace around her throat, the cold stones resting against her heated skin. "Riccardo…"

"Riccardo what?" Humor deepened his voice. "Tear the dress off?"

"Get the hell away from me."

"Because you don't trust yourself when I touch you?"

"Because this is a *charade,*" she hissed. "And when we aren't in public you *don't* touch me."

He fastened the clasp of the necklace. "Do you remember how we christened this?"

She stared down at the row of diamonds encircling her throat, sparkling against her skin like a ring of fire. As if she could ever forget. They had been out for dinner, wholly unable to keep their hands off each other, and he'd slapped his credit card on the table as soon as the entrées were removed and taken her home, where he'd ravished her with such urgent, sensual demand she had never been able to wear the necklace again without going back to that moment.

The fleeting sensation of his lips on her bare shoulder made her jump under his hands.

"You look stunningly beautiful in this dress, *tesoro.*

You could easily convince me to forget all about tonight and play hookey."

She would have replied, except his teeth nipped gently into her skin and a wave of heat swept through her. That would be one way of avoiding the fashion show…

Not worth the consequences.

She yanked herself out of his arms and fixed him with a glare. *Remember how he broke your heart. Remember this is only for six months…*

He watched her with a hooded gaze. "I take it that's a no?"

"Not ever," she agreed icily. "Shall we go?"

He inclined his head, stepped toward the closet and stripped off the towel. She averted her eyes and left to wait for him downstairs—but not before she got a full-on shot of his firm, beautiful behind.

CHAPTER FIVE

THE BALLROOM OF the historic hotel near Central Park glittered with light, muted laughter and a sense that time hadn't really moved on—it was just different souls passing through it.

Lilly stood at the entrance with Riccardo and took in the ambience with that same feeling. Massive chandeliers five feet in width still dominated the room, still exuded the elegance of decades past, the band was timelessly tasteful, filling the space with rich classical music, and the black-coated wait staff could have been from any time period. It was *her* that was different. Once she had walked in here with naive, trusting eyes that had seen only the sparkling beauty of so much loveliness in one place. Now she saw it for what it was—a backdrop for the rich and powerful, a symbol of how beauty could destroy and disfigure.

If you let it.

Her gaze shifted to the long runway that ran the center of the room. In an hour she would be up there, modeling Antonia Abelli's dress. If she didn't throw up first. It was a distinct possibility.

Heads turned. The open stares began. Her fingers dug into Riccardo's forearm as the room seemed to ignite with speculative conversation. The press had been all over them since the divorce party, coming up with a multitude of creative, vicious angles as to why they were back together.

Lilly was pregnant—thus her "added pounds," one tab-loid had said. Riccardo had had his fill of his mistress and wanted to start a family, said another. Worst of all had been the dirt they'd dug up on poor Harry Taylor—a former girl-friend citing his low libido as the reason Lilly had left him.

Riccardo looked down at her. "Just ignore them," he said quietly. "Ignore the rubbish they say and be true to yourself."

Lilly wished she had just an ounce of his self-confidence right now—or his supreme ability to focus on what was important and let everything else go.

"Let's get a drink," he murmured, sliding an arm around her waist. She leaned into him and allowed herself to absorb the innate strength that had once made her think nothing and no one could ever hurt her.

How wrong she'd been.

They procured martinis at the bar and were soon caught up in a rolling series of conversations with people eager to see if the rumors were true. Were the De Campos *really* back together?

Lilly tried to focus on the conversation, but the closer it got to nine o'clock and the fashion show the weaker her legs felt. She could feel the cold, assessing looks being thrown her way by the socialites who had claimed the limelight in her absence. And her stomach started to churn.

Riccardo shot her a look with those perceptive eyes of his, warning her to liven up. But Lilly was finished with the acting job she'd done for years. He wanted her as a wife? Then he was getting the real Lilly—not some plas-tic, manufactured replica of herself.

"Riccardo!"

The shrill voice of an outrageously beautiful blond just about took her ears off. About her own age, and so deli-cate a puff of wind might blow her away in her silver lamé dress, she threw herself into Riccardo's arms and landed a big kiss on either cheek before Lilly could blink.

Riccardo set the diminutive blond down, a smile pulling at the corners of his mouth. "Always a dramatic greeting, Victoria."

A rough-hewn, handsome man in a tux stepped up to shake his hand and clap him on the back. "She always did prefer you, De Campo."

Riccardo smiled—a guarded smile that didn't quite reach his eyes. "Alessandro Marino. This is the last place I'd expect to see you."

"My wife." Alessandro inclined his head with a rueful look. "We had a family wedding in the city. And of course my fashion-obsessed wife couldn't miss this."

Riccardo pulled Lilly forward, his hand firm at her back. "I don't believe you've met *my* wife. Lilly, this is Alessandro Marino, my former teammate, and his wife Victoria."

Lilly felt his fingers digging into her back. Surprised, she looked up at his face. He looked firmly in control, as always, but there was a tightness in his face that belied his easy smile. *Alessandro Marino.* It hit her. The man who had taken Riccardo's place as the star of TeamXT. She'd seen a cover story on him recently. He'd been described as "unbeatable."

Alessandro leaned forward and pressed a kiss to both her cheeks. His wife followed suit.

"So *you're* the woman stupid enough to walk out on Riccardo…" Victoria stood back, giving Lilly a once-over, her blue eyes assessing her as thoroughly as she might a prize filly. "Another few months and you might have been out of luck, with all those women lining up to catch him when he fell."

"Victoria." Alessandro bit out the word. "Not appropriate."

His wife shrugged. "It's the truth."

"How is the wine business?" Alessandro asked Riccardo. "De Campo's doing well."

"We had a good year. And you," he said, nodding at the other man. "You're at the top of the pack. Congratulations."

Alessandro shrugged. "You left big shoes to fill. No one is a daredevil like you, De Campo. I had to work on my style."

"Well, it's obviously working."

"He was the best, you know." Alessandro flicked a glance at Lilly. "He'd have a couple championship titles by now if he'd stayed."

Lilly nodded. "So I've heard."

Racing had always been a taboo subject with her and Riccardo. Anytime she'd brought it up her husband had shut down. As he looked like he was about to do right now, judging by the granite-hard expression on his face.

Their conversation with the Marinos deteriorated into an awkward, stilted back and forth that Lilly escaped as soon as she could with a trip to the ladies' room. When she returned to her husband's side he excused himself from the group of men he was speaking to and took her arm.

"Finished your little temper tantrum?"

"It wasn't a temper tantrum. I'm bored, and I'm tired about hearing how much women love you. I get it."

"Then why is smoke coming out of your ears?" He exerted pressure on her arm until she followed him through the crowd.

"Why didn't you defend me?" she burst out. "Why didn't you say something, like, *Good thing I'm madly in love with my wife,* or *anything* that would have made me feel less like an idiot?"

"What do you care? This is just an act for you, isn't it?"

She glared up at him. "I *don't* care. What bugs me is that all these people think we're back together and madly in love and *you're* letting *her* get away with *that.* You always do with women who fall all over you. You *eat* it up, Riccardo. You get that same look on your face like you had when you were standing on the podium splashing champagne over everyone after winning a race."

His jaw tightened. "All men like attention, Lilly. Especially when you get none from your wife."

Oh. She swung away from him before she hit him. "Is it unrealistic to expect you to stand up for me? You never reassure me. It's humiliating."

He led her onto the dance floor. "You know what's humiliating? Me having to tell everyone we know you've left and not knowing what to say because I didn't know why."

She absorbed that as he pulled her into his arms and wrapped his fingers around hers. "You brought it on yourself, Riccardo. Don't try and make me feel bad for you. One week with me out of the house and you were probably acting like 'Ravishing Riccardo' again."

His gaze sharpened at her use of the tabloid nickname for him. "You have a wicked mouth—you know that, *cara?*"

She stared mutinously at his chest as he pulled her closer. So he'd had to answer some questions about why she'd left? It couldn't possibly have matched the jealousy and humiliation *she'd* felt every time he'd left the house without her, wondering if he was with Chelsea. Wondering why she wasn't enough for him.

She studied his hard, proud profile. Maybe it hadn't been right for her to run as she had. She was sure it had been a knock to his pride for a man who was built around pride and honor, who had a public image to uphold, to admit his marriage had failed. But if she'd stayed in that house one more day she would have cracked in half.

Guilt lanced through her. "What did you tell them, then, when they asked where I was?"

He looked down at her, his expression cold and forbidding. "I told them we were taking some time off. And I let them talk. It was our business, not theirs."

"And you think I should do the same?"

"Let them think what they want. They can't hurt you if you don't let them."

"Have you ever read what they say about me?" she challenged. "Even once?"

"I don't have time to read those rags."

Her mouth tightened. "Today they called my figure 'less than fashionable' and insinuated I was pregnant."

"So what?"

So what? She clamped her mouth shut before she said something she'd regret.

"You need to recognize jealousy for what it is," he said impatiently. "They want to be you. That's why they try and tear you down."

She gave him a vicious look. "What would you know about it? You're Mr. Perfect. You have an affair and it only makes you sexier to them."

His eyes went so black she took a step backward. His fingers tightened around hers, drawing her forward in a slow, deliberate movement that wouldn't attract attention. His tone as he pinned her to the spot with his gaze was ice-cold. "Get over this obsession, Lilly. I did not cheat."

She swallowed back the nausea that circled her insides like a shark waiting to pounce. Eight time-lapse photographs didn't lie.

"I want to go."

"Well, we're staying. This is what you signed up for."

She hated him. At that moment she hated him as she'd never hated anyone in her life. "We should never have done this," she murmured huskily. "Look what we're doing to each other."

"We should have done this a long time ago," he disagreed roughly. "My big mistake was giving you time and space when what you really needed was for someone to shake some sense into you."

Her throat tightened. "What does it matter? We're past fixable."

A hard light glittered in his eyes. "That remains to be seen."

"No, it doesn't." She lifted her gaze to his. "This is a short-term solution, Riccardo. You become CEO and we're done."

It was as if her words bounced off his Teflon coating. His expression was inscrutable as he regarded her from beneath lowered lashes. "Matty told me I was a bad husband today."

Her mouth dropped open. "He did?"

"I expect I have been at times."

"At times?" Lilly was past being diplomatic. "That last year you couldn't have cared if I was on Mars as long as I showed up for whatever social function you dictated I appear at. So I could charm the Mayor or sweet-talk a difficult client."

He frowned. "That's an exaggeration. We supported each other. We were a team."

"A team?" She let out a bark of laughter that made a couple near them stare. "If by 'team' you mean I supported you while you ran roughshod over my career every time it was inconvenient for you, then you'd be right."

"Now you're being ridiculous."

"*Really?* You know why I was late that night we had dinner with the owner of Jacob's?" She waited while he paused, then shook his head. "Because I was consulting on the treatment for a little boy's legs. A little boy who'd just lost his mother in a car accident. I was crushed, devastated by what had happened, and all you did when I told you was nod and tell me to get to the table before the appetizers got cold."

"I did *not*. You did not tell me that story."

Her mouth tightened. "Oh, yes, I did. You just couldn't be bothered to listen. And you know what, Riccardo? I helped that little boy. I worked by his side for six months until he was walking again. I might not have been able to bring his mother back but I gave him the use of his legs back. And I'm damn proud of that."

"And so you should be. Lilly, I've always thought what you do is amazing."

"As long as it didn't interfere with the grand plan," she agreed bitterly. "With your obsession to win the CEO job."

A dark flush spread across his cheekbones. "It's my birthright to run De Campo. Why couldn't you ever understand that?"

"I understand it matters to you to the exclusion of everything else in your life. Please forgive me if I don't want to go along for the ride."

A muscle jumped in his jaw. "It won't last forever. Once I'm appointed CEO things will change."

"It'll never change. I think you left a piece of yourself on that racetrack, Riccardo. Nothing you do lives up to that, but you'll never stop looking, *needing* that adrenalin."

The color in his cheeks darkened to a deep, livid red. "Don't try and play psychologist, Lilly. You're not even close."

But she knew she was. She could see it in his face. And finally she felt she was starting to understand him. "Your need for a challenge will always be there. And everyone around you suffers. Our kids would have suffered if we'd been foolish enough to have had them."

"You know that would have changed things."

"No, I don't. We couldn't even keep a dog alive, Riccardo. How would a child have worked?"

The stormclouds in his eyes turned black and dangerous. "That's a ridiculous comparison. Brooklyn was a wild dog. There was nothing we could have done to prevent her death."

She knew he was right. From the day they'd found Brooklyn, a German Shepherd puppy, injured on their street and taken her in, she'd never lost her lust for adventure or for chasing cars.

"You promised you'd train her," she said roughly. "Just like you promised to be around more and you never were."

His mouth flattened into a grim line. "You just can't take your fair share for what happened, can you? You shut me out until I was tired of being verbally slapped in the face every time I walked through the door. And I'm the bad guy for not being around enough? You have a distorted view of the world, Lilly."

The couple beside them suddenly seemed awfully close, their curious gazes on the two of them. Lilly waited until Riccardo had steered them away. "We can talk until we're blue in the face but it isn't going to change the things that were wrong with us."

His fingers tightened around her waist. "Every marriage has its ups and downs. You work through them. You don't run away."

She swallowed hard. If only he knew how badly she'd tried to stick it out. To be what he needed.

His gaze burned into hers, radiating a warning that was impossible to ignore. "We are not over, Lilly."

"We will be in six months."

"And what a six months it's going to be…" He lifted his chin. "Buckle up, *tesoro,* it's going to be quite a ride."

A shiver ran through her. The flicker of the gorgeous two-carat canary-yellow diamond he'd bought to replace the one she'd told him she'd lost shimmered where her hand rested on his shoulder. If he seemed angry now, it would be nothing compared to how he'd react if he knew the truth about what had really happened to the ring.

The organizer of the fashion show waved at her. Her heart lifted to her throat. *She did not want to do this.* The guillotine seemed preferable. But she nodded back at her. The sooner she did this the sooner it was going to be over.

"I have to go."

The tremulous note in her voice drew her husband's eye.

He slid his fingers under her chin and drew her gaze up to his. "What's the matter?"

"Nothing."

"You're nervous."

"I'm not."

She waited for him to release her, but he pulled her closer instead, his eyes flashing as he anchored her against his hard, muscled length. "There was always one way to cure your nerves…"

Lilly started to protest, but he'd already brought his mouth down on hers. His palm cradled her jaw, holding her still while he explored the soft curves of her lips so thoroughly it felt as if he was memorizing them all over again. The heat that flashed between them was undeniable, as life-giving as it had been destructive. She told herself to stop, to end it, but it was impossible not to rise on tiptoes and kiss him back.

No one kissed like Riccardo. No one.

She stepped back, her gaze on his face, wanting him to feel as shaken, as flustered as she was. All she saw was a man still so firmly in control he looked as if he could have been carved out of stone. "Now you have color in your face," he murmured, releasing her and giving her a tap on the behind. "Off you go."

Confused, not sure which way was north and which was south, Lilly did as she was told, following the organizer, Kelly Rankin, to the temporary fitting rooms. Funnily enough, she *did* feel calmer.

Antonia Abelli stripped Lilly down to her underwear. "*Buon Dio,*" she breathed, casting a critical eye over the demure bra and panties Lilly had on. "Really?" She disappeared and came back with flimsy, lacy, non-existent underwear. She told Lilly to put it on. "They're yours. Riccardo will thank me later."

No, he wouldn't. Lilly tried to tell herself that as she closed the curtain on the tiny little changing space and exchanged her own "nothing" underwear for the exquisite lace. This was not a real marriage. And she was definitely not sleeping with Riccardo.

"You need to give me the dress," she told Antonia, peeking around the curtain. "I'm not going out there like this."

The designer whipped the curtain away and gave her a critical look. "You look hot in those."

"Yes, well—" She gasped as Antonia grabbed her arm and yanked her out. Shoulders slumping, cheeks on fire, she stood there, in the middle of all the pre-show chaos, a multitude of mirrors surrounding her, wanting to sink into the floor. Riccardo might have said he liked the changes, but there was too much flesh on her butt for comfort, and too much in her cleavage too, if the truth were told. And her thighs—well, they just looked big. She'd bet five of her extra pounds were *there,* as if she'd reached down and slapped a piece of chocolate cake on them.

"Turn," Antonia ordered, whipping her around with firm hands.

Lilly did her best to ignore all the rail-thin women being dressed around her. But it was hard to because that was her ideal. That was what she thought she *should* look like.

"You have an unrealistic view of your body that has nothing to do with reality." Her therapist's words echoed in her ears. *"You need to change the input you give your brain."*

She tried to look at herself objectively, but it was impossible to concentrate in the middle of a gazillion bodies racing around tucking people in, touching up hair and makeup and waving clipboards. She felt dizzy just watching them. Or was that because her chest felt so tight it was hard to breathe?

One pass down the runway, she told herself, pressing clammy palms together. That was all she had to do.

Antonia pulled the stunning white gown emblazoned with vibrant purple roses over her head and knelt to adjust the hem. Lilly's eyes connected with a hard-looking blond's in the mirror. "Hell," she muttered, her throat tightening. Lacey Craig. Gossip columnist and bitch extraordinaire. The woman who'd begun the end of her marriage.

Lacey sauntered up. "Nice to have you back on the scene."

Why? Because you missed having a punching bag? Lilly looked down at Antonia's updo for fear she might lose it. Lacey had been the worst of the worst when it had come to her and Riccardo's breakup. She'd splashed lurid details— some of them true, some of them not—across the pages of Manhattan's most widely read tabloid. And would have done worse if Lilly hadn't stopped her.

"You might want to watch the weight, though," Lacey commented, running her gaze over her. "Wouldn't want your sexy husband straying again."

Antonia rose to her full five-foot-two inches and nodded at a security guard. "Get her out of here."

Lacey shrugged. "Just a bit of friendly advice. You might have forgotten just how competitive the scene can be."

As if Lilly could ever forget her husband's infidelity. The room swayed around her, the floor tilting under her feet. Perspiration broke out on her forehead and she reached out an arm to steady herself against the wall. It must be a hundred degrees in here...

Antonia grimaced as the security guard ushered Lacey out. "Why can't she ever behave?"

Lilly closed her eyes and told herself to focus. To put the nasty words out of her head and concentrate on getting through this. But visions of those photos flashed through her head like a film strip that wouldn't stop. Riccardo in Chelsea Tate's apartment, standing face-to-face with her in intimate conversation, his dark head bent to hers as he kissed her. Remembering the rest of the blurry series made her stomach churn anew.

Bile rose up in her throat. The sense of betrayal had

been all-consuming. Had sucked her down into a cauldron of self-doubt so deep it had been impossible for her to climb out.

Antonia handed her some water. "Forget that horrible witch," she murmured as she slipped a different pair of shoes on Lilly, then decided she liked Lilly's own better with the dress. "You have a real woman's body that most would die for."

Lilly only barely registered the designer's words. Lost in the world that had destroyed her, she twisted her hands together and stared down at the blindingly beautiful ring on her finger.

The stage manager called for the models. "You need to go," Antonia said. "Keep your head up and don't slouch. I've left the hem a bit long."

She lined up behind the other women at the entrance to the stage, fourth in the queue, but she wasn't really there. All she could see was the brilliant smile on Chelsea Tate's face as she pulled Riccardo in for that kiss.

She ran the back of her hand across her damp forehead. The woman in front of her went out. The show director motioned that she was on.

"Go," he said, giving her a nudge.

She stepped onto the runway. The lights blinded her. The beat of the music pounded in her ears. She started walking, but her legs were shaking so much it was hard to make any progress. The hundreds of faces in rows around the stage were a blur. The long catwalk stretched like an endless sea of white in front of her.

She stumbled, looked down to gauge where she was. Her gaze collided with a handsome blond man sitting in the front row.

Harry.

He smiled at her. She couldn't move her lips out of their frozen curve. Of course he would be here. He worked for the hospital. Her gaze slid down the row to Riccardo, her stomach giving a sickening lurch. *Had they talked to each other?*

She forced herself to keep walking, but her trembling limbs made her misstep again. Her foot slid sideways in her shoe and she stumbled forward. *What the*—? she stuck a desperate hand out to steady herself, but the momentum of her body weight sent her careening off the side of the runway. A choked scream escaped her as the wooden floor rose up to meet her.

Bracing herself for impact, she felt the air hiss from her lungs as a pair of strong arms closed around her and hauled her in.

Winded and dazed, she stared up into the face of Harry Taylor.

"*Hell,* Lilly, are you okay?"

The pounding music made her head spin. The crowd gathering around her was claustrophobic.

She nodded. "I don't know what happened. I—"

"Lilly—" Antonia pushed through the crowd, a horrified look on her face. "I forgot to do up your shoe."

Lilly grimaced and put her hand on Harry's shoulder. "It's okay. I'm fine. You can put—"

"Her down." Riccardo stepped in, his gaze not leaving Harry's face.

No thanks for saving his wife from breaking a few bones. Not even a curt acknowledgement of what he'd done. Her husband stood glaring at Harry, his expression so dark Lilly was convinced most men would have dropped her and run.

But not Harry. He lowered her gently to the floor and held her steady as Antonia knelt and did up her shoe.

"You okay?" he asked again, keeping his hands on her arms until he was sure she had her balance.

Lilly nodded, humiliation washing over her until she wanted to shrivel up into a little droplet of water and disappear between the floorboards.

Kelly Rankin stepped forward. "I am *so* sorry, Lilly," she murmured. "Are you okay to get back up there and continue?"

Riccardo slipped an arm around her waist and pulled her to his side. "She's had enough. Go on without her."

Lilly's humiliation degenerated into a slow, explosive burn. He had been the one to make her do this. He had insisted on her doing something she clearly wasn't comfortable with. *How dared he act so concerned?*

If she didn't get back up there and hold her head high she would never get over it. Pressing her lips together, she turned to Kelly. "I'm fine. Let's do it."

The organizer gave her a relieved look and went backstage. Harry stepped back and went to his seat. Lilly went on tiptoe and put her mouth to Riccardo's ear. "Never, *ever* speak for me in public again."

Then she turned and followed Antonia, leaving her stunned husband staring after her.

"Good for you, getting back up there."

An attractive fifty-something brunette gave Lilly an encouraging smile as she touched up her lipstick in the ladies' room. "I'm not sure I would have."

Lilly flashed her a polite smile. "Not much else I could do."

The woman shrugged and tossed her perfume in her purse. "Well, you looked gorgeous. I hope you get to keep the dress."

She did, in fact. Riccardo had it outside, in a monogrammed Antonia Abelli bag that also held her own less-than-spectacular underwear. Although she doubted she'd ever wear the dress again. Not after tonight. Not after she'd crashed and burned so spectacularly in it.

She nodded at the woman and left. No less than a dozen people had come up to her since the show had ended. It would have been more if Riccardo hadn't acted as gate-keeper.

Her husband's mood had gone steeply downhill since she'd ended up in Harry's arms, and she'd been relieved at his suggestion they leave shortly after. Determined to avoid as many people as she could, she walked around the edge of the crowd toward the entrance.

"Lilly."

Harry Taylor stood in front of her, a determined look on his face.

"I wanted to make sure you're okay."

She smiled and gave him a kiss on the cheek. "More embarrassed than anything. Thank you for rescuing me."

His gaze sharpened on her face. "You sure? You looked like a ghost up there—not like yourself at all."

She nodded. "I'm fine, really. Just tired. We're leaving now."

He pulled at his tie and gave her a pained look. "You know I meant what I said the other day. I don't think Riccardo is the right guy for you. And I'm always here if you need me."

Lilly bit her lip. "Look, I shouldn't be talking to you, Harry—Riccardo will hit the roof."

"That's exactly what I mean," he pointed out, frowning. "Why should you have to worry about that? Dammit, Lilly, if that bastard starts treating you badly I swear I will—"

"What?"

She spun around to find her husband standing behind them, a barely restrained look of violence on his face.

"What will you do, Taylor? I'd like to know."

Harry stepped forward. He wasn't a short man, but Riccardo had three inches on him easily. That didn't seem to faze Harry as he stood toe to toe with him. "I will hold you accountable."

Riccardo gave him a silky look. "My wife and I and our

personal life are none of your business. Accept the fact that you never stood a chance, Taylor."

Harry's face turned bright red. Lilly stared as a man who never lost control balled his hand into a fist and sent it arcing toward her husband's face. Riccardo's reflexes, honed by years as a competitive athlete, were lightning-fast and he caught the other man's wrist in his hand before it connected.

Light exploded around them. Lilly looked up to see a half-dozen cameras pointed at them. *Oh, my God.* How could this be happening?

"Guys," she pleaded, pulling on Riccardo's arm. "Stop."

Her husband dropped his hand away but stayed toe to toe with Harry. "You come near my wife again and I will take you apart piece by piece."

Harry lifted his chin. "You don't scare me, De Campo. You—"

"Harry!" Lilly had the hysterical thought that if he'd acted more like *this*—more manly, more aggressive—he might have done it for her. She took a deep breath and gave both men a level look. "We are leaving. Goodnight, Harry."

Riccardo drove home like he was on a racecourse instead of in the middle of Manhattan, and was shocked when no police officer appeared to pull him over. Lilly was out of the car and flouncing up the walkway before he came to a complete stop in their driveway, but she'd forgotten he was the only one with keys and had to cool her heels while he parked and strolled leisurely up to the door. She stood back while he inserted his key and pushed it open, then swept by him, her head held high, fury in her hazel eyes. Her heels clicked on the hardwood floor as she charged upstairs without another word.

His own safety valve about to blow, he walked into his study and poured himself a Scotch. *"I don't think Riccardo is the right guy for you..."* Taylor's smug pronouncement:

"I'm always here if you need me." His blood burned in his veins, snaking through him like a river of fire. Taylor was there in the wings, waiting for her. Waiting for *him* to screw up. And what had he done to deserve it?

He took a swig of Scotch and stifled the urge to go back there and finish Taylor off. *He* was the only man Lilly was ever going to run to. He knew it and she knew it.

It was time he proved it to her.

He downed the Scotch in two gulps, slammed the glass down on the sideboard and took the stairs to their bedroom two at a time. When he arrived in the doorway Lilly was standing in front of the closet, her shoes in her hands. He sucked in a breath. She had taken her dress off and stood there in a very sexy, very skimpy lacy white panties and bra.

Desire slammed into him, hot and hard.

Lilly flicked her gaze over him, her cat eyes wary and defiant. "Get out."

He shook his head and leaned back against the door frame. "I don't think so."

Her eyes grew larger—big, bottomless pools of amber and green he could lose himself in. Her spine stiffened as she turned fully to face him. She was afraid of him, and with a savage inner growl he acknowledged that he didn't care.

He moved toward her, his steps slow and purposeful. "I warned you not to talk to him."

She planted her hands on her hips. "I fell off that runway because *you* insisted I model that dress. Harry just wanted to see if I was okay."

His mouth twisted. "He wanted to remind you he's still around."

"Good thing he was, or who would have caught me?"

She knew her mistake the minute he stepped in to trap her against the door. "You think I'm never there for you, Lilly? Well, here I am."

He could hear her agitated breathing, see the confusion and fire that swirled in her eyes. "Go to hell," she blazed, her shoulders pressing back into the door.

"I'd rather go down on you," he murmured, sliding the back of his hand over her rosy cheek. "I know how sweet you taste, *tesoro*. How much you love it when I— Ah—" He caught the hand she swung at him and twisted it behind her back. "Don't do that."

She bit out a curse and fought against his hold, but he held her firm. "Dammit, Riccardo, let me go."

He dropped her hand and stepped in closer, until his body was pushed up against hers. "Time to talk in the only way we know how."

She squirmed against him as he imprinted her with *his* brand of honesty—the hard, throbbing truth of his lust, which was quickly sending him over the edge. But she wasn't being very convincing and he could hear how her breathing had quickened.

"Give it up, Lilly," he murmured, lowering his mouth to hers. "We both know how this is going to end."

She said something against his lips and he replied with a hard, bruising kiss that was about control, not pleasure. She'd always liked it when he dominated, and he knew that hadn't changed.

She pressed her lips mutinously shut as he slid his tongue against the crease and demanded entry. Smiling at that, he trailed his hand down over the newly voluptuous curves of her breasts, over the nipple that jutted through the lacy material that covered her, and rolled the hard nub between his fingers. She made a sound low in her throat and twisted against him, but it wasn't the movement of a woman who wanted to go anywhere. Her eyes were closed and her lips had softened, and when he swept his thumb over the hard tip and made it come to full erectness she sagged against him.

Melted into him.

He buried his hands in the thick swath of hair at the nape of her neck. Then he kissed her again, and this time she opened for him and let him take the kiss deeper, into an achingly intimate caress that told her exactly what he wanted to do to her with his tongue and with his body.

The broken sound that came from her throat told him the battle had been won.

"*Basta,*" he murmured. "Enough denying ourselves what we both want."

Lilly pressed her hands back against the door as he ran his palm down the trembling flatness of her stomach. "Ric—"

He slid his hand underneath the silk that covered her and his fingers delved into the hot cleft between her thighs. She gasped and arched against his hand. A primal surge of heat flashed through him. She was wet—oh, so wet for him— and he nearly lost it right there. But he savagely yanked back his control and stilled his fingers to growl, "Tell me you love it when I touch you, *tesoro.*"

She nodded, but kept her eyes shut.

"Say it."

"Dammit, yes. Please—"

"And I'm the only man who's ever going to touch you like this?"

She moaned her assent. Satisfied, he slid his fingers against the warm silk of her and indulged his craving to touch her in every way possible.

Her sudden intake of breath and her hands against his chest took him off guard.

"Get your hands off me."

He drew back. "Lil—"

"That's what this is about, isn't it?" Her voice rose in furious accusation. "Control. *You* being the only one to ever have me. *Me* doing what you want."

He frowned. "You were as into that as I was."

"I was being stupid. *Stupid.* How could I forget what this

is all about? You—always you, Riccardo." She pushed her hair out of her face. "Claiming what's yours."

"You're being ridiculous."

Her eyes glittered. "No, I've finally got my head back. Lord forbid *I* forget to keep my eye on the prize. You certainly haven't."

He shook his head. "What are you talking about?"

"I am not something to be conquered," she said thickly. "I am your wife. You just can't understand that."

"Lilly—"

"Get out." Her face was a blotchy patchwork of red. "Get out or I will walk out of here and never come back, deal or no deal."

Deciding there was no reasoning with her while she was in this state, he turned on his heel and left, hearing the door slam behind him.

He took a cold shower in the guest bedroom, letting the freezing water pound down on his shoulders. *Was* he demented for even attempting this plan of his? To want to make Lilly pay for everything she'd done to him? The humiliation she'd caused him? Because he wasn't sure who was winning—her or him.

CHAPTER SIX

"*THIS IS YOUR* idea of convincing the board you're the man to lead De Campo?"

Gabe shoved a folded newspaper under Riccardo's nose.

He sat back in his office chair and glanced at the tabloid. It was the same one Lilly had waved in his face this morning on her way to work. Having the juiciest of all the coverage of the charity event, it sported the headline "Trouble in Paradise—Already?", which was set over a montage of three photos of him and Lilly laid out in timeline fashion.

The first was of him kissing her on the dance floor. He studied it critically. They *looked* very much in love, despite the fact they hadn't talked in days. The second was of Lilly falling off the runway into Taylor's arms. His mouth tightened. *That* he'd like to forget. The third was a shot of himself restraining the surgeon after he'd thrown that punch.

All in all, fairly damaging.

"What can I say?" He shrugged. "It's a slow news day."

Gabe lifted a brow at him. "What the hell happened? Fisticuffs aren't usually your style—although lately I have to say you're doing a pretty good job of it."

Riccardo spread his fingers in an expressive gesture. "He threw a punch."

Gabe sat on the edge of his desk. "Why?"

"He cornered Lilly and made it clear he was going to

be around to pick up the pieces when I broke her heart. I took offense at that."

His brother let out a low whistle. "I'm surprised you didn't slug him."

"That would have been giving the board far too much ammunition."

"And Lilly falling off the runway?"

"The designer forgot to do up her shoe."

"You're kidding?"

He crumpled up the paper and tossed it freethrow-style into the garbage can he kept across the room for exactly that purpose. "She was a trooper. She got right back up there and did it again."

"That's Lilly." His brother grinned. "She has *spirito*."

Until the end. When she'd become a shadow of her former self. When she'd had that same look on her face she'd had before going up on that stage *every* night before they'd gone out. As if she'd been dreading it.

A wave of remorse settled over him. He'd been the son-of-a-bitch who'd made her go up there. And, even though he had no idea what had set her off, it had been wrong to do it.

Dio. He picked up his coffee and glowered into it. Lilly had used to be comfortable in the center of it all. They'd been nicknamed the Golden Couple for their ability to work a room.

So what had changed?

She had accused him of never being there for her. The symbolic act of Taylor rescuing her and not him had been a brutal shot to his ego. Not just because he'd been five feet away and Taylor had sprung out of his seat like Sir Galahad on a white steed. But because it had once again reinforced the fact that she'd left him. That he wasn't the one she wanted. The fact that he had no clue *who* she really was.

His hand tightened around the coffee cup, red-hot anger slicing through him. It was time he and Lilly had a long conversation about a lot of things—not the least of which was what had really happened to her during those last few months of their marriage. Why she'd frozen him out. Become a ghost of who she'd been. It had to be about more than Chelsea. And he was sure that last night held the key to at least some of it.

Gabe glanced at his watch. "You ready?"

Riccardo nodded.

The cold war between him and Lilly couldn't go on forever. Not with this battle with the board and his father ahead of him. Not when he was intent on claiming what was rightfully his. Both at home and in the boardroom.

There was a knock on the door. He got to his feet as Paige, his PA, came in.

"The meeting's about to start."

He nodded and slipped on his jacket. It was possibly the most important meeting of his life, in which he was to lay out his plans for De Campo's future to the board, and here he was obsessing over his wife. His mouth twisted. Lilly would find that bitterly amusing, he was sure.

He picked up his laptop and followed Gabe out of the room.

"Ah…Riccardo?" Paige lifted a brow at him as he walked past her.

"Mmm?"

"Want the blueprints?"

The blueprints of their new restaurant in SoHo. The centerpiece of his presentation. He grimaced and took them from her. "What would I do without you?"

Antonio had the same salacious tabloid Riccardo had now seen twice this morning tucked in front of him when they walked into the room. Riccardo swept his gaze around the table. So did Phil Bedford and Chase Kenyon. *Hell*. Was his life a walking soap opera?

"Smoothing the way, I see," his father murmured as he

took his place beside him. "Did you know Phil Bedford plays golf with Harry Taylor?"

Riccardo deposited his laptop on the table with slightly more force than was necessary, picked up his father's paper and waved it in the air. "Looks like most of you have seen the paper this morning?"

Matty's mouth dropped open. Gabe looked fascinated. All the other extremely senior heads of their corporations sat there silently and stared at him. He shifted his gaze to Phil Bedford, the portly CEO of a consumer packaged goods company pushing fifty.

"Harry Taylor wants to date my wife. I don't consider that a valid proposition since she is *still* my wife. So I acted on it." He threw the paper down on the table like the trash it was and eyed the room. "If anyone would like to crucify me with this please do so now, so we can get on with business."

Phil Bedford stared down at his coffee. Chase Kenyon doodled on his notepad.

"Fine." Riccardo looked at Antonio. "All yours."

He could have sworn his father was holding back laughter as he got to his feet and opened the meeting. Antonio gave a holistic presentation on how the De Campo Group was performing worldwide, every bit the elegant global wine baron as he talked through the slides in his thick accent, then turned the meeting over to Riccardo for an update on the restaurant business.

Riccardo opened with an overview of the division's strong growth prospects, then ran through a presentation on the new jewel in the De Campo restaurant crown—Zambia, the SoHo restaurant set to open in six months. He saw the lights go on in the board members' eyes as he spoke of the twelve percent overall profit increase the restaurant division would bring in, and knew he'd driven home his message of where the future was for De Campo.

He sat down, his jaw clenched with satisfaction. He had nailed it.

Gabe stood to give an update on the California operations. Another board member gave a presentation on how lessons learned from the packaged goods industry could be applied to wine. Then they broke for lunch.

Antonio followed him into his office. *"Buon lavoro, figlio."*

Good job, son.

Caught off-guard by the compliment, he warily inclined his head. *"Grazie."*

"You keep this up and I might just throw my weight behind you."

He froze. *The son-of-a-bitch.* Even after the results he'd just presented Antonio was still stringing him along.

He dragged in a breath and let it out slowly. "I will be single-handedly responsible for that twelve percent profit you just gloated over. You start putting recognition where it's due or so, help me God, I will leave this company and not look back."

His father set his chin at that haughty angle he favored. "A De Campo would *never* utter those words."

"This one just did." Riccardo jammed his hands in his pockets and paced to the window. "Just out of curiosity, how long do you intend to make me pay?"

Antonio narrowed his gaze on him. "Is that what you think I'm doing?"

"I *know* that's what you're doing."

"Maybe I think Gabe would do a better job."

He stiffened, white-hot rage slicing through him. "We are not Cain and Abel, with you playing God, Antonio. I will *not* compete with my brother. Make a decision, but do not try and drive a wedge between us. Neither of us will tolerate it."

His father shrugged his broad shoulders. "Some think Gabe has the true love for this business. He's aggressive, with just the right amount of conservatism."

"Then why didn't you choose him to run the company while you were ill? You had the opportunity."

Antonio met his combative stare with one of his own. "Because, despite the fact that you dishonored this family by choosing a racing career over your heritage, you have the heart of a lion, Riccardo. You have the vision to take this company where it needs to go."

"So does Gabe."

His father shook his head. "Not like you. You have the ability to be brutal. To make the decisions no one else wants to make."

"Then do it," Riccardo gritted out. "Because I'm not waiting much longer. I've sacrificed too much."

Antonio pointed a beefy finger at him. "How long have I been waiting to hear you say that?"

Riccardo frowned. "What?"

"Sacrifice. You view De Campo as a sacrifice. As an impediment to your personal freedom. Not as the majestic birthright that's been handed to you."

"I love this company. I have killed myself for this company. I do *not* view it as a sacrifice. But I *have* sacrificed for it." He trained his gaze on his father. "As you did."

"Prove it." His father flicked his hand in the air in a dismissive motion. "I'm retiring in three months. The job is yours to lose."

"You might just kill me one of these days."

The big, burly football player wiped the sweat from his face and stepped off the treadmill. Lilly smiled and made a note of the time in her chart. What would normally have been a walk-in-the-park run for Trent Goodman had been a one-mile endurance test on a knee that had a whole lot of healing ahead before he stepped back on a football field.

"Admit it—you like coming to see me."

"Are you kidding?" He dropped the towel in his bag and slung it over his shoulder. "It's the highlight of my week.

The pain I can take, when I'm getting the inside scoop on all the gossip. You get more press than I do—and frankly," he admitted sheepishly, "that's not a good thing."

Lilly laughed. "Believe me—I'd happily pass it along if I could."

"I bet you would." He grinned. "That photo of your husband tangling with the doctor? Priceless."

Maybe somewhat less than priceless. She was now back as a fixture in all the gossip rags. She'd spent the weekend fuming at Riccardo's caveman tactics. Both with Harry and in the bedroom.

"He has his moments," she murmured, looking back at the clipboard. "Same time tomorrow?"

He nodded and blew her a kiss. She smiled and watched him leave. Muscular, gorgeous, charming and making millions…Trent would have had most women on their knees with his overt flirtatiousness. Lilly, however, was fixated on her own brutish male.

What in the world had gotten into her? She'd nearly toppled. Slept with him and done something she'd have sorely regretted. All because she still couldn't keep her hands to herself when it came to Riccardo.

She twirled a chunk of hair around her finger. They had exchanged a total of about a hundred words since that scene in the bedroom. If he was in the kitchen when she came down, she took her coffee onto the patio. If she came down first, he went and watched the news in his study.

It couldn't go on like this.

Unresolved issues lay between them like unexploded mines. Yet Saturday night had proved beyond a shadow of a doubt she never wanted to live the life of Riccardo's society wife ever again. That she'd been right to leave when she had.

That she wasn't *capable* of living it beyond the six months she'd committed to.

So why did everything feel so wrong? Why couldn't

she just do what she needed to in public and to hell with how things were at home? She tossed her clipboard on her desk and grabbed the notes on her afternoon patients so she could file them. She had pushed a set of notes into a folder and slid it back into the drawer before realizing she'd completely mixed the two patients up. *Damn.* She pulled the two folders out again.

A loud piano piece filled the air. She frowned. *Her new ringtone.* Note to self: change that. She pulled her phone out of her pocket and held it to her ear while she fixed the notes.

"Lilly Anderson."

"De Campo," Riccardo's rich drawl oozed across the line. "Really, Lilly, you have to get with the program."

"I don't use your name professionally. You know that."

"I don't like it. I'm calling to ask your permission to ask Katy to clear your schedule for Thursday and Friday."

Her husband's drily delivered request made Lilly frown and push the drawer of the filing cabinet shut with her foot. Riccardo asking for her permission to do something? Was he sick? On some type of mood-altering medication?

She cleared her throat and chose her words carefully. "I have clinics at the hospital on Thurdsay and Friday. Is it important?"

"I'd like to take you to Barbados for the weekend."

"The Caribbean island of Barbados?"

"The one and only," he confirmed, amusement lacing his tone. "A friend of mine offered up his place for the weekend."

She stuck a finger in her mouth and chewed on her nail. "So it's a business thing?"

"No." His voice deepened to that silky tone that made her toes squish in her shoes. "Definitely not business."

Heat filled her cheeks. "Riccardo—"

He sighed. "We need a truce. We need to talk, Lil. Somewhere by ourselves, with no photographers, no one interrupting us, neither of us rushing off to work… Just us."

She couldn't deny that. It was just that it sounded sort of...*terrifying.* She rested her hip on the corner of the desk and the guilty thought came to her that maybe, *maybe,* if she'd talked to him from the start instead of shutting down things *would* have been different.

A snapping sound filled the air. She pulled her finger out of her mouth and stared, horrified, at her broken nail. She hadn't bitten her nails in exactly twelve months.

"You still there?"

"Yes."

Another sigh. "I'm pretending I'm asking, but I'm not really, you know."

She smiled. At least she knew her husband hadn't been abducted by aliens. She stared down at her wreck of a nail and swallowed hard. "To be clear—this is a discussion? That's all?"

"A discussion," he agreed firmly. "That's all I'm asking for."

"Okay, then, yes." It would be closure for them both.

"Good. Will you tell Katy or will I?"

"I will."

"*Bene.* I'm off for dinner with the boys and Antonio." His voice took on a sardonic edge. "Wish me luck."

"Keep your cool. You'll be fine."

A meaningful silence came down the phone line. "Already lost it. *Ciao, bella.*"

"*Ciao.*"

Lilly pressed the end button, her skin tingling from the effects of those two softly spoken words. Would there ever come a day when *that* didn't make her want to throw caution to the wind and do exactly what she wasn't supposed to do?

She fought the sinking feeling she had just made a huge mistake and dialed her sister.

Alex answered with a distracted, "Hello."

"It's your sister. Got a sec?"

"Always. How are you holding up? Riccardo mix it up with anyone lately?"

"Very funny." Lilly pulled a pristine nail out of her mouth before she trashed that one too. "We have to reschedule brunch. I'm going to be away this weekend."

"What lifestyle-of-the-rich-and-famous event is he taking you to?"

"None. We're going to Barbados together."

"*Damn. I* would put up with him for a weekend like that."

Lilly smiled. "Gabe's still in town, you know."

"Mmm, yes—well, I'm afraid I'm not up for twenty-four-seven sparring. Dr. Overlea just called to say he's scheduled Lisbeth in for some pretreatments next week. I'm going to head home and keep her company so she doesn't stress."

Lilly's throat tightened. "I didn't think he was going to be able to get her in so soon."

"He needs to do this before he schedules treatment with the clinic in Switzerland."

"Right." She swallowed hard. "I—" *Hell.* The conversation with Riccardo was important, but her sister's health was more so.

"Lil—it's fine. I'll go." Her sister's voice softened. "You guys need time together."

She chewed on her lip. Alex probably thought she and Riccardo were having hot reunion sex every night… She so desperately wanted to tell her that, no, they weren't, that they were hardly talking to each other and she was hopelessly confused, but she couldn't. Not if she was to keep her and Riccardo's deal.

"You'll call me if you need me? I'll come right back."

"I will. I promise."

Her shoulders sagged. "Okay."

"By the way—one of the girls here just showed me some

of the stuff the tabloids are saying about you. Please tell me you're not reading it?"

"I'm not reading it." Only a bit. One or two particularly horrid pieces...

"Yes, you are. I can tell. You have to stop it, Lil. It's awful, destructive stuff and not a bit true. I've never seen you looking so good."

Lilly sighed. "I'm fine, Alex. I promise." Only her sister knew how deep her body issues went and she called her on it when she needed to.

"You sure?"

"I gave my whole wardrobe to charity," she said drily. "Riccardo almost had a fit."

"The whole thing?" her sister squeaked.

"All of it."

"I can't tell you how glad I am to hear you say that."

"I know... Al?"

"Yeah?"

"Do you really think people never change?"

She sighed. "Are you talking about Riccardo?"

"Yes."

And why, exactly, was she?

Her sister cleared her throat. "When we were looking at those tabloids this morning, one of the girls here looked at that photo of you and Riccardo kissing—which is dreamy, by the way, and I don't *do* dreamy, as you know—and she got this stupid, expression on her face and said, 'I just want *that*. To be that much in love.'"

Lilly felt the stitches she'd triple-sewed around her heart rip, leaving it jagged and raw. *She* wanted to be that much in love again. But that wasn't her and Riccardo anymore, and telling herself that was possible was foolish.

"So," her sister continued, "while I think he might be the most arrogant son-of-a-bitch I've ever met, I know what you have is special, Lil, and that man is crazy about you in his own demented way. Which leads me to believe he's going to do whatever it takes to keep you."

Lilly stood there, wishing she'd never asked the question in the first place.

"Do me a favor?" Alex's voice lost its sarcasm and took on a serious note.

"Name it."

"Whatever you do, don't get pregnant."

Lilly stared at the phone, horrified. Then remembered her sister didn't know. Didn't know this was all a charade. "Of course I won't. That would complicate everything."

"Exactly."

Exactly. She glanced at her watch. "I'm done for the day, and Riccardo's out with the boys. You up to swimsuit-shopping? You're the only one I know who'll give me an honest opinion."

They made arrangements to meet and Lilly hung up, more worried with every passing moment that a "conversation" in Barbados with her sexier than hell husband was a disaster waiting to happen.

One thing she knew for sure. She could never, never tell him about why she'd entered into this deal. About Lisbeth. Because she didn't trust him not to use that against her. And Lisbeth was all that mattered.

CHAPTER SEVEN

LILLY STOOD ON the patio of Charles Greene's very beautiful, very exclusive Barbados estate overlooking Heron Bay. The sparkling, water-soaked playground of the world's rich and famous, the bay was dotted with luxury hotels and villas that sat on heavenly golden sand beaches and the most stunning clear turquoise water Lilly had ever seen.

If you were the world's most famous golfer you took over Heron Bay's five-thousand-dollar-a-night marquee hotel for a sunset marriage featuring heads of state, rock stars and movie icons. If you were Charles Greene, British billionaire and heir to a heavy machinery fortune, you bought this gorgeous six-bedroom villa on the ocean and kept it for yourself.

Charles and Riccardo had done business together on a few occasions, and had formed a close personal relationship in addition to their working one. With Charles away on business in the UK, the villa was theirs. A private oasis in paradise.

At any other time in her life Lilly would have been ecstatic to be here. But not tonight. Not when she was about to learn the truth about her marriage.

She kept her feet planted firmly on the concrete. Tonight was not about running. It was about facing her demons.

She drank in the sheet of shimmering perfect blue sea in front of her, its color morphing from light to dark turquoise, then to a marine blue the further out the eye traveled. Were relationships like that? she wondered. Were there gradations and depths she and Riccardo had yet to explore? Or would this be the end for them?

"I'm leaving now."

Mrs. Adams, the housekeeper who had greeted them and shown them to their rooms, appeared on the patio with a bottle of wine and a cooler in her hands. "Mr. De Campo thought you might enjoy a glass of wine while he showers."

Lilly forced a smile to her lips. "Thank you. He's off the phone, then?"

She nodded. "He said to tell you he'd be down in a few minutes." She set the cooler down on the table and took some glasses out of a cupboard. "Did you say you'd been here before?"

"Yes. A year ago."

Riccardo had come here on business and brought her with him. It had been right after news of his affair had surfaced and she'd spent the whole week trying to convince herself she shouldn't doubt him. Trying to save her marriage.

Until she'd seen the photos.

"It's a beautiful island," she murmured, realizing the woman was waiting for her response. "We stayed further up the coast."

Her brief response had the desired effect. The housekeeper nodded and stuck her hands on her hips. "I'll be back tomorrow to cook breakfast. Would you like me to pour you a glass of wine?"

"No, thank you. I can pour it."

"Okay, see you tomorrow, then."

"Goodnight."

Lilly kept the plastic smile on her face until the housekeeper had disappeared into the house. Her body vibrated with a tension that hadn't left her since they'd climbed aboard the De Campo jet and flown the five hours south to the island—a flight the entire duration of which Riccardo had worked. She pulled in a breath to steady herself, but the shallow pulls of air she managed to take in didn't help much.

She turned back to the sea and laced her hands together. *"Stay in the moment. Allow yourself to feel and move through the pain..."* Her therapist's words were a grounding force when all she wanted to do was run. It had been her coping mechanism since she was a teenager and her parents had been having their no-holds-barred fights to run when she was in pain. To refuse to feel it.

Making herself stand here was like being asked to walk over red-hot coals.

"You haven't had any wine."

Riccardo's low, smooth observation contrasted sharply with the imminent hysteria she felt building within her. This had always been the pattern with them. Him handling everything with reason—with well-thought-out premeditation. Lilly shooting from the hip—driven by emotion.

She turned around, a sharp condemnation on her lips. But he was so breathtakingly handsome in jeans and a navy polo shirt, his square-jawed, dark good looks only intensified by the casual attire, that the words fled her head.

He was beautiful beyond the meaning of the word. Charisma oozed out of him like oxygen for the female race. And she knew then that this had been a big, huge mistake.

Just as it had been to think she could claim ownership over a man every woman wanted.

She turned back to look at the ocean. "You can pour me some now."

The knot in her stomach grew to an almost incapacitating level as she heard him walk across the patio and pour the wine. The sound of bubbling liquid hitting glass was deafeningly loud on the night air.

He came to stand beside her, the smoky, spicy scent of him wrapping itself around her.

"What's wrong?"

She swiveled to face him. "You've been talking on that phone non-stop since we left. I thought we had a no work rule."

His mouth tightened. "It's off now. I just had a few last things to go through with Gabe. By the way," he added, raising a brow, "he asked Alex out for dinner and she turned him down flat. Said she was going back to Mason Hill for the weekend." His gaze narrowed on her face. "You two *never* go home. Is everything okay with your family?"

She blanched. "Everything's fine. Can we just get this over with?"

He kept that watchful dark gaze on her. Then handed her the glass of wine.

She wrapped her fingers around the stem. The glass shook in her hand.

"Lil—" His eyes moved from her shaking fingers to her face.

"I'm fine," she murmured. "You—you start."

He exhaled harshly, the nostrils of his perfectly straight Roman nose flaring.

"What happened the night of the fashion show? Why were you so afraid to do it?"

She blinked. She had not expected that to be his first question. "You know I've never been comfortable in that type of setting. I told you that when we first started dating."

"But you got over it. You thrived on it."

"I hated every minute of it. I trained myself to do it so I wouldn't let you down."

Confusion flickered in his eyes. "Why? Why would a woman like you have confidence issues? You had the position, the wealth, the looks to back you. Why would you feel inferior?"

She gave a twisted smile. "I come from a town of two thousand, five hundred people, Riccardo. I will always feel small-town, no matter how you dress me up or how many places you take me or how many etiquette rules you teach me." She shook her head. "You swept me up into this glamorous life I had no coping skills for, tossed me into the deep end and expected me to swim."

He frowned. "But you never said anything. To me—you were just fine."

Her shoulders stiffened. "I was doing what I had to do. That was my *job*. My role as Lilly De Campo."

He exhaled heavily. "No one would ever have known you felt that way."

Her lips twisted in a bitter smile. "I became extraordinarily good at faking it. And why not? I faked my way through our entire marriage."

His gaze sharpened on her face, a dangerous glint firing in its dark depths. "I think you'd better explain that."

"I never wanted that life, Riccardo. I told you that when you knocked me off my feet in that bar in SoHo. But you wouldn't listen…you kept pushing until I said yes."

"We were in love with each other," he growled.

"We were infatuated with each other," she corrected. "There was still time to recognize how wrong it was for me. How self-destructive all the attention and criticism was."

"How so?"

She set her wine down on the railing and pushed her hair behind her ears. "I've never been secure in the way I look. It's always been a tough one for me. But as your wife I couldn't put on five pounds without the tabloids noticing and pouncing on me."

"I told you. Stop reading them."

"That's overly simplistic. They were everywhere. I couldn't avoid them all."

His brows drew together. "But where does it come from, then, this insecurity about your looks? Beyond what the tabloids say?"

She turned away from his penetrating barrage of questions. But her therapist's words haunted her, refused to let her back away. *"Above all be honest, Lilly. Be honest with yourself and those around you."*

She took a deep breath. "I was very unhappy as a teenager. My parents' marriage was a mess for a long time. The farm wasn't doing well and the stress of having no money was getting to them. The kids—we had no life. We spent all our time helping out on the farm. We barely had time for schoolwork, let alone social lives."

"I knew you weren't happy at home and that's why you left," he said quietly. "But I didn't know it was that bad."

She nodded. "My parents' fights would dissolve into screaming matches. Plates would fly and my mother would threaten to leave. My dad had an affair with the farmer's wife down the road." She hugged her arms around herself and looked up at him. "It was a disaster. A huge mess."

There was a pregnant silence. His face paled. *Yes,* she thought viciously. *That's why what you did hurt so much.*

She kept going, afraid that if she stopped she'd never tell him the truth. "David seemed immune to it all. Lisbeth was too young to know what was happening. Alex dealt with it by getting into trouble—running with the wrong crowd. I internalized it. I thought if I could control everything about my life beyond them, beyond what was happening at home, I'd be okay."

Her mouth felt wooden, her lips thick, and the desire to stop talking was so strong it was hard to make herself form the words. "My big thing was food. I hated the way I looked so I controlled everything I put in my mouth." She swallowed hard. "To the point where I was hardly eating."

His eyes darkened with an emotion she couldn't read. "But you can't ever have been fat. Why in the world would you hate yourself so much?"

"I was a 'chunky, healthy, solid-boned farmgirl,' as my mother would say," she said with a derisive smile. "And I hated it. No one wanted to date me. No one wanted to be with me."

"I find that hard to believe."

"It wasn't until I was in my twenties that I bloomed. Came into myself. You met me not long after that."

He frowned. "So why is it still so bad? I've seen men lust after you, Lilly. You know they do. That must give you some confidence."

"Yes." She turned back to look at the brilliant sunset staining the sky now, the giant ball of orange and red sinking into the horizon. She swallowed past the hard, round mass in her throat that felt as if it was choking her, as if revealing her shameful secret might bring her to her knees. "But not before I developed anorexia."

There was a long silence. He scraped his hand over his jaw and stared at her. "I had no idea."

She made a face. "It's not something you drop into casual conversation, like the fact I had a dog named Honey when I was little."

"*Dio,* Lilly." He stepped forward and took her by the shoulders. "That's not what I'm talking about. This is key to who you are. Essential information I need to know about you. I would never have put you through any of this if I'd known that."

She lifted her chin. "I didn't want you to know."

"Why?" He threw up his hands. "Because for once I might see who the real Lilly De Campo is?"

"No, I—"

"Lilly, we've been as intimate as two people can be. We've spent hours devouring each other. Yet you still can't tell me these profound truths about yourself? No wonder we're messed up."

She shook her head and took a step back. "Sex and intimacy are two different things."

"They most certainly are," he agreed tightly. "And the minute you turned into the Ice Queen and froze me out any intimacy we had was blown to bits."

She winced. "I wasn't trying to hurt you. I was trying

to protect myself. My anorexia was my deep, dark secret. It was the thing no one knew about me in my new life. The thing I never wanted anyone to know about me. Most of all you."

A muscle jumped in his jaw. "Why?"

She pressed her lips together. "You're a perfect human being, Riccardo. Everything about you is so damn perfect that everyone wants you, everyone admires you. I've never felt I could live up to it. *Be* that woman who's worthy of you."

"That's ridiculous."

She stamped her foot. "*It's how I feel, dammit*. Everything—*everything* about my life with you was about keeping up appearances. Making sure we were that Golden Couple. And the balance I'd tried so hard to inject into my life in order to stay healthy went out the window. How could it not when I was constantly in the spotlight? Constantly being judged?"

He raked his hand through his hair. "I wish you'd told me so I could have helped you."

Her heart throbbed in her chest. "I didn't want to add myself to your list of issues. You had enough going on with De Campo business."

He shook his head. "Did *I* ever put any pressure on you about your weight?"

"You never reassured me."

"I *always* told you how gorgeous you looked."

"Yes, but when I said things like, 'I feel fat,' to get some reassurance from you, you told me to go to the gym."

"That's because that's what *I* do when I feel like that. I work out, get the tension out, and I feel better about myself. *Hell,* Lilly…" He was staring at her as if she was a creature from another planet. "Has there ever been any doubt about how much I love your body?"

Her gaze skipped away from his. "I've put on weight since we were together."

"And that scene the other night wasn't enough to convince you I like the changes?"

"Why wasn't I enough, then?" She yelled the words at him, her control snapping. "If you think I'm beautiful, if I'm *enough* for you, then why did you have to have an affair with Chelsea Tate?"

All the color drained out of his face. "It didn't happen. You're the only woman I want, Lilly. Chelsea never came close to meaning anything like that to me."

"*Then tell me the truth,*" she raged, pointing a finger at him. "This is my life, Riccardo. Not a tabloid page. When I left you I was in the fetal position for three days. *Three days.* And if Alex hadn't come along to dig me out I might still be there. So do *not* tell me any more lies. I can't take it."

He stared at her with the glazed look of a man who didn't know where to go. What to do. She watched him take a deep breath and steady himself and felt her heart sink into the depths of hell.

"You need to give me a chance to explain…"

She bit back the bile that rose in her throat. "Believe me—you have my full attention."

He raked a hand through his hair and set his jaw. "Chelsea and I were once close—you know that. But once I met you that all ended and you were the only woman in my life. The *only* one, Lilly." He frowned when she gave no reaction. "When things got so bad between us I was completely at a loss as to what to do. It was impossible to believe a marriage could go from one-fifty to zero in a matter of months—but somehow ours did, and I couldn't figure out why or what to do about it. You refused to be with me, my pride was stinging, and I think we were both questioning our marriage."

She forgot to breathe. Forgot she *had* to.

"I was hurt at what had become of us. Angry at what you were doing to me." His mouth flattened into a grim line and his eyes half closed, as if he couldn't believe what he was saying. "So I called Chelsea and invited her to dinner."

Lilly felt as if a train was headed for her, but she couldn't move. Couldn't do anything to avoid it.

"I wanted to prove I didn't need you—I didn't love you," he continued hoarsely. "And maybe I wanted to hurt you too. Make you hurt as much as I was hurting."

Lilly pressed her hands to her ears, but he stalked forward and dragged them away.

"I drove her home, I went up to her apartment with every intention of taking her to bed. And then I kissed her and everything felt wrong."

Lilly felt the ground sway beneath her and, cursing, Riccardo scooped her up in his arms. He carried her over to the bench and sat down with her cradled against him. A tortured expression filled his eyes as he stared down at her. "You haunted me. No matter how much you pushed me away you were the only one I wanted."

She sat there in his arms like a strange, disembodied presence that could hear what he was saying but couldn't actually register it. When she managed to speak, her voice was low and thready. "You kissed her but you didn't sleep with her?"

He nodded. "I came home to you and never saw her again."

Something reached inside her and tore her heart out. "What kind of a kiss was it?"

He cursed low under his breath. "You can't torture yourself like that."

"*Yes, I can!*" she shrieked, stumbling off his lap and facing him on shaking legs. "You betrayed me, Riccardo. I saw those photographs. You didn't just kiss her. You had sex with her!"

He frowned. "There were no photographs taken of us. We were in Chelsea's apartment."

"There were *eight*. Eight photos of you in various states of undress. Dammit, stop lying."

He stood up and took her by the shoulders. "You will watch your tongue and tell me what you're talking about."

"Lacey Craig," she threw at him, knowing this might well put the final nail in their marriage, but past caring. "After we got back from Barbados I called her up and asked what proof she had to support her story. She showed me photos of you and Chelsea. *Intimate* photos of you. And she let me buy them to spare me the humiliation of having them splashed across every gossip magazine in the country."

He blinked at her, a look of complete incomprehension on his face. "Let me get this straight," he said slowly. "You called a gossip columnist, demanded information about my infidelity and paid her for fake photos?"

"They weren't fake," she cried. "Everybody in New York knew you were having an affair! Too bad I was the last to know."

His fingers tightened around her shoulders. "They *are* fake photos because I did not sleep with Chelsea Tate— ever—after our relationship began."

His rage and the icy, menacing look on his face vibrated through her like a sledgehammer. Riccardo had never lied to her. Not once in their marriage. Until Chelsea. Truth was like a badge of honor to him—it was the De Campo creed, the way he conducted his life. Better to be brutal and get it over with.

What if she was wrong?

"Lilly?"

She yanked herself out of his grasp and turned away. Her brain moved wildly through the possibilities. Photos could be doctored. They were doctored all the time. Maybe those *hadn't* been shots of him and Chelsea. It had been hard to see their faces after that initial shot of them kissing…

A cold, buzzing feeling descended over her. Would Lacey Craig have dared to sell her fakes? Wouldn't she have been worried Lilly would take them straight to Riccardo, who would have pronounced them as such and sued the hell out of her?

Or maybe Lacey hadn't known they were fake...

Oh, God.

Riccardo took a step toward her, his face hard and determined. "How much did you pay for those photos?"

She shook her head.

"How much?"

"One hundred thousand dollars."

"A hundred thousand?" His brow furrowed. "They wouldn't give you a full-page ad for a hundred grand..."

Lilly felt her world fall apart.

His gaze sharpened on her face as understanding dawned in his eyes. "That was the money you said you sent your parents?"

"Yes."

He sucked in a breath, his fists clenching at his sides. "You trusted me so little you would do that without talking to me?"

"You kissed her, Riccardo! You went home with her, intending to sleep with her. Where in that is there anything that says I should have trusted you?"

His jaw clamped shut. He was silent for several long moments, each one driving the stake that was impaling her heart deeper and deeper.

Finally he raised his gaze to hers and asked quietly, "Was there ever any point in our marriage you were happy?"

She fought the fire burning the back of her eyes. "That first year after we married was the most amazing year of my life. I loved you, Riccardo. I worshipped the ground you walked on. You were my knight in shining armor who'd swooped into my life and made it whole again. But somewhere along the way I lost my glitter when it came to you. You didn't want me the same way you did before. And it was torturous for me to be with you like that." She looked down at the sparkling ring on her finger. "So I left."

"You left because you thought I didn't love you anymore?"

"I left because we were destroying each other. You became obsessed with that job—obsessed with having your birthright. And you left me alone to deal with the fallout of being Lilly De Campo. Something I couldn't do on my own."

He was silent, a granite mask stretching across his face. She hugged her arms around herself and listened as a chorus of tree frogs filled the air with their haunting, rhythmical song.

"You never once thought I might be struggling too? That I might need my wife?" He said the words quietly, deliberately, his face devoid of emotion.

"How would I have known? You're like Mount Vesuvius. You keep everything inside until you explode. And when you do there's nothing for me to respond to but the anger."

His dark gaze rested on her. "I could say the same about you."

"Yes, you could." She nodded. "I have a ton of baggage, I know. But at least I acknowledge mine."

His mouth pulled tight as her arrow hit home. He swung away and walked to the edge of the terrace, rested his elbows on the railing as he looked out at the sea. "I always thought if you wanted something bad enough you made it happen. That we could resolve our differences because we loved each other that much."

The lump in her throat grew so large it felt as if she was aching all over. "Sometimes," she choked, "love isn't enough."

He turned around, his broad shoulders silhouetted against the setting sun. The dull look on his face made the rest of her shrivel away.

"A marriage needs trust to survive. And between the two of us I think we've proved we have none."

And there it was, she thought miserably. Their marriage summed up in one glaring truth.

"It was never going to work."

Her words sat flat and lifeless on the night air between them. Riccardo's head snapped back, a flare of angry color slashing across his cheekbones. His steps as he closed the distance between them were jerky, full of a barely leashed rage that made her suck in a breath. When he stopped in front of her, his furious glare leveled on her face, her heart seemed to stop.

"We may have spoken a lot of truths tonight, Lilly, but do not, *do not* absolve yourself of the responsibility you carry for this marriage. You checked out. You left me. You *chose* to give up. And you *will* own that."

She pulled in another breath, but it wasn't enough, and desperately she dragged in another. There never seemed to be enough oxygen on the planet when she was with Riccardo because he sucked it out of her. Stripped her bare.

He stared at her for a long moment, waiting for her to respond, waiting for her to give him what he demanded of her, but she couldn't force the words out of her mouth.

He spun away and stalked toward the French doors.

"Ric—"

"I need some space."

He disappeared inside. Lilly watched him go, too numb to react. *Where was he going?* The sound of the front door slamming made her heart drop. *He was leaving?*

She ran to the front door and threw it open, but only the glaring darkness of the Caribbean night stared back at her. She would have heard the car if he'd taken it. He must have gone on foot.

She closed the door and fumbled with the deadbolt to lock it. Unsure of what to do next, she turned and leaned against it, pulling in deep, long breaths. Then she slid down to the floor and did the thing she hadn't let herself do since the week she'd left Riccardo.

She sobbed her heart out.

Tears streamed down her face in a barrage that it seemed would never end. Her worst fear about her marriage had been both proven and unproven in one explosive conversation that had left her so raw and exposed she wasn't sure she would ever be able to close herself back up again.

Riccardo had kissed Chelsea Tate with the intent of sleeping with her. And even though he hadn't been able to do it, the fact that he'd kissed Chelsea—the *thought* of him kissing her—splintered Lilly's heart into a million pieces.

How could he? The man who'd promised to love and protect her that day in the cathedral when they'd been married, whom she'd let down all her barriers for, had betrayed her in the worst way possible. Because, she thought numbly, wasn't kissing the most intimate act of all?

Somewhere, someplace deep down inside her, she'd been hoping she was wrong. That Riccardo had been telling her the truth when he'd said nothing had happened between him and Chelsea and that her early naive belief that nothing could touch them was true.

But it wasn't something she could hang onto anymore. She and Riccardo *were* fallible and his message had been clear. *She* had driven him into Chelsea's arms. He had wanted to hurt her as she'd been hurting him. And that, she realized, swiping the tears from her face, was something she'd never thought of. That cool, hard-as-rock Riccardo could be hurt in any way. That *she* had the power to hurt him like that.

But in the end it had been as she'd always known it would be. She hadn't been capable of being what he needed. She hadn't been enough for him. Otherwise he never would have gone to Chelsea.

Her severed heart throbbed with a misery that said there was still some life in it. She closed her eyes and breathed.

To leave had been her survival mechanism. To stop trying to be something she could never be.

But Riccardo's relentless assault continued to unpeel her layers, as if once started it would never stop. Emotions that had been bottled up far too long bubbled over and tumbled into her consciousness. She remembered that perfect day before everything had unraveled, when they'd rescued their dog, Brooklyn, from the street, taken her to the house in Westchester and spent the weekend there. Her gorgeous husband had scooped up Brooklyn in one hand and Lilly in the other and tucked them all into bed. Throwing out the heart-stopping comment as the puppy lay snoring at their feet that maybe they should make theirs a family of four.

She'd been so excited, her mind whirring like the hamster's wheel from her childhood, that she hadn't slept that night. Like the luckiest of little girls on Christmas morning, she'd felt as if she'd been given everything she'd ever dreamed of. She had Riccardo, a great career and a home. A *real* home, where love reigned—not dramatic tension that would take her who knew where next. And for the first time since she'd left Iowa as a teenager, scared and unsure of her future, she'd known everything was going to be okay.

She would have a family of her own—one that wasn't living a hand-to-mouth existence. A family that wasn't a dysfunctional, sordid mess.

Dreams could come true, she'd told herself, falling asleep in Riccardo's arms at dawn.

The impossibly perfect memory made her suck in a breath.

She was still in love with her husband.

No matter how hard she tried to deny it, no matter how much she told herself they shouldn't be together, it was never going to go away. That deep, gnawing pain that had started when she'd left him and never stopped.

She pried her eyes open and stared dully up at the grandfather clock in the hallway. Its rhythmical tick-tock was deafeningly loud in the still villa. She was mad about a man who'd spoken of their love in the past tense tonight. As if he was as sure as she was they'd done too much harm to each other ever to be able to recover from it.

And he was right. About all of it. She *had* shut down on him. She should have told him about her anorexia. She should have told him about the photos. Instead she'd run, like she always did.

But he had kissed Chelsea. And that wasn't something she was sure she could forgive.

She bit her lip, vaguely registering the metallic taste of blood. The clock droned on…tick-tock, tick-tock. She had made huge mistakes in her marriage. But at least tonight she'd taken her first step forward. She'd told the truth. And that was something.

She bit her lip, refusing to give in to the fresh set of tears burning the back of her eyes. If it was clear they were over, then that was for the best. They had closure. In six months she was going to have to walk away from Riccardo, this time for good.

She was going to have to move on.

At least now she could.

She got to her feet, splashed cold water on her face and went back out to the terrace to wait for Riccardo. Two, three hours passed—she wasn't sure. A million stars blanketed the dark Caribbean sky as she drank wine and listened to the rhythmic pull of the ocean.

Her eyes started to drift shut.

The clocks chiming midnight woke her. Disoriented and half asleep, she padded inside to a dark, empty villa. And realized her husband wasn't coming back.

CHAPTER EIGHT

RICCARDO ENDED UP nursing a glass of ten-year-old rum on the front steps of a local rum shack in Holetown. Neat, as the grizzly old proprietor had suggested.

He'd needed a place he could think, away from the glitzy west coast hotels and restaurants. A place where he could digest his mind-blowing conversation with his wife. Because if he'd suspected before that he didn't know all of her it was now brutally apparent he hadn't even scratched the surface of who Lilly De Campo was.

Mind reeling, he'd wandered down the road from the villa until he'd come to the local hotspot—a red-and-cream-painted clapboard house emblazoned with the logo of a local beer company, one of dozens of such dwellings scattered around the island. There had been a handful of Bajans sitting on the front steps, chatting about last night's cricket game, and zero expectations of socializing.

Perfetto.

He took a sip of the rum and was glad the proprietor had talked him into drinking it neat. It brought out the oaky molasses flavor of the blend and right now he needed its smooth burn. Needed to quell the tumult raging through his brain.

His wife had trusted him so little she'd paid a gossip columnist one hundred thousand dollars for pictures that weren't even of him. Then she'd lied to him about where the money had gone.

Che diavolo.

He pulled in a deep breath. What state of mind must she have been in to do something like that? To air their dirty laundry to a tabloid journalist and expose their private lives rather than come to him? He wanted to shake her. To chastise her for being so stupid. Except it had also been his fault. *He* had given her reason to be jealous. *He* had violated the trust in their marriage.

He had almost smeared the past in her face without knowing it by being unfaithful to her like her father had her mother.

He uttered a smothered oath. The bombshells had just kept coming. His wife had been suffering from an eating disorder he hadn't known about. She had been struggling with a disease only made worse by the limelight she'd been thrust into and *he hadn't noticed.* How had he not noticed? It was inconceivable to him. He wasn't an expert on eating disorders, but didn't women usually make themselves throw up when they had one? He knew for sure he hadn't missed that. Lilly hated throwing up, and when she did so because of her migraines she was miserable.

So where had been the signs he'd been supposed to see?

She'd always been tall and thin, and he'd thought that was her natural predisposition, but now that he thought about it she *had* been curvier when they'd met. She'd consistently lost weight throughout their marriage until she'd been ultra-thin at the end, but he'd thought that was because she'd wanted to fit into the designer dresses she'd worn. In hindsight, he admitted, shifting uncomfortably on the steps, her penchant for skipping meals near the end should have raised alarm bells. It was just that he hadn't been home enough to monitor it.

A memory of Lilly, exhausted and seemingly emotionally spent, begging him to let her stay home the night of the financial district's Christmas ball filled his head. He'd thought she was just being difficult and had insisted on her attending because it was a De Campo-sponsored event.

She'd obviously been struggling.

His hands tightened around the glass. He could have destroyed her by not knowing. By continuing to push her. Had he really been that oblivious? Was he so set on perfection in those around him she'd felt she couldn't come to him? Couldn't talk to him?

Had he been, as Lilly had accused, so caught up with his obsession of becoming CEO he hadn't seen anything but the end goal?

An intense feeling of shame washed over him. There had been one month in that last year when he'd only been home one night because he'd been traveling so much, opening restaurants. *One night.*

And maybe there had been more months like that...

"You left me alone to deal with the fallout of being Lilly De Campo."

Was that what he'd done?

He took a swig of the rum and stared out at the cars whizzing by on the snakelike coastal road. Their ability to hurt each other was monumental. The breakdown in communication between them breathtaking. How had something so good gone so wrong?

He watched as a new arrival joined the other grizzled old men on the steps. They clapped him on the back and kept on talking about last night's game, which apparently had been a barn-burner. He was struck by how absolutely insane his life had become. He was a machine, not a man. He no longer remembered what it was like to live because he was too busy planning for tomorrow.

He nursed the glass between his hands and stared down at the brilliant amber liquid. It was time he simplified his life. Step one had been this weekend with Lilly, to discover the truth. Step two would be in three months, when

Antonio ceded control to him. Step three was going to be about honesty.

"I faked my way through our entire marriage."

The statement had made his blood boil. He might have done things all wrong but Lilly had owed him honesty. She had owed that to their marriage. And nothing, *nothing* made up for the fact that she'd walked out on him. And left *him* to deal with the fallout of their marriage.

"It was never going to work."

Her words danced in front of him like a red cape, egging on an enraged bull. If his wife thought she was going to check out again now, when the honesty had just started between them, she was sadly mistaken. Lilly was about to find out what it was like to follow through on a promise. What it was like to pay as he'd been paying for the past year. Because De Campos didn't divorce. They stuck it out—even if they were in a loveless partnership like his parents.

He drained his glass and set it down with a thud that drew the eyes of the faction of grizzled old men. Standing up, he went back inside and slapped his glass on the counter. "Another," he said hoarsely. "Make it a double."

This time he *had left* her.

Lilly stood on the balcony of their villa, staring at the ocean as it sparkled in the moonlight. It was pushing one o'clock and still her husband hadn't come home. He had decided the muddled, mass of confusion his wife undoubtedly was wasn't CEO wife material. Wasn't worth the effort.

Hot, silent tears ran down her cheeks. She'd kept her secrets because she'd known if she'd told the truth about who she was she'd lose him. But in the end it hadn't mattered. She'd lost him anyway.

Had he been repulsed by her secret—by the anorexia that had been her Achilles' Heel? Or had it been the dishonesty? The lies she'd told to save herself?

She didn't blame him for not wanting her. She'd only just started to learn how to appreciate herself.

"I thought you'd be asleep."

Her husband's deep voice came from behind her. She spun around, her heart in her mouth as her gaze moved over his strained, somber features.

"You came back."

"Of course I did." He closed the distance between them. "I told you this is not over between us."

That had been before tonight. Before they had annihilated each other.

His gaze moved over her face. "I've never seen you cry."

She raised a hand to swipe the tears from her face. Telling him she still loved him, that she'd thought she'd lost him forever, wasn't going to happen. Not when she was sure he hated her for what she'd done to him. But she couldn't stop the emotion that was suffocating her, threatening to spill over into something she couldn't control.

His eyes darkened and the strain on his face deepened, looking even harsher in the moonlight. "This is not over," he repeated. "Get that through your head, Lilly. We are only getting started."

How could that be? This reconciliation of theirs was only for six months. And it wasn't real. But tell that to her brain. He did away with the last few inches between them, a look of intent on his face so deliberate her heart stopped in her chest.

"Ric—"

The hand she held out to ward him off was captured and folded against his chest as he pulled her into him. "No more talking," he murmured, moving his lips to the upper curve of her cheek, where the tears were still falling. "We've done enough talking for a lifetime tonight."

She knew she should protest, but then he was kissing away her tears one by one, following the hot, salty path down over the curve of her jaw. As if with every one he dispensed with he was wiping the past away. A sigh was torn from deep inside her as she arched her neck back. If this was supposed to be comfort she couldn't quite envision it, because he was setting her blood on fire.

His big hands swept the straps of her négligée aside so his lips could continue their exploration down the sensitive skin of her neck and over the roundness of her shoulder.

The honesty of this—the honesty of them together like this—had never been in question. And tonight she needed for him to heal them.

To hell with the consequences.

She moved willingly against him as he pulled her up on tiptoes and kissed her—a slow, drugging caress she felt down to her toes. It was like an anesthetic to her soul, his touch, as if the only thing she'd been put on this planet to do was kiss him in these deep, never-ending caresses that devoured the essence of each other.

A shiver ran through her—anticipatory, all-consuming. She buried her fingers in the thick muscles of his shoulders, rediscovering the feel of him under her hands, the way the sharp tug of her teeth on his bottom lip made him groan low in the back of his throat.

"You are killing me," he murmured, sliding his hands down over her silk-covered bottom and yanking her closer.

The feel of his big, warm hands on her, shaping her against the muscular hard length of him made her whimper. His thick erection made her gasp.

"*Esattamente,*" he muttered, scooping her up into his arms. She breathed in the familiar, heady male scent of him as he carried her into the bedroom. It was like coming home.

Light from the big, fat, almost-full moon flooded the beautiful blue-and-white-striped bedroom that looked as if it had come straight out of a magazine. But all Lilly had eyes for was her husband as he let her slide down his body to the floor, the silk catching between them. He was the most smoking hot man she'd ever encountered on so many levels.

Intense, like the night. Exciting, like a summer storm that made everything electric. Earthy, like a man who knew how to savor every moment like the fine wines his family created.

Her heart thumped at the foot of her throat as he slid his fingers under the straps of her négligée and dropped it to the floor. She closed her eyes as his gaze moved over her naked flesh. She had never been perfect but she was definitely less than that now.

"Dio, Lilly. *Come sei bella."*

His raspily intoned observation made her eyes fly open. The look of pure lust on his face made her knees go weak. "I don't look like I used to," she whispered.

He slid his hands down her back to her bottom and tugged her forward, until her naked flesh was flush against his still clothed body. "I told you," he murmured. "I love the curves... If anything, I want you more than I did before."

Oh. Liquid fire raced through her veins as his fingers tangled in the hair at the nape of her neck and he tipped her head back to receive his kiss. Open-mouthed, and hotter than Hades, it immersed her in a pool of want that threatened to eat her alive.

Her control snapped. The depth of her emotion for this man was frightening, endless, but to have him again like this made her frantic, desperate.

"Ric," she muttered against his mouth. "Please."

He abandoned her lips in favor of a fingertips to bare skin exploration of the weight of her breasts. "Do you know how hard it's been for me to keep my hands off you?" he breathed, brushing his thumbs over the tips of her nipples. "I took down a ninety-foot tree in Westchester, I was so crazed."

Lilly squeezed her eyes shut as her nipples hardened beneath his touch. "I can't believe you didn't kill yourself."

"Gabe helped. Matteo got in the way."

She smiled and wriggled against him, trying to get closer, but he closed his hands down hard over her shoulders and held her away.

"Not so fast, *tesoro*. It's been a long time since I've had you like this."

She eased back reluctantly. "Did you really go a year without sex?"

"I'm a man, Lilly. I found ways to ease the tension."

"Oh."

His soft laughter filled the night air. "Don't worry—you were still the star attraction."

The erotic image of him pleasuring himself—stroking that beautiful muscular body of his and thinking about her—sent another hot flash through her body that made her feel vaguely feverish. But then he was kissing his way down her throat toward the sensitive spot at the base of her neck—the spot he knew drove her crazy.

Hot. So hot.

She moved desperately against him.

He slid a hand down over her trembling stomach, over her navel to the juncture of her thighs. "Spread your legs for me, sweetheart."

Lilly swallowed hard and relaxed her grip, letting him push her legs apart.

"Did you ever touch yourself, thinking about me?" he questioned, sliding his fingers against the most private part of her.

"Ric—"

"The truth," he insisted.

"Yes," she murmured. God help her, yes, she had.

He rotated his thumb against the hard, aching center of her. "But it wasn't as good as the real thing, was it? Because I know it wasn't for me."

"No," she groaned. "It wasn't."

He lowered his head and kissed her, made her remember exactly how good he could make her feel. She grabbed a hold of his shirt to steady herself as he slid a finger inside her, his touch so unbearly good she thought she would scream.

"More," she murmured against his lips.

He withdrew and slid two fingers inside her, filling her deeper, harder. She arched against his hand as the ache inside her became unbearable.

"Please," she moaned.

He dropped to his knees in front of her. Lilly made a sound of protest, reaching down and grabbing his arms to pull him back up to her. She felt too exposed, too raw to have him do this to her right now.

But he shook her hands off and looked up at her, eyes glittering. "Immersion therapy, Lilly. Relax and enjoy it."

She squeezed her eyes shut, too hot, too aroused to do anything but obey. And then he was parting her with gentle fingers, his raspy, "*Bella...*" filling the air before he bent and feasted on her. She held the back of his head as he slid his tongue against her aroused flesh. The rush of pleasure that swirled through her was so incredibly good she felt as if every nerve in her body was concentrated right *there*.

"Ric—I need—"

"I know," he murmured against her skin. "Let go, Lilly."

Her legs started to tremble wildly. He slid his fingers inside her again and shot her into another stratosphere. *God.* She just needed him to curve his fingers like—*that*.

"*Oh.*"

He kept his fingers there and flicked his tongue over the hard bud at the center of her. Her insides contracted as she came in a rush of such sweet, hot pleasure he had to hold her upright. It was white-hot, blinding. All-consuming.

She was floating on a sea of pleasure when he got to his feet, scooped her up into his arms and carried her to the bed. "You are so sexy," he murmured, leaning down to kiss her. "Your reactions...everything about you turns me on."

The taste of herself on his lips was unbearably intimate. And she felt her last barrier come tumbling down.

He left her to pull his shirt over his head, his impatient, jerky movements so unlike him she smiled. "Need some help with your pants?"

He stepped closer and brought her hands to his belt.

She took in the hard muscles of his torso, the perfectly defined six-pack, the undeniably hot vee that disappeared beneath his jeans. She had undressed him hundreds of times, but this time her hands were shaking and her throat was dry.

She worked his belt buckle open and fumbled with the button of his jeans.

"Lilly," he murmured, covering her hand with his. "Are you okay?"

She nodded and bit her lip. With a smothered curse he stepped back and shoved his jeans and boxers off. The masculine beauty of his body made her want like a woman who'd been stranded in the desert far too long. When he sank down on the bed and reached for her she straddled his muscular thighs, wanting to give him as much pleasure as he'd given her.

He was hard, aroused, barely leashed male power beneath her, and she wanted him inside her more than she wanted her next breath.

He buried his lips in her shoulder, a tremor running through his big body. "I can't play around like this much longer..."

"Who's playing?" She sat back on her haunches, her eyes riveted to his beautiful toned body. "I'm not," she assured him, sliding her fingers to the insides of his thighs.

His gaze moved to her hands. *"Lilly..."*

She curved her fingers around him and reveled in his sharp intake of breath. He was smooth and hard like steel, pulsing underneath her fingers. With a muffled curse he sank his hands into her waist and lifted her over him, the movement bringing her swollen flesh into contact with his engorged length.

Ruddy color dusted his cheekbones. "*Maledizione, Lilly…*"

She slid the thick head of him inside her, her body so aroused, so wet, she accommodated him easily. He cursed under his breath, the muscles of his arms bulging as he braced them on either side of himself. She took more of him, and more, until she felt as if she couldn't go further. She'd forgotten how big he was, how the length of him caressed every last centimeter of her. Closing her eyes, she focused on taking him, adjusting her hips until he slid in to the hilt.

Her gasp split the air.

He stayed completely still beneath her while her body adjusted to his, his jaw clenched, his face a picture of grim self-control. "Are you okay?"

"Fine," she breathed, relaxing into him. "You're just so damned big."

He closed his eyes. "That's not usually a complaint."

"It's not, it's j— *Oh, God,* you feel so good."

"*I'd* feel better if I could move," he rasped.

She leaned down and kissed him. "Let me."

She rode him slowly, deliberately at first, every movement designed to drive him wild. He twisted his hips and tried to control the rhythm but she shook her head. "Like this."

He clamped his jaw shut and let her take the lead. Lilly shut her eyes and just *felt*. Felt the size and girth of him stroke her, reach every nerve-ending. Her body clamped around him as she remembered the pleasure he could give her, cried out desperately for it.

No man had ever been able to turn her on this much. Only Riccardo.

She threw her head back and let herself go. Every powerful stroke of his body up into hers was filling her from the inside out—filling the lonely place inside her that had never gotten over the loss of him. And when she looked down at him the dark glitter in his eyes told her he felt it too.

"Are you with me?" he demanded hoarsely. "Please tell me you're with me."

"Always," she whispered.

Something tilted in his face. A look of such raw, uncensored emotion that she felt it in a place she'd never felt it before. He might not love her anymore, but he wasn't devoid of emotion.

She committed it to memory, held onto it as he surged up inside her and demanded she ride him harder, faster. Something told her she was going to need it as he made her drown in the sensations he was creating. As he branded her with his touch and found that sweet spot he knew would take her over the edge. Her fingernails dug into his shoulders as he stroked her deliberately, repeatedly, until she felt the white-hot beginning of her release. Once, twice, three times he drove into her, and she screamed, her body contracting around his in an orgasm stronger and more shattering than the first.

He cursed under his breath and fell back onto his elbows, his body surging up inside her. She felt him throb even bigger, watched his face as he lost control. His hands clamped down on her hips and his body shook in a release that rocked them both.

Winded, shaken to her core, she collapsed forward onto his chest, listening to his heart thunder beneath her ear. This was the time when he'd used to whisper that he loved her in Italian. When he'd tuck her into his side and cradle her until she slept. When she had been sure beyond a shadow of a doubt of his feelings for her.

The hot, humid Caribbean air throbbed around them—heavy and full. A loaded silence stretched between them. They stayed like that for several long minutes. Then Riccardo lifted her off his chest and tucked her beneath the sheets.

"You need to sleep."

She wanted to beg him to hold her. To prolong what they'd shared for just a few more minutes. She heard him snap off the lights and come back to the bed, felt the mattress dipping beneath his weight. Then he reached for her and pulled her into his arms, curving her back against the warm length of him. She exhaled in a long, slow breath. This was enough. Being back in the place where everything felt right. Even for one night.

She fell asleep almost immediately.

Her pounding head woke her at two a.m. She stumbled into the bathroom and grabbed her painkillers out of her bag. She had unscrewed the bottle and downed two tablets with a glass of water when the unthinkable occurred to her.

In the hustle of traveling this morning she'd forgotten to take her birth control pill.

It had been almost twenty-four hours since she had.

"Do me a favor." Alex's words rang in her ear. *"Whatever you do, don't get pregnant."*

She pulled the birth control pills out of her bag and desperately shoved one in her mouth. It hadn't even been twenty-four hours... It would be fine.

But even as she reassured herself she knew it had been stupid, *stupid.* How could she have complicated a relationship in which the only thing that *was* clear was that it didn't need complicating?

CHAPTER NINE

LILLY WOKE UP with such a supreme feeling of well-being she thought she might have been accidentally transported to a land of paradise, where everything was silk sheets, hard male and a bone-meltingly familiar sense of satisfaction she never wanted to end.

Turning her head from its face-down planting in the pillow, she slid her palm across the sheet in search of more warm, hard male. Nothing but silk. Her eyes flickered open. She was alone in the huge king-sized bed.

She flipped over, settled back against the mountain of pillows and stared out at the brilliant blue sky. She might almost think it had been a dream, the ridiculously hot sex she'd had with her husband. But the ache between her legs begged to differ. And in the blinding light of morning everything seemed magnified by ten.

She'd let the man she was still madly in love with, who didn't love her anymore, strip her of the defenses she'd spent a decade building. Then she'd slept with him in a moment of madness without using protection, which demonstrated exactly what a moment of madness it had been.

Damn.

She squeezed her eyes shut. It had been a monumentally stupid thing to do. The one thing she'd never been able to deny was the connection they'd had in bed. And once that took over all bets were off.

It was the reason she'd refused to see him for so long. Because she didn't trust herself around Riccardo.

Her stomach churned. Both she and Riccardo had extremely fertile families. But hadn't it taken her girlfriend, Darya, forever to conceive? Surely it wouldn't happen in one night?

Finding the whole thing entirely too disconcerting, she threw back the covers and swung her legs out of bed. Riccardo would have been up hours ago. He'd probably swum fifty lengths of that Olympic-sized pool and gone through every set of weights in the exercise room by now.

She padded restlessly over to the patio doors and threw open the curtains. The humid heat hit her immediately, and the perfume-soaked, salty, heavy air was filled with the scent of dozens of exotic flowers. It begged complete lethargy—a sunchair, a book and a drink, followed by a cool swim.

She blinked and shaded her eyes against the brilliant sunlight. And found her guess had been right. But rather than laps her husband was slicing through the ocean with a powerful front crawl that ate up the distance between the raft that bobbed about a mile out and the beach.

She watched as he hit the shore and walked up the beach, water sluicing down over his washboard abs. The drool that formed in her mouth was swift and uncontrollable. As if having him so completely last night had done nothing to stem the urge she had for him.

He lifted a hand to swipe the water from his face. And saw her standing there.

A heart-meltingly sexy smile curved his mouth. He walked up the beach and came to stand below the balcony, a fully relaxed, content-looking Riccardo who turned her insides to mush.

"You coming down?"

A smile twisted her lips. "If you'll come swimming with me. I'm sweating already."

"We have fifteen minutes before breakfast is ready. Get your suit on and get down here."

She slipped off her négligée and pulled on the fuchsia bikini she'd bought with Alex. She might have made the huge mistake of sleeping with Riccardo last night, but that didn't mean she had to continue her foolish behavior today. She needed to focus on keeping her head. She bit her lip as she pulled on a short cotton dress over her bathing suit. So what was she doing, running down to swim with him? And what had he meant when he'd said, *"This is not over. We are only getting started"?*

It didn't matter what he'd said! She swiped some sunscreen across her cheeks and nose. Riccardo *was* a lethal banned substance for her. Best to accept that last night had been inevitable between them, like a storm reaching its conclusion, and find a way to make it through the next six months without killing each other.

Hot sex wasn't going to accomplish that.

A rational brain would.

Tell that to her hormones, she thought as she joined Riccardo on the tiny private beach in front of the villa, the sand as smooth as silk between her toes. Because the intensity of her husband's dark gaze on her was making her overheating problem a virtual crisis.

"You'd better lose the dress," he advised. "Nowhere down here to leave it."

She darted a self-conscious glance around her. The bikini wasn't French Riviera material but it was revealing enough. She would rather have just gotten in the water, but since there really wasn't anywhere to leave her cover-up on the beach she walked up to the terrace, draped it over a chair and headed back down to him, self-conscious in her halter top bikini.

The smell of bacon wafted through the air. "Mrs. Adams is cooking?"

He nodded. "We thought we'd let you sleep in. You needed it."

She walked toward him, ultra self-conscious in her halter top bikini.

Her husband took her in from beneath veiled lashes. "And here I thought we had declared a truce."

She frowned. Looked down at herself. *Pink.* Her swimsuit was pink.

Heat filled her cheeks. "It was the only suit that didn't make me look like an adult movie star."

He reached for her, his fingers closing over her forearm. "Why go for modest when you look that good, *cara?*"

She sucked in a breath as he pulled her against his hard, dripping wet body. "Did you listen to a word I said last night?"

"*Si.* I am intent on desensitizing you."

She pressed a hand against his chest to balance herself. "You can't just wave your fairy wand and cure me, Riccardo. Anorexia is something I'll carry with me for the rest of my life, even if I have it under control."

"I know," he said, bringing his lips down on hers as he swung her up in his arms. "But I'm going to do it anyway."

She smiled at his arrogance. His lips were warm from the heat of the sun, his kiss as leisurely as the mood he seemed to be in, and she found she just didn't have the willpower to fight him.

He walked into the sea, and the water was so warm it barely registered on her heated skin. Then he wrapped her legs around him so they floated on the buoyant sea.

"Riccardo…"

"What?"

"I—I don't think this is appropriate."

He gave her an amused look. "We're married. What's inappropriate about it?"

She focused her gaze on his Adam's apple. "Last night

was…amazing…but I think anymore of that is just going to complicate things between us."

He lifted her chin with his fingers. "If you mean sex, Lilly, then I'm going to have to disagree. Sex breaks down the barriers between us, and if you think, now that we're finally talking, I'm going to let you put them up again, you're mistaken. By the end of this weekend there isn't going to be anything I don't know about you."

She went rigid. "There isn't anymore to say."

He pressed his lips together. "How did you keep it from me? I never saw the signs."

"My anorexia?"

He nodded.

She pressed her hands against his chest to put some distance between them, but he kept his arms firmly banded around her. "I was better when I met you. I'd gotten control over it. I'd spent my career practicing physiotherapy, learning how incredible the human body is—how strong it is—and how much more important it was to honor your body than do what I'd been doing to it."

She swallowed hard. His gaze on her face was making her feel as if she was under a microscope.

"It started to get bad for me again after that first year, when our honeymoon with the media wore off and they made a game out of criticizing how I looked or what I wore."

"Which they do with anyone who's in the limelight like that," he interjected.

"Yes. But for me it was harder. Anorexia isn't something with a lot of outward signs. It's insidious. I withdraw. I stop eating. It becomes impossible for me to look at my body objectively. Everything gets distorted."

He frowned. "I thought it was a vanity thing. The need to look perfect."

A rueful smile curved her mouth. "The need to not hate myself would be more accurate."

His jaw hardened. "Was I really that impossible to talk to? Did I really demand that much perfection from you?"

"It comes with your life, Riccardo. It's *expected* from those around you."

His jaw hardened. "We could have made adjustments to our life to make things easier for you."

She shook her head. "You're going to be the head of a ten-billion-dollar conglomerate when you take over from your father. You couldn't make those changes even if you wanted to."

His dark eyes glittered. "We could have. We could have done what was necessary and let the rest go."

"You're a dreamer," she bit out. "You needed a new wife. And you refused to admit it."

His lip curled. "I did not need a new wife. I needed a wife with the guts to tell me what was wrong. I needed a wife who was there for me at one of the lowest points of my life and instead you were *gone*."

She recoiled. "I had lost myself, Riccardo. I had lost the ability to keep myself in balance. If I hadn't left I would have reverted back to my old bad habits and destroyed myself."

A muscle jumped in his jaw. "You couldn't have waited until I'd gotten back? Been there for me?"

She pushed hard against his chest and this time he let her go. Finding the sandy bottom with her feet, she stood facing him. "What happened in Italy? All I knew was that you'd been summoned there on Antonio's orders."

He scraped his wet hair out of his face. "It doesn't matter now. We're talking about why you left."

"Goddammit, Riccardo." She took a step closer and jabbed her finger in his face. "We *are* talking about why I left. You never talk. You never tell me how you're feeling. What the hell happened in Tuscany?"

His face tightened into a stony stillness. "I knew the restaurant business was the future for De Campo. Knew we needed to diversify. Antonio didn't agree. He forbade me to proceed with the plans I had for Orvietto." He paused. "I signed the lease anyway."

She let out a slow breath. "He lost his mind…?"

"He threatened to strip me of my title and kick me out of the company."

"What?" Her mouth dropped open. "He wouldn't have done that."

"He would have!"

She took a step back as he practically yelled the words at her.

"The only reason he didn't was because my decision was right. I *proved* him wrong. Orvietto proved him wrong. But when I came back to New York that night I thought I'd lost everything. I'd given up the sport I loved for an old man who didn't give a damn, I was about to lose my job at De Campo, and then I walked into our house—into our *empty* house—to find the only person who could make me feel better and a teary Magda informed me you'd gone. *Gone.*" His gaze, dark and tormented, swept over her. "I hadn't slept in forty-eight hours. I just looked at her and said, 'Gone? What do you mean, gone?'"

Lilly felt a wave of nausea sweep over her. She'd been so lost in her own private hell she'd been numbed against the bizarre, disjointed tone of his voice when he'd called that night from overseas.

"I'm sorry," she whispered, tears stinging the back of her eyes. "I'm so sorry."

He looked away, the sun reflecting off the hard line of his jaw. "It isn't always about you, Lilly."

She wrapped her arms around herself. "I never thought it was."

The waves lapped gently around them, the only sound in this private slice of paradise.

"How did things ever get so bad between you two?"

He looked back at her. "Between Antonio and I?"

She nodded.

"The day of my graduation from Harvard I told him I'd signed with TeamXT. It was a once-in-a-lifetime opportunity I couldn't say no to. I'd been driving every summer, whenever I could, but this—this was my chance. I told Antonio I needed a couple of years to get it out of my system—that I'd join De Campo after that." He shrugged. "I knew he wasn't going to be happy, but I thought, given the opportunity, he might understand." A bitter note filled his tone as he continued. "I should have known better. He gave me an ultimatum instead. Join De Campo or forget ever being a part of it."

"You walked away?"

"We didn't speak after that until he became ill and asked me to take over."

"He expected you to come back after all that?"

He exhaled roughly. "You have to understand Antonio's background. His father was a tyrant. He browbeat Antonio into running the business when all my father ever wanted to do was work with animals. He wanted to raise prize-winning racehorses, not prize-winning vines, but his father had built a thriving business and Antonio was expected to take over."

"So by following your dream with racing you became everything he'd ever wanted to be?"

"Sì. I was the ultimate insult."

"So why not choose Gabe to head the company? He has such a love for it."

He grimaced. "Antonio is old-fashioned. He could never get past the fact that his eldest son should carry on as CEO. And, despite the animosity between us, we have always been the same. Tough sons-of-bitches who know how to get what we want."

How true *that* was. She blinked, trying to absorb it all. "And what about your mother? She didn't interject through all of this?"

"You've met her," he said roughly. "My mother toes the party line. Their marriage is based on mutual ambition. Emotion doesn't have anything to do with it. Not with her boys, either. She would have carted us off to boarding school in true aristocratic fashion if my father hadn't insisted we learn the wine business."

Emotions swirled inside her. Suddenly she wasn't certain of anything anymore. Whether she'd been right to leave him. Whether she should have worked harder at her marriage. It was all riddled with intricacies she had no way of assimilating.

"So what now?" she asked huskily. "You wait while Antonio strings you along?"

He shook his head. "He's retiring in three months. He's promised to hand De Campo over to me then. *If,*" he murmured bitterly, "I continue to prove to him I deserve it."

She flinched. "You could walk away. Go back to racing…"

His expression turned black as night. "I can't go back."

"You can do anything you want. You're a winner, Riccardo. You move mountains when you need to."

"You think I don't want to?" The words exploded out of him. "Every morning when I was driving I woke up feeling lucky to be on this planet. I was free. I was *alive*. Everytime I stepped on that racetrack I challenged the very core of myself. I was the *best*. The adrenalin, that charge that came at the starting line from driving a vehicle more powerful than any other on the planet—it *defined* me."

"So do it," she urged. "You don't owe Antonio anything. This is your life, not his."

His broad shoulders stiffened. "This is about honor. Not about doing what I want. Something I'm not sure *you* know much about. You walked away from your family and you walked away from me. But sometimes you have to hang in there, Lilly. Sometimes you have to fulfill the promises you've made. Even if it interferes with the grand plan."

His anger rippled through her, the depth and fury of it rocking her back on her heels. It was too much. Too much had passed between them. There was no going back.

"I think we should get some breakfast," she murmured, needing to break the intensity. "Mrs. Adams must have it ready by now."

"By all means." He nodded savagely. "Wouldn't want the eggs to cool while you do a little soul-searching."

She turned her back on him and started walking. Five and a half months. She could do this.

If it was possible to spend the day in heaven and feel as if you were in hell, then Lilly had managed to capture perfectly that peculiar and miserable experience. She'd spent the day on the private beach with an introspective version of her husband, surrounded by a shimmering sexual tension that was impossible to ignore despite the fact it seemed they were a million miles apart.

Somehow guilt had taken center stage. She should have been there for Riccardo when he'd been struggling. His account of coming home to find her gone had torn her heart out. No matter what she'd been going through, she should have been there for him.

She'd been incredibly selfish. Not only with her marriage. With her life. She'd had a dream for herself. To leave Mason Hill and never look back. But in pursuing that dream she'd hurt a lot of people. Her parents, Lisbeth—who'd been left alone and defenseless, even if she *had* been too young to come with them—and her brother, who'd been left with her and Alex's work on the farm. And, although she would do the same thing over, she'd had to leave to be who she was now, she was starting to realize that by being so wrapped up in herself she'd neglected the people she loved.

Her heart gave a painful squeeze. Even now she was

here and not with Lisbeth, helping her through her treatment.

When she got better, Lilly was going to bring her to New York to stay with her. She was going to make up for leaving her alone in Iowa.

"What are you thinking about?"

Riccardo's idly delivered question was one of the few he'd uttered over their evening meal at the beachfront restaurant on Barbados's south coast. It pulled her out of her thoughts and focused her attention on the man sitting across from her. Not that she'd been able to avoid acknowledging how good he looked. Dressed in jeans and a gray T-shirt, he had a relaxed and dangerously attractive air about him that every woman in the restaurant had already noticed. Including the Hollywood A-lister and the Mediterranean Princess sitting at right angles to them.

He hadn't looked at one of them.

"So?" He lifted his hand and waved it at her.

She took a sip of her wine—just because Riccardo had refused alcohol tonight it didn't mean she had to. "Is this going to be your new occupation? Analyzing me at every moment?"

His gaze narrowed. "Until I'm sure you're telling the truth—*si,* it is."

She waggled her fingers at him. "No secrets left here. I'm an open book."

Except I still love you desperately.

"You're thinking about something."

About how she'd like to skip dessert, rush home and enjoy that incredible body of his as the final course... Which was absolutely, positively not going to happen.

His mouth tilted up at the corners. "You know the rules. You look at me like that—we leave." He reached into his jeans pocket and threw his wallet on the table.

She stared at the wallet, her heart pounding. "I wasn't

looking at you like that. And we should at least look at the dessert menu."

"Why? You never eat dessert." He handed his credit card to the waiter. "Tell me what happened to your wedding rings."

She set her glass down with a jerky movement. "I told you I'm not sure where they are."

He lifted a brow. "I may be a lot of things, *tesoro,* but I'm not a fool. You're far too careful with things to lose them. So where are they?"

Her gaze slid away from his. "I'm not sure you want to know."

He lifted his brow higher.

"They might be in the East River."

"Scusi?"

She swallowed hard. "I threw them off the Brooklyn Bridge."

His jaw dropped. "You threw your fifty-thousand-dollar engagement ring off the Brooklyn Bridge?"

"I was angry."

"You were *angry?*" For the first time in their married life her husband looked speechless.

She lifted her chin. "The day I left I was so mad, so hurt. I had a clinic in Brooklyn and on my way back I lost it. I felt so betrayed—about Chelsea, about what you'd done to us—that I asked my cab driver to stop and I just…"

"Threw them in," he finished grimly.

"Sure I can't get you anything else?" Their waiter popped a leather folder on their table.

"I wanted to have a liqueur." Lilly searched desperately for anything that wouldn't involve them being alone together.

"We can have one at the villa."

"I'd prefer to have it here." She looked desperately at the little bar that sat beside this restaurant on the beach. There was loud Calypso music playing and lots of locals hanging out on the front patio. "Why don't we have one *there?* It looks like fun."

He followed her gaze. "Trying to avoid the inevitable, Lil?"

"I'm trying to have a good time. You might try that every once in a while."

The antagonism that flared in his gaze made her stomach do a little flip. He threw some money on the table and stood up.

"One drink."

Breathing deeply at her momentary reprieve, Lilly settled herself on a stool at the beachside bar and smiled at the tall, dreadlocked Bajan bartender.

He eyed them up. "On your honeymoon?"

Lilly choked.

"I wish we were," Riccardo interjected drily. "The *signora* would like a drink."

Mr. Dreadlocks, whose hair reached further down his back than her own, shifted his oh-so-cool gaze to her. "What can I get you?"

"How about the house specialty?"

He blinked. "The house specialty?"

"Sure. Sounds good."

"Lewis," he introduced himself, sticking a hand out. She took it, then he did the same to Riccardo. "The same?"

"Wouldn't miss it. But make mine a half—I'm driving."

Lewis pulled about five different bottles off the shelf and started mixing. Lilly could tell she'd made a big mistake by the time he got to bottle number three, which had no label on it and looked as if it was a home brew.

Riccardo held his glass up to hers, a challenging glitter in his ebony eyes. "Bottoms up."

It was so strong it was all Lilly could do not to plug her nose and drink it that way. Those who liked straight alcohol might have found it passable, and Riccardo wasn't having any trouble with it, but for Lilly, who wasn't used to drinking liquor neat, every sip felt like a fire in her mouth and throat.

Every sip was also making her feel looser and much less inhibited. She permitted herself a good look at her drool-worthy husband. Imagined stripping off that T-shirt and exploring every inch of his hard pecs and chest. *Would allowing herself one more night be such a huge mistake?* After all, it wasn't as if this was easy, being here in such a romantic place. Maybe after this weekend, back in New York, she'd be able to keep a much firmer grip on her head.

Determinedly she rattled on to Lewis about how much she loved the island and asked him a million questions about himself.

Riccardo drained his glass and set it on the bar. "Time to go."

She scrunched her face up and downed the rest of her drink. She was going to need it. She was definitely going to need it. Lewis waved goodnight and made them promise to come back.

Their walk to the car was filled with a weighty silence that played on Lilly's nerve-endings like a bow. Her whole body felt as if it was on fire.

"What the hell was in that drink?" she muttered, leaning against the car while Riccardo opened her door.

He whipped the door open, then pushed her back against the Lamborghini. "I'm not sure I want to know."

Her fingers curled into his shirt as he leaned down and took her mouth in a hard, punishing kiss that told her he was still furious about the rings. But it was the heat behind it that made her feel light-headed.

This was going to be off the scale.

Riccardo considered himself a skilled driver, but there was no finesse in the way he handled Charles Browne's sleek sports car as they drove the windy coastal road home. Lilly was all over him. It was all he could do to keep the car on the road with her unbuttoning his shirt and sliding her hands over his chest.

"Lilly," he groaned. "What are you doing?"

"What's the matter, Mr. Racecar Driver?" she taunted, sliding her hands to his belt. "A little distraction and you can't cope?"

He sucked in a breath as she tugged hard on the leather. "I never should have let you have that drink."

"So true," she murmured. The rasp of his zipper was agonizingly loud in the quiet confines of the car. "Too late now."

Her fingers brushed over him. He jerked so hard the car went sliding across the road. He shoved her away from him and yanked hard on the wheel to avoid a ditch. "If you want to live, keep your hands off me."

She slunk back against the seat. He glanced at her impatient expression. *Dio.* What had gotten into his wife? He hadn't seen this Lilly since—when? He couldn't remember.

His body throbbing with an urgency that was near combustible, he started inwardly reciting the specs of the engine under the Lamborghini's hood. One after another he went through the parts, until he'd exhausted every single screw and cap and they were on the side road to the villa.

He brought the car to a growling halt in the garage, walked around to Lilly's side and pulled her out. "You're paying for that," he promised, pushing her in front of him and out of the garage. "That was seriously stupid, Lilly."

His wife appeared not to care. In fact she stood there, her cat's eyes challenging him, focused on him, as he unlocked the door to the villa. He urged her inside and locked it. The want in her gaze undid him.

He threw her over his shoulder and headed upstairs.

"You know I like this," she teased.

"Your payment hasn't even begun."

He set her down on the floor of their bedroom, then shrugged out of his shirt, ripped off his belt and ditched his pants. Lilly's eyes were big as saucers as he pushed her against the wall and ran his hand over the soft flesh of her breasts, temptingly full under her cotton dress, then down over her trembling stomach.

"Ric—"

He moved his hands over her hips and under the flirty dress that had been driving him crazy all night. Her flesh was warm, and toned, and control was in short supply.

"Feel free to tell me when the punishment is over."

He pushed her thighs apart and slid the heel of his hand up over the heat of her. "You will know."

She was trembling under his hands. He reached up, snagged his fingers in the sides of her barely-there thong and pulled it down over her long legs. She was beautiful and intoxicating, his Lilly, and she whispered something unintelligible as he stood and buried his fingers in her hair, kissing her senseless. She had the most perfect lips he'd ever encountered in a woman—full, perfectly shaped, and without a collagen injection in sight. And if he hadn't been so intent on teaching her a lesson he would have suggested she wrap them around another part of his anatomy.

But payback was paramount. He slid a hand between her thighs, seeking and finding her hot wetness. She moaned and pressed closer, inviting him in as he slid a finger inside her.

"Ric—"she said brokenly, shaking like a leaf.

"Not over," he said harshly, adding another finger and working her in a rhythm he knew would send her close to the edge.

Her breathing was quick and tortured against his mouth. Her hips writhed against his hand. And he knew the point at which she would beg…

"Please—I—"

He removed his fingers from her and pushed her toward the bed. "I never make a promise I don't keep, *amore mio*."

The front of her knees butted up against the edge of the

mattress. He placed a palm in the small of her back and pushed her forward until her hands were braced on the bed.

"Almost over," he murmured. "Because I know you like it like this too."

She bit back a gasp as he pushed her dress up and nudged her legs apart.

"Ric—"

"Shh." He leaned over and pressed a kiss against her back. "Keep your hands there and don't move."

She stayed where she was. He felt his composure waver as he brushed himself against the wet heat of her, hard steel against soft velvet. Lilly groaned and grasped the bedcovers. She was as hot for him as he was for her, but he kept a torturous hold on himself as he slid into her slowly, inch by inch. She was incredibly vulnerable in this position and he needed her trust.

"Good?" he asked hoarsely, giving her body a chance to adjust to the size and girth of him.

She let out a strangled, urgent moan. He closed his eyes and let himself go. Let the desperate urgency of a man who was haunted by a woman take over as he drove into the tight, wet heat that embraced him like a glove.

Too long he had wanted her. Too much he had missed her.

His hands tightened on her hips as he took her close to the edge, then pulled back, wanting this to last, wanting to torture her as she'd tortured him. Wanting to give them both maximum pleasure. But his body tensed and swelled; his mind fixed on the torturously perfect fit of being inside of her again. Then the world splintered apart.

He wanted, *needed* her to be there with him, and he almost cried out with relief when he felt her body contract around his, drawing out his own release until his harsh moan split the night air. The tightening of her body rolled over him like a shockwave, sending surge after surge of explosive pleasure through him.

Dio. He scooped her trembling body off the bed and sat down with her limbs wrapped around him. She buried her head in his shoulder as if she couldn't bear to break the connection. And the force of his emotion hit him like a tidal wave, stealing his breath.

He was not over her. He was not even close to being over her.

She had walked out on him without a backward glance. He had spent every night after that for at least a month thinking she would change her mind and come home.

She hadn't.

He stood up with an abrupt movement and deposited Lilly on the bed. She stared up at him, a dazed look on her face, all tangled long limbs and physical satiation.

Great sex, he told himself. *That's all it is.* But it was enough to severely mess a man's head up.

"I'm going to go make sure everything's locked up," he said roughly.

She was curled in a ball on her side of the bed when he came back. A tightness seized his belly so strong he almost reached down to gather her in his arms. But he kept his hands clenched tightly by his sides.

She deserved to suffer.

He'd suffered every night for a year. Let her feel his pain.

CHAPTER TEN

LILLY PEEKED HER head around her sister Lisbeth's hospital room door, checking to see if she was awake. Their brother David, who'd driven Lisbeth down to New York last night for a series of tests before her treatment abroad, was sitting in a chair by the window.

"Lilly!" Lisbeth practically screamed the word across the room at her, her blue eyes shining brightly. "You're here!"

Lilly crossed the room, gave her older brother a hug, then pressed a kiss to her sister's cheek. Lisbeth had an IV tube sticking out of her arm and looked so pale and small that a lump formed in her throat. This had to work. There was no alternative.

"Where is Riccardo? Did you bring him?"

Lilly shook her head and sat back. She needed to tell Riccardo about Lisbeth, and soon, because she and Alex intended on going to Switzerland with her. But it never seemed like the right time—not with the rollercoaster of emotion going on between them. "I will soon, sweetie. How are you feeling?"

Her sister made a face. "Crappy, but the doctor's hoping after all this I'm going to feel a whole lot better."

Lilly's heart contracted, feeling too big for her chest. "Six weeks, Lizzie. You can do it."

"Does you and Riccardo being back together mean I can

come stay with you guys when I'm better?" Lisbeth looked at her with eager eyes.

Lilly kept her face straight, because to do anything else would be to reveal far too much to her sister and brother about her and Riccardo's relationship. "You can come stay with us anytime."

You can come stay with me *anytime.*

A satisfied smile curved her sister's lips. "I think I need a life."

Lilly squeezed her hand. "Conserve your energy so we can fight this battle together. Then we'll talk about it."

They stayed until Lisbeth got tired and David had to leave for home. Kissing their sister goodbye, they walked out into the hallway.

"She's going to be okay, right?" Lilly asked, looking up at her older brother.

David pulled her into a hug. "Of course she is."

She hugged him tight, her head feeling far, far too full. She loved her serious, hardworking sibling, even with his strict sense of right and wrong—which had clearly labeled her and Alex's defection nine years ago *wrong.* Seeing him again after so long—what had it been? A year and a half? Two years—reminded her how much she missed him.

Her brother pulled back. "You okay? You look like hell, sis."

No. She most definitely was not okay. But she couldn't talk to David about it.

"I'm fine. Just worried."

"Pretty damn amazing we can get her this treatment. She'll be fine, Lil. We didn't raise her to be a strong, sturdy farmgirl for nothing."

She nodded. "You sure you want to head back tonight? You could stay and start out early tomorrow. A few hours isn't going to make a difference."

"It will the way things are now." Her brother rubbed a hand against his face. "Even with the extra money you've been sending and the extra help we've hired we've all been working from sun-up till sun-down."

Guilt mixed with the maelstrom of emotion swirling through her. She felt as if she was hanging on by a thread. "I'm sorry," she whispered. "You know we had to go."

The lines of fatigue softened around the corners of his mouth. "I know. In some ways I think Mom and Dad even understand too. But staying away isn't going to change the past. It's only driving the wedge deeper and deeper between you guys."

"I know." And she knew she had to do something about it. "Are things any better between them?"

"Not unless you count the fact they've given up fighting with each other." He lifted his shoulders. "I think they're just numb to it all now."

She wasn't sure if that was a good or bad thing. "I was thinking of coming home for Mom's birthday."

"She would love that. She misses you, Lilly. She doesn't say anything—you know Mom—but she does."

A lump formed in her throat. "About Lisbeth..."

He shook his head. "She needs to get out. We can't keep her where she doesn't want to be."

"But the farm..."

"We'll manage. The extra money is helping a lot."

At least something good was coming out of a reconciliation that only seemed to get more complicated with every day that passed.

Speaking of which... She glanced at her watch. "I need to go. I'm late for dinner with Riccardo."

She hugged her brother, watched as he headed in the direction of the parking garage and then pushed through the front doors of Memorial Sloan Kettering. Flagging a cab, she slid in and gave the driver directions to the restaurant where she was to meet Riccardo.

She rested her head against the seat and closed her eyes. It had been seven weeks since her and Riccardo's weekend in Barbados. Seven weeks during which she'd been telling herself she could walk out when their deal was done. Then she'd walked into her doctor's office this morning to confirm what she'd been desperate to deny.

She was pregnant. Exactly seven weeks pregnant. With her soon-to-be ex-husband's baby.

If she'd consciously set out to create a bigger disaster, she couldn't have done so.

How was a baby going to fit into all this?

She stared numbly out at the rush-hour Manhattan traffic, bumper to bumper, horns blaring. She'd spent the past seven weeks trying to blend her and Riccardo's lives in a way that eased confrontation. She'd done the things she had to do for her practice, refused to give up the friends and essential things that had made her life her own over the past year—*and* fulfilled her commitments as Riccardo's wife. Surprisingly, it had worked rather well.

Riccardo seemed bent on reducing the stress placed on her, and had instructed Paige to accept only the social invitations that were essential to De Campo's interests. He was like a guard dog, monitoring her with annoying persistence. And it made her wonder if there would have been a different outcome for them if it had been like this all along.

Pain stabbed at her insides. The ache inside her was deep and all-consuming. She'd been trying so hard to ignore her feelings for him—to keep herself intact. But every time she tried to put distance between them Riccardo would knock the walls down. He came home early, insisted they eat together, and this time around they actually talked. About which way the board was leaning toward a CEO. How delayed tiles meant Zambia would open a week late. About Antonio being a piece of work.

And then there were the nights… He had followed through on his promise that there would be sexual intimacy. And it was the one thing she couldn't deny him. Or herself.

It was becoming harder and harder to remind herself that

this was a business arrangement when in so many ways this was the marriage she'd never had.

The cab swung to a halt in front of Toujours, a new, eclectic French bistro in the financial district which Riccardo was courting to stock De Campo's new Napa Valley vintages. She had met the owner, Henri Thibout, formerly a chef in Paris, at a party a few weeks before, and knew Toujours was at the top of her husband's expansion list.

Henri stood as the maître d' ushered her to the table. Lilly's eyes widened when she saw the tall man standing behind him. *Antonio.* What was he doing here? Riccardo hadn't mentioned anything about him being in town.

"Lilly." Henri, a short, balding man in his mid-fifties, who made up for it with bucketloads of charm, brushed twin kisses to her cheeks and introduced her to his head sommelier, Georges, and his wife Joanna.

Riccardo stood and brushed a similar kiss to both her cheeks. She felt the tension radiating from him. *Great,* she thought, turning to Antonio. Exactly what she needed tonight. The battle of the De Campos.

The big, burly, aristocratic man, with his hook nose and formidable features, failed to intimidate her tonight.

Maybe because she was *pregnant.* If she said it ten more times maybe she'd believe it.

Henri reached for the sparkling wine chilling on the table and pulled Lilly's glass toward him. "This will do the trick after a long day," he said jovially. "Riccardo says you work long days."

"None for me, thank you," Lilly said quickly. "It *has* been a long day. I might actually fall flat on my face if I do."

Riccardo shot her a quizzical look. If there was anything Lilly loved it was a good sparkling wine. She averted her gaze and answered Joanna's question about what she did for a living.

The five-course tasting menu was superb, but the smell

of seafood was making her nauseous. She did her best, but by the time she'd forced herself to eat half of her third course chicken dish she thought she was going to choke. She set her fork and knife down in an abrupt movement that sent the clang of fine china echoing throughout the restaurant.

Conversation stopped. "Is it not to your liking?" Henri enquired, frowning. "I can get you some—"

"It's delicious," Lilly assured him. She reached for her water. "Apologies—my appetite is a bit off."

Riccardo kept that watchdog look on her, his gaze darkening. She stumbled through the sorbet and cheese course, so desperate to be home alone with her thoughts that she almost jumped out of her seat at the end of the meal.

"Thank you," she murmured to Henri after he'd promised Riccardo feedback on the wine list by next week. "It was lovely to see you again."

Antonio stayed behind to enjoy an aperitif with Henri. She watched her husband's mouth tighten at the interaction. Antonio was in town without Francesca, as usual, who preferred not to travel to North America. He and Henri had obviously hit it off.

Riccardo led her through the restaurant, his firm grip on her elbow keeping her by his side. When they'd stepped out of the busy restaurant onto the sidewalk he spun her around.

"What is up with you? *Dio.* It's like you've had a gallon of coffee in one go."

She pulled her arm out of his. There was *no way* she was telling him her news on a busy Manhattan sidewalk.

"Like I said. It's been a long day. What was Antonio doing here?"

"Sticking his nose where it doesn't belong, as usual," he growled. "Don't deflect, Lilly. You were a disaster in there. You hardly ate a thing. In fact you've hardly eaten a thing for weeks. This is ending *now.*"

She focused her gaze a centimeter to the right of his. "I'm feeling a bit nauseous, that's all."

"Then we're going to see your doctor," he said grimly. "I will not have you go through this again."

"I did see my doctor. I'm fine."

"Then what's wrong?" He stalked closer and captured her wrist in his. "We are not moving until you tell me."

"I think we should—"

"Lilly!" The valet who had been headed toward them stopped in mid-stride as Riccardo bellowed the word at her. "Spit it out."

His anger, her terror, and the complete loss of control she was feeling all hit her at once. "I'm pregnant!" she yelled at him. "I'm pregnant, goddammit, Riccardo. There—are you happy?"

He went chalk-white under his olive skin. The valet swiftly changed direction. The two of them faced off like prize fighters on the busy sidewalk. Then Riccardo grabbed her arm and pulled her under the awning of the restaurant, away from the flow of people.

"Is it mine?"

Her jaw dropped open. "I can't believe you're asking me that."

"It could be Taylor's."

She put a hand on her stomach. "I'm seven weeks pregnant. *Exactly* seven weeks pregnant. It's yours."

He went even paler, raking a hand through his hair. "We're not having this conversation here."

"I was trying to avoid it," she muttered. "And I sincerely hope that valet doesn't realize what a scoop he has on his hands."

Riccardo walked over to the valet stand and said something to the young guy, who practically ran to the lot across the street. He came back minutes later with the Jag.

Riccardo opened the door. "Get in."

They didn't talk for the entire drive home. Her husband's

knuckles were white on the steering wheel, his attention focused on the road. When they got to the house he opened the door, slammed it behind her and directed her inside.

She flicked on the lights in the front sitting room and sat down on the sofa. Riccardo poured himself a Scotch and paced the room like a restless, lethal animal that had no idea what its next move would be.

Finally he stopped by the fireplace and rested an elbow on the mantel, his gaze sinking into her. "It happened in Barbados if that's the timing."

She nodded. "I forgot my pill that morning we flew down. I didn't realize it until after we'd had sex."

His gaze narrowed. "You didn't see fit to tell me?"

She pressed her lips together. "The chances of anything coming from it were minuscule."

"Well, it happened," he growled. "You should have told me."

She got to her feet, feeling too vulnerable while he towered over her. "What difference would it have made? It happened. Now we're going to have to decide how we're going to deal with it."

He was in front of her so fast her head spun, his fingers biting into her arms. "We are *having* this baby."

"Of course we are." She stared at him, aghast. "Well, technically *I* am having this baby, and *we* are going to have to figure out how it'll work after we separate."

"Separate?"

She watched him digest the word as if it were a particularly tough piece of steak.

"We are not carting this baby back and forth between the two of us, Lilly."

"What are you suggesting, then?" she demanded flippantly. "That we stay together and live happily ever after?"

His lips curved in a smile that showed his teeth. "That's exactly what I'm suggesting, *tesoro*. Glad you're keeping up with me."

A feeling akin to shock settled over her. She studied his face, searching for some sign he was joking, but other than his twisted smile there was nothing but grim determination. Her chin lifted. "There is no way in hell I'm staying in an unhappy marriage. I know what it's like to grow up like that, and I won't do it to a child."

"You think it's better to subject them to a tug of war between two adults?"

"I think it's better to create an amicable separation where we both have this baby's best interests at heart."

"*Buona prova,* Lilly," he drawled. "But I'm not about to let your baggage destroy the future of our child. You contest this and I'll make it a court battle of epic porportions."

She shrugged out of his hold. "You are crazy. *This* is crazy." She looked at him desperately. "It will never work."

"It will work because we'll make it work." He crossed his arms over his chest and stood looking down at her like the impenetrable force he was. "Haven't we proved the last few weeks we can compromise?"

"About our social schedule," she said dully. How would a child fare in a marriage based solely on sex? In a marriage so far gone there was no pulling it back?

He lifted her chin with his fingers. "We have been good together lately, Lil. And we once had a fantastic marriage. We can make this work."

Or the bitterness between them would consume both them *and* their child, just as it had her.

She went for the jugular. "Don't you remember what it was like to live as part of a business partnership? Do you want that for yourself? For your child?"

"If what we've been doing in bed is a business partnership, then I'm all for it," he returned with a mocking smile. "Sign me up."

"You are—" She spun away, frustration burning a path of fire through her.

"A man who wants the family that was promised to

him," he rasped. "You are having my child, Lilly. De Campos don't divorce. So this is it. And I want more than one. My brothers are the most precious thing I have. I want that for our child."

Once she would have been sure he would say *she* was the most precious thing he had. Wrapping her arms around herself, she stared up at him. "So you were never going to let me walk away?"

"You would have been free to walk when our deal was up. But I would never have remarried."

Why? She wanted to scream it at him, but her throat felt as if it was closing over as the inevitability of what had happened hit her. How could she have been so stupid as to allow this to happen? To do the one thing that would bind her to the man she loved forever when she would never have his love back?

"I'm tired," she said abruptly, sure that if she attempted one more word she was going to sob. "I need some rest."

He let her go.

Overwhelmed and exhausted, she climbed the stairs to the bedroom, unzipped her dress and left it on the floor. She washed her face and brushed her teeth and slipped beneath the silk sheets of their bed. The dark, silent room finally allowed a refuge for her tears. They ran hot, silent, down her face.

What once would have been the news that completed her and Riccardo's dream had only driven them further apart.

She cried for that dream. She cried for her childhood. She cried for Riccardo's. She cried for the damage they had done to each other. And when he came after her and reached for her with strong, comforting hands she curled into him and let him hold her until her tears soaked his shirt.

"Don't be sad, *amore mio,*" he murmured. "The past is the past. *We* are in control of our future and I promise you we can make this work."

My love. He'd said it not in the taunting tone he'd adopted of late, but the way he'd used to say it to her. Her sobs gradually subsided into big, hiccuping breaths that shook her body. When she was silent against him he undressed her and moved over her, kissing every inch of her skin. His passionate tenderness revealed more to her than he ever could have said with words.

They had a chance. He might not have meant the words literally—maybe they had just been to comfort her—but as her head rested on his chest and the solid warmth of him put her to sleep her heart told her differently. She had seen that look on his face before.

He cared more than he was saying.

Could she hope his feelings would eventually turn into love again, for the sake of their unborn child? Or was she just fooling herself in a very dangerous game?

CHAPTER ELEVEN

WHEN LILLY WAS a little girl she'd dreamed of attending a Hollywood movie premiere on the arm of a handsome man, with paparazzi flashbulbs exploding in her face as they made their way down the red carpet. She would blink, steady herself on his arm, and continue on, a big smile on her face as she showed off her very fabulous dress.

Never once, outside of those dreams, had she allowed herself to believe she would actually live that life. Not Lilly the awkward, shy farmgirl. Not even Lilly the graduate physiotherapist with a budding career in front of her, living in one of the most exciting cities in the world where red carpets were a star-studded fixture.

Then she'd met Riccardo. And her life had *become* that dream. Only for her to realize how lonely and empty a life it was.

She walked into her office and shut the door, feeling as if her life had come full circle. Tonight she was to walk the red carpet for the premiere of this summer's hottest blockbuster with her very own dark and dangerous male. The man she was falling more in love with every day she was with him.

She didn't want the dream. She wanted what was real. She wanted *him*.

She sank down in her office chair and dropped her head into her hands. She had married Riccardo for the man he'd been early in their marriage. And ever since they'd returned from Barbados she'd seen glimpses of him again.

He'd been by her side through all the doctor's appointments and tests, asking the pertinent questions her scrambled brain didn't think to. He'd made her sit down to a proper meal every night, and sent her to bed early. And when he did he would stay for a few minutes before he started working again. He would cradle her against him and talk to her, even confide in her if his mood was right. She was realizing how complex a man her husband was—that she'd never really *known* him in their two years of marriage.

Or one, if you counted the year they'd stopped talking.

He'd sacrificed so much for De Campo. And she was starting to see what becoming CEO would do for his soul. It was the final piece in the puzzle that was Riccardo De Campo.

She wondered how she'd never seen it before.

Weariness swept over her and she closed her eyes just for a moment. The weight of the decision she had to make was killing her. Was she going to follow her heart, agree to stay with Riccardo and hope she was right about his feelings for her? Or was she going to run and fight him all the way to the bitter end for custody of a child who would become a pawn in their tug of war?

She'd promised herself she would stop running. Which also meant running from herself.

She blinked to keep herself awake, so exhausted she wanted to crawl onto her desk and sleep there. She had nothing to wear tonight that fit, and hadn't had time to shop since she'd really started showing.

She wanted to walk the red carpet like she wanted a hole in her head.

But it was important to De Campo, this sponsorship, and she didn't really have a choice.

A knock sounded on the door. She pulled herself up off

her desk, expecting to see Katy. Instead Riccardo strolled through the door, looking as if he'd just slayed ten dragons and was ready to move on to the next. The smile on his face faded into a frown when he saw her wipe a trail of drool from the corner of her mouth.

"*Dio,* Lilly, you're sleeping at your *desk?*"

"Resting," she corrected, sitting up straight and smoothing her hair. "Wasn't I meeting you at home?"

"My meetings were canceled this afternoon." He walked over to her desk and leaned against the edge of it, his gaze resting on hers. "This is ridiculous. You're asleep on your feet."

"I'm fine," she murmured, standing up. "Just give me a minute to gather my stuff."

He waved her on. She shoved a file she was working on in her briefcase, along with the antacids that had become a new food group for her, and went to retrieve her sweater off the coat rack near the door.

"Jim—Riccardo here."

She turned to see her husband on his phone.

"Lilly and I can't make it to the premiere tonight. Can you and your wife attend in our place?"

Her eyes widened. She waved at him to say she was fine, but he held up a hand.

"Great. We'll drop off the tickets on our way home."

She stared at him as he disconnected the call. "I can't believe you just did that."

He lifted his shoulders. "Jim's the head of North American sales… It'll be a great networking opportunity for him."

"I would have been fine."

He crossed over to her. "I know you would have. You've been a trooper, *tesoro.* But enough's enough. I'm worried about you."

She pushed her hair out of her face. "It just hit me how tired I am."

"You're not getting enough rest." He ran his fingers down her cheek. "You have big black bags under your eyes."

"Heartburn," she lied. "But I am glad you canceled."

"Because you have nothing to wear?" His dark gaze slashed over her in a reprimand. "You refuse to go buy new clothes, because that would be admitting you're gaining weight, and you don't like the way you look. So I went out and bought some for you."

Her jaw dropped. "You mean you had Paige get me a dress for tonight?"

"No, *I* bought you a dress for tonight—plus the rest of the wardrobe you need." He shrugged. "I'm sure I forgot something, but it's a start."

"You went shopping?"

His teeth flashed white. "I run one of the world's top ten beverage companies, *cara*. A trip to a recommended fashion house isn't beyond my means."

She couldn't believe what she was hearing. "How did you know my size?"

He lifted his hands. "I told them you were this tall and like this." He arced his hands in the shape of an hourglass.

"You did?"

"I did. It's all in the car." He looked supremely satisfied with himself as he took her sweater and pushed her out the door in front of him. "I think I have pretty good taste."

He had exquisite taste. In everything. Lilly stared at the cream silk sweater draped over her arm. It was exactly the right size and style she would have chosen. As were the T-shirts, blouses, jeans and gowns he'd picked out.

He had forgotten nothing.

A lump the size of Mount Everest formed in her throat. The little pieces of her heart she'd thought shattered forever started to put themselves back together again.

His attention to detail wasn't surprising. What got her

was how in tune a big, macho man like him could be with what she loved. Who she was.

She pulled the last couple of items out of the bag—a sexy lilac-colored silk nightie she was sure Riccardo had chosen with himself in mind, and a pair of yoga pants. Fuchsia yoga pants. Her mouth twisted in her first real smile of the day.

She slipped her too-tight pants off and pulled on the pink pair. And sighed. To be in something that fit, that didn't make her feel like an overstuffed sausage, was heavenly. She added a T-shirt, pulled her hair into a ponytail, and went downstairs to find Riccardo.

She found him in the den—a cozy, comfortable room that housed their big screen TV and library.

"I ordered us Chinese," he told her. "Should be here in a few minutes."

"I've decided you are always to shop for me," she murmured, moving toward him. Lifting on tiptoe, she brushed a kiss across the light stubble that dusted his cheek. "Since you do such a good job."

He slid his arms around her waist. "I closed my eyes when I handed the woman the yoga pants."

"You get bonus points for those," she murmured, lifting her chin and inviting his kiss. She was rewarded with a hard, possessive one that left her breathless.

"You need to cut down on your schedule."

"I'm not taking any new patients. It'll gradually lessen."

He pressed his lips together, consciously controlling his automatic response, which she was sure would have been, *Cut it down now.*

"You also have to accept the changes in your body. They're natural and healthy."

"I'm getting there," she murmured. "It's just hard when it feels like my body is out of control. The control part is the hardest for me."

He spread his hands wide. "Just hand it over to me, *cara,* and I'll take care of it for you."

She made a face at him. "You would love that, wouldn't you?"

He caught her hand in his much larger one, the teasing light in his eyes darkening into seriousness. "No more keeping things inside, Lil. If you're struggling you need to tell me."

"I will. I promise."

He put some classical music on—a haunting piece of Mozart she knew was his favorite—then pulled her into his arms on the sofa while they waited for the food. She closed her eyes and rested her head against his chest. *This* was what she'd always wanted. The way they were when they were together like this.

At that moment she knew with certainty that everything he'd been holding back, everything he hadn't said to her these past few weeks, had been because she'd hurt him so badly. Because she'd deserted him when he'd needed her the most.

Because she had failed him.

"Ric?"

He pressed his lips to her hair. "Mmm?"

"I'm sorry for walking out on you. I'm sorry I gave up on us."

He stiffened. Then his arms tightened around her. For a long moment silence bound them together, her husky admission sitting on the air between them. Then he bent and pressed a kiss to her shoulder. "I've made so many mistakes too," he said thickly. "It wasn't just you."

Her eyes burned. Her throat was clogged with so much pent-up emotion she wasn't sure she could articulate it all. "I hurt you."

He turned her around so their gazes met. "We hurt each other."

"I want to make this work." Her voice came out husky, edged with the fear she felt.

His eyes were razor-sharp. "What do you mean?"

She sucked in a shuddering breath. "I was so angry with you at first—threatening to turn this into a custody battle, not giving me any choice in the matter. But then I realized you were right. It's time for me—for *us*—to move on. To let go of the past. To give this marriage the shot it deserves. To give our *baby* the home it deserves."

An emotion she wished desperately she could identify flashed in his eyes. He lifted his hands to frame her face.

"But I want *you*, Riccardo," she said shakily. "I don't want the Golden Man from the Golden Couple. I want the Riccardo De Campo who charmed me out of my phone number in that bar. The man who just wanted to be with me."

His gaze darkened to midnight. "You will have him," he promised huskily. "You have always been the only woman for me."

"You won't want me in a few months," she murmured. "I'll be so far from the woman you married you'll be repelled by me."

A smile curved his lips. "Don't you know there's nothing you could ever do to make me want you less? You're like a fire in my blood, *cara.* I want you all the time."

The heat in his eyes stole her breath. The reverence of his hands as he slipped her T-shirt over her head and cupped her breasts in his palms made it catch in her throat. And when he stripped the bra from her and set his mouth to her flesh she moaned her appreciation.

The pink yoga pants went next, landing on the floor in a heap. "This part you hate so much," he whispered, sliding his hands up over her hips, "allows you to carry my baby. And *that* is a miracle."

Her heart turned over and emotion so sharp it was almost painful sliced through her. When he was touching her, when he was holding her like this, his reverence eclipsed her insecurities and made her feel like the most beautiful woman on the planet.

She got the buttons undone on his shirt, divested him of his jeans and boxers, and then there was only his magnificent body, free for her to touch at will. She dropped to her knees and worshipped him, moved her lips over his perfect chest, his powerful abs, then down over the hard, throbbing length of him that telegraphed his desire for her. Reveling in his sharp intake of breath, she teased him until he begged—begged for her to take him into the heat of her mouth—and then, when he'd had all he could take of that, he begged for her to end the torture.

She crawled up his body and hooked her legs around his waist. Slowly, torturously, she took him inside her, prolonging it until sweat beaded on his forehead and he cursed out loud.

Her gaze locked with his. She wanted to look away, *needed* to look away, because surely her love for him was written across her face. But she'd promised honesty. To herself and to him. She kept her eyes on his as he allowed her to drive him crazy with shallow, then deeper twists of her hips. His eyes were closed. His big body was shaking with need. She had control. But she knew it was an illusion. She was about to take the biggest risk of her life. Bigger even than that day when she and Alex had driven out of Iowa, a dust cloud rising up behind the beat-up old car they'd paid a hundred dollars for, which had barely been moving, with nothing but hope and determination in their hearts.

He could cheat on her again. He could actually cheat this time. And there was nothing she could do but believe he would never do it. And she did. Because he was the only man who could turn her world from dark to light.

She could only hope that this didn't turn out to be her biggest mistake. That once he saw the messy, frightened truth of her he didn't run in the opposite direction.

Pleasure coursed through her, wave after wave, as his body swelled inside her, making it impossible to think. To worry. She closed her eyes and rocked her hips and took him over the edge. And let go of everything except her love for him.

CHAPTER TWELVE

THE DEEP TIMBRE of male voices greeted Lilly as she let herself into the townhouse. Her husband's smooth, rich baritone slid down her spine in a delicious reminder of how he'd woken her up this morning. A husky prompt to get out of bed, her own teasing reply, then a spark that burst into a flame that put both of them fifteen minutes behind schedule.

She kicked off her shoes. She was happy—so happy she felt as if she was floating on air. As if she'd figured out the secret of life.

Gabe's voice floated in from the terrace. A male with a deeper, more heavily accented tone responded. *Antonio?*

A twinge of disappointment sliced through her. She'd been hoping for another quiet night at home with Riccardo. Tonight she'd intended on telling him about Lisbeth. She couldn't hold off any longer because she was to fly to Switzerland in a couple of weeks. Finally she felt sure enough of what she and Riccardo had to tell him.

She was making peace with the past. She'd gone home for her mother's birthday a week ago. It hadn't been perfect. But it was progress. And now she would wipe any remaining secrets from her and Riccardo's relationship.

She waved at Magda in the kitchen before joining the men on the terrace.

"Cara." Riccardo's dark eyes lit with pleasure. "You're just in time to celebrate with us."

She crossed to his side and smiled up at him. "Celebrate what?"

Antonio strolled over and pressed a kiss to her cheeks. "I've just told Riccardo I am backing him as the next CEO of De Campo."

Her gaze lifted to her husband's. A quiet gleam of satisfaction burned in his eyes.

"Congratulations," she murmured, reaching up to brush a kiss across his cheek.

His lifted brow told her she would do better than that later. She smiled and tamped down her anxiety at the confirmation of what she'd known was coming but had secretly been dreading.

They had just gotten themselves back on track. Now the craziness would begin.

"Content to tend your vines?" she teased Gabe, walking over to greet him.

He smiled that serious Gabe smile she loved and kissed her. "The most crucial job in the company—*si.*"

She laughed and drew back. "But of course."

"I intend to endorse Riccardo tomorrow at the board meeting," Antonio said, nodding at his son.

Her throat tightened. *It was all happening so quickly.*

She moved back to Riccardo's side and slipped an arm around his waist. He would make a far better leader for De Campo than Antonio had. He would inspire the best in those who worked for him without using fear or intimidation as a threat. And she—she would shine for him. Riccardo needed her by his side, needed her to be the softness when everything else was a million-dollar decision. And this time she would not let the pressure get to her. She had the tools in place to manage her stress.

The De Campo men stayed for dinner. Tonight there was no need for Gabe to be his usual buffer between Antonio and Riccardo. There was rare harmony at the table. And she wondered, moving her gaze over her handsome, quietly confident brother-in-law, what it must have been like always to be the peacekeeper—always to be second best. In any other company Gabe would have made a brilliant CEO. Instead he made brilliant wine.

And maybe that was all he wanted.

After dinner Antonio excused himself to make a call. Lilly checked with Magda about dessert, then slipped out onto the terrace to get a breath of fresh air. The summer night was on the chilly side and she wrapped her arms around herself and stared up at the sky. It was so rare to see stars in Manhattan that the smattering overhead held her attention.

"My son's about to become one of the most powerful men on the planet." Antonio stepped out of the shadows and slid his mobile phone into his pocket. "Are you ready for this, Lilly?"

She wrapped her arms tighter around herself. What was it about these De Campo men, always trying to intimidate her?

"You must think I can or you wouldn't have mandated our reconciliation."

"Scusi?"

She gave him a level look. "Your condition, Antonio, for throwing your weight behind Riccardo. I take it our reconciliation has cemented your choice?"

He lifted a brow. "The performance of the company dictated my choice."

"But you wanted us to reconcile?"

He shrugged. "You're good for my son. I've always thought you had an excellent grounding effect on him. But it had nothing to do with my decision."

Her brain spun in a confused circle. "But you made our reconciliation a condition for your support."

An amused look spread across his face. "If Riccardo

said that he was using it as a way to get you back. You must know my son by now... He is solely focused on getting what he wants and damn the consequences."

She felt the blood drain from her face. Either Antonio or Riccardo was lying.

She prayed it was her father-in-law.

An icy numbness spread through her limbs. She lifted trembling hands to her face. "I—I think I'm going to go back inside. It's getting chilly out here."

She was halfway across the patio when Antonio's voice stopped her. "You look upset—but why? Riccardo may be ruthless in going after what he wants, *mia cara,* but is it so bad if he loves you that much?"

It *was* bad if he had lied to her without compunction. If he had preyed upon her in a moment of weakness, dangling a divorce in front of her she now wasn't sure he'd ever intended to give her.

"De Campos don't divorce."

He had never intended to let her go.

She excused herself from dessert, uncaring of her husband's concerned glance, sweeping upstairs before he had a chance to press her. She immersed her three and a half months pregnant body in a hot bath, desperate for something to soothe her. Desperate not to believe the man she had fallen in love with all over again could have lied to her like that when he had demanded honesty from *her*.

Damn him. She struggled to come up with a reason, an alternative explanation for why he'd done what he'd done. But there weren't any. There was nothing that excused what he'd done.

She closed her eyes and let the steaming water attack the numbness that had consumed her. Riccardo hadn't technically lied when he had talked about what had happened with Chelsea Tate. But it had been a lie by omission. And now he had lied again.

It was crazy. She'd *wanted* him to want her that much.

She'd *wanted* him to do exactly as she'd fantasized in the limo the night of their divorce party. To ride down her street on a white horse, climb through her window and carry her home.

But now she was afraid he was still the same old Riccardo, just cloaked in a new suit. The Riccardo who would use any weapon at his disposal to get what he wanted.

No. She slapped her hand against the water, sending bubbles flying. He had stood there on that terrace in Barbados and sworn to her they were going to create a marriage based on honesty and trust. And she had eaten it up like the naive Iowa farm girl she obviously still was.

Her insides crumbled. She'd made herself completely vulnerable to him. She had trusted him with her darkest secrets, trusted him to take care of her and their baby. And he had violated that trust.

Just like with everything else in her past—every time her parents' relationship had gone through a good patch and they'd actually been happy together, every time the farm had gone into the black and she'd been able to buy a new dress, or that bittersweet moment in Westchester when she'd thought she had everything she'd ever wanted—this brief moment of happiness had been taken from her. Just as she'd feared it would be.

She didn't know what was real anymore.

The moment he entered the room she sensed him. The air thickened around her. His grim appraisal as she opened her eyes made her sink further under the water.

"What's going on, Lilly?"

She swallowed past the lump in her throat. "You promised me honesty. You promised we could trust each other."

He nodded, his dark gaze fixed intently on her. "*Si.* Have I given you any reason to doubt me?"

She sat up and reached for the sides of the tub with shaking hands. "You *lied* to me, Riccardo. You lied to me about this whole crazy deal."

He paled. "What did Antonio say to you?"

"That you're a selfish bastard who'll do whatever it takes to get what you want." She stood up and jabbed a finger at him. "I trusted you. You told me we were starting over without any lies between us."

He took a step toward her. "I might have taken some artistic liberty with my wording, but Antonio *did* want us back together."

"You told me Antonio's support *depended* on us getting back together." She was shaking so hard she could hardly get the words out. "It was a bold-faced lie."

"What was I supposed to do?" he shot back tightly. "You wouldn't see me, you wouldn't talk to me, but you knew I wasn't going to give up."

Heat blazed through her. "You were supposed to *woo* me. You were supposed to come sit on my doorstep every night for a week, like you did when we first started dating. You were not supposed to *coerce* me into a reconciliation."

She stood there shivering violently. He grasped her wrists and pulled her out of the tub, wrapped a towel around her.

"Wooing wasn't working."

"The deal was a lie," she said dully. "And the only reason I accepted it was because of Lisbeth."

"Lisbeth?"

"Her leukemia is back. She needed treatment and I needed the money. So I agreed to your deal."

His expression darkened. "You agreed to reconcile with me because Lisbeth needed treatment? *Hell,* Lilly, what kind of a monster do you think I am that I wouldn't have given you that money if you'd told me?"

"I didn't want to be beholden to you. I didn't trust you. And look—" she threw her hands up in the air "—guess I was right."

His mouth flattened into a thin line, the nostrils of his Roman nose flaring. "You accuse *me* of not being completely honest when you are withholding things like that from me?"

"It has nothing to do with us."

"It has *everything* to do with us. We are a family, Lilly. We support each other."

"Well, now you've got your family," she bit out, feeling her world fall apart. "Wife, baby—you've got everything you ever wanted, just like you always do."

He closed his eyes, his long dark lashes sweeping down over his cheeks. "It was never about that," he denied huskily. "I swear to you—it was never about that. I was—I was desperately in love with you, Lilly, and I needed you back."

Her heart stopped. She took a deep breath, forcing herself to breathe, forcing her heart to start again—because surely he would not use that tactic on her now. Not after she'd spent weeks desperate to hear him say it.

She pulled the towel tight around her, fingers clenching the material. "How many other things have you lied to me about?"

"Nothing." His voice vibrated with emotion. "Lilly—"

She held up a hand. "No more."

He ignored her and pulled her into his arms. The strength and breadth of him dwarfed her, so achingly familiar she wanted to howl at the want in her.

His gaze bored into hers. "You are not a possession. You and this baby we are going to have are the most precious things in my life. How could I have let myself lose you? I couldn't let that happen."

Hot tears escaped her eyes, running down her cheeks like a river of fire. She beat her hands against his chest, desperate for him to hurt as much as she was hurting. "I needed this to be real. I needed *us* to be real this time."

"We are. Lilly—"

"No." She wrenched herself out of his arms, the towel falling into a heap on the floor. "You know what Alex said to me before we left for Barbados? 'Whatever you do, don't get pregnant...' Because that was the one thing that would complicate a relationship that didn't need complicating." She closed her eyes. "And what do I do? I let exactly that happen. And *now* look at us."

He eyed her wild, naked stance apprehensively, as if she were a keg of dynamite poised to go off. "Let's get some clothes on you," he suggested quietly, "and then we'll talk."

She stalked past him into the bedroom and reached for the first piece of clothing she could lay her hands on. He followed, watching as she pulled on a T-shirt and jeans.

"Listen, I know you're emotional, *cara,* but—"

"I am not emotional." She wrenched her hair from underneath her T-shirt and whipped to face him. "I am crushed and I am saddened and I am *disappointed* in you. But I am *not* hormonal."

If she sounded insane she was past caring. "I need some time to myself," she muttered, turning back to search for a sweater. "Away from here. Away from you."

"You are not running away again."

"You're right." She swiped a sweater off a chair and shoved her arm in a sleeve. "I'm walking. Maybe to the Brooklyn Bridge. Who knows?"

He moved forward, took her by the shoulders and spun her around. His eyes were black, stormy. "You can throw away a million rings and I will still come after you."

She squared her shoulders. "I need time. Do not follow me. Don't have anyone follow me, for that matter. Or I swear to God you'll push me over the edge."

She turned and walked out the door. The stars were still shining brightly when she climbed into Riccardo's Jag and reversed it down the driveway. But this time she didn't look up.

CHAPTER THIRTEEN

RICCARDO KNOTTED HIS tie with fingers that weren't quite steady. This should have been the most important day of his life—the day his father anointed him the new head of De Campo. It should have been the crowning glory of three years spent proving to Antonio that he had what it took—that this was *his* company and his vision was the future. That the passion in his veins ran as deep as it did through his father's.

But his wife was gone. His *pregnant* wife was gone. And he had no idea where she was, what her state of mind was, or what he was supposed to do with the unfamiliar feeling of helplessness pulsing through him. Giving a speech to the board that painted a vision of De Campo's future seemed inconceivable.

His hands dropped away from his tie. Lilly had made it clear she needed space. If he had denied it to her, gone after her, he would have lost her.

If he hadn't already.

He shrugged on his jacket, lifted his collar clear of the dark gray Armani that was his good luck suit—the suit he'd been wearing the night he'd met Lilly in that bar—and refused even to contemplate the possibility. Instead he thought about the twists and turns life could take. Antonio had wanted to raise racehorses. He'd ended up with vines and a company that had brought him success beyond his wildest dreams. Motor racing had been *his* passion, but he'd grown to love the business that was bigger than him, bigger than his brothers and his father now. De Campo had come to signify luxury and refinement on a global scale. It was bigger than all of them. He would be the man who took it to new heights. Who exploited its raw potential.

Sometimes things happened that were beyond your control.

Sometimes you made them happen with your own arrogance and stupidity.

He stared at his reflection in the mirror, searching for some sign of life in his perfectly tailored appearance. A machine stared back at him. None of this meant anything without Lilly. He could handle the dull throb he woke with every day he wasn't racing as long as she was by his side. But he could not fathom the future without her.

His chest ached with the need to have his wife back.

Shaking it off—shaking it off because he had to—he straightened his shoulders and went downstairs to where Tony was waiting with the car. His longtime driver said hello, gave him a quick look, and eliminated his usual witty banter.

Riccardo slid into the backseat and pressed his head against the leather. He'd felt justified in coercing Lilly into the deal because it had been the only weapon he'd had against her refusal to see him. Because he loved her. He was so used to having to fight tooth and nail to get what he wanted from Antonio he'd carried that same demeanor into his personal life. Strategize and conquer. But with all of his and Lilly's trust issues he should have known better. He should have at least come clean when he'd had the chance to in Barbados.

Muddled thinking from a man who had seen the destructive effects of secrets harbored.

He clasped his hands together in his lap and looked down at the gleaming gold wedding band Lilly had placed on his finger. He'd been forgiven once. Would he be forgiven again? Or had he made one mistake too many?

The urge to put his fist through the bulletproof window overwhelmingly strong, he switched his attention to the traffic on Fifth Avenue instead, curling his fist on his lap. Lilly had called in to her clinic to say she wouldn't be in. After she hadn't picked up her cell he'd called Alex, to see if she was with her. Which had, in turn, opened him up to her sister's sarcastic demand to know what he'd done *now*.

He ran a hand over his chin, his uneven shaving job making him frown. Where in *Dio's* name was she? And why wouldn't she at least pick up the phone and let him know she was okay?

Paige handed him a stack of messages when he walked in. He crumpled them up and threw them on his desk.

"Everyone's here," she murmured, moving her gaze from the wad of paper back to him. "You okay?"

Did he *look* okay? He gave her a curt nod, dropped his briefcase by his desk and took his laptop out.

His father gave him a nod as he walked into the boardroom. *"Siete pronti?"*

"Pronto." Ready.

Gabe took the chair beside him. "You look like hell, *fratello*. Too much champagne last night?"

"I can't find Lilly."

His brother blinked. *"Scusi?"*

He powered up his laptop. "We had a fight last night and she needed some space."

"You have no idea where she went?"

"None." His jammed his palm against the table. She was pregnant. Driving his far too powerful car. And emotional.

Antonio opened the meeting and ran through the agenda. Riccardo looked down at the notes for his speech. There were only five words on the cue card. *Vision. Courage. Expertise. Timing. Domination.* They would define De Campo's future.

His father began his pitch to endorse his son as CEO. Riccardo checked his messages on his phone. *Nothing.*

"As you have seen over the past three years, my son Riccardo has transformed De Campo into the multifaceted global brand that it is today…"

Antonio's voice droned on, blurred into nothingness. It was only when his father turned to him and put his hands together, and the board followed suit, that he realized it was time.

"I am throwing my full support behind Riccardo De Campo for the position of CEO of this company."

The board members stood and clapped.

It was happening.

This time as he made his way to the podium and shook Antonio's hand there was no mistaking the pride gleaming in his father's eyes. He felt strong and weak at the same time—as if he was both that boy who'd trailed after his father into the vineyard asking a million questions and the man he'd become.

He cleared his throat and stepped to the microphone.

"For the last three years I have watched the De Campo Group grow from a fledgling global brand to a force to be reckoned with in the industry. We gambled. Our vision was big. Our vision was ambitious. But our vision was right." He paused and cast his gaze around the room. "And now we sit poised on a precipice. We can either move with the future or we can lose our way, as so many other brands have done. I say we move—that we have the guts and the vision to—"

Paige stepped into the back of the room. It was highly unusual for her to interrupt a meeting of this importance, and the look on her face stopped him cold.

Lilly. He knew it as instinctively as he knew the sun rose in the east.

"Excuse me." He stepped down from the podium and walked toward the back of the room. Antonio frowned and stood up as he passed. The buzzing in his ears got louder the closer he got to Paige. Her eyes were glued to his face and she stood wringing her hands together—something his PA never did.

Antonio announced they would take a quick break.

"I have Lilly on the line," Paige whispered to him. "Riccardo, she doesn't sound good."

He sprinted to Paige's desk and picked up the line. *"Lilly?"*

"Riccardo?"

"Yes," he barked. Her voice was faint. Not right. "Lilly, where are you?"

"I—I'm not feeling well. Ric, I—"

"Lilly?"

The line went dead. He slammed the receiver down and stood staring at it.

Paige's hand flew to her mouth. "She said her phone was dying."

He was already halfway into his office. "Call the security company and have her phone traced. *Now.* I need to know where she is."

Antonio and Gabe joined him in his office.

"What the hell are you doing?" his father demanded. "They're waiting to hear from you."

"There's something wrong with Lilly," he said grimly. "I've got to find her."

Antonio gave him an incredulous look. "Surely it can wait fifteen minutes?"

"No, it can't!" Riccardo roared. "Gabe, I need your keys."

His brother dug them out of his pocket. "I'll come with you."

"You should stay here and hold down the fort."

"I'm not sure you should—"

He ripped the keys out of his brother's hand. "I'll call when I know something."

Mid-morning traffic was still thick. He crawled forward, trying not to think about how weak and scared Lilly had sounded. Why had he let her go last night?

Paige called. Lilly had last been tracked in Westchester. *She was at the house.* He changed lanes and headed for the interstate, relieved, and then his heart started to pound as all sorts of disturbing images crammed his head. What if something was wrong with her pregnancy? The house was on the water. What if she'd taken one of the boats out and started to feel ill? Or gotten weak while swimming?

What if she was lying somewhere helpless?

He put his foot down on the accelerator and gunned the Maserati, weaving in and out of traffic as if he was in the Monaco Grand Prix. When he hit the interstate he put the pedal to the floor. The powerful car ate up the miles, but it wasn't fast enough. Not for the torturous images running through his head.

The guy in front of him was driving like his grandmother in the left lane. He jammed his foot on the accelerator and sent the car to twice the legal speed limit, passing him on the inside.

The sirens started ten minutes out of Westchester. Red flashing lights blazed in his rearview mirror. For a split second he contemplated ignoring them. He could outdrive them in this car, he knew. But the whir of a helicopter overhead convinced him the cop on the ground wasn't the only one after him.

He slowed down and pulled onto the side of the road. The cop pulled in behind him and got out of his car. He'd just explain what was going on and then he'd be on his way…

A tall, beefy cop stopped by his window. "License and registration."

Riccardo handed it to him. "Officer—I—"

"Do you have any idea how fast you were going, sir?"

"About a hundred. But, Officer, I—"

The cop jabbed a finger at him. "You, sir, are a danger-ous driver. You aren't walking away with this car today. I can tell you that."

"Look, I—"

The officer looked at his license and started to laugh. "You're kidding me? Riccardo De Campo the racecar driver?"

"Former racecar driver," Riccardo corrected. "I can ex-plain why I was driving so fast. My—"

"Save it. You're not the first superstar to think you can flaunt the rules."

"*Officer!*" Riccardo yelled. "My wife is sick. She's preg-nant. I was racing to get to her."

The cop blinked. "Where?"

"Our Westchester house. It's ten minutes from here."

"Did you call an ambulance?"

He closed his eyes. "No." *Why hadn't he?*

The cop gave him a considering look. "You better be telling the truth."

"I am," Riccardo rasped desperately. "Can I go?"

"You will follow me," the cop said sternly. "You so much as step one inch out of line and I will impound both you *and* your car."

Riccardo nodded and gave him directions. The cop put on his siren and thankfully was no slouch in the speed de-partment either, getting them to the house in just under fifteen minutes.

He found Lilly in the living room, lying on the sofa.

"Cara." He dropped down on his knees beside her. She was curled in the fetal position, her face about five shades paler than it normally was.

"I didn't mean to scare you," she murmured. "The phones here aren't working and my cell phone died."

"They've been working on the lines out here. Lil—" He took her hands in his. "Can you tell me what doesn't feel right?"

She bit her lip. "I don't know. I—I'm nauseous and I'm having bad pains."

Riccardo looked up at the cop, who'd come in behind him, but the officer was already on his radio, calling for an ambulance.

A tear rolled down her cheek. "I didn't want to bother you. You had that meeting…"

He gripped her hands tighter. "I don't care if I'm having lunch with the Pope. You need me—you call me."

A river of tears ran down her cheeks.

"Are the pains getting worse or better?"

"Worse. There's more of them now."

His insides went cold. "When did they start?"

"A couple hours ago." She closed her eyes as a tremor ran through her slim body. "Ric—something's wrong. I don't feel right."

He sat down and pulled her into his arms. "It's going to be all right, *tesoro,* I promise you. The ambulance is on its way."

She burrowed into him. The tension in her body made his own stiffen with fear.

"I'm so sorry. You should be in that meeting, and if I screw up your ch—"

"Ssh." He pressed a kiss against her hair. "You're the most important thing in the world to me, Lilly."

"Yes, but the job is—"

He pressed his fingers to her mouth. "The job is nothing without you. *I* am nothing without you. Haven't you realized that yet? I do these stupid things because I love you. Because I can't bear the thought of losing you."

Her lashes fluttered down over those beautiful hazel eyes. "I spent the morning walking along the river, thinking."

His heart jammed in his chest.

The tears streamed harder down her face now, running

over the edge of her chin. "I love you, Riccardo. I've never stopped loving you. Not even for a minute."

He felt as if the sun had come out on this dreary, overcast summer day. The flash of joy that swept through him was powerful. Followed by sick, overwhelming relief that he hadn't lost her.

"Please forgive me," he whispered. "That was my last big mistake. Ever."

She shook her head. "It was my running too. I can see that now. I was so scared that once you saw the truth of me—how messed up I am still—you wouldn't want me anymore."

He brought her hand to his mouth and pressed his lips to her knuckles. "We all have our baggage, *cara*. Look what you've done with your life. You help little boys walk again. Nothing I've ever done comes close to that."

Her eyes glittered with an emotion that stole his breath.

"We have to be honest with each other. No more lies. No matter how little or how painful the truth."

"Agreed." He held her tightly as another shudder racked her body and glanced up at the cop. The officer held up two fingers.

"I mean it." Lilly bumped her hand against his chest. "Three strikes and you're out, Riccardo De Campo."

"Then it's a good thing I don't need anymore," he murmured. "*You* are all I need."

"Ambulance is here." The cop abandoned his post at the window. "Let's go."

Riccardo picked up Lilly and strode outside. She was going to be fine. She *had* to be fine. There was no other way to think.

CHAPTER FOURTEEN

THE GRAY-HAIRED emergency room physician walked into the waiting room where Riccardo, Gabe, Alex and—surprisingly—Antonio, who'd shown up a couple of hours ago sat, just over three hours after they'd taken Lilly in. He wore the unsmiling, grim look of a man who'd been working too many hours straight.

Riccardo's heart dropped to the floor.

The elderly physician stopped in front of him, a tired smile curving his mouth. "They're both fine. Lilly's suffering from pre-eclampsia—a high blood pressure condition associated with pregnancy. Very common, but she'll need to see her doctor often."

His shoulders sagged with relief. "And the pain?"

"Under control. You can take her home as soon as we can do the paperwork, but you'll need to schedule an appointment with her obstetrician as soon as possible. Get some more detailed tests done."

He released the breath he'd been holding in a long, heavy exhale. *Lilly was fine. Their baby was fine.*

Thank God.

The doctor smiled. "Glad I could give out some good news today. There hasn't been a surplus of it."

"*Grazie,*" he murmured huskily. "I can't say it enough."

The doctor waved him off and headed back into the chaos. Alex went in and spent a few minutes with her sister before Riccardo took her home. Gabe went to get him a cup of coffee for the ride.

He rested his elbows on his thighs and dropped his head into his hands. Moisture stung the backs of his eyes, mixing with a relief so profound it was all-consuming.

A hand gripped his shoulder. "Your mother suffered from pre-eclampsia. Lilly will be fine."

He looked up at Antonio through glazed eyes. He'd been shocked when his father had arrived and waited with them without a word. The emotion darkening his father's silver eyes shocked him even more.

Antonio straightened, as if the show of affection had thrown him off balance. "You don't need to worry about the board," he said roughly. "I made sure you have a hundred and ten percent of their support."

Riccardo held his gaze for a long moment. *"Grazie."*

He had Lilly. Now he could think about the future.

Lilly prided herself on the toughness at her core. It had carried her out of Iowa and into a life she could only have dreamed of. It had helped her give that same strength to her patients when they were intent on giving up. But the vulnerability she felt walking toward the front door of the hospital was so soul-searing it was hard to keep walking in a straight line.

A nurse pushed the door open for her and she walked out into the light drizzle to Riccardo, waiting with the car at the curb. Her legs trembled as her husband walked toward her—tall, imposing, with a determined set to his mouth that made her want to fling herself into his arms.

What if he hadn't come after her? What if she'd lost him?

Her knees wobbled as he took the last couple of steps and pulled her into his arms. She closed her eyes and absorbed his strength, that determination. It was enough for both of them.

"Let's go home," he said quietly.

They made the drive back to Manhattan in silence, an acknowledgement of what they'd almost lost heavy in the air. Riccardo held her hand in his lap the entire way, as if he couldn't bear to let her go.

Their stately old limestone townhouse awaited them— the scene of her rollercoaster marriage which had run from perfect to miserable to all she'd ever wanted. Majestic, it glimmered in the late-afternoon sunlight, so solid with its heavy brick façade it would stand forever.

She stepped out of the car, her mind traveling back to that night four and a half months before, when limos had lined up in this driveway to witness the destruction of her and Riccardo.

Tonight it was unusually quiet. There were no limos. No drivers chatting. No false illusions of perfection on either part. There was only the here and now and what they chose to do with it.

Riccardo came around the car and slid his arm around her waist. "What are you thinking?"

"We have a blank slate," she said huskily. "The story is ours to write."

He tugged her closer and lifted her chin with his fingers. "I predict a very happy ending."

She drank him in—the hard, strong lines of his face that could soften into devastating humor, the sensuous pull of his lips that could make her crazy for him. He loved her. He was crazy about her. That much she was sure of. And that was enough.

Her lips curved. "You think so, Signor De Campo?"

"I know so, Signora De Campo."

He swung her into his arms and carried her up the front walk.

For her and Riccardo this past year had been simply a twist in the road of a lifetime together.

And tomorrow was another day.

EPILOGUE

Westchester, New York

"I DON'T KNOW about you, but I think he needs a strong, manly name to match his personality."

"Papà."

One-and-a-half-year-old Marco ducked under Lilly's arm and ran as fast as his short, stumpy legs would carry him across the terrace to where her husband stood, indecently attractive in a navy pinstriped suit. Her heart contracted as her son flung himself around Riccardo's legs. The two males had a love affair going on that was a joy to watch.

She would normally have let herself drool a little longer over the suit that set off her husband's swarthy good looks to perfection, but the squirming bundle of fluff in his arms demanded her attention.

It looked suspiciously like a chocolate-brown Labrador Retriever puppy.

"*Cucciolo!*" Marco squealed, tugging on his father's pant leg. "*Giù,*" he ordered, in an imperious tone that was already so close to his father's Lilly was afraid he was going to skip the baby stage entirely and move straight to domination.

Riccardo bent and set the puppy on the ground. Marco

grabbed onto its fur so hard the puppy backed up and cowered against Riccardo's leg.

"*Dolcemente,*" her husband instructed, scooping the puppy up in one arm and Marco in the other. "You are a brute, Marco De Campo."

"Just like his daddy." Lilly sighed. "Well, most of the time anyway," she teased, standing up on tiptoe to kiss him. But between the squirming, licking puppy and the delighted Marco it was a pretty fruitless effort.

"Hold that thought," Riccardo murmured. "I have a surprise for you too, but you'll get it later."

Heat rose to her face.

He laughed—a low, sexy rumble that did jittery things to her insides. "*That* is a given, *tesoro*. But I also stumbled upon something else I thought you'd like."

Mortified that her thoughts always seemed to involve her husband and some sort of naked activity, she took the puppy from him and felt her heart melt at the tiny bundle of fur, the big brown eyes and giant paws. "I thought this was happening in the spring?"

He lifted his shoulders. "The breeder had someone cancel at the last minute. I made the mistake of going to see him, and well…"

She smiled as the puppy licked her face with boundless enthusiasm. "I wouldn't have been able to resist him either."

"His name's Dutch. But we can rename him."

She lifted a brow.

"Dutch chocolate?"

She hated it. "We'll rename."

"Thought so. You were about to swim?"

She nodded. "We didn't expect you for hours."

Her husband's gaze rested on her face with that singular intensity he devoted to everything he focused on. "I ducked out early. I missed you."

A lump formed in her throat. Her life was as close to perfect as a life could be. So perfect, in fact, that some days when it seemed *too* perfect, as if it could never last, she retreated to the back porch of the house here in Westchester, where they'd move for the summer, and stayed there until her heart stopped racing and the feeling went away. It was where Riccardo inevitably found her. And instinctively he'd always know what to say, because this beautiful, autocratic man who'd suffered plenty of his own heartaches knew her better than anyone.

He'd been there every step of the way.

She ran her fingers down the hard lines of his face. They still had their blow-outs—and, boy, were they blow-outs when they happened. That had never changed. But they were few and far between, and beneficial from the point of view that they both got their feelings out and moved on.

Marco scrunched up his face and shoved a beefy little hand against Riccardo's chest. "Swim. *Cucciolo.*"

Lilly laughed. "Maybe no swimming for the puppy today. But we can."

They splashed in the shallow end of the pool and Riccardo changed, then joined them. Lilly sat on the edge of the pool, dangling her legs in the water while her husband tossed Marco high. Her son's delighted yelps filled the air.

Her husband lifted a brow. "Enjoying your part-time life?"

"Oh, yes." She'd opted to cut back to part-time hours after Marco had been born, sharing her workload with another physiotherapist who also had a family. It allowed her to focus on work *and* her family, and she was loving every minute of it.

Marco slapped his hand on the water and sprayed water in Riccardo's face. Her lips curved. He was not only a solid little dark-haired mirror image of his father he was just as much of a daredevil. Fearless. Willing to try everything. Nothing like his mother had been like as a child. And she was glad for that.

Marco Alfonso De Campo. Named after Riccardo's racing hero and former teammate Marco Agostino, who'd died in a crash just weeks before their Marco had been born. His second name was after Riccardo's grandfather, who had built the first De Campo vineyard in Tuscany.

She blinked, her eyes stinging with the bittersweet emotion that seemed to define her life now. With the naming of Marco her husband seemed to have moved on, to have made amends with the past. He no longer shut down if racing came up. He acknowledged the subject, then moved on.

She had moved on too. It would never be a perfect relationship, but she was making strides with her parents. They were in love with Marco, and she visited a few times a year to give them a chance to spend time together. And somehow that was enough.

Riccardo caught her eye across the water. "Lisbeth's met an investment banker. She had stars in her eyes when he dropped her off the other night."

Oh, no. Of all the men in New York, investment bankers had to be the most arrogant. "Did you *do* something about it?"

A smile tugged at the corners of his mouth. "What was I supposed to do? Put the fear of God in him?"

"Yes. You should have." Her sister had been in remission for six months now. She'd come to live with them in New York after her treatment and was set to start college in the fall. She was so much like her former vibrant self it felt almost as if a miracle had happened, but Lilly was still fiercely protective of her. She was so vulnerable in so many ways.

But then again, she reminded herself, she'd been the same way when she'd moved to New York, and it had done her a world of good to stand on her own two feet in a city as tough as Manhattan.

"On second thought," she murmured, "maybe this is a good thing. She *should* have her heart broken a few times. It'll teach her how to deal with you alpha males."

His dark eyes glittered. "Maybe so. You've figured out how to have *this* one hopelessly within your power."

She glanced at him from beneath lowered lashes. "You think so?"

"Undoubtedly."

She put the heat in his gaze on hold while they enjoyed the afternoon, took care of the puppy, then fed and put their son to bed. Riccardo read to Marco while she changed. Her soft, cream-colored jersey dress that showed an ample amount of cleavage was meant to put his theory to the test. Her husband's deep velvet stare as she walked out onto the terrace gave her the answer she was looking for.

Just tamable enough.

He finished mixing their drinks. "New dress?"

"Yes."

"Come here."

Her heart went pitter-patter in her chest as she closed the distance between them. "What is *that?*" she questioned, staring at the murky dark liquid in the glass he handed her.

A satisfied smile touched his lips. "It so happens Lewis, our Bajan bartender friend, has become an international celebrity. The recipe for his house specialty has made it into one of the top food and beverage magazines."

"You're kidding?"

"Would I lie to you about something like that? He calls it his 'love potion'. The 'ultimate aphrodisiac.'"

An all-over body flush consumed her. *A love potion?* She could only think of three words. Hottest. Sex. Ever.

Riccardo read her expression. "Exactly," he drawled. "Drink up."

She took a sip. "Doesn't taste any better than I remember."

"It gets better the more you drink. Remember that?"

She sipped on the potent drink, wincing as the alcohol hit her empty stomach.

"What's that?" she asked, pointing at the tabloid he'd set on the bar. "I thought we weren't reading that stuff."

"You should read Jay Kaiken's column."

Ugh. "Really?"

"Yes. Read it."

She took another sip of her drink, thinking she might need it. Jay Kaiken's column was an account of the posh benefit she and Riccardo had attended for former super-model Gillian King's Manhattan clinic for eating disorders. A friend of Gillian's, Lilly had instantly seen the value of a place where women could go to be surrounded by those who were going through the same thing they were. And when Gillian had asked her to speak at the event she'd decided it was time for her to tell her story publicly. Even if it only helped one person, that was enough.

"Perhaps the most poignant moment of the evening was Lilly De Campo's account of her struggle with anorexia," Kaiken had written. *"Courageous and truthful, its honesty no doubt made an impression on everyone in attendance. I'm pretty sure there wasn't a dry eye in the crowd."* And, in true Kaiken tongue-in-cheek fashion, he'd added, *"PS— can I say how good it is to have the De Campos back together? I always did want to believe in fairytales..."*

She looked up at Riccardo, her vision blurring.

"It *was* very courageous of you," he said quietly. "But then again you're the most courageous woman I know, Lilly De Campo."

She stepped in to kiss him as she'd wanted to this afternoon. Heat swept through her veins, licked at her nerve-endings as he claimed her mouth in a thorough, possessive kiss that seemed to promise a million forevers.

"I love you," she whispered. *"Io ti amo per sempre."*

I will love you forever.

He pulled back, his gaze so dark it was almost black. "Finish that drink," he muttered roughly. "Dinner can wait."

She downed the last gulp and gasped when he swung her up in his arms and headed for the stairs. Up he climbed, to the bedroom that overlooked the river, the room where her dream of their family had begun. It occurred to her as Riccardo slid his hands to the back of her dress and unzipped it, letting the silky material slip to the floor, that her dream had finally come true. The puppy sleeping downstairs in a basket in the kitchen had been the final piece.

She smiled and wrapped her arms around her husband's neck, pulling his mouth down to hers.

From a divorce party to forever. Who would have known?

* * * * *

AN EXQUISITE
CHALLENGE

BY
JENNIFER HAYWARD

For my editor, Carly, whose impeccable advice made this book what it is. Thank you!

For Victoria Parker and Kat Cantrell, the two best critique partners a writer could have. Your advice and support mean everything to me.

For winemaker Jac Cole of Spring Mountain Vineyard in Napa, who graciously offered his time to teach me about the fine art of blending and bringing a wine to market. I can only hope Gabe's wines are half as wonderful as yours!

CHAPTER ONE

IF LIFE WAS a glass of Cabernet, Alexandra Anderson wanted to live right in the lusty, full-bodied center of it. The thrill of the chase was paramount—the stickier the challenge, the better. If she wasn't sure she could do it— that's where she wanted to be. That's when she got even better. That's where she thrived.

As for the intricacies of that particular varietal versus California Zinfandel and Merlot? For a girl who'd grown up in the backwaters of Iowa tossing back beers with the undesirable crowd, it wasn't something that kept her up at night. Who gave a toss as long as it tasted good and did something to alleviate the interminable boredom of yet another cocktail party that was all work and no play?

Certainly not the sentiment of the man who'd just strode into Napa Valley's annual industry fundraiser for the homeless, a massive scowl on his face. Those grapes that made bubbly go fizz for her were an obsession for Gabriele De Campo, the visionary behind De Campo Group's world-renowned wines. His raison d'être.

She stood watching him from her perch on the balcony overlooking the mezzanine of the Pacific Heights hotspot Charo, where the event was being held, with only one goal in mind: to indulge in one of those adrenaline-seeking ventures she so loved. To convince Gabriele De Campo to let her PR firm handle the two massive upcoming launch events for De Campo's most important wine in a decade. It was her chance to finally win a piece of the internationally renowned winemaker's communications portfolio, and she didn't intend to fail.

She took a sip of the glass of wine she'd been nursing for an hour and a half while she'd schmoozed every key player in the California wine industry, doing every piece of reconnaissance she could to learn who was who, what made these people tick and what would make a knockout launch for De Campo.

A warning shiver snaked up her spine. Was she crazy to even be attempting this?

It had all happened in a rather mind-numbingly quick fashion. This morning she'd been sleeping off one too many martinis from her girls' night out in Manhattan when she'd been woken at 6:00 a.m. with a panicked phone call from Katya Jones, the head of De Campo's marketing department. An old colleague of hers, cool-as-a-cucumber Katya had sounded unusually flustered. Gabriele De Campo had just fired the PR agency handling his Devil's Peak launch for its *"atroce"* ideas three and a half weeks before simultaneous kickoff events in Napa and New York. "I need you," Katya had groaned. "And I need you *now*."

Alex might not have been so inclined to drag her sorry butt out of bed for a chance to work for her sister's brother-in-law if she hadn't just lost her three-million-dollar-a-year diamond client this week in a hostile takeover. It had been a huge blow for Alex's fledgling PR firm that had just taken over a ritzy new space on Fifth Avenue. If she didn't find another big client soon, she'd be closing her doors before she even got started. So she'd shaken off her fuzz, canceled her appointments and jumped on a plane to San Francisco in time to make this party.

There was only one problem with the whole scenario. Katya didn't know Alex's relationship to Gabe. Didn't know he had a strict no-working-with-family policy he'd never bent from, no matter how much she'd tried to convince him to give her De Campo's business. Didn't know she and Gabe were like oil and water. *Always.* When Gabe said white, she said black. It was just the way it was.

Which had no bearing on the here and now, she told herself, tucking a wayward strand of her long, dark hair back into her chignon, squaring her shoulders and starting for the winding staircase that led down to the mezzanine. Her combative relationship with Gabe was inconsequential when a two-million-dollar contract was on the line. *When her future was on the line.*

She curved her hand around the mahogany banister and took a deep, steadying breath. Her steps down the staircase were slow and deliberate, designed not to attract attention. Gabe was in the middle of the crowd, speaking to the head of the local farm workers union, his attention immersed in his subject as it always was—that single-minded focus his trademark. But as she continued her descent, that familiar awareness flickered across the air between them, charged, electric. Gabe's head came up. His gaze froze as it rested on her. His eyes widened.

As if he was surprised to see her.

Oh, Lord. Katya had told him she'd hired her. *Hadn't she?*

She started to get the awful feeling that no, somehow her old colleague had not passed along that crucial piece of information as she descended the second flight of stairs, her heart thumping in tandem with each step. Gabe's thick, dark brow arched high, his gaze not leaving her face. Surprise. Definitely surprise.

This was so, so not good.

Or maybe, she countered desperately, as he broke off his conversation and strode over to stand at the base of the stairs, it was actually a very good thing. Having the element of surprise over control freak Gabe could work in her favor. Allow her to slide in some sound reasoning before he brought the gavel down.

Her knees, as she descended the last flight and took him in, felt a little too weak for a woman facing a man who was essentially family. Which might have been due to the superbly tailored suit that fit Gabe's tall, muscular body like a glove. Or his black-as-night hair worn overly long with perfectly cut sideburns.

Some women pointed out the sexy indentation in the middle of his chin as outrageously hot. She preferred the drown-yourself-in-them forest-green eyes. His formidable self-control she was fairly certain would come crumbling down for the right woman…

She pulled in a breath as she negotiated the last step and stopped in front of him. *Utterly to die for. Utterly off-limits. Get a hold of yourself, Lex.*

His mouth curved. "Alexandra."

The rich, velvety texture of his voice stormed her senses, sending goose bumps to every inch of her skin. His use of her full name was formal, his gaze as it rested on her face probing. "I had no idea you were on the West Coast."

Dammit, Katya. He really had no idea. She swallowed past the sudden dryness in her throat and tipped her head back to look up at him. "Your internal radar didn't signal I was close?"

His mouth quirked. "Something must have been scrambling the signal."

She braced herself against the smoky, earthy scent of him as he bent to brush his lips across each of her cheeks, but his husky *"ciao"* decimated her composure.

"What *are* you doing here?" he murmured, drawing back, his gaze lingering on her face. "I can't imagine anything less your style than an industry party like this."

Hell. She lifted her chin. "You haven't spoken to Katya yet today, have you?"

"Katya Jones?"

"Yes, she was going to call you. She—I—" Alex planted her gaze on his and held on. "She hired me, Gabe. To do the events."

His eyes widened, then darkened. "That isn't possible. I approve those decisions."

"I'm afraid it is," she said calmly. "Have you checked your messages? She must have left you one."

He scraped his hair out of his face with a tanned, elegant-fingered hand and scowled. "I haven't had two seconds to think today, let alone check email."

And there you had it. She plastered a breezy, confident smile on her face. "You have coast-to-coast launches in three and a half weeks, Gabe. Katya knows I'm the only one who can pull them off at this point, so she called me in to help." She waved a hand at him. "I'm here to save you."

"*Save* me?" His frown deepened. "You know I have a firm policy against working with family."

"I don't think you have a choice."

He screwed up his aristocratic, beautiful face and sliced a hand through the air. "I need a drink."

Excellent idea. So did she.

"So, I can have a theme to you in forty-eight hours," she said brightly, trailing along behind him to the bar. "I looked at the ideas the other agency put together for you and I agree, they're crap. I've got some much better ones."

"Alex," he growled, slapping his palm on the bar, "you are not doing these launch events."

She slid onto a stool, her chin tilted at a mutinous angle. "Katya hired me. *I'm* brilliant at my job. You know I am."

"*That* is irrelevant." He barked a request for drinks at the bartender, then sat down beside her. "I know you're the best, Alex. I would have hired you already if you weren't family. But you are, and it's not happening."

Desperation surged through her. She rested her elbows on the bar, locked her gaze on his and went for the jugular. "You backed the wrong horse, Gabe. You chose the wrong agency and now you're in too deep. Executing two massive back-to-back launch events in Napa and New York with this little prep time is an almost suicidal assignment. There are only two PR people besides myself in this country who are even capable of pulling it off. One," she emphasized, "is presently sailing up the Nile with his wife. I *know* because I just got a postcard from him. The second is in Houston doing an event with five extra staff she just hired to make it happen. You will not," she pronounced, "be getting any personal service there."

He slid a glass of wine across the bar to her, his broad shoulders rising in a dismissive shrug. "We'll figure it out. I'm not breaking my rule."

Fire singed her veins. There were a few things Alex was sure of in life. One was the fact that no one was better at their job than she was. Hands down. He *needed* her. "Do you *want* your launches to fail?" she demanded. "You've spent eight years, *eight years* getting De Campo to this point in Napa, Gabe. Eight years gaining the respect you deserve for your Californian vintages. You have one chance to make a first impression with this wine. I can make sure it's the launch of the year."

He set his glass down and cursed under his breath. Alex stared at him. She had never, *ever* heard Gabe say that word.

"Let me help you," she murmured, reaching out and laying her hand on his forearm. "I can do this."

A current of electricity zigzagged its way from her palm to her stomach. She pulled her hand away and tucked it under her thigh. It was always this way between them, a gigantic pulse-fluttering awareness of each other that defied reason.

"You didn't think it was a really bad idea jumping on a plane before you had *any* idea if I was going to take you on?" Gabe muttered with a dark stare that was equal parts frustration and something else entirely.

"Katya *hired* me. As in gave me the job, Gabe."

"I can unhire you."

"You wouldn't."

He shrugged. "You know it's a bad idea."

"It's *fine*." She sank her teeth into her bottom lip. "I'll stay out of your way. I'll be so invisible you won't even know I'm there."

"That," he murmured, wry humor flashing in his eyes, "is a physical impossibility for you. You're like a fire-engine-red poppy in a sea of Tuscan green."

"Gabe—"

He held up a hand, his gaze flicking over her shoulder. "I need to talk to a couple of people, then I have a ton of work to do at home. Sit here, wait for me and I'll drive you back to your hotel. We can talk on the way."

She wanted to retort she wasn't a dog, that she didn't take orders, but this was the part where she needed to prove he could work with her.

"Fine," she murmured sweetly. "Here I sit, waiting for you…"

He narrowed his gaze on her face, looked as if he was about to say something, then shook his head and stood. "Ten minutes."

She watched his tall, imposing figure cut through the crowd. *Holy hell, Katya. Really?*

The chicly dressed West Coast crowd buzzed around her, drawn to the shining mahogany centerpiece of a bar like moths to a flame. She settled back on the stool, enjoying the relaxed, chilled-out vibe that was so far from the New York scene she was used to, it was like night and day. Sipped her wine and wondered how to approach this Gabe she wasn't familiar with. He rarely got into a mood, he was iron man, the man most likely to walk through a burning building unscathed, his Armani suit intact. Yet tonight he was antagonized, edgy. Harder to predict.

The only thing to do was stick to the end goal, she told herself. *Get the job.* She hadn't spent the last eight years slugging it out in a big, prestigious Manhattan PR firm to go back to working fourteen-hour days on brands that bored her to tears. Functioning like a corporate robot to pad someone else's bottom line. Anderson Communications was *hers.* Her ticket to complete financial independence and security. She was not going to fail.

For her, freedom was everything. Misplaced testosterone had no part in it when her future was on the line.

She ran her gaze over the crowded bar with a restless energy that contrasted with the easy vibe. Continued cataloging the attributes of her target audience. A fortysomething salt-and-pepper male on the other side of the bar caught her eye.

It couldn't be.

It was.

The one man she'd truly hoped never to see again.

Her heart stopped in her chest. Tall, lean and sophisticated in a dark gray designer suit, chatting to a quirkily beautiful blonde, he looked exactly the same. Except, now he had the gray where before he hadn't and there were visible lines around his eyes when he smiled. That smile he knew dropped a woman at fifty paces.

It had her.

She whipped around on the stool, but not before he saw her. The shock on his face rocketed through her, made her dizzy, disoriented. She got unsteadily to her feet and walked blindly through the crowd, destination undetermined, anywhere that was far, far away from him. The faces around her blurred into a haze of polite laughter and bright lights. *Of course Jordan would be here tonight.* He was the CEO of the biggest spirits company in the U.S. Everyone who was anyone in the wine industry was here....

Why hadn't she anticipated it?

A hand came down on her shoulder.

"Alex."

She spun around, her heart jump-starting and racing a mile a minute. Jordan Lane. Her former client. The man she'd made the biggest mistake of her life with.

The man she'd loved and hated in equal measure.

"Jordan." She forced the words past her constricted throat. "What a surprise."

His gaze narrowed on her face as if to say he knew she'd seen him, but he played the game, capturing her hand in a deliberate gesture and brushing his lips across her knuckles. "You look beautiful. Age agrees with you."

Meaning she'd been twenty-two when she'd met him and far too unsophisticated to ever have been able to handle a man like him. Heat roared inside of her, dark and all consuming. She pulled her hand back and pressed the trembling appendage to her side. He had used her inexperience to play her like a bow, to mold her into what he'd desired.

The charm was still there, but the predatory instinct in those startling blue eyes was clearly visible to her now. *How had she not seen it before?*

"How about," she suggested icily, "we pretend I took that as a compliment and you go back to your flirtation? At least she doesn't look half your age."

His eyes darkened to the wintry color of the Hudson River on a stormy day. "How about we have a drink and talk about it?"

"No. Thank. You." She turned her back on him.

"It's about work."

She spun around. "I wouldn't work for you if you were the last client on this planet."

"It takes two to tango, Alex."

"Funny," she bit out, "I didn't even know I was dancing."

His mouth tightened. "I need branding work done. I know your work and I trust you."

Trust. Her stomach lurched. The very thing he'd taken away from her when she'd had so little to start with. She clenched her hands into fists and drew herself up to her full height, her gaze clashing with his wintry silver one. "You lied to me and dishonored your wife, Jordan. You almost destroyed my career. Don't talk to me about trust."

"Let me make it up to you." He thrust his hands in his pockets and shifted his weight onto both feet. "I heard you lost Generes. Let me give you some work."

She lifted her chin. "Go to hell."

Head held high, she pushed through the crowd, anger stinging her eyes, stinging every part of her. How dare he so cavalierly dismiss what he'd done? How dare he think she'd even want to talk to him, let alone work for him? She was almost to the front doors when a hand grasped her arm. Sure it was him again, she swung around, intent on giving him a piece of her mind, but it was Gabe standing in front of her.

"Everything all right?"

She nodded. "I just need some fresh air."

"You know Jordan Lane?"

Damn. He had seen them. She struggled to wipe the emotion from her face, to wipe away any evidence she had ever known the man who had almost destroyed her. "Yes—" she nodded "—he was a client at my old agency."

A frown creased his brow. "He was coming on to you?"

"No." She raked a hand through her hair and looked

away from that penetrating green gaze. "He was offering me a job."

"He's not the kind of guy you want to work for, Alex."

She set her chin at a belligerent angle. "Then give me the job and I won't have to."

He was silent for a moment. If there was one person she couldn't read in this world, it was Gabe. He guarded his feelings with a security worthy of Alcatraz. "I'm ready to go," he said finally, pulling the sweater out of her arms and holding it out for her. "You look exhausted. Let's go."

She slipped her arms into the sleeves, letting him wrap it around her. His deliciously male scent enveloped her, sending her senses into overdrive. And not the kind of overdrive that had anything to do with business.

The valet brought Gabe's car around. He held the door open for her and she slipped into the luxurious interior of the silver-blue Porsche and sighed. So much better to be out of that crowd.

On the way to her hotel, Gabe wanted to know how his nephew, Marco, Lilly and Riccardo's rambunctious two-year-old, was doing. She gave him an update, smiling when he asked her what he should buy him for his birthday present, because Gabe inevitably bought Marco totally inappropriate toys. No one saw fit to correct him because, really, how could you tell a proud uncle that a two-year-old, however clever Marco undoubtedly was, was not capable of building a suspension bridge by himself?

They hadn't even begun discussing the events when Gabe parked outside her boutique Union Square hotel, cut the engine on the powerful beast of a car and looked at her. "Talk over a drink?"

She nodded, even though every bone in her body told her it was a *bad idea*. She wasn't sure if it was seeing Jordan tonight that made her nervous about having a man in her hotel room or if it was just that it was Gabe, but her cozy little suite suddenly seemed far too small as they entered it and he shrugged out of his jacket and loosened his tie. *Steady on,* she told herself, turning some lights on as he folded himself into the sofa in the little sitting room. It's just a drink.

He looked tired, she noticed, the lines at the sides of his mouth more pronounced than usual, the hand he used to rub his eyes shifting back to cradle his neck. The stress was getting to him.

She walked over to the bar. "Scotch?"

"Soda and lime if you have it. I have to drive back to the vineyard tonight."

"Aren't you swamped back in New York?" he asked as she handed him his drink and perched on the sofa beside him. "How can you possibly take on a job like this?"

"Some things have moved around in my calendar." Moved permanently, as in *out* of her calendar, but he didn't need to know that.

He sat back and took a sip of his drink. "Us working together is a bad idea, Alex."

"These are extraordinary circumstances."

"We will kill each other."

"No," she countered, "we will learn to work together. I haven't even *tried* to be nice to you."

His smile flashed white against his olive skin. "That thought terrifies me."

She gave him an earnest look. "I'm the only person who can do this, Gabe."

He set his drink down and pushed a distracted hand through his hair. "*If* I gave you the business, and I'm not insinuating anything here, would you do the work yourself or will it be a case of bait and switch with the juniors doing everything?"

"I've never done a bait and switch in my life," she said matter-of-factly. "If you hire me, you get me."

Oh. That didn't sound right. She hadn't meant *get her.* But he knew what she meant, right?

He shot her a sideways look. "What is *wrong* with you? Sit down properly, for *Cristo's* sake. You're completely on edge."

She pushed herself deeper into the sofa. She *was* on edge, dammit. It was stupidly hard to concentrate with Gabe plastered across the sofa of her hotel room looking hellishly hot in a shirt and tie that would have been ordinary on any other man but made him look like stud of the century.

"Alex?"

"Sorry?" She lifted her gaze to his face.

He sighed. "What's wrong?"

She shook her head. "It's been a long day."

He pursed his lips. Took a sip of his drink. "Convince me I should let you do this."

She got up, found her briefcase and pulled out a file. "Here are five case studies of events I've pulled off in this amount of time," she said, handing it to him. "I can make this the most spectacular debut for your wine. I promise you that."

He flipped through the folder. "This is impressive."

"So make the call."

He put the folder down on the coffee table and sat back. The movement drew her attention to his superb, muscular thighs. They were so good they were impossible not to ogle.

"Even if I did agree you are the right choice," he said evenly, "we still need to discuss our other *problema.*"

"What other problem?"

"*That* problem."

She frowned. "I have no idea what you're talking about."

He lifted a brow. "Tell me that was not a distinctly lustful look."

"That was not lustful. That was—"

"Alex." He angled his body toward her and captured her gaze. "You've been jumpy since the minute we walked into this hotel room and we both know why. You keep wondering what it would have been like to have that kiss in Lilly and Riccardo's garden and so do I."

Ahh. The almost kiss. The thing she couldn't get out of her head no matter how hard she tried. She'd been slightly tipsy, standing on a stool unstringing lanterns from a tree after all the guests had left her sister's welcome-to-summer party, when Gabe had come looking for her. She'd been caught so off guard by his sudden presence she'd nearly fallen off the stool. He'd caught her and swung her to the ground, but kept his arms around her waist. The knowledge that he had been about to kiss her had made her grab her slingbacks and run.

She scowled at him. "I'm working on about four hours' sleep, that's why I'm jumpy. Maybe you should just say yes to the contract so I can get some rest and—" She stared at him as he moved closer. "What *are* you doing?"

He lifted his hand and splayed his fingers across her jaw. "Figuring out how bad this particular *problema* is before I make up my mind."

"There is no problem," she croaked. "And if we're going to be working together, I—"

"I haven't said yes yet," he cut in, his gaze purposeful. "Right now we have no working relationship whatsoever."

They did have heat. *They definitely had heat.* She swallowed hard as it washed over her and made her pulse dance. "If I make this really bad you'll say yes?"

His gaze darkened. "It isn't going to be bad."

No, she acknowledged, heart pounding, it wasn't. Slicking her tongue across dry lips, she told herself she just needed to stay in control. Prove to him this attraction between them was wholly avoidable. But when he shifted his thumb to the seam of her lips in the most erotic opening to a kiss she'd ever experienced, she caved like a ton of bricks.

Her first taste of Gabriele De Campo lived up to every fantasy she'd ever had. Hot, smooth and utterly in control, his mouth slanted unhurriedly over hers, exploring every dip and curve with a leisurely enjoyment that made her want to curl her fingers into his shirt and beg. She resisted with the small amount of willpower she still possessed, but it was like being dangled over a ledge a hundred feet above the ground and told to hang on when you knew you were eventually going to fall.

She'd known he'd be good. Just not *this* good.

For a minute, for just one glorious minute, the temptation was too great and she let her mind go blank. And let herself savor what she'd been craving for a very long time.

He sensed her softening. Slid his hand to the back of her head and took her mouth in a drugging, never-ending kiss that upped the hotness quotient by ten. Off balance, she *had* to dig her fingers into his shirt and hang on.

"Lex," he murmured, sliding his tongue along the seam of her lips. "Give me more."

She was going to stop this in about five seconds. She was. He demanded entry again and she gave it to him. The feel of his tongue sliding sensuously against hers made her insides coil tight. This was more than a kiss, it was a full-out assault on her common sense.

And it was working.

She yanked herself out of his arms, her chest moving rapidly in and out. Her five seconds were definitely up. Way past up.

"That was not fair."

"You need to admit you have a problem to solve it," he murmured dryly. "Now we know."

"We also know we can control it," she pointed out.

"Look it's done. Presto," she said, waving her hand at him. "Never to be had again. Curiosity's over."

He picked up the file and got to his feet. "Be at my office at ten tomorrow."

She stared at him incredulously. "You're leaving me hanging?"

He waved the file at her. "I need to read this."

"That kiss was nothing, Gabe."

"I'd like to see what something is."

She watched as he straightened his shirt. Mortification sank into her bones. Why the hell had she allowed that to happen? She was supposed to be convincing him of her professionalism, not her skills in the necking department.

She followed him to the door. "You won't regret it if you give me this job, Gabe."

He gave her a long look. *"Che resta da vedere."*

She scrunched her face up. "What does that mean?"

"That remains to be seen."

He left. She picked up her shoe and threw it at the door. His soft laughter came from the other side. "Use the deadbolt, Alex."

Despite her bone-deep fatigue, it took a hot shower and an hour of fretting to get herself anywhere near sleep. Gabe had been playing her and playing her well. Establishing a reason *not* to give her the business. She'd just been too busy being a spineless fool who couldn't resist his Italian charm to see it.

After all these years of walking away, it had taken *jet lag* to do her in.

She whacked her head against the pillow and closed her eyes. If she got another chance, *if* he gave her the job tomorrow, she wasn't making the same mistake twice.

CHAPTER TWO

MORNING BUMPER-TO-BUMPER traffic on Highway 101, with every motorist in northern California fighting their way into San Francisco with an aggressive zeal that said they were ten minutes late for a meeting and short on temper, wasn't helping to improve Gabe's mood. In fact, it had sent it to a whole other level.

He cursed, checked his blind spot and accelerated into the left-hand lane, which appeared equally blocked, but the movement at least made him feel as though he was doing *something*.

"Maledizione," he muttered. "I should have stayed in the city last night."

"One of San Francisco's most eligible bachelors, devoid of a date on a Thursday night?" His brother Riccardo's taunting voice sliced through the high-tech speakerphone.

"I was at an industry party." He scowled at the tinny box. "Mention the bachelor thing one more time and you'll be talking to empty air."

His brother chuckled. "I'm just jealous I never made the list."

As if. Riccardo had dated five times a man's usual share of the styled-down-to-their-pinkie women who inhabited the island of Manhattan and it hadn't been until he'd met Lilly and fallen flat on his face for her that the parade had ended. His mouth twisted in a wry smile. "They probably figured they were doing the female population a favor."

"Maybe so." Humor flavored his brother's response. "Speaking of women, talk to Matty lately?"

"No." It struck him as strange now that he thought about it. Matty and Gabe were close and usually talked once a week. "What's up?"

"A woman, I think. He won't talk about it. You should call him."

Gabe wasn't sure his cynical attitude of late was going to be of much use to his younger brother. Matty was the Don Juan of his generation—he thought love made the world go around. Gabe wasn't sure how he'd acquired that notion in *their* particular family, but that was for Matty to figure out. Not his problem. Matty's issue was likely of the which-one-do-I-pick variety, anyway.

"What happened to the Olympian?"

"I don't know. He hung up shortly after I asked him if her flexibility was useful in bed."

"You don't say?"

His brother's tone turned businesslike. "How are the events going, by the way? Do you need me in Napa or can I just do NYC?"

Gabe's fingers tightened on the wheel. "They're getting there. We're working through some kinks at the moment." He checked his rearview mirror and moved back to the center lane. "New York's fine. I can handle Napa."

"*Bene.* The doctor said to keep a close eye on Lilly for the next few weeks."

"You should be there," Gabe muttered distractedly, his brain on five hundred people at his vineyard in three weeks. "How did Marco take the news of a little brother?"

"He's *estatico.* Already picking out which trains his little brother can and cannot use."

Gabe smiled. "Already a De Campo."

"Was there ever any doubt?"

"Nessuna." Marco was an exuberant brute of a little boy so much like his father and the rest of the De Campo brothers it was like watching one of them as a child. Gabe was glad the little guy was going to *have* a brother, because his had been a lifeline in a childhood marked by his parents' coldness. His father's survival-of-the-fittest regime had reigned supreme in Montalcino, his mother's lack of interest in her children blatantly apparent. A business merger between two important families did that to the family dynamic.

"I heard," Riccardo said evenly, "that Alex flew over there to do the events."

Gabe grimaced. "I fired the PR firm. They were spewing out garbage that was all wrong for the brand."

"*Three weeks* before launch?"

"It wasn't working."

"So you're letting Alex step in?"

"I'm thinking about it." Truth was, Alex's portfolio was brilliant. The campaigns she'd included had all been for established brands launching products with breakout potential. Just like The Devil's Peak. Not only had her campaigns been sophisticated and clever with the big buzz potential he was looking for, they'd also been exactly the tone and feel he'd wanted in the last PR agency's ideas.

"The board is only giving me so much leeway with the Napa investment." Riccardo's quietly worded warning came through the speaker. "At some point they're going to rein us in, and I'd prefer that time be when you've had a chance to make things happen and they're compelled to keep investing."

Gabe stiffened. "You think I'm not well aware of that?"

"A launch event is a launch event, *fratello,* not the second coming of Christ. Get it done. Don't let yourself get in the way of your success."

Old animosities surged to life—charged, destructive forces that skimmed just beneath the surface. If he'd inherited his father and grandfather's wine-making brilliance and the ability to play with the chemistry of a wine until it melted on the tongue, Riccardo had mastered the ability to see the big picture. It was the one trait, Gabe was sure, that had catapulted his brother over him to CEO, aside from the fact that Riccardo was the eldest, and Antonio was traditional to the hilt.

He scowled. "Are you questioning my judgment?"

"No," his brother said matter-of-factly. "I'm saying we're treading close to the line."

Which was true. He'd seen the latest profit-and-loss statements for the Napa operations and they weren't pretty. They weren't meeting profit targets they'd established at launch eight years ago and there were reasons for that, yes, like the fact that The Devil's Peak and his other star wine had matured faster than they'd expected and he'd invested in bringing them to market. But the board didn't know they were about to reap huge financial rewards. To them, he was a number.

He let out a long breath. "These risks we're taking—they're going to pay off. You know that."

"There isn't a doubt in my mind."

The quiet confidence in his brother's reply made him sink his head back against the headrest. *"Dispiace,"* he murmured. "It's been quite a week."

"Get yourself laid. It'll help."

"I'm too busy to get laid."

"A man is never too busy to get laid."

The gospel according to Riccardo. Gabe shook his head. "Do you have a problem with me hiring Alex?"

"I'm staying out of this particular discussion," his brother returned dryly. "Better to leave it to your impartial judgment rather than face my wife's wrath. But I will say, I've heard she is the best in the business."

Gabe wouldn't describe his attitude toward Alex as impartial, particularly after last night. But *this* wasn't personal, it was business.

He and Riccardo debated which quarterback would prevail in the weekend's football game, arranged to talk after Gabe's meeting tomorrow with a restaurant chain they'd been courting and signed off.

Traffic started to move. He put his foot down on the accelerator and forced himself to focus on the decision at hand. Hiring Alex was the right thing to do. She might be the only person who could save him. The fact that she made his blood pressure rise by about ten points just by being in the same room shouldn't have anything to do with it. And yet…the feel of her soft, lush mouth under his last night slammed into his brain with a force that was distinctly off-putting. The hazy desire in her big blue eyes when she'd pulled away. *That* was what was making him hesitate. Alex's ability to get under his skin.

She was the type of woman you took to bed once, got out of your system then banished from your head forever. But given their familial ties, he couldn't do that. He *had* to see her on a regular basis. So he'd restrained himself. Until that night in Lilly and Riccardo's garden. Until last night. And even though he'd now assured himself she'd be spectacular in bed, she was off-limits. It pained him to admit it—but he needed her. In a couple of hours she'd be working for him. And if there was one thing he never did, it was mix business with pleasure.

Alex was two large coffees into an official snit when Gabe deigned to make an appearance at his airy warehouse office space in downtown San Francisco. It had surprised her at first, the modernity of the building, given De Campo's historic lineage, but Gabe, his chatty PA Danielle had told her, was contemporary both in his design taste and in the way he chose to make his wines in Napa, using a blend of new and old-world techniques.

She sat up straighter in the cream-colored leather chair, her senses switching to high alert. Gabe was dressed in another of those beautifully tailored suits, this time a charcoal-gray that made his green eyes pop, and it took her pulse from zero to fifty in a second flat.

His gaze slid over her. "*Scusa*. Traffic was murder."

She bit her tongue. "No worries."

"*Buongiorno*," he murmured to Danielle, requesting an espresso and for her to move his next meeting, before waving Alex into his office, an equally large, open space that offered a superb view of the city.

She sat down in the chair he pointed to and took in the hard line of his jaw. "You're not going to give me the job."

He shut the door, walked around the desk and sat down opposite her. "I want to get a few things straight before I give you my answer."

She felt the need for a preemptive strike. "If it's about the kiss, I—"

"Are you even capable," he asked harshly, stripping off his jacket, "of muzzling that mouth of yours while I lay this out?"

Whoa. Someone had gotten up on the wrong side of the bed this morning... His face was all hard lines and tense mouth, his broad shoulders ramrod straight under the crisp light blue shirt. "Okay," she agreed carefully, "I'm a mute until you tell me I can speak."

His eyes flashed and she had the feeling he would have taken that comment elsewhere had he not been so focused on the subject at hand. He leaned forward and rested his forearms on the desk. If that was supposed to intimidate her, it didn't. "I will let you manage these events on four conditions."

It was on the tip of her tongue to snap back that he needed her as much as she needed him, but she pressed her lips together and sat back in the chair.

"One," he began, "I brief you today, you put an idea I like on my desk by Monday and you're in."

She nodded. She was nothing if not good under pressure.

"Two. If for any reason creative differences make it impossible for us to work together, I can fire you at any time."

Hot anger singed her veins. "You are too much."

He held up a hand, an icy, calm expression on his face. "You're a mute, remember?"

She was going to be a killer in a second.

"Three," he continued. "You have nothing to do with Jordan Lane. He is the competition and you will not do work for him. And four—" he trained his gaze on hers "—what happened last night doesn't happen again."

"You started it," she burst out like a three-year-old.

"And now I'm ending it." His lips tilted downward. "This is the most important launch of De Campo's modern history, Alex. There is a ten-million-dollar ad campaign behind it. We don't get to screw up."

No kidding.

He pushed her portfolio across the desk. "I looked at this. You're incredibly talented."

She glowed at that. "Thank you."

"I want you to work on the events. I know you're right for this. Which means," he added grimly, "we need to learn to work together. We need to put our personal differences aside. Put this *inconvenient attraction* we have for one other aside. And get this done."

Inconvenient attraction? She supposed that's what it was, but she didn't like the distasteful way he said it. As if she were a bug running across the gleaming wooden floor he wanted to crush.

His gaze was on her, expectant. She lifted a brow. "Am I allowed to talk?" He nodded. "Sooo," she began, "I'm all for that." She had precisely one month's office rent in reserve and she'd like to pad that, not kiss him again. "I also have no interest in working for Jordan Lane."

"Bene." He leaned back in his chair and crossed his arms over his chest, his dictatorial terms secured. "This is the way it's going to work. You show me the theme—I approve. Then I see everything at every step in the process. Invitations, decor, suppliers.... Any major decision—I approve it."

Alarm bells started to ring in her head. "Look, I know you had a bad experience with the last agency and the pressure is on, but that's not how I work."

"It is now."

She reined in the urge to tell him he'd lost touch with reality. "We have *three and a half weeks* to pull these events together, Gabe. We're going to have to move at lightning speed and even then, it's going to be a minor miracle if we pull it off."

His face was hard, implacable. "Tell me now if you can't do it."

"I can do it," she barked, leaning forward and resting her palms on the desk. "But I think it's nuts. You're the vice president of De Campo Group. You have a wine to get out the door in a few weeks. You really want to be approving catering menus?"

"I'm creating a brand," he returned harshly. "Everything depends on first impressions. So if I want to approve a catering menu, I will."

"What about one of your marketing people back in New York? Surely they can work with me?"

"They're not close enough to the ground."

"Then *get* them here."

His scowl grew. "This launch is mine, Alex. The culmination of years of blood, sweat and tears. I want to be intimately involved. You play by my rules or you don't play at all."

She pressed her lips together. "Do I need your approval to go to the bathroom, too?"

"Scusi?"

"Nothing." She tapped her fingernails on the desk in a staccato rhythm. "Those poor buggers," she muttered under her breath, feeling sorry for the last agency. But maybe it should be poor *her*. Because she was going to have to spend the next month of her life working for *him*.

"What *did* you say?"

She looked up at him, the tilt of her chin defiant. "I said, 'poor buggers.' As in I feel sorry for the old agency to have had to work with you. Are you sure *they* didn't quit?"

His eyes glittered. "Are you sure you want to talk to your boss like that?"

"You're not my boss yet." She threw his words from last night back at him, wishing that didn't put her head squarely back on that kiss. "I haven't signed the contract yet. You realize I could walk out of this office right now and you'd be screwed, right?"

"But you aren't going to do that." He waved her portfolio at her. "I thought it was odd you weren't booked solid, so I did some homework this morning. You just lost your biggest client, Alex. Swallowed up by a multinational. You *need* me."

Her stomach dropped. "It had nothing to do with our work."

"I'm sure it didn't. Your reputation is exemplary." He threw the portfolio down on the desk. "What remains are the facts. It's me or Jordan Lane, and I can guarantee you, you want to pick me."

She could guarantee that, too. She stared mutinously at him, hating nothing more than being boxed into a corner, but unfortunately, that's exactly where she was. "You know what they say about great leaders, Gabe? They surround themselves with good people, they don't get caught up in the minutia and they let their disciples make them look good."

His gaze cooled. "Earn my trust, then. Although something tells me you are far from trainable."

She held her hands up in the air in mock surrender. "You'll get every menu. You might want to consider joining us at the hip, though."

Her attempt at a joke didn't seem to have the intended effect and she wondered if she'd hit a nerve with the leadership thing. "Elena has a room ready for you at the house," he said abruptly. "It makes more sense for you to be there where you'll have much more access to me."

And why did that sound like a very, very bad idea? The kiss from last night flashed through her head again. Her burying her hands in his shirt and begging for more. Him walking away. Sure, it would be more convenient for her to stay at the winery, given the event was going to be held there, but her and Gabe in the same house? Was that *asking* for trouble?

"I can stay in one of the bed-and-breakfasts," she suggested. "So I'm not underfoot."

"You'll stay at the house." He pointed to the conference table. "Shall I walk you through the brief?"

She nodded. They moved to the table and Gabe took her through the brief he'd given the other agency. Five hundred people, an outdoor venue where weather could be a factor, VIP tours of the winery and a press junket to see the wine-making process. Oh, and no theme in existence.

Totally doable in three weeks, right?

She almost turned around and ran out the door. Except

the desire to conquer was stronger. And maybe the urge to show Mr. Perfection she was a whole lot more than he thought she was.

She might have been describing her entire life.

CHAPTER THREE

How could she be freezing now?

Uttering a string of purple prose that would have made a trucker proud, Alex got up from her PC before she did something crazy, like throw it across the room. She stalked to the window and looked out over the vineyard, lush and green on a hot summer day. The sunroom Gabe had given her to work in was a wonderful, quiet space, but right now it felt like a prison. She'd said she wouldn't leave until she had a theme. But it wasn't coming. At all.

The only thing she'd been able to spew out thus far was a lame idea about how the rich boldness of De Campo's new wine, The Devil's Peak, was a feast for the senses.

Ugh. Clichéd. Boring. Done. It could have been coffee for all its originality. Which she'd had more than enough of by now, by the way.

She rubbed her fatigue-stung eyes. Of all the moments for her to have a total creative meltdown, *this* was not the one she would have chosen. She had forty-eight hours left to conjure up an event theme that would have De Campo on the lips of every wine lover on the East and West Coasts, but nothing was coming.

She picked up her bottle of water and abandoned her office for outside. The De Campo homestead was done in an open-concept, New England–style design that blended in perfectly with the beautiful countryside. Huge floor-to-ceiling windows let in the gorgeous Napa light, bounded by a wraparound porch, terrace and pool area. Up the rolling hill in front of her sprawled the vineyard. Maybe some sunshine and a walk into the vines would inspire her. Impart some fantastic *oh, my God* idea into her brain.

She walked up the hill and into the Cabernet vines, which stretched all the way up to the edge of the escarpment. A band of green topped by the pure blue Napa sky. Harvest, Gabe had told her, would be the end of summer or early fall, but the grapes on the vines already looked like perfect replicas of the most glorious still lifes. Smaller and more perfectly rounded than a supermarket grape, they were a vibrant, luscious purple. Inspirational, certainly.

Channeling hard, she tried the word-association games they used to brainstorm at the agency. Nothing came. Nada. She was officially in a slump. A ninth-inning slump, at that. A building sense of panic tattooed itself through her veins. It was Saturday. The invitations had to go out by Tuesday, latest, if they were to get into people's busy summer calendars. Which meant Gabe had to approve a theme and invites by Monday. She had confidence in her graphic designer's ability to turn a concept and invitation around in twenty-four hours. He was brilliant. But she needed to give him something to work with.

"A feast for the senses" was just not going to cut it.

She plopped herself down in the middle of a row, drew her jeans-clad knees up to her chest and propped her elbows on them. The Devil's Peak, Gabe's star wine, was a Cabernet blend. Cabernet was the most popular grape in Napa, compromising a whopping 40 percent of the harvest. Complexity, Gabe had said, the way the varietals were blended together, was the key to this wine. But what the hell did *complexity* mean?

That was what was freezing her brain. She didn't understand the product. Didn't understand what she *should* be brainstorming about. What was The Devil's Peak's key differentiator?

Gabe found her there a half an hour later, still staring glumly at the beautiful purple grapes. Her fried brain took him in. Clinging T-shirt plastered across a muscular chest, dirt-stained jeans and a sweaty, man-working-hard look provided more inspiration than the last half hour had in total.

He gave her a once-over. "You look like hell."

"Thank you." She pushed a self-conscious hand through her hair. Too bad she didn't rock the disheveled look like he did.

"Elena said you were up before her."

At five, to be precise. One rose with the birds when severely agitated. "I have to nail this theme."

He held out a hand. "Looking for inspiration?"

She could have said he was doing just fine in that department, but that would have violated their nothing-personal rule. So she curled her fingers around his palm instead and let him drag her to her feet. Unfortunately, his perspiration-covered, hard-packed abs were now staring her in the face. Looking down or up wasn't an option, so she stepped back instead.

"I think I'm getting sunstroke along the way."

He frowned down at her. "Have you had enough water?"

She held up her bottle. Took a deep breath. "I don't understand what makes this wine special. I need to know what its key differentiator is to come up with a theme, and to me a Cabernet is a Cabernet."

He looked down his perfect, aquiline nose at her, as if to ask why she hadn't said something sooner. "You were with Pedro in the winery," she said defensively. "I didn't want to bug you."

His frown eased. "On a scale of one to ten, how much do you know about wine?"

She winced. "Three." That might actually be pushing it.

He sighed. "You need to understand the process from beginning to end if you're going to understand what makes the wine special." He glanced at his watch. "I can give you a tour before my call and shower later. I just need to grab some water from the house."

They started the tour in the rows of De Campo's prize Cabernet vines. Maybe it was the passionate way Gabe spoke about the growing process or maybe it was because one of the hottest men on the planet was delivering the information, but wine was getting more fascinating by the minute. This Gabe, the relaxed, visionary version of the man she'd never seen before, was darn near irresistible and it was doing strange things to her ability to focus.

"You still *pick* the grapes?" she asked incredulously. "I thought there were machines for that."

He nodded. "There are. For mass production that's fine, but the machines can't distinguish between the desirable and undesirable grapes, so for the premium wines such as the ones that come from these rows, we harvest them by hand."

"Got it." She nodded toward the vine he held. "So how can you tell when they're ready to pick? They look ready to me."

A smile curved his lips. "Try one."

She popped one in her mouth. "*Oh.* It's a bit tart."

"It needs another couple months for the tannins to mature."

She wrinkled her nose. "I still don't understand those."

He lifted a shoulder. "It's not the easiest concept to grasp. Think of it like the structure our skeleton gives us. Tannins give that to a wine. They're derived from the skins, stems and seeds of the grapes."

Finally, a concept that made sense to her.

She shoved another in her mouth, swiping a hand across

her chin as a rivulet of juice escaped. "Yep. Can definitely taste it's not quite ready. Must take skill to know when the exact right time to pick is."

"Years of practice." He reached up and swept his thumb over the corner of her mouth. "You missed some."

The roughness of his flesh, callused by years in the fields, made her lips tingle long after his thumb fell away. Her gaze rose to his. The sexual awareness she saw there made her heart stall in her chest.

A no-touching rule might have been prudent.

Skipping that kiss even better.

His mouth flattened into a straight line. He stepped back, out of her personal space, and she started to breathe again. "Shall we move on to the winery?"

She nodded. Sucked in an unsteady breath. What the hell was wrong with her?

Whacking herself over the head with a big mental stick, she followed him into the winery. Built around the foundation of the original historic building, it gleamed with modern efficiency. Huge stainless-steel tanks in which the grapes were fermented nearly reached the ceiling, lined up one after the other—the scale of it was breathtaking.

"Why do you move the wine to barrels?" she asked. "Why not leave it in the vats?"

"To complete the maturation process and add character to the wine." He led her into a room that was lined with beautiful, honey-colored barrels stacked three rows high. "These are Chardonnay. Some of these barrels have been used for multiple generations of wine. Each one adds a unique flavor depending on where it's from—French oak or American, say—and how old it is."

He took a glass from a shelf and used the tap on the top of the barrel to pour a small amount. "Young wine is usually rough, raw and green and needs to settle," he told her, handing her the glass. "This one's done in a French oak barrel to add that oaky flavor you often get in a Chardonnay."

She took a sip. It was too light and fruity for her taste. "I prefer reds."

"We're getting to those." He led her downstairs to the cool, underground cellars where the premium wines were stored. Dark-bricked, high-arched ceilings supported by columns of stone were complemented by the beautiful dark woods of the original cellar. Quiet and hushed in the middle of the day, the rich, atmospheric space seemed to whisper of years gone by and the historic vintages that had been nurtured there.

"It's unbelievable," she whispered as he walked her into a large room with stacks of oak barrels displayed on both sides and a huge rustic table running down the center of it. A crystal chandelier hung from the ceiling. This must be the formal dining room Lilly had spoken of, where the events were held.

Gabe threw her an amused look. "Why are you whispering?"

She shrugged, spooked by the feeling there were souls down here other than their own. "It just feels like there's so much history in the air."

The grooves around his mouth deepened. "If you mean ghosts—there are. *If* you choose to believe the folklore."

Her skin went cold. If there was anything she was afraid of, debilitatingly, horrifyingly afraid of, it was ghosts. "Do not play with me, Gabe. That's not funny."

He picked up two glasses and handed them to her, then took two more and motioned for her to follow him. "The story goes that the original owners, Janine and Ralf Courtland, held a huge celebration in honor of Dionysus one summer night. Half of Napa came."

She frowned, following him out of the room. "Who is Dionysus?"

"The Greek god of wine and revelry." He looked back at her. "Didn't they teach you that in school?"

"Greek mythology at Mission Hill High School?" she murmured dryly. "Not quite."

"I meant in university."

"I didn't go to university."

"College, then. Wherever.'

Heat swept across her skin, this particular conversation humiliating when it was happening with ever-so-brilliant Gabe. "I pretty much flunked out of high school. They only passed me to get rid of me. It was a relief for all of us, I think, to have me gone. And that's as far as I went."

His gaze sharpened on her face. "I don't get that. You have a razor-sharp brain. You must not have applied yourself."

She recoiled at the rebuke. "It's clear I'm not approaching the level of perfection you are, Gabe. But I did *apply* myself to work my way to the top of the PR industry."

"That's not what I meant." Ruddy color dusted his cheekbones. "I was merely trying to understand how such an intelligent woman would have almost flunked out of school."

"I was a bad girl," she said sharply. "Let's leave it at that, shall we?"

He gave her a long look. She stared him down until he started moving again, leading the way into the room across the hall. "Apparently the Courtlands' party was something else. Boatloads of Champagne, British royalty, a famous Vegas singer…" He leaned down and poured a glass from one of the barrels, this wine a light magenta. "Dionysus is known for instigating a frenzied madness among the celebrants. He's all about extreme self-gratification and things can and do go very wrong."

She and Dionysus would have been best buddies when

she was younger, she was pretty sure. "And…things went wrong, I presume?"

He leaned down to pour a second glass. "Apparently Janine was in love with the Courtlands' head winemaker, not her husband. During the celebration they lost their heads and were found down here in flagrante delicto by Ralf."

Her jaw dropped. "No way."

He nodded. "Ralf stabbed the winemaker and his wife to death with an ornate dagger."

Oh, my God. Her huge mistake with Jordan Lane fresh in her mind, she stood there gaping at him. "That's awful."

He shrugged. "Some would say Janine Courtland got her due."

A buzzing sound filled her ears. "Sometimes things aren't so black-and-white."

"And sometimes they are." His voice had taken on a dark intensity, his gaze on hers. "Wouldn't you put cheating in that category?"

Obviously yes. Watching her father destroy her mother with his affair with a local farmer's wife had been devastating for her entire family. But what had happened with Jordan had shaken her. He had lied to her and told her he was divorced. But should she have seen past the lies? Seen the signs?

She licked suddenly dry lips, realized he was waiting for her response. "I agree," she nodded. "There is no excuse for infidelity."

He led her to another room, where he poured two more glasses of a richer-looking red. Alex tried to shake off the darkness that had invaded her. "Any particular reason the reds are down here?"

He pointed to the gravel lining the earth floor. "They're the premium wines. Keeping them down here, where the humidity is high and the barrels rest on the earth, preserves as much of the wine as we can." He ran his hand over the smooth surface of the barrel. "If we get three hundred bottles from this one, we'll still lose a liter and a half along the way."

"That much?"

He nodded. "Winemakers like to call it the Angel's Share."

She smiled. "I love that."

"Very apt, no?"

They took the wine back to the dining room and sat at the ornately carved showpiece of a bar. "So where was she murdered?"

His mouth tipped up on one side. "In the last barrel room we visited."

"And *whose* ghost is supposed to be down here?"

"Janine's. Apparently she paces the cellar demanding to be brought back to life. She considers the whole situation unjust." He shrugged. "I say *apparently,* because I haven't heard or seen her since I've been here."

Thank God for that. Her breath left her in a whoosh. "Time to drink."

"Alexandra Anderson," Gabe drawled slowly, studying her face. "You aren't afraid of ghosts, are you?"

She waved her hand in the air. "Let's just say they're not one of my favorite things."

"Interesting." He lowered his tall, lean frame onto the stool beside her and slid a glass across the bar. "We'll start with the lightest ones. First the Zinfandel."

She took a sip. "Too fruity."

"Lots of people find that."

Next came the Pinot Noir. It was better. Smoky, maybe? She wrinkled her nose. "Too light."

His mouth quirked. "What are you, Goldilocks?"

She smiled. "Next?"

He pushed the second-deepest-toned red toward her. She took a sip. This time the smoother, richer tone of the wine curled itself around her tongue in a mellow greeting she was fully on board with. "Mmm. This one is good."

"I should hope so." Humor darkened his eyes. "It's our gold-medal award-winning Merlot."

She took another sip. It really *was* good. Rich, smooth and so easy to drink... A warm glow began to spread through her body as the combined effect of the different wines and a lack of sleep hit her. She pushed her empty glass toward him. "Next."

"Easy, tiger. You still have two more to go."

"Two?"

"Our Devil's Peak is behind the bar. Just getting it labeled." He flashed her one of those schoolteacher looks of his. "What did you notice about the last wine?"

She frowned. "I dunno. It's heavier but still soft."

"Exactly. Merlots are softer and fruitier than a Cab, yet display many of the same aromas and flavors—black cherry, currant, cedar and green olive. You can even have mint, tobacco and tea-leaf tones in them."

She snorted. "Green olives? You don't actually believe all that mumbo jumbo, do you? I mean, have you *ever* tasted green olive in a wine?"

"Sì." He gave her a condescending look. "I have."

She surveyed the twist of his lips with an inner growl. He was so smug. So confident. She wondered what it would take to knock him off his peg. To kiss him again, except this time ruffle that deep, dark packaging and see what happened.

Which couldn't happen, given their agreement. But fun to think about nonetheless...

"And this one?" She summoned her best dutiful-school-girl look. "Must be a Cab."

He nodded. "From 2006. Our best year. Try it."

She tasted it. It was rich and dark and so good she wanted to eat it up. *"That* is a wine."

"The king of all reds, *infatti*. Cabs are the world's most sought-after grape—they take five to ten years to achieve an optimal flavor, and they're worth every minute of it." He gestured toward her glass. "You should taste plum, cherry, blackberry and a hint of tobacco in that one."

She frowned. "I'll take your word for it."

"Lex," he said darkly. "Focus. You aren't going to get a feel for this unless you try."

She took another sip, rolled it around her mouth and swallowed. "Maybe the spice?"

"Not *spice,* tobacco."

"I can't taste it."

His lips moved but no sound came out. He looked as though he was counting to five. *Was he counting to five?*

"Gabe…"

He shook his head and waved a hand at her, as if he'd given up. She pouted. *Really?* Could it be this hard?

He walked around the bar and pulled out a bottle without a label. "Now for The Devil's Peak."

She perked up. *This* was what it was all about.

He poured them some. She pulled her glass toward her lips. "Lex—" He muttered a curse and came around the bar. "You don't drink wine like you're slinging beer. You savor it."

"That's pretentious garbage."

He grabbed her wrist and pulled the glass away from her mouth. "It's not pretentious garbage, it's how to drink wine. First," he instructed, guiding her wrist in a smooth, circular movement, "you swirl it in the glass to smell the bouquet. It's important to get that first scent of the flavor to taste it correctly." He pushed the glass toward her nose. "Now you inhale." She did and lo and behold, an intense shot of berry filled her lungs.

"Cherry," she crowed triumphantly.

"Hallelujah." He held his hands up. "So what's the other grape it's blended with?"

She bit her lip. Thought hard. "Merlot?"

His teeth flashed white against his swarthy skin. *"Esattamente."*

She tried to ignore how everything he said in Italian sounded sexy. How he was standing so close to her she could smell that earthy, spicy aftershave of his, bringing back heady memories of *the kiss*. Hell. She forced herself to focus on the issue at hand. The wine was rich like the previous Cab, smooth like the prize-winning Merlot, but there was also something else…something special she couldn't put her finger on. "Lots of wines blend Merlots and Cabs, though, right? What makes *this one* so special?"

He lifted his shoulders. "Chemistry. We add the mystery ingredients, play with the yeasts and use our proprietary processes to get that perfect blend."

So how did that play into her theme? She racked her brain. Tossed around a couple of ideas. Then a lightbulb went off in her head. Maybe that *was* her theme…

Chemistry. There were a million innovative ways she could make it come to life at the party. It was *perfect*.

"You," she pronounced, poking her finger into his chest, "are brilliant."

"I'm glad you've seen the light," he responded dryly. "Care to share?"

"Not yet." She wasn't stupid. She needed to have this idea fully baked before she put it in front of Mr. Flawless here. "On Monday when I can show you the full concept."

"Prudent of you."

She ignored the tilt of his mouth. She *could* be prudent when she needed to. She did have *some* restraint. Another sip of the glorious wine kept the ideas flowing. She rolled it around her mouth. Yes, she could definitely get inspired about *this*.

"We haven't talked about who's going to speak to the media about all this brilliance." She lifted a brow. "You? Antonio?"

"Me. Riccardo doesn't want to leave Lilly alone and Antonio isn't coming."

She frowned. "Why? The press eat Antonio up. They love his big personality, his theatrics. He can do the big-picture historic stuff."

His face tightened. "I'll do it. Antonio isn't available."

"What do you mean *isn't available?* How can he not be available for this?"

He picked up the bottle and jammed it on the shelf behind the bar. "Antonio doesn't believe in this venture. He doesn't believe a decent bottle of wine can be made outside of Italy and if he were to come, he'd say something damaging that would hurt us. I don't *want* him here."

"We can message him so he doesn't go off track. Make sure he knows what he can and cannot say. I really think—"

"No." The force behind the word stopped her in her tracks. His face was a thundercloud of black emotion. "Find another way to get press coverage, Alex."

And that was that. He excused himself to take his call. Alex sat there finishing her wine, wondering what kind of a father showed such a lack of support for his son in the most important venture of his life. She knew from Lilly that the De Campo men were not close to their father, but she'd never had any idea the rift between Gabe and Antonio ran this deep.

Her insides twisted with a hurt so old it had been healed fifty times over. She knew all about rifts. How you said you didn't care, but they ate away at you until you couldn't let another person in for fear you'd drive them away, too. *Her* father had written her off as unrecoverable at such an early age, nothing she'd done since had compensated. None of the career ladders she'd climbed, none of the praise lauded on her by some of the world's leading companies had helped. She could be the first woman president of the United States and he'd still have the same low opinion of her.

She pushed the glass away and took in the dark, historic cellar around her. Gabe De Campo had demons, too. Go figure.

She was pretty sure she'd just scratched the surface at that.

CHAPTER FOUR

MONDAY MORNING AND Alex was once again cooling her heels in the reception area of De Campo's San Francisco office. This time Gabe was on a call. She tapped her foot on the floor, the small amount of patience she did have fading fast in light of the amount of work she had in front of her if Gabe deigned to give the go-ahead on this concept.

Her tapping foot drew Danielle's eye. "He shouldn't be much longer," the PA murmured sympathetically. "I saw the light go off on the line a few minutes ago. I'm sure he'll be right out."

Alex checked her watch and glared at the door. He was forty minutes late now.

"Does he always have so little respect for other people's time? I'm sure that thinking you own the world inevitably leads to thinking your time is more valuable than everyone else's, but I would—" She broke off midsentence as Danielle's gaze slid to the right and her eyes widened. *Oh, no.* She turned around and found Gabe leaning against the doorframe, his tall body arranged in a deceptively relaxed pose.

"Per favore," he murmured. "Go on. I was getting some keen insight into what you really think of me."

She lowered her gaze, the sickening feeling she might have just blown it flooding through her. "I was just venting. You're supposed to be in your office, not sneaking around the back way."

"I've been on calls since seven. Nature called."

She stood up, refusing to cower in the wake of the arrogant tilt of that nose. "If we're going to make this into a contest, I've been up since five."

His eyes glittered. "I wasn't, but how very five-year-old of you."

Danielle was watching them as though they were a prime-time reality show. Gabe inclined his head toward his office. "Shall we do this?"

Alex picked up her storyboards and followed him in, laying them out on the oval conference table near the window. The designer had done an inspired job on the visual representations of the concept and event. "On our tour," she began, "you said the complexity and individuality of a wine depends on the chemistry—how *you* as the winemaker make the choices. Whether to use man-made or naturally occurring yeasts, how long the different varietals should be aged, the proportion of one versus the other."

He nodded.

"I started playing around with the concept of chemistry. How that would work as an event theme. And came up with these concepts." She flipped to the first storyboard. "The initial touch point is the invite. Guests are invited to fall in love with their 'match' at De Campo's The Devil's Peak launch." She flipped to the next board. "When they arrive, they're handed a computer generated 'chemistry' match, someone attending the event who is like-minded. It can be either a networking match or a romantic one. Throughout the evening, they're tasked with finding their match and exploring it."

He arched a brow. "What if they're the jaded, unimaginative type who couldn't be bothered?"

She flipped to the next board, which had a photo of the

De Campo Tuscan vineyard on it. "We incent them. We offer them something fabulous, like a trip to the motherland. But only if the matches sign in during the evening and prove they've met."

He looked skeptical. "Go on."

She flipped to the next board. "Everything that happens throughout the evening is about chemistry. The decor, the quiz at the bar to match guests with their perfect De Campo wine, the gift bags tailored to each individual's chemistry and finally," she said, smiling, "the fireworks at the end of the night. They represent the chemistry of The Devil's Peak. We end with the tasting of the wine and the fireworks for a big last impression."

He rubbed his hand over his jaw. "I like it. I'm not sure about the chemistry matches, though. Will this type of a crowd do it? Will the New York crowd do it?"

She nodded. "I've found from experience if you incent people well enough, they'll do anything. It doesn't have to be a trip to Tuscany. We can make it a selection of chemistry experiences to pick from…"

His mouth twisted. "And how do we not make the matches look like quackery?"

She'd wondered the same thing. It had to be real science. "There's a firm here in San Francisco that specializes in just this. It's run by scientists with human-behavior backgrounds. We supply details on the subjects, they input them into the computer and presto, they spit us out real, scientific matches."

He gave a rueful smile. "What about liability issues with the romantic matches?"

She gave him a long look. "This isn't an escort service. It's a lighthearted meet and greet with a like-minded person."

"Run it by our lawyers," he instructed. "We have five

hundred people attending this event. You're going to have time to pull information on all of them?"

She nodded, anticipation flaring inside of her as he seemed to increasingly buy into the concept. "The joys of the internet. People say far too many personal things on social media."

"We won't be seen as stalkers of people's personal information?"

"Most people put it out there to be seen."

He gave the storyboards a long look. Her heart rose to her mouth as she watched him debate. *Please, God. It's a great concept. Go for it.*

Finally, he nodded. "*Bene.* Make it happen."

Her heart jumped *into* her mouth. "Make the whole event happen? As in, you're giving the contract to me?"

He smiled, the effect of it so dazzling when he put the effort into it, it was impossible to resist. "Katya was right. You're brilliant."

She could have hugged him except there was that no-touching rule she'd imposed on herself. "You won't regret this," she declared. "This is going to be the event of the year."

"I might actually believe you *are* Superwoman if you pull it off," he murmured.

"My cape is in my room," she confided cheekily. "I need your approval on the invite before I go."

They went through it. For about five minutes of their relationship they had harmony. Might have been six. Then he started picking the invitation apart piece by piece. Twenty changes in all. On one measly invitation. A picture of how this was going to be formed in her head. It was worse than she'd even imagined. She was going to have to figure out a way to convince him to back off—fast. Because if she was going to pull these events off, she needed to fly without someone looking over her shoulder every five minutes.

She took a big breath of the salty, clean San Francisco air as she walked out of the building to her car, her irritation fading as it sank in that she'd done it. Gabe had given her the contract. *She was still in business.*

Just as quickly as her euphoria arrived came the stomach-clenching reality of what she now had to do. She had three weeks to execute one of the most complex events she'd ever created.

A feat that might or might not be possible.

CHAPTER FIVE

THE NEXT FEW days passed in a blur of logistical activity. Alex met with the graphic designer, finalized the invitations and took a last look at the guest list. It was missing a few VIPs the other agency had overlooked, as well as included a few undesirables she didn't think should make the final five hundred. Gabe had seen the list twice, according to Danielle, so she made the changes, marked it as final and sent it off to the printer.

The most pressing job done, she called her two Manhattan-based staff and told them to get on a plane. Convinced her transplanted New Yorker friend Susan James, one of the most talented designers she'd ever worked with, to do the event decor with her. Then she secured the catering company Susan preferred and signed a contract with the matching firm.

And breathed.

The pure scope of the event left her and her team exhausted and stumbling into bed in the wee hours every night. She wouldn't call their execution flawless, exactly—there were just too many moving parts and not enough time to get them done. Flying by the seat of their pants was a better description. Just the way she liked it. Except her clients usually weren't overbearing control freaks—like Gabe—who had to have their hands in everything. *Everything. Earn my trust,* he'd said. She was trying very, very hard to do that. But Gabe's insane schedule meant they had to take everything to him in between meetings and after he'd come up from the winery at night, which meant late, late nights for everyone. Not to mention his habit of disappearing when he said he was going to be somewhere. *The power's out at the winery,* Danielle had said one day, "supply problems" another.

He was making them crazy. Putting them behind by adding a whole other layer of complexity. So Alex put Operation Control Freak into effect. She deluged Gabe with paper, every single piece of minutia approval she could find: the color of the napkins on the bar, the type of chocolate in the gift bags, the musical selections for the band. At some point, she figured, he'd give in.

He didn't. He powered through it all in his own sweet time with a grim determination that made her wonder if *he* was the one who was superhuman. So she gave up on that plan and took matters into her own hands. *Only give Gabe crucial things he must see,* she told her staff. *Give me the rest.*

He was still killing them.

On Tuesday he made an imperious demand for Ligurian anchovies to be added to the appetizer list. "Ligurian, as in the coast of Italy?" she'd asked, sure he must be joking. "Is there any other?" he'd muttered back and gotten into his car. She'd bitten her lip and called the caterer. By Thursday, he still hadn't approved the cost to fly them in *and* the chef was having a hissy fit about the fact he still hadn't okayed the final menu. Her fireworks supplier was threatening to double the price if they didn't settle on a run schedule by the end of the week and her Champagne fountain, the centerpiece of her cocktail area, was apparently leaking, without a replacement structure in sight.

Total chaos.

At two a.m. on Friday, she declared herself officially

brain-dead and fell into the big, soft king-size bed in the suite at the far end of the hall from Gabe's. A wise placement, she'd decided. But her mind kept spitting out things she'd forgotten to do, so she got out of bed, grabbed her notebook and headed to the kitchen for some hot milk, which was usually foolproof in putting her to sleep.

Hot milk in hand, dosed with a liberal amount of cocoa and sugar, she turned away from the stove and walked straight into a wall. Or Gabe, to be precise. Hot cocoa went flying. Alex squealed. Gabe cursed. She jumped back, stared at his soaked T-shirt and gave a low moan.

"Please tell me I didn't burn you." He pulled the soaked material away from his skin, hissed in a breath as he did so and lifted it. Red, blotchy skin stared back at her, but nothing worse. "Oh, God," she choked, shoving her mug onto the counter. "I am *so* sorry. I thought you were in bed."

He grimaced. "Still working."

Of course he was. He was a *machine*.

His gaze slid down over her. "You might have ruined that."

She remembered what she was wearing. Short. Silk. Heavy on the cleavage.

Damn.

She crossed her arms over her chest. A little too late, as his focus had already moved from the curve of her breasts down over her hips and bare legs. His gaze slid leisurely back up to hers, taking in every last inch. Heat, molten heat, stole the breath from her lungs. He would be smooth. He would be generous. And he would take his time.

She sank her teeth into her bottom lip. Suddenly no-touching, no-attraction clauses seemed like an abstract concept that did not pertain to this particular situation. Not when his eyes were flickering with a warning that his iron control was wavering, and a part of her wished desperately it would.

There was a period of one, maybe two seconds where she wasn't sure where this was going to go. The air was so charged she found it too thick to breathe. She dragged in a breath because breathing *was* necessary. Then his face hardened and a chill fell over those amazing green eyes.

"I need to get back to work. Any milk left?"

"In the pan. Gabe—I need those approvals. The catering stuff is urgent."

He walked to the cupboard and pulled a mug out. "I'll give you feedback on all of it tomorrow morning."

"It's got to be first thing."

"I'll do it before my meeting in town." He turned around. "And Lex? I think we need a dress code."

A wave of heat engulfed her. She picked up her half-full mug—no way was she going near him to get more—and lifted her chin. "I'll remember that the next time you have me working until two a.m."

She flounced up the stairs and went back to bed. Her body sang with a dose of raging hormones she had no idea what to do with. *Power through the list,* she told herself, picking up her pad of paper. But the look on Gabe's face kept replaying itself over and over in her head. *That* had been lust.

"He's done it again."

Emily, Alex's star junior exec with exactly three years' experience under her belt but about ten times that in wisdom, planted herself in front of where Alex was measuring the dance floor the next morning, an exasperated look on her face. "He told me ten a.m. to meet about the catering and Elena just informed me he's left for the city."

Alex straightened and pushed the hair that had escaped her ponytail out of her face. Gabe had also promised her feedback on three other crucial things. She was going to kill him. They could not afford to get any further behind.

"Leave it to me," she said grimly. "He has a meeting here this afternoon. I'll stake him out and get the sign off on all of it."

"Great." Emily sighed as only a twenty-three-year-old could and stretched. "If he wasn't so good-looking I might hate him."

"I'm past that," Alex muttered. She was so tired she wanted someone to shoot her right now and put her out of her misery. "Call the caterer and tell her we'll let her know on all of it today, including the anchovies."

She wrote down her measurements, nabbed a coffee from the kitchen and sat down before she fell down. She needed a dose of her sister's calming Zen powers. Lilly had the ability to pull her down a notch when she felt as if it was all spinning out of control.

Lilly answered on the third ring. "I was wondering if you were still alive…"

"You could always ask my boss," Alex suggested dryly. "He's the one trying to kill me."

"How's that working out?" Amusement laced her sister's tone.

Alex chewed on the end of her pencil and stared up at the workers adjusting the netting in the vineyard. "You know how I feel about him. It's been interesting."

"No, I don't, actually." There was a pause. "Do you?"

"Lil."

Her sister sighed. "One of these days you're going to have to figure it out, you know."

No, Alex disagreed silently, she didn't. Particularly when it was now a ground rule not to.

"I worry about you, Lex," her sister continued. "I'm worried you're going to spend the next ten years of your life pursuing this giant ambition of yours and then realize that it's about so much more than that."

Here we go again. "I'm only twenty-eight. I'm *supposed* to be climbing the corporate ladder."

"What about babies?"

"I don't want babies."

"You don't *know* if you want babies. There is a whole legion of women out there putting off pregnancy for their careers. Then they wake up one morning and realize *it's too late.*"

Alex shut her eyes and prayed for patience. "I *know* I don't want babies. In fact, maybe I should let them harvest my eggs *now* so one of those poor women has a fighting chance."

Her sister gasped. "You *wouldn't.*"

"Did we not share the same childhood?"

"Yes, but—"

"Lil. I understand you are sickeningly happy with your machismo husband and your gorgeous little boy, soon to be brother of a gorgeous little girl, I'm sure. But leave me out of the baby discussions."

Lilly sighed. "Fine."

Alex looked up to see the sound technicians she'd hired pulling into the parking lot. "If you don't hear from me in a while it's because I am either snowed under *or* I've actually gone ahead and committed murder on your brother-in-law. How are you feeling, by the way? Following doctor's orders?"

"Riccardo will barely let me move without commenting. I might kill *him* before this is all over."

Lilly had suffered from preeclampsia with her first pregnancy and they'd all walked on needles throughout most of it. For once, Alex didn't blame her controlling husband for being that way. "This may be the only time I ever tell you this, but listen to your husband. He's right." She stood up and grabbed her clipboard. "I gotta go. Give said husband a sock in the head for me."

* * *

Gabe stared at the guest list and decided he must be delusional at this point, because he had not put *that* name on *this* list.

He hit the intercom button. "Danielle," he growled. "You sent me the wrong list."

"Let me check." She walked into his office a minute later. "Nope, that's the final one."

"It can't be," Gabe replied as patiently as he could manage. "Darya Theriault is on it."

His PA whitened. "It's the master list. Alex had a last look at it."

His fingers curled around the paper. "She *changed* it and didn't get my final approval?"

"She said you'd seen it twice."

White-hot anger sliced through him. "Get her on the phone, *now.*"

"Frank Thomas is here." Danielle gave him an uncertain look. "Do you want me to make him wait?"

The desire to put his hands around Alex's beautiful neck and strangle her almost made him nod, but finding out what Jordan Lane was up to was more important than bloody murder. "Give me two minutes, then send him in."

She nodded and left.

Alex had put his ex on the guest list. His ambitious lawyer ex who'd left him for a senior partner with a note that had said, "I don't love him like I love you but it's a smart move and I'm marrying him."

Just like that. Propped up beside his coffee mug when he'd walked in the door from a trip to New York.

Worse than that, this RSVP list said Darya was attending. With her husband.

It was the last straw. He slammed the list down on his desk. He'd managed to overlook Alex and her team's blatant misuse of his time. The decisions she was making she thought he wasn't noticing. But *this*. This was too much. *Troppo*.

As was the creation she'd sashayed into the kitchen wearing last night that had screamed *take me*. *Merda*. There was only so much a man could take. He'd dealt with the insubordination; he'd even managed to handle the smart mouth. But he could not get his mind off of how good she'd felt under his hands that night at the hotel— sleek, smooth and undoubtedly worth every last husky sigh. Or the way that negligee had put her perfect body on display, hugging the lush curves of her breasts and hips. His body tightened under his fitted suit trousers. They were the type of curves that made a man want to put his hands all over her—in no particular order.

Dannazione. He jammed his hand against the desk and ruthlessly pushed the image away. It had taken him ten pages of sales figures to wipe it from his head last night, but apparently it was of the recurring variety. Not a positive thing, when she was the employee he intended to tear a strip off of as soon as he could get his hands on her.

He stood to greet Frank. This afternoon he was getting rid of *that* particular problem. One way or another.

Frank Thomas, a fifty-two-year-old cop–turned–private investigator, gave Gabe's hand a hearty shake and made himself at home on the leather sofa. Gabe followed and stood opposite him, too restless to sit down.

"The rumors are true," Thomas announced. "Jordan Lane is developing a Devil's Peak look-alike."

His heart dropped. "How do you know?"

"A source in the restaurant industry. He's been chatting it up, apparently."

"How close is it?"

The investigator shook his head. "Talking's all he's doing. But I hear close."

Gabe shoved his hands in his pockets and paced to the

window. "It doesn't fit with his current strategy. I don't get it."

"I think that's the point. It isn't about strategy. He's after *you*."

A sense of foreboding settled over him, an uneasy feeling pulling deep down in his gut. The Devil's Peak wasn't your run-of-the-mill, ordinary blend. A great deal of proprietary processes and ingredients had gone into it that hadn't been done in a Californian wine before.

He looked at Thomas. "He's got someone on the inside."

"My thoughts exactly." The wily investigator cocked a brow at him. "Any idea who it could be?"

No. He thought about Pedro, his head winemaker, whom he'd brought with him from the Tuscan De Campo vineyard after the older man's wife had died. The men and women he'd handpicked to work alongside Pedro. "No—I trust them all implicitly."

Thomas pursed his lips. "Someone in the office? Suppliers, distributors, customers?"

Gabe shook his head. "They wouldn't have the knowledge. You can't copy the structure, the composition of a wine without knowing what you're doing."

"Then you've got to go through your people again. Take a closer look. See if you've missed something."

He nodded. The uneasy feeling in his gut tightened. He was close, so close to achieving what he'd set out to do eight years ago—to put De Campo in the upper echelon of Californian winemakers. So close he could almost taste it. He would not, *could not* allow a disloyal team member to destroy his dream. There was another wine, a far more important wine, in the works, too. The wine only he and Pedro knew about.

He had to find the bad apple before whoever it was found out about that wine as well. The game changer. *If* it wasn't too late.

"Give me an hour and I'll get a list to you," he said to Thomas. "We've done background checks on everyone, but dig deeper. See what you can find. Meanwhile, I'll go through them all with Pedro. See if anyone sticks out."

Thomas nodded. "If there's something there I'll find it."

Gabe got back to the vineyard at two and went directly into another meeting. Alex waited until she saw one of the men leave at three-fifteen, tucked the folder with the approvals she needed under her arm and marched into the house, determination fueling her every step. Down the gleaming hallway to Gabe's office she went, a closed door greeting her. She knocked and reached for the handle. Elena held up a hand. "I wouldn't—"

"Bother him," Alex finished. "I know." She turned the handle and swung the door open, her legs planted wide in a fighting stance. "This time your guard dogs aren't going to work. I need y—"

Two men were seated near the window, staring at her. She did a double take. *Oh.* Only one had left.

"Whoops," she muttered. "I thought you were done."

The room was silent. Gabe said nothing, his gaze resting on her with a stillness that drew her attention to the furious gleam in those spectacular green eyes. "We're almost done," he said in a deadly quiet voice. "Would you wait for us in the living room?"

She backed out, thinking she really might have done it this time, but past caring because he was impossible and she had to get her job done. Closing the door, she retreated to the kitchen instead, a tiny rebellious part of her refusing to let him order her around.

"Lemonade," she murmured in response to Elena's curious look.

"You're in trouble?"

"I would say so." She retrieved the carton from the fridge and sloshed some into a glass. "Got any advice?"

"Normally I would say appeal to his reasonable side. But these days?" Elena shrugged. "Keep your head down."

Which was obviously *not* what Alex did when Gabe found her there ten minutes later, chatting with his housekeeper. "You," he snarled. "In my office."

She followed him, wincing as he slammed the door behind her.

"What the *hell* do you think you're doing walking into the middle of my meeting?"

"I didn't know it was still going on," she said calmly. "I'm sorry."

"I told you I'd come get you."

She set the lemonade down on his desk. "You keep disappearing, Gabe. We are behind. *Significantly* behind. Emily needed an approval on the catering yesterday, I need an approval on this interview list *now* or we aren't going to have any one-on-one media interviews at the event."

"To hell with the media," he roared, making her take a step backward. "They can wait."

Her stomach clenched at the fury streaking across his face. "There's no need to shout," she murmured. "And they can't wait, Gabe. You need them if you want this launch to be a success."

"What do you think, Alex? That I'm working twenty-hour days because I don't?" He took a step closer to her, then another, until two hundred pounds of pure male aggression was staring her in the face. Her heart started to pound furiously in her chest. She tumbled back in time to another room, to another big male bearing down on her, laying his hands on her, and her breath came quick and hard. *This is Gabe,* she told herself, sucking in a breath, *not him.*

Breathe.

Gabe scowled. "I want you to stop disobeying my orders and start doing what I say, because you are treading very, very close to the line."

That snapped her out of it. "What line?" she demanded.

"The creative differences line. The one where I fire you."

"Fire me?" She let out a bark of laughter, releasing the tension inside of her. "I only *wish* you would fire me, you're such a pain in the ass."

His hands clenched at his sides. "I am *not* having a good day, Alex. Rein it in."

"No." She stuck her chin out. "You are killing us, Gabe. You need to start letting us make decisions."

"Like adding people to the guest list I haven't approved?"

She frowned. "Your PR agency missed some key influencers."

"You *added* my *ex-girlfriend* and her husband."

"Oh." Her fingers flew to her mouth. "Who is that?"

"Darya Theriault."

She thought hard. "Right. Yes, well, she and Peter are a Bay Area power couple. Don't you think you can swallow your pride for one night and do what's right for the event?"

"No, I cannot," he yelled at her. "She is not coming to this event."

She squeezed her eyes shut. This was getting just a *little* out of control. "Okay, maybe I should have checked with you on that. I *should* have checked with you on that. But it isn't my fault you fired the last agency and left us with zero time. It isn't my fault you can't prioritize what's important and it isn't my fault you are a serial perfectionist."

He gave her a dangerous look. "A serial perfectionist?"

She opened her eyes, looked up into his furious face. "You have me chasing down Ligurian anchovies. How stupid is that? *Ligurian anchovies, Gabe.*"

"It is a treasured cultural food for Italians," he bit out.

She waved a hand at him. "It's ridiculous. *Ridiculous*. However, I would be inclined to pander to your little whims if you would just give me my *goddamned* approvals before we all go down in a big, fiery flash."

"You are driving me crazy," he rasped, taking another step forward until she was backed up against the desk. "You have been deliberately antagonizing me. You don't like someone to control you, so you decided to bury me in paper. I ask you to do something, you do the opposite. And when all of these things don't work, you go your own renegade way and do exactly what you like."

"I do *not* do the opposite of what you say."

His gaze flashed. "I asked you to wait in the living room and found you in the kitchen."

She stared at him. "Do you *know* how ridiculous you sound? It's control freak gone crazy." She shook her head. "Is this how you are in bed, Gabe, because I'm gobsmacked that so many women in this day and age would go for it."

"You'd be surprised," he grated. "Maybe that's why you were strutting around in that outfit last night? Because you still can't admit you'd like to try it on for size?"

She winced at the innuendo. At the hard heat of his body that had her trapped against the desk. "*This* is not professional."

"This hasn't been professional since day one."

"Still—" Her pulse went into overdrive as he reached up and slid his hand into her hair. "Gabe—"

"Shut the hell up, Alex."

He brought his mouth down on hers in a hard, punishing kiss that held more than its fair share of anger. She should have stopped it, should have immediately pushed him away, but unfortunately intense sexual frustration made her highly susceptible to the command behind it. To the insistence she open her mouth and let him in. She did and he made a sound in the back of his throat and explored her with an erotic thoroughness that made her hot all over. Desperate for more.

The desk was hard against her back. She moved against him and he picked her up and set her on it. Braced his hands on either side of her and took her mouth in another heated exploration that sent her pulse soaring.

"Gabe," she murmured, hoping to inject some sanity into the situation. He dragged his mouth down the line of her neck to the raging pulse at the base of it. "I think we should—"

His hands moved to the top button of her shirt. The second. His mouth at her most sensitive place between shoulder and neck, teeth scraping across her skin, made her shiver with want. Somehow she couldn't make herself move or get the rest of the words out. He pushed her shirt aside, his gaze hot on her. "*Dio.* You are so beautiful."

Alex forgot her name then, squeezing her eyes shut as he ran his thumbs over the hard tips of her breasts. Shaped the weight of them in his hands. It felt good, so exquisitely good to finally have them on her that she let out a low moan.

He moved his mouth back up to her lips, set them ablaze with another scorching kiss and slid his hands around to the back clasp of her bra.

She stiffened. *He was her client. She could not have sex with him on his desk.*

"Gabe—" She pushed a hand against his chest. His fingers stilled on the clasp. "We—we can't do this."

He pulled back and looked at her, the hazy desire in his eyes sending another wave of heat through her. Strength, she needed strength…

"We— I—" she stumbled, "whatever is happening here, we need to figure it out and not…do this."

His mouth tightened. His hands fell away from her. "Fix your shirt."

She moved trembling hands to the buttons. "Gabe—"

"Fix your shirt."

She did the buttons up with unsteady fingers that didn't seem to want to work. Tucked her shirt back into her skirt. Gabe shoved his hands in his pockets and walked to the window. "You're right," he muttered harshly. "That shouldn't have happened."

Only for a million different reasons. She offered up the most convenient excuse. "We're both stressed."

"Yes," he agreed, sarcasm lacing his tone. "Let's go with that."

She pushed off the desk. He turned around, his face grim and forbidding.

"I'll have the catering menu to you within the hour. What else do you have?"

"It's all in here." She pushed the folder across the desk. "The menu and the interview schedule are the priorities."

"Bene."

"Gabe—"

"Leave it alone, Alex. That was an act of insanity on both our parts. Enough said."

She swallowed hard, tried not to be intimidated by the coldness coming off him like an arctic current. "I know how much this means to you. Let me do my job and I will not let you fail."

He looked at her for a long moment, then his dark lashes came down to veil his gaze. "No more executive decisions, Alex. Or two days, *two hours* before the event, I will fire you. I promise you that."

She nodded. And got the hell out of there before she did something else that was incredibly stupid.

CHAPTER SIX

GABE SPENT THE next week reviewing every person who'd ever been involved in the development of The Devil's Peak with Pedro, from those who'd supervised the pruning of the vines to get the tannins just right, to those in the lab who were intimately familiar with the finished product, hoping to find something, *anything* that would point to a leak.

They racked their brains but could find no one with the right combination of access, motivation or strange behavior of late to warrant looking into. Thomas' background checks didn't turn up anything. It was distressing, to be sure, that a Devil's Peak imitator supposedly existed, but Gabe wasn't prepared to go on a witch hunt and alienate his employees on the basis of rumor. He didn't even know how close the wine was to his. Which meant he hadn't told Riccardo or Antonio about it and didn't plan to until he had more to work with.

He sat back in his chair and looked over at Pedro, the sixty-two-year-old, third-generation winemaker who'd taught him everything he knew about blending. "We need to get our hands on Lane's wine. You have any friends in the valley who can help?"

Pedro shrugged. "No one wants to cross him. But I can try."

"Grazie." Jordan Lane was the undisputed king of wine

in California. No one wanted to touch him, because they'd be blackballed within a minute of doing so.

Pedro sharpened his gaze on him. "Have you thought about moving our special project up? Going with that instead for the fall campaign?"

"It's not ready."

Pedro shook his head. "*You're* not ready. The wine is."

"You know the plan," Gabe reminded him, a tad defensively.

"*Sì.* You are focusing on The Devil's Peak because you know Antonio will support a traditional blend more than the Malbec."

"It's not about what Antonio wants. It's about doing the right thing for the market. Launch a superior wine that gets us noticed to pave the way, then hit them with the game changer."

"You may not have a choice."

No, he conceded. He might not. But what he needed to focus on now was what he *could* control, which was getting The Devil's Peak out the door. And these bloody launch events, which were eating him alive.

He stayed and went through some approvals for Alex, but every time he looked at the gleaming desk in front of him, a vivid picture filled his head of what had almost happened between them. He couldn't say he would have stopped. *Infatti,* he was pretty sure he wouldn't have. The desire to assuage the frustration she roused in him as easily as taking her next breath had been too strong.

Was still too strong for reason. *Cristo.* He tossed the pen down and raked his hands through his hair. She was making him lose it. Lose the control he was legendary for.

She had stopped him from breaking his own rule.

One complete loss of control with a woman was enough for a lifetime.

Darya had stolen his breath the night he'd met her at a

cocktail party in Pacific Heights. Younger and less jaded then, he'd fallen for her long blond hair, sparkling blue eyes and aggressive desire for him. Bright, on the fast track at the partnered law firm she worked for, she'd whispered something overtly sexual in his ear in the middle of a crowded party and they'd ended up in bed together that night and every other night for the next eight months. She'd pretty much moved into his San Francisco condo and the rumor had flown: Gabe De Campo might finally have been caught. He, in his misplaced belief that he could have a relationship that rose above his parents' business partnership, had thrown himself into it like a man without a brain.

Big mistake. Maybe he should have seen it coming. Maybe he should have seen how Darya's ambition was a match for his, how she never would have been happy running the vineyard with him instead of climbing the corporate ladder. Maybe he should have recognized the distance growing between them as they pursued their separate agendas. But he hadn't. He'd been too blind with the bright light Darya had been, until the Sunday when he'd returned home from New York to find that note. The note that had taken his uncertain belief in relationships and crushed it as easily as his machines annihilated a ton of grapes.

His mouth tightened. He hadn't tried to call her. Hadn't tried to get her back. Because from that moment on, before he'd even heard the senior partner had left his wife and married Darya, Gabe had ceased believing in love. His parents' marriage might rival the arctic in its coldness, but it worked. And that's what he would have. It was simpler that way.

Which made him wonder exactly where his fascination with Alex lay. He watched her out on the lawn, directing traffic like a law enforcement official. She drove him *pazzo,* no doubt about it. But on another level, he had to admit she intrigued him. Not just the fact she'd been bright enough to make it to the top of her profession without postsecondary education. *That* didn't surprise him in the least. It had been the look on her face when she'd admitted that chink in her armor to him. Those words from that day in the cellar kept coming back. *I was a bad girl,* she'd said, as if she'd expected that to shut him down. Instead he wanted to know more. Much more.

He rubbed his fingers over the stubble covering his chin. That was a problem. *She* was a far bigger problem than he'd pegged that night at the hotel. The way he'd wanted her from the beginning had multiplied into an inconvenient obsession to have her. He needed to fix this before he crossed the line.

Taking someone *else* to bed was a possibility. Maybe Riccardo was right. Maybe that was *exactly* what he needed.

He picked up his smartphone, pulled up the contact details of the opera singer who'd been all over him at a party a few weeks ago and dialed the number. Five minutes later he had a breathy acceptance of a dinner date.

If only solving all his problems was that easy...

Things had gotten better AE—after the explosion, as Alex liked to call it. Whether Gabe had decided to trust her or had finally acknowledged he didn't have time to micromanage, he was letting her run with the event. They were finally knocking things off at the speed they needed to.

If she could just forget how blindingly hot that moment in his office had been. But even her best efforts at denial couldn't completely wipe it out of her head. She had had a taste of what Gabe would be like now. And it was impossible to forget.

In the end, she reverted back to what she knew was true. Men were fickle. Gabe might have an "inconvenient" attraction to her—but it didn't go beyond craving her female assets. Not worth a career-limiting move guaranteed to trash her future. She knew, because she'd suffered through an almost fatal one.

Wasn't about to go there again.

"That's it." Susan shoved the tape measure into her hand and got to her feet. "I have all the stuff I need. Let's get out of here and blow off some steam."

Alex wrapped her hand around the tiny silver square, her lips twisting in a rueful smile. "It's Thursday night in Napa. Where do people go to do that?"

"There's a little restaurant in St. Helena where everyone goes on Thursdays. It's *the* night to be there. And the chef's from the Culinary Institute, which means yummy food."

Oh, her stomach liked that idea. Her workload, however, did not. "Sorry," she said, shaking her head. "I have two hundred people left to research for my chemistry matches. I'm not going anywhere except the kitchen to beg Elena for dinner while I surf the Net. Care to join me for some exciting entertainment?"

"You need to get out." Susan cast a critical eye over her. "No offense, but you look like crap."

"I have a multimillion-dollar event in eight days," Alex murmured dryly. "It's not about looking good at this point—it's about survival."

Susan stuck her hand on her hip. "If I promise to help you with half of those names tomorrow, will you come out for a drink? We need to catch up."

Alex eyed her as though she was suddenly plated in eighteen-karat gold. "I have some tough ones you could help with."

"You buy the drinks—you're on."

Feeling like an escapee from prison, Alex packed up her things and checked with her team to see if they wanted to come. They pleaded fatigue, so she stripped off her jeans for the first time in weeks and put on a flirty summer dress. "Very cute bartender there," Susan alerted her in the car. "You'll like him."

She was pretty sure she'd love anything that wasn't a run sheet or budget tonight. And she did love quaint little St. Helena, the most adorable town in the heart of Napa, with tree-lined streets and cute shop fronts. In addition to its boutiques and restaurants, St. Helena also featured a campus of the Culinary Institute of America, giving it a bustling, hip atmosphere that was exactly what she needed tonight.

The chic restaurant was buzzing as they stepped inside. Done in a breezy, clean California style with original works of art on the whitewashed walls, it featured a long cherrywood bar that ran the length of the restaurant. The bar area and tables were packed with an affluent-looking Napa crowd.

They were lucky enough to score seats at the bar when a couple left. Which was fine with Alex, because Susan was right—the bartender was serious Scandinavian eye candy—tall, blond, built and funny to boot.

They ordered drinks and flirted with the Swede, who was a student at the Culinary Institute. It was hot in the jam-packed space, steaming hot, so she slipped off her sweater and turned to slide it over the back of her stool. The sight of Gabe tucked in an intimate little booth opposite them with a sleek-looking brunette who possessed more natural style in her pinkie than Alex had in her entire body stopped her cold.

He was dressed in jeans and a collared shirt, a lazy, confident smile playing about his lips as he focused on his dining partner. Her stomach did a swooping dive. What did the De Campo men always say? *Take a woman out for dinner, flatter her outrageously, and you're as good as there.* She was pretty sure she'd never heard *Gabe* say it, but there was no doubt in her mind looking at the lazy smile on his face and the animated interplay between the two that that was exactly what Gabe had on his mind.

Her fingers tightened around the back of the stool. She had no claim on Gabe. She should be happy he was out with another woman so they could avoid the dangerous attraction between them. But really. How *could* he look at the other woman like that when he'd kissed *her* like he had just days ago?

Gabe's gaze drifted away from his date to scan the room idly. And collided with Alex's. She jerked her head back and aimed a look of pure nonchalance at him, but not before, she feared, her "I hate you" message was broadcast loud and clear. His eyes narrowed on her and he murmured something to his dinner companion and stood up. She calmly arranged her sweater on the chair.

"Who are you looking a—? *Oh.*" Susan's voice lowered to an earthy purr. "Your brother-in-law. Damn if he isn't the finest-looking man in Napa. Problem is…no one can catch him."

"That isn't Napa specific," Alex murmured dryly, her stomach tightening as Gabe strode toward them. "He has unrealistic expectations of perfection."

"What a nice surprise." Gabe stopped in front of them and kissed Susan on both cheeks, making her pale skin glow bright pink. Then he turned his attention to Alex. "I had no idea you were going to be here tonight."

No doubt. He likely would have beelined it in the opposite direction, given their lack of interaction this past week. *"Surprise,"* she announced brightly. "What fun."

His mouth twisted. "How are you, Susan?"

Her friend chattered on, babbling in her attempt to charm Gabe. Alex finally had enough. "You should have brought your *friend* over," she interjected. "Or were you too far down the flattering-outrageously route to bother?"

A warning gleam flashed in his eyes. "Please come over if you'd like to meet her."

Alex tossed her hair back and waved her hand at him. "We'll pass. I'm having a boss-free night tonight, thank you."

The grooves on either side of his mouth deepened. "*Bene.* Everyone needs one."

Like he needed a night out with a hot woman. Alex inclined her head toward the brunette in the booth, green jealousy driving her.. "She's lovely. Should we make sure she's on the list for the party?"

"Samantha's already been invited, but she's out of town next weekend."

Of course she had been. The urge to take the Black Forest cake arriving at Gabe's table and shove it in his face was appallingly strong. What was *wrong* with her? This thing between her and Gabe was nothing but a stupid fascination that was going nowhere. "Oh, look," she said desperately, "your dessert has arrived. You should go share."

"I should." He gave her a hard look. "I think you need some food to go with that martini."

"No doubt. My boss has been working me like a madman…my tolerance seems to have disappeared."

His mouth opened, then slammed shut. "Feed her," he instructed Susan. "*Buonasera,* ladies. Enjoy yourselves."

Susan waited until he was out of earshot to shoot her a sideways look. "What the hell was that?"

Alex shrugged. "Gabe and I tend to rub each other the wrong way."

"I don't think *he* could ever rub me the wrong way," Susan murmured dreamily. "In fact, I'd be all in for a full-on rub*down*."

"Try big doses of him," Alex suggested. "You'd change your mind in a heartbeat."

Her friend didn't look convinced. "The Italian's so sexy."

She conceded that point. "Who is *she,* by the way?" She nodded her head in the direction of the brunette presently spooning a piece of cake into Gabe's mouth. "I have three Samanthas on my list."

"That's Samantha Parker, daughter of the former mayor of San Francisco and celebrated opera singer. She," Susan murmured, her eyes glittering wickedly, "might be able to satisfy the unrealistic-perfection thing. She's supertalented and, apparently, quite nice—no ego. *With* the added bonus of being able to open up a hell of a lot of doors for Gabe."

Alex picked up her drink and downed the rest of it. Gabe didn't even like her. He'd kissed her because there was this *thing* between them, but she knew she wasn't his type. Had always known that. So why did it bother her she wasn't an opera singer? That she didn't have the type of pedigree that would open doors? Slam them shut, more likely, with all her skeletons…

She was willing to bet Samantha Parker had never felt the cold slap of handcuffs around her wrists. Seen what the inside of a jail cell looked like.

"Alex?" Susan was looking at her with a raised brow. "You want something to eat?"

They ordered appetizers. One drink blended into two and more flirtatious chatter with the bartender. Alex laid it on thick, as it made her feel better to know that *he* thought she was beautiful. And if Gabe was noticing—even better. She had other options, too.

But as the night went on, it became her fervent desire that Gabe would spirit his companion out of there and do the dirty deed already. She just couldn't stomach it. She couldn't. But apparently her plea to the martini fairies had not been heard. By ten she was so exhausted she was in serious danger of doing a face-plant into her glass. And the two beautiful ones were *still* enjoying their bottle of wine, Samantha Parker, gifted vocalist, staring dreamily into Gabe's eyes.

"I want to puke," she muttered, pushing her empty glass away.

Susan gave her an amused look. "If you like him, Alex, why don't you just tell him?"

"Like him?" She stood up with a dismissive movement. "That would be confusing antagonism with attraction."

"O-kay." Susan darted a look at the bartender. "What do you intend to do with him? *He* thinks you're going home with him."

"What?"

"You've been flirting outrageously with him, Alex."

Alex stared at her friend. "So were you. *We were flirting.* That's all. Are the rules that different in California?"

"Oh, boy." Susan pointed to the washrooms. "If *that's* where you're headed, go. I'll clean up your wreckage, settle the bill and get you home for some sleep."

Alex waved her hand at the stool. "Money's in my purse."

She made her way to the ladies' room without a glance at Gabe's table. She'd only had an appetizer with the two martinis, not exactly evoking rational thought. Better to stay away.

"Alex."

Gabe's voice stopped her in her tracks in the corridor outside the bathroom. An instinct of self-preservation made her start moving again, her hand curving around the handle of the door, but Gabe was faster, setting his down on top of hers.

"Dio," he muttered, spinning her around. "What is *wrong* with you?"

"Nothing." She looked at the wall behind him. "We're on our way out."

"With the bartender?"

"No." Anger mixed with the unusually high amount of alcohol in her system to form a lethally intoxicating combination. She lifted her gaze to his and glared at him. "Although it is astonishing to me how quickly men move on. You kiss me like you did in your office, then you appear on a date with Ms. Opera Singer, all cozy and canoodling." She tossed her hair over her shoulder. "I think I may need a lesson on that, because it is truly impressive."

He stared at her. "You're jealous."

"As *if.*"

"So why the bitchy behavior?"

She shrugged. "Maybe I can't turn my feelings on and off like you can."

"Oh, I'm feeling them all right," he corrected grimly. "I was trying to have enough sense for the both of us."

"About what?"

"Don't play coy, Alex."

A frission of excitement coursed through her, dangerous, forbidden. She closed her eyes and fought it. "Go back to your table, take your opera singer home and do the sensible, or not-so-sensible thing—whatever you want to call it—and take her to bed. I'm all for it."

"How can I?" he rasped, "when all I can think of is having *you* in my bed?"

Her eyes flew open. "You were letting that woman drool all over you."

His gaze heated. "Like the bartender was over you?"

"He was *entertainment.*"

"Cristo, Alex." He raked a hand through his hair, that thing he did, she realized, when he was hot and bothered. "You are making me nuts. I'm on a date with someone else and I'm thinking about you."

His confession mixed with her intense jealousy elicited a dangerously heady feeling. It wasn't rational; it was the aching need to experience that sweet shot of adrenaline she knew he could give her, no matter how wrong it was. She rose on tiptoes and kissed him. Went after what she wanted. He hesitated, his mouth still beneath hers, and for a heart-stopping moment she thought he wouldn't kiss her back. Then, with a muttered imprecation, he slanted his mouth roughly over hers and took control. His kiss was hungry and demanding and everything she'd been craving since that day in his office. Frustration had her moving closer, seeking more, wrapping her arms around his neck and reveling in the magical connection they shared.

"Lex," he muttered against her mouth. "This isn't—"

She pressed her fingers against his nape and brought his mouth back to hers. Hot, uncontrollable, she wanted the kiss to go on forever.

"Oh my God." A muffled cry from behind them split them apart. Samantha Parker stood there, blue eyes huge, hand to her mouth. Her face whitened as she looked from Gabe to Alex and back before she turned and fled.

Gabe cursed under his breath. Alex's fuzzy brain struggled to comprehend what had just happened.

"Go after her," she bit out when she finally recovered the power of speech.

"Alex—"

"Go." She pushed into the ladies' room, the door swinging shut behind her. Her legs trembled; bile pulsed at the base of her throat. She had never even spoken flirtatiously with someone else's man since Jordan. Never even *looked* at a man unless she had irrefutable evidence he was single and not harboring secrets. But she had just kissed Gabe in a crowded restaurant in front of his date. *Deliberately kissed him.*

She sank down on the leather bench, rested her forearms on her thighs and pulled in deep breaths. The night Cassandra Lane had walked in on her and Jordan in bed in his apartment flashed through her head like the recurring nightmare it was. The one that had never gone away. Jordan laughingly insisting on getting out of bed to get them more wine, the sound of a strange woman's voice in the hallway, then the appearance of Jordan's redheaded wife in the bedroom, her face dissolving at what met her there.

Alex had been so disorientated, so confused as to what was happening she hadn't been able to move. A *wife?* Jordan had a wife? He was supposed to be divorced.

After that, everything had been a blur. Cassandra had lost her mind. Jordan had had to physically remove her from the room while Alex recovered her brain and dragged on her clothes.

Her six-month affair with the man she was in love with had ended the next day with a flower delivery to her office and a thank-you note.

Well, she *wished* it had ended there. But it hadn't. As much as she'd wanted to bury her head in the sand and nurse her wounded heart, damage control had to be done. A thirty-million-dollar divorce settlement—in which her firm was inextricably involved because of her—was in play. A five-million-dollar-a-year account her agency depended on hung in the balance. It had been a disaster. Alex was problem child number one yet again, after a youth filled with that label.

She lifted her head as a woman came in and stared curiously at her. Sat up straight and ran her fingers through her hair. Only her boss's contacts and efforts had prevented the story from being dragged through the tabloids. Kept her career and reputation intact. And yet here she was displaying the same type of reckless behavior.

She was the woman least likely to ever become a De Campo, with a past that could bring the family tumbling down faster than a deck of cards. So why was she making a total and complete fool of herself over him?

It didn't matter what was between her and Gabe. This had been wrong. Very wrong.

She collected herself and walked back into the restaurant. Susan eyed her paper-white face, asked her if she wanted to talk, then hustled her out to the car when she said no.

This was why she didn't allow emotion to rule, she told herself in the car as Susan drove her back to the vineyard. Because this was how she messed up people's lives. How she'd messed up a great deal of her own.

Whatever was happening with Gabe—how she was allowing herself to feel things for him—it had to stop. He was dangerous, lethal to her because of it. She had to end it before she messed up this opportunity she'd been given to keep herself in business. To keep her life on track.

At first, Samantha Parker refused to let Gabe drive her home. Her bag clutched to her chest, she stood outside the restaurant and blasted him with at least five minutes of insults in a combination of English and Italian before she took a breath. Too bad most of the world's great operas had been written in Italian, he thought ruefully as he endured the barrage, because Samantha had a very good handle on his native language.

She eventually agreed to let him drive her home when he explained that getting a cab to the city would be both difficult at this time of the night and cost a small fortune. The silence in the car was deafening and he deserved it in every way. No apology seemed to help. How could it? He wasn't about to tell her the truth, that he'd wanted the woman he'd been kissing back there for what seemed like an eternity, and nothing he did got her out of his head. He could tell her he regretted it, because he did. He'd never acted that way with a woman in his life. But when Samantha had put her hands on her hips outside the restaurant and asked what Alex meant to him, he'd been devoid of an answer. Maybe because he didn't have one.

So he'd said nothing. That had gone over well.

Now, walking up the front steps to Samantha's expensive Presidio Heights home, he flinched as she walked in and slammed the door in his face. *Bene.* He deserved that. But *Cristo,* he had never navigated waters as murky as these. What was he doing? He'd told himself to forget about Alex and focus on Samantha, yet every time Alex had laughed at something that hulk of a bartender had said, he'd wanted to smash his fist through the guy's face.

He strode back down to his car and got in, bracing his forearms on the steering wheel. He had the scary feeling the only way forward for him and Alex was to face their attraction for each other. Get it out of their systems. And maybe that was the path they'd always been on. It's just that neither of them had cared to admit it.

The fact that it was a bloody inconvenient time didn't seem to matter. Neither did his rule. Avoidance was definitely not working.

He revved the engine and pulled away from the sidewalk, the car's throaty snarl matching his inner one. His orderly life was in chaos. Ever since Alex Anderson, mistress of mayhem, had landed in the Bay Area, he'd gone from being the logical, sensible De Campo, the one Antonio and Riccardo called in to smooth things over with ruffled clients, to being a complete wild card at a time when he should be, *needed to be* concentrating on the most important launch of his life.

It was complete insanity. And it needed to end. He jammed his foot down on the accelerator. The nagging doubt that Alex was like an iceberg—with way more beneath the surface than he could see, and likely far more than he bargained for—wasn't enough to stop him.

A wise man would stay away. Resist temptation. But he couldn't seem to help himself.

Alex felt Gabe's presence before she saw him. Feet dangling in the pool that was the jewel and center point of the De Campo gardens, moonlight slanting over her shoulder, she felt the air pick up in intensity—a charge went through it. She swiveled around and took in his openlegged stance, his hands in his pockets, the slight frown that marred his brow.

Confrontational.

"I take it your date didn't end as planned." She almost laughed after she said it, because that was the understatement of the evening, except nothing about this was funny.

He stepped out of one shoe, then the other and came to sit beside her. Close enough to disturb everything about her. Far enough that they were just two people talking.

"She's furious." He slid his feet into the water. "I don't blame her."

"Neither do I." She watched the moonlight dance across the surface of the oval-shaped pool rather than look at him. "I'm sorry. I don't know what I was thinking."

"Probably the same thing I was thinking in my office," he said dryly. "We knew from the beginning we had a problem, Lex."

"We could forget it happened?"

"I don't think that's an option anymore."

Her heart stuttered. She jump-started it with a determined pull of air. "We're a week away from the most important event of both of our lives. I'd say it's a mighty fine option."

He braced a hand on the pool ledge and swiveled to face her. "What happened *tonight* is not an option. What happened in my office is not an option."

She turned to look at him then, wishing immediately

she hadn't, because he was so handsome in his jeans and rolled-up sleeves, his hard, strong profile silhouetted against the moonlight. "We have a business agreement," she said curtly. "I *need* this to be about business. I cannot lose this job."

He sighed. "That ground rule is gone. I was a fool to think we could ignore what's between us and so were you."

No, they weren't! She inched another centimeter away from those rock-hard thighs. "I think it's better to try and keep this under control."

"You think *tonight* was under control?"

"We have to do better."

His breath hissed through his teeth. "I've wanted you since the first insult you threw at me at Riccardo and Lilly's engagement party, Lex. This is not going to get better—it's going to send both of us over the edge."

Her heart tripped over itself. "Gabe—"

He waved a hand at her. "It's more destructive for us *not* to face this than to try and ignore it."

She pulled in a breath. "What *exactly* are you suggesting?"

His gaze was steady on her face. "One night to get it out of our systems."

A buzzing sound filled her head. "You're suggesting we have a one-night stand?"

He rolled to his feet. "Either that or we shut this thing down for good. Your call."

She tried to say something, anything, but she had no words.

"Think about it. You know where to find me."

She watched as he walked around the pool edge toward the house. The smooth, glassy surface of the water, so tranquil minutes before, shifted into a murky, shark-infested pool of black. She couldn't remember a time when she hadn't wanted Gabe—consciously or unconsciously.

But tonight, in kissing him, she had taken a step down the rocky road toward the self-destruction she was so adept at. It was a slippery slope to losing everything she'd worked for.

One night to get it out of our systems.

His words sliced through her like a knife, opening wounds she'd thought long ago healed. They gaped raw under the unrelenting moonlight, pulsed with an insidious throb that brought back everything. The way Jordan had bundled her off like a used piece of furniture the night his wife had arrived home, so clearly dispensable, as though she'd been barely a blip on his stream of consciousness. As though she'd *never* mattered to him.

She had thought he'd loved her. Had finally allowed herself to believe that one man, *one man* in her life would not hurt her. That finally someone had seen through the facade that was Alex and still wanted her, warts and all. That somehow her dream of escaping the past could be a reality.

She dipped her foot into the water and flicked it up, sending a ripple of diamonds through the air. Her affair with Jordan had taught her that she was no one's long-term prospect. That she would always be the Iowa trash everyone over the age of eighteen in Mission Hill had thought she was.

She sent another river of shimmering beaded droplets through the air. Gabe was right. They *were* a disaster waiting to happen. But somehow she'd hoped he would be the one to think more of her. That this endless tension between them was something bigger than lust. Something neither of them dared address for fear of facing it head-on. But apparently she was once again allowing herself to believe things that were just not true.

She blinked, desperately seeking to restore some sense to her head. If she was going to consider Gabe's proposal, she needed to be real with herself about what it was. Each of them slaking their mutual hotness for each other. Nothing more, nothing less. She had not suddenly morphed into Alex the respectable, even if she had the job and the clothes to fake it with. She was still just the girl for now.

The moon inched higher in the sky. She pulled her feet out of the bathtub-warm water and let them dry on the concrete. Was one night with Gabe even something she *could* consider? Would it finally get this particular monkey off her back and get her mind back on business where it belonged? Or would it make her other bad decisions look like child's play?

CHAPTER SEVEN

THE ONLY THING that kept Alex going for the next week was knowing the end was almost in sight. For the Napa event, anyway. With a week's rest in between that and the New York launch and most of the kinks worked out in California, she would have a chance to breathe and, more importantly, restore her equilibrium.

It was sadly lacking right now. She'd chosen to ignore Gabe's proposal in favor of ensuring the VIP/media tour schedule was set, she had enough staff to cover everything and attendee numbers were finalized.

But she couldn't avoid it forever. She needed to get this event out of the way—knock Gabe's socks off—then she could wrap her head around what she was going to do. Avoiding him hadn't worked for more than four years now. So aside from the fact that he was her client and the family dynamic wasn't likely to get any smoother if they slept together, she was contemplating it.

Anything to get that intense, rabid curiosity about how he'd be out of her head. Would he be *that good?*

Thus, anything that occupied her conflicted brain that week was where she wanted to be. Which meant superhuman efficiency on her part. It seemed like a minor miracle when she and her team went through their final checklist at nine o'clock the night before the party and everything was done. She sent Emily and Darren back to the B&B,

stretched her sore body with a big yawn and thought of only one thing: the hot tub. It might be her favorite feature of the De Campo estate. Perched on the hill looking out onto the vineyard, it was glorious at night. And she was going there *now* before she collapsed into bed.

She poured herself a glass of chilled white wine in the kitchen, put on her bikini and a cover-up, and shoved a cracker and cheese in her mouth. The light was on in Gabe's study as she whipped by. She gave the door an uncertain look. Better to leave him to it, she decided. He'd been grumpy Smurf lately trying to perfect his mystery wine, which seemed to be something of a big deal, and she'd gathered it wasn't going very well.

Heading to the west wing, she pushed open the French doors, padded her way around the pool and stepped up to the level where the hot tub sat with that incomparable view. She jerked to a halt. It was occupied. By six feet, three inches of magnificent, grumpy Smurf.

Oh. Her heart started to work again, this time pumping at a slightly higher rate than usual. Gabe's eyes were half-closed, his dark hair slicked back from his face. The lines of fatigue that had been carved around his mouth and eyes for the past couple of weeks were relaxed, less defined now. His bronzed, muscular body, clad in a pair of navy trunks, was mouthwatering.

Damn, but he was hot. An insanely delicious piece of male anatomy it would be a revelation for any woman to get her hands on.

Hands. Mouth. Tongue…

He could be yours.

She turned around. Later was better.

"Lex."

Crap. She swiveled back. "I thought you were asleep."

"You'd leave a sleeping man in a hot tub?"

Humor was definitely more appealing than grumpy Smurf. She stepped back up on the ledge.

He slid those sensational green eyes over her, eating her up. A wave of heat engulfed her that wasn't in any way connected with the steam coming off the tub.

He brought his gaze back up to her face. "All set for the event?"

"Amazingly so, yes. Usually I'm crawling into bed at 2:00 a.m. the night before."

"You seem to have been…supercharged this past week."

Uh-oh. Irresistible Gabe was back.

He tilted a brow up. "You getting in?"

"I don't want to disturb you."

"That's just baseline with you, Lex. Get in. You look exhausted."

She thought about how revealing her bikini was. Wished she had something more modest on, but it didn't exist in her wardrobe.

His mouth quirked. "This isn't the first time I've seen you in a bathing suit."

Yes, but it was the first time he would do so after propositioning her. And with the location being a steaming hot tub. Still… She looked longingly at the bubbling water. She had knots in her shoulders the size of kiwis. It was an eight-person tub. Surely that was big enough to house their attraction?

Gabe flicked water at her. *"Non essere un gatto scaredy."*

"I can guess what that means," she murmured. *Run,* said a little voice inside of her. But Alex was all about the challenge, unfortunately. He gave no quarter, keeping his gaze on her while she stepped out of her flip-flops and slid the dress over her head. Lowered herself into the water as quickly as humanly possible.

"Oh." She sank down slowly into the almost unbearably hot water. "You've turned the temperature up."

"I like it *molto, molto caldo.*"

Right. She could have figured that one out, too.

"You speak more Italian when you're tired." She wondered if that happened in bed as well. She'd bet it did, and she'd bet it was hot. "So," she murmured desperately. "How's your mystery wine coming?"

His face darkened. "Not perfect yet."

"It will come. You're a brilliant winemaker, Gabe. Everyone says so."

"It needs to come soon."

She frowned. "Why the rush? I thought The Devil's Peak was your focus."

"I may need to move that wine up."

He didn't look too happy about that. Thus the grumpiness.

"Maybe you need some inspiration."

His gaze rested on her face, hard and challenging. "Got any suggestions?"

She shifted uncomfortably. "I was thinking about your chemistry explanation. What do you think is missing?"

"If I knew that, I'd be doing it."

"Oh." She pointed a finger at him. "You really are a grumpy Smurf."

He lifted an elegant brow. "A *what?*"

"American TV." She sank back into the jets and stifled a moan as they attacked her shoulders. "I heard you tell Pedro this one is a big risk. Why?"

"It's a new varietal for California. The market isn't mature yet."

"And you're going to have to fight Antonio on this one, too," she guessed.

His face tightened. "Antonio, Riccardo, the board. All of them."

"Will Riccardo support you?"

"I'm hoping so."

"What was it like being passed over for him?" She had always been so intensely curious about that. Gabe was the brilliant winemaker—but Riccardo had gotten the top job after gallivanting around the world driving race cars.

A shuttered look crossed his face. "I've always loved the wine-making part of the business."

"That's not exclusionary from being CEO. Some would have said you were the natural fit."

"My brother is a fine CEO," he said harshly. "He's done an incredible job expanding De Campo into the restaurant business and I support him fully."

"But you must have wanted it to be you?"

A muscle jumped in his jaw. "Don't put words in my mouth."

"But you did…"

"Lex."

She sighed. "I'm a branding expert. I know you need help with the name. Give me some details."

"I can't."

"You don't trust me."

"I don't trust anyone with this wine."

"Fair enough." She wriggled her toes as her throbbing feet started to unwind. "Then give me the brand attributes you're going for. How do you normally name your wines?"

He shrugged. "We've been using American landmarks for the Napa wines. The Devil's Peak, Yellowstone, etc. But I want something special for this one. Something out of the ordinary, because the wine is out of the ordinary."

"Key descriptor?"

He slid a reproving glance at her.

"One word."

"Ethereal."

"Fancy word coming from a man."

She sank farther down in the water and brainstormed in her head. Ethereal. Special. Heavenly. Celestial. A smile curved her lips. "How about the Angel's Share? There is just something so magical about that expression. Your wine is *that* rare. To be coveted."

She watched him turn it over in that analytical brain of his. There was nothing knee-jerk about Gabe. Ever.

"Maybe it's been used before?"

"Not that I know of." He gave her a thoughtful look. "I like it. It's exactly where I wanted to go with the brand. Aspirational…"

She shrugged. "It's a great n— *Ouch.*"

"What?"

"Cramp," she breathed, squeezing her eyes shut as a tiny ball of excruciating pain seized the arch of her foot.

"Give." He held out his hand.

"Mmm, no." The ball seized tighter. *"God."* She shoved her foot at him. "Make it stop."

He pulled it onto his lap and ran his fingers over the soft underside of it. "Where?"

"The arch," she croaked. His fingers moved to the curve of her foot and found the lump. Started kneading it out with a firm pressure that was so painful she almost snatched it back. But then the knot started to give under his fingers and she sighed and leaned back against the tub. "Don't stop."

He didn't. Kept kneading her flesh until the ball of tangled muscle was gone. "That could be enough," she murmured.

He took her other foot in his hands. "You're a mess," he said gruffly.

"My boss is a taskmaster." She sighed as he dug into her sole. "You've done this before."

"Feet are a highly erogenous zone for women."

Her stomach curled in on itself. She bet he knew where they all were.

"I took a massage course once."

"*You* took a massage course?"

"A girlfriend decided we should do it together."

"Right." She closed her eyes and tried not to imagine him kneading her flesh—all over. Susan was right. It would be a beautiful thing.

"Have you thought more about my suggestion?"

His smoothly delivered question made her eyes fly open. "I've been too busy to think about it."

His gaze darkened to a smoky, sultry green. "Liar."

She met his stare head-on. "You have a big ego."

He pressed his fingers into her arch and she yelped. "Relax," he murmured. "Out of curiosity, if you were to agree to one night, how would you like it, Lex? Hot and heavy or long and drawn out?"

Her insides seized. "I don't think so, Gabe."

"We're just talking," he drawled, eyes glittering. "Hypothetically, of course."

She should have shut him down, but she couldn't resist a challenge. And then there was that curiosity about him that was burning her up.

She gave him a thoughtful look. "I like both. But I think I'd start with long and drawn out."

He nodded. "Good choice. It's been a while, after all, hasn't it?"

"Excuse me?" She tensed and tried to pull her foot away, but he held it firm.

"When's the last time you were on a date?"

She was *not* admitting it had been a while.

He smiled. "Exactly as I thought. So theoretically, if I were to be the one to break your slump, *I* would move my hands up over your calf like this and work those muscles, too, first this leg, then the other. Make sure you were loose, relaxed."

She swallowed hard as his fingers kneaded the tight muscles of her right calf. *Dear Lord, that felt good.*

"Then," he continued, "when I was sure you were in the zone, I'd move over there, slowly, making sure you knew my full intentions. You'd give me that fight-or-flight look of yours. I'd wait until you bit your lip in that way you do when you want to be kissed, because you *would* want to be kissed. That would be my cue to give you one, and I would, but only a teasing, fleeting pressure. Just enough to generate heat. When you'd gotten into it, I might want to taste that bottom lip myself."

She closed her eyes as he dug more firmly into her calf. "You with me?" he murmured.

"Yes." Her voice was low, thready, nothing like her.

"*Bene.* Next, I'd put my mouth to that sensitive spot at the base of your neck, where your pulse is, because I know that works for you. Another one of those erogenous zones…*and,* in this hypothetical scenario, it'd be racing and you'd have that trickle of sweat dripping down into the cleft between your breasts, just like you do now. Which would prove irresistible to me, since I'm a big fan of that part of the female anatomy. I'd relieve you of your bikini top shortly after that."

"Gabe—" She licked dry lips. "I think that's enough."

"Don't you want to know how it ends?"

"No," she croaked.

"Just a little more." His eyes gleamed with humor and something, darker, primal. "So then I'd be aching to get my hands on you and I *would* put my hands on you. I'd take those beautiful breasts of yours into my palms like I did in my office, but this time I'd use my mouth on you and you'd arch into me and moan." He lifted his broad shoulders. "At this point you'd be begging for me to touch you in other places and we'd pretty much have to make a call as to whether we go all hot and steamy and you let me—"

"Enough," she broke in shakily. "I get the picture."

"You *sure?* I was just getting to the good part."

She waved her hand at him. "Who *are* you, anyway? Where did conservative Gabe go?"

He shook his head. "Never conservative in the bedroom, Lex."

God. She pulled in an unsteady breath. "When, exactly, were you planning on stopping, *just out of curiosity?*"

His gaze burned into hers. "I wasn't."

Heat slammed into her, hard and fast. She had the shocking feeling if she'd let him continue he could have made her do things...experience things completely out of her control. Just by talking to her...

She sank her fingers into the concrete ledge, poised to run for her life. Gabe's hand came down on hers. Her heart careened into the wall of her chest as she stared at him.

"Stay. I think I've had enough."

What? He levered himself out of the tub and flashed her one of those blinding smiles. "I'm going to go make sure no one's using that name."

She stared after him, pulse pounding, stomach in knots. Had he really just done that? Had she really just *let* him do that? She winced as another cramp hit her left arch and reached down to massage it.

Gabe was right about one thing. This had to end, one way or another. The scary thing was—her wild-child alter ego seemed to be making an extended appearance.

A loud thump woke Gabe.

He jackknifed into a sitting position and glanced at the clock. *2:00 a.m.* What in *Cristo's* name had that been?

A string of curses filled the air. *Alex?*

Heart in his mouth, he ran to the door, whipped it open

and headed for the stairs, terrified she'd fallen down them. A glance down the winding staircase found her sitting at the bottom, holding her right arm cradled in her left. *Merda.*

"Stai bene?"

He ran down and knelt in front of her. Her face was white, her slim body trembling. His heart thumped hard in his chest. *"Stai bene?"* he asked again. She stared vacantly back at him. *He was speaking in Italian.* "Alex," he murmured, taking her shaking hands in his. "Did you hurt yourself?"

She recoiled like an injured animal, a panicked light filling her eyes. "Stay away from me."

What in Cristo's name? He took her by the shoulders. "Lex, are you okay?"

She ripped herself away and sprang to her feet, the wild-eyed look of a hunted animal in her eyes. "Get your goddamned hands off me."

He froze, heart pounding. "Lex," he said slowly. "What's wrong? Did you fall?"

"Stay away from me!" She backed into the corner and wrapped her arms around herself. "You have no right to touch me."

His heart rose in his throat. "I think you need t—"

"Y-you c-call my f-father right now." She waved her hand frantically at him. "You c-can't keep me here."

A tingling feeling went through him. Something was very wrong here. "I don't think I can do that, Lex," he said calmly. "It's the middle of the night."

She came at him then, nails like talons. "You bastard," she screamed, digging them into his arm. "I didn't know anything about it. You can't keep me here. I want to go home!"

He cursed as her nails dug into his forearm. Grabbed her arms and twisted them behind her back. She wasn't talking to him, he realized. She was having a nightmare. *She was sleepwalking.*

"*Let me go,*" she raged, twisting away from him. "*Dammit,* you let me go right now."

He kept her arms pinned behind her back. What were you supposed to do with a sleepwalker? Wake them up? Or was that dangerous? Unsure and recoiling from the terror in her eyes, he released her wrists and scooped her up, holding her tight so her blows landed ineffectually on his back. Her curses echoing in his ears, he carried her to the living room and dumped her on the sofa. She came at him again with her nails and he grabbed the lethal little instruments and pinned her hands by her sides. Panic raged in her face. He swallowed hard. Who was she fighting and how could he get her to stop?

"*Lex—*"

"I hate you," she yelled. "You son of a bitch. You were just waiting for this chance. Waiting to get your hands on me." She twisted her wrists and tried to pull out of his grip. "Let. Me. Go. *Damn you.*" When he refused, she kept repeating the words over and over again like a mantra, until her voice grew hoarse and her head fell to his shoulder. "Please," she begged. "Call my daddy. Let me go home."

The tears that started to fall tore his heart in half. Hot torrents of them ran down her cheeks and soaked his shirt. He wanted to wake her up so he could make them stop, but he was afraid shocking her out of it now would do more damage than good. So he pulled her into his arms and rocked her and told her she was home. That she was safe. Slowly, she relaxed against him, her hands releasing their death grip on his shirt. Her sobs turned to sniffles, then to quick intakes of breath.

His heart slowed. Thank *Dio.* "*Stai bene,*" he murmured into her hair. "You're okay."

When she was finally quiet and unmoving in his arms,

he carried her upstairs and tucked her into her bed. She grabbed her pillow and hugged it like a lifeline. Something in Gabe tore wide open. What the hell had happened to her? Who had been touching her? Someone in authority? Had that person let her go?

He lowered himself in the chair beside the bed, raking trembling hands through his hair. He shut the thoughts out of his head, because he couldn't go there when she couldn't give him an answer.

He sat back in the chair, his gaze on her pinched, drawn face. He couldn't leave her—what if the nightmare started again? What if she'd hit her head when she fell? And regardless, he could no more sleep now than he could forget the terrified look on her face.

In the end, he fell asleep. Woke in the chair at four a.m. to find Alex sleeping like a baby. He crawled into his own bed to catch a couple of hours of sleep before the big day. And told himself whatever he'd seen on Alex's face couldn't be *that* bad.

Alex woke to the buzz of her alarm with the heavy feeling she'd taken a journey while she'd slept. Pushing herself into a sitting position, she slapped her fingers against the clock to turn it off and blinked to clear the fuzziness in her head. Her shoulder throbbed. *Weird.* She hadn't been doing any heavy lifting yesterday. She rotated it around and winced as a stab of pain shot through her arm. *What in the world?*

With no time to worry about aches and pains, she slid out of bed and headed for the shower. Today was game day. The day she threw an incredible party everyone would remember. Padding to the window, she glanced out. Sun. Excellent. Just like they'd predicted.

She stepped into the shower, the steaming-hot water proving an effective antidote for her sore shoulder. Adrenaline hummed through her veins. Today had become personal. Not just a job. Gabe's wine was brilliant. She wanted to win this for him.

A T-shirt and jeans was the uniform of the day. She pulled her hair into a ponytail, winced as her arm throbbed and went downstairs in search of coffee. Gabe was sitting at the breakfast bar with an espresso and a newspaper. She flicked him a wary glance, their encounter in the hot tub burned vividly into her mind.

He looked up. *"Buongiorno."*

"Morning. Did you stay up playing with the name?" she asked blithely, reaching for the coffeepot.

He put his mug down and focused on her. Dark shadows smudged his eyes. His olive skin stretched tightly across his face. "A bit. *Grazie*. I think it's going to be *perfetto*."

"Good." Unsure of what to do next with that penetrating stare on her, she reached up and took a thermos mug out of the cupboard.

"Lex." His low address skated across her skin, made the hair on the back of her neck stand up. "Do you remember what happened last night?"

She turned to face him, heat invading every cell of her body. "We— I went to bed."

"I'm talking about what happened afterward."

Afterward?

He grimaced. "You don't remember, do you?"

She stiffened. "Remember what?"

"You were sleepwalking, Lex."

Oh. The heavy feeling in her head. The throbbing in her shoulder. She frowned. "Did I *fall?*"

"I think so. I found you at the bottom of the stairs holding your arm."

Her stomach tightened into a mortified knot. "Did I wake up?"

His face was grim. "No."

She put the mug down. "Was it the good one or the bad one?"

"The bad one."

She felt the color drain from her face. She turned, picked up the coffeepot and sloshed some into her mug, cursing as half of it ended up on the counter. "I'm sorry you had to witness that."

His stool scraped the floor. Footsteps sounded behind her. She flinched as he took the pot from her hand and jammed it back into the machine. "Tell me what happened."

She shook her head.

He planted his hands on her shoulders and turned her around. The worry and confusion in his eyes made her shrivel inside. "You were hysterical. Frantic."

She twisted out of his hands. "I don't want to talk about it."

His jaw hardened. "Lex—"

"No." She bit her lip and laced her hands together. "I can't talk about this. Not now. Not today. I need to get out there and prep for the arrivals."

His hands clenched by his sides. "Who was it?"

She turned and reached for the lid to her mug.

"I need to know he didn't hurt you."

The vibrating emotion in his voice made her stop. She swung around and stared at him. The haggard lines in his face, the dark shadows under his eyes were because of *her*. She bit hard into her lip, the urge to fold in on herself, to deny it had all happened immense. But she lifted her chin instead. "He didn't hurt me," she said huskily. "I scared him off."

He stared at her. She saw him fighting the urge to keep asking questions, which was good, because she had to get out of here. "The caterers will be arriving any minute. I need to get out there."

He nodded. Rubbed his palm over his forehead. "*Bene,* but if you—"

"*Oh, my Lord.*" She stared at the jagged red scratches on his forearm. "Please tell me I didn't do that to you."

"Unless there was another female in my bed last night I was unaware of," he said grimly, "yes."

She failed to see the humor in that. The gouges looked deep and angry, scrawling across hard muscle. "Did you clean them?"

He inclined his head. "It's fine."

"At least they'll be covered tonight," she muttered. "I am so sorry."

His mouth curved in a wry smile. "The men would just think I had a night of wild sex."

Instead she'd been a wild animal. She picked up her coffee. And fled.

CHAPTER EIGHT

NORMALLY WHEN ALEX was in event-day mode, she was tunnel visioned, unflappable and 100 percent on her game. Today she felt off kilter, unusually indecisive and decidedly *off* her game. It must be the residual effects of the sleepwalking. And the fact that Gabe had witnessed it. It made her feel that much more self-conscious and vulnerable.

If she brought a bit too much intensity to her interactions with the chef who was acting like a prima donna in Elena's kitchen or the fireworks provider who deemed it acceptable to store potent explosives alongside propane tanks, so be it. The stakes didn't get any higher than they were tonight. They had to wow every VIP, journalist and socialite attending this party. Nail the big reveal of The Devil's Peak at ten. Convince them De Campo had arrived in Napa.

Equally important was that everyone talked about it. At the water cooler, on social media, face-to-face. These were influencers attending. She needed them to influence.

She finished the setup, made sure everything was on schedule, then jetted into town to get her hair done. A big dress required big hair. And since her L.A. designer friend, Stella, had made her a big dress for tonight, hot rollers were a necessity.

At six o'clock, half an hour before the guests were to arrive, every glass, every torch, every staff person was in place. She surveyed the grounds with a satisfied nod and nipped inside to get dressed.

The champagne silk creation Stella had made her fluttered to her ankles as she slid it on. Not in a million years would she have ever been able to afford *this* dress, but Stella had given it to her in exchange for Alex's promise to talk it up tonight.

It was Hollywood glam at its finest. Excessively form-fitting, it clung lovingly to every inch of her body. Its spaghetti straps and low neckline emphasized her cleavage, while the back dipped almost to her waist. *And the beading.* It was magical, sparkling from every centimeter of the dress like hundreds of tiny diamonds.

She was not the princess, believer-of-fairy-tales type. But this dress put her first real smile of the day on her lips. She was ready now. *The game was on.*

She glanced at the clock. Six-fifteen. Time for her to walk Gabe through the grounds and make sure everything was perfect. She slipped on matching champagne-colored stilettos and her only pair of real diamonds—her very real two-carat drop earrings. They sparkled in the light like white fire. Any guilt she'd felt for keeping the earrings Jordan had given her had long disappeared with the knowledge they reminded her of his betrayal. Reminded her never to make that mistake with a man again.

She never would.

Her legs shook slightly as she took her first step down the stairs. The fact that she was headed toward Gabe might have something to do with it. Would he think she looked beautiful? Or would he think she was a messed-up piece of work after last night?

Not that he would be wrong on that.

She paused by his office door. He sat at his desk reviewing some papers, looking devastatingly severe in an exquisitely tailored tux that played up his dark good looks. She stood there silently, drinking him in. And realized there wasn't one centimeter of him she didn't want. From his complexity carved by the need to prove himself in a family of titans to the undeniably hot body and sex appeal. She wanted it all. And in that moment, she knew where her nervousness had been coming from all day.

She'd made her decision.

Gabe looked up, as if sensing her. His expression was distracted, his broad shoulders tense under the beautifully fitting jacket. He focused, zoned in on her, subjected her to an inspection that brought every nerve ending raging to life.

He stood up. Walked around the desk. "Determined to break some hearts tonight?"

"I don't let men close enough to break their hearts."

He joined her at the door, besting her by a good three inches even in her heels. "I think I'm going to say my suggestion expires tonight."

She lifted a brow. "You're putting a time limit on it?"

He dipped his chin. *"Sì."*

"Why?"

"Because," he admitted roughly, "I can't take it anymore."

She walked Gabe through the grounds, every step she took punctuated by the insistent drumbeat of her heart. The vineyard looked stunning, fire and light blazing from every corner. Torches burned at the end of the long, sweeping driveway to greet the guests, the cocktail area on the main patio was lit by lanterns and the vineyard itself was cast in spotlight as it meandered its way up the hill. It felt magical. As if fairies had visited and set everything aglow.

A four-piece band played jazz on the patio, mixologists waited to create individualized cocktails for the guests and staff stood ready to give VIP tours of the winery. Even the recalcitrant Champagne fountain was working, shooting a stunning golden spray into the air.

"All in all, a rather Dionysian feel, if I do say so myself," she murmured to Gabe.

"It looks fantastic. Do you think Janine will put in an appearance?"

Alex rolled her eyes. "Are you okay with everything, then? Happy?"

"I will be at midnight, when this is all over and people are raving about my wine."

She studied the tension in his broad shoulders. "They will be," she said softly. "It's a brilliant wine, Gabe. Relax and enjoy the moment."

She left him to ensure her beautiful young staff were at their station near the front gates, ready to meet the guests. They stood with beautifully embossed boxes containing each guest's scientifically chosen match, written in calligraphy on a blue card—De Campo blue. "*You* are not to be connected with," she reminded them firmly. They were eye candy—meant to inspire—nothing more. At too many of her parties she'd found them being admired by a guest in a basement closet. Or snorting a banned substance with a politician in the bathroom.

Not happening tonight.

The guests began to arrive like clockwork, one after another, in limos, dark sedans and even a motorcycle draped with a denim-clad Silicon Valley millionaire. "Black tie," the invites had said, but who was she to reject Jared Stone? His rebel persona was worth a fortune and anything he did made news. "Enjoy your match, Mr. Stone," she said smiling and handing him his notecard. "Make sure you seek her out."

She knew exactly whose name was on the card. It was the one and only match she'd tampered with, because to have Jared hook up with a top—one hundred pop singer at her party? Priceless.

When the bulk of the guests had arrived, she found Gabe to do his introductory remarks. He'd refused her help on them, of course, insisting that he had it. And as she listened to him begin, her mouth curved. He did.

"Eight years ago I came to California with the dream of making a De Campo wine on Napa soil that was every bit as brilliant as the Tuscan wines my family has been making for over a hundred years. To create a wine that possessed all those attributes but also had that unique, mellow beauty of a Napa Valley wine. No problem, I thought," he drawled, flashing that brilliant masculine smile of his she was sure felled every female in the crowd instantly, "I've got this." He paused, a rueful expression crossing his face. "Well, how wrong I was. It took six seasons before this vineyard produced a wine I considered worthy of the De Campo name. But somewhere along the way we got it right. We harvested what I knew was here all along. And tonight you will get to taste the fruit of that labor—The Devil's Peak." He raised his glass. "We think it's brilliant and we hope you agree. *Salute!* And enjoy your evening."

She swallowed hard, a burning sensation at the back of her eyes. She couldn't have written anything more impactful. Could not have captured his passion the way he had. And in the end, for a great speech, that was all that mattered.

The evening flowed smoothly after that. Almost every guest on their list had showed up, an eclectic mix of Silicon Valley types, wine bloggers, politicians, the arts crowd and the business elite. To her surprise, almost everyone seemed curious to seek out their match, incentive or no incentive. There was lots of networking going on and even a couple of flirtations, one of which was Jared Stone and

Briana Bergen, the stunning German pop singer she'd handpicked for him.

They were standing close to each other at the bar now, his hand on her bare arm. Alex's mouth curved. How predictable men were. All it took was a busty blonde and the right opportunity.

She tipped a photographer off to the liaison, watched as he took off in glee to capture the shot, then added a couple of extra staff to the bars to deal with the lines.

The sight of Gabe talking to Darya Theriault and her husband, who had to be ten years older than she, had her lingering by the bar. Gabe's face was blank, a painfully polite smile touching his mouth. Darya's husband had a possessive arm around her back, and the blonde, who Alex had to grudgingly admit was stunning with her platinum hair and blue eyes, was eating Gabe up.

Jealousy searing through her, she tore her gaze away. Had Gabe broken her heart as he had a string of other women's? A suitable reminder to guard her own, she told herself. Self-protection was definitely an asset when it came to the De Campo men.

She made herself busy, and by the end of the evening she was ready to drop. One more media interview, the big reveal and fireworks and they were done. She could hardly believe it as she sought out the notoriously tricky wine columnist for San Francisco's largest daily newspaper. Three weeks of insanity and here they were, an hour away from success.

She located Georges Abel and led him down into the cellar where the interview with Gabe would take place. The corridor echoed as they walked down it, the hallways even darker and spookier at night. The click of a woman's heels had her spinning around.

No one was behind them.

"Did you hear that?" she hissed to Georges.

The big Frenchman gave a wary nod. She turned around and kept walking.

Click, click, click.

They both spun around again. No one. Alex's heart thumped in her chest. What the hell?

Georges made a joke about her trying to scare him off before the interview. She laughed, but it was a hollow, petrified cackle. *Oh, my God.* Was Janine Courtland walking around down here? She led Georges into the tasting room, her knees knocking together. Gabe and Georges shook hands.

"Janine Courtland is walking around," she hissed to Gabe.

He gave her a frowning look as if to say this wasn't the time for jokes. "We both heard it. I wasn't imagining it. It was a *woman's* shoes."

"I told you this was the night that might bring her out," he murmured facetiously, and sat down with Georges. She sat at the table and half listened, a tremor running through her. Was Janine prowling around? And what did she want?

The chat went smoothly until Georges started probing about Antonio in a fascinated, lengthy fashion that was disproportionate to the subject at hand. Gabe humored him at first, but as the conversation went on she could see him growing more short fused.

"How much does Antonio have to do with the Napa operations?" Georges questioned. "I'm assuming he's made as big an impression here as he has in Montalcino."

"He's actually retired now."

"Before, I mean?"

Gabe's jaw tightened. "Antonio is a guiding force. His impact is always going to be felt."

The journalist sensed him hedging. "*How much* would you say he's been involved? Put his stamp on things?"

"Enough," Gabe growled. "Try the wine and see for yourself how you think we've done."

Alex ended the interview and kept Georges for a few minutes after Gabe left to feed him some other information that might fascinate him versus the storyline that was undoubtedly circling his head—a father-son feud.

She practically ran through the cellar on their way out, but this time they didn't hear any footsteps. And she wondered what Janine was up to.

At ten o'clock sharp, Alex sent the staff out into the crowd with trays of The Devil's Peak. "Get one in every person's hand before the toast," she instructed them. Then she sent Gabe to the front of the crowd. The guests halted their conversations and waited with a hushed anticipation as Gabe lifted his glass.

"Signore e signori," he said, "please meet The Devil's Peak."

He toasted the crowd, then lowered his glass to drink. Everyone followed suit, a dazzling display of fireworks lighting the sky. This was it, she thought, lifting her glass to her mouth. Her hands shook so much she could hardly get the glass to her lips. It all came down to this. The buzz in the crowd was palpable. *They had to love it.*

The fireworks popped and crackled as they hissed across the sky in an explosion of color. Alex thought she might pop along with them. Then voices started to penetrate her consciousness. "Brilliant," she heard the man beside her say. "The wine of the year," his companion agreed. "Where Cabs will go this season," said another.

Gabe was surrounded by the crowd. She saw Georges walk up to him, speak to him, then a smile that lit the night came across Gabe's face. Georges shook his hand. Then everyone pressed in to congratulate him. Their excited faces said it all.

They loved it. Gabe had done it.

A lump formed in her throat, so immense she could hardly swallow. To stand there and watch his dream come true was a soul-baring experience she had no idea how to handle. Which was also true of the rest of her feelings toward him.

She blinked and took a sip of the brilliant wine. *She had done it.* She had pulled this insane, crazy idea of an event off in three and a half weeks. The tattered, ragged girl who'd dragged herself out of Mission Hill, Iowa, on a wing and a prayer, thinking that life could be different, had been right. She had *made* it different.

She was the captain of her own destiny.

The sting of tears blinded her. She brushed them away with a shake of her head. *Take it in,* she told herself. *Stay in the moment.*

She wasn't sure how long she stood there, clutching her glass, watching the fireworks.

"Taking in your success?"

She tore her gaze from the blue starbursts streaking across the inky-black sky to find Gabe standing beside her. "And yours," she said huskily. "Congratulations."

"Grazie," he murmured. "You've earned my trust, Alex."

His words sent another dangerously powerful surge of emotion through her. She bit her lip, unsure of how to verbalize what she wanted. But she knew beyond a doubt she did. "Gabe—"

He reached a hand up to run his thumb across the smooth skin of her cheek. "I have two questions."

She stared at him, her body buzzing as though she'd had twenty cups of coffee.

"What happened last night—are you vulnerable because of it?"

He didn't want to take advantage of her. Her heartbeat

became an insistent pounding in her ears. "That nightmare is from way in the past. I sleepwalk when I'm stressed. It's—it's a trigger for me."

"Are you stressed now?"

"Depends on what kind of stress you're talking about."

His mouth curved. "Did a man give you those earrings?"

"That's three questions.'

"Answer the bloody question, Lex."

"Yes, but he doesn't mean anything to me."

His gaze flickered. "Take them off."

CHAPTER NINE

THAT HUSKILY WORDED command was the last she heard or saw of Gabe until the party was over. He was swallowed up in a groundswell of congratulations that lasted well past midnight, and she was busy wrapping everything up. It was one a.m. before the last of the guests left, their headlights disappearing in a snakelike formation down the long, winding driveway.

Her stomach seemed to go along with them. She made arrangements with the caterer to come back tomorrow to finish their cleanup and collect all of their materials, then walked back up to the house. The vineyard felt deathly quiet without the band, without the buzzing conversation of hundreds of guests and the pop of the fireworks.

Or maybe it was just that the sound of her heart pounding in her chest was almost deafening.

She picked out Gabe's tall figure sprawled on a chair on the front porch. The knot in her stomach grew to gargantuan proportions as she walked up the stairs, avoiding the gaps in the boards with her thin stilettos. He had taken his jacket and tie off. A glass of scotch sat on the arm of his chair. His relaxed yet intent expression was one she hadn't seen since she'd come to Napa. This was the Gabe she knew—focused, watchful, *deadly*.

"I told you to lose the earrings," he drawled.

She lifted her hands to her ears in a self-conscious

movement. "I couldn't exactly stash them on a corner of the buffet."

His purposeful stare suggested she lose them now. Excitement roared through her, licked at her nerve endings. She reached up and pulled the outrageously expensive jewelry from her ears and secured the backs with trembling fingers.

He took them from her and set them on the table. "Nice gift," he murmured. "Cost of a small car and all."

Green eyes tangled with blue. "I like to think of them as a reminder of how untrustworthy men can be."

His brow lifted. "Are we talking one particular man here or the species in general?"

"I'd have to go with the great majority," she responded. "Lilly would say I should say present company excluded, of course. She thinks you're one of the good guys."

His mouth quirked. "And what do you think?"

She lifted a shoulder. "Does it matter? This is about sex, isn't it?"

He picked up his scotch and took a long sip. Set it down with a deliberate movement. "I've never seen a more jaw-droppingly beautiful woman in my life than you tonight."

Her heart stuttered in her chest. *Dammit,* he was smooth. And hell, did she feel reckless. She'd just thrown the party of the year. She was on top of the world.

"First move's yours, Lex," he murmured. "After that, all bets are off."

Never one to resist a challenge, she leaned down, braced her hand against his shoulder to steady herself and set her mouth to his. Explored his beautiful, sensuous lips as she'd been desperate to do for days. He allowed her to take her leisure, let her have her fill of him. Then he reached up, tangled his hand in her hair and brought her down on his lap. Hard, dominant male greeted her silk-covered thighs. His kiss when he took control was gentle and fiery at the same time. Touched something deep inside of her. And if she'd ever had any doubt that making love with Gabe would strip her bare, it went up in smoke now.

A tremor slid through her. He pulled back, his gaze questioning. *This was why she'd never gone here. Because she wasn't sure how she'd come out the other side.*

She plastered a careless smile across her lips. "I think I'm having performance anxiety."

His mouth tipped upward. "Maybe I'm not that good."

"Maybe you're better."

He set his lips to her jaw. "Why don't you find out?"

She decided that might be the way to go. Doubt gave way to sensation as he pressed kisses to the vulnerable line of her neck. Blazed a trail down to the pulse pounding at the base of it. A shiver skittered through her as he lingered on the ultrasensitive spot between her shoulder and neck. He'd been right in the hot tub—it was her Achilles heel. The thing that just did it for her.

And he kept doing it for her. His fingers, deft and purposeful despite their size, slid underneath the spaghetti straps of her dress and drew them down, so exquisitely slowly it made her self-conscious in a way she'd never felt before. No hesitation with this man. He was getting right to the point. She felt exposed, wanton as he drank her curves in. There had been no place for a bra with this dress, nothing shielding her now from the heat of his gaze.

"You *are* beautiful," he murmured reverently. But unlike his seduction in the hot tub, this was hands-on, his palms cupping her flesh, the pads of his thumbs bringing her nipples to hard erectness. To watch her flesh pucker and respond to his touch in the moonlight was achingly erotic. The slow slide of his tongue over the hard point of her nipple as he bent his head to her so exquisitely pleasurable she squirmed against the hard pressure of his thighs.

A gentle nip of his teeth punished her. "Stay still," he murmured against her skin. "Long and drawn out, remember?"

She closed her eyes. "I might have made an error in judgment on that one."

"Live with it."

She sucked in a breath as he moved to her other breast and lavished the same treatment on it. There had been times in her life when being with a man had made her feel shame. But nothing about Gabe's touch made her feel that way. His hands and mouth on her skin savored her—treasured her—as if she were one of his fine wines. She closed her eyes and savored *him*. His touch. She was stone-cold sober, had only had that half a glass of The Devil's Peak during the toast. And yet she felt as if she'd consumed way beyond her limit.

He took her other nipple into the heat of his mouth. This time he stayed longer, made her ache for him inside. "Gabe—" she gasped, digging her fingers into the fine material of his shirt.

"Rilassarsi," he murmured, sliding his hand over her hip and down to where her dress bunched under her knees. Every centimeter of her skin glowed with scorching awareness as he slid his fingers under the edge of the silk and brought the dress up to her thighs in a slow, deliberate movement that made her body clench. "What did you think of my foreplay last night?"

She closed her eyes as he traced the edge of her panties with his fingertips. "Mean. It was just mean."

"That wasn't mean," he countered huskily. *"This,"* he suggested, moving his thumb to the center of her, "is mean."

Alex burrowed her head in his shoulder and caught her lip between her teeth. He rotated his thumb against her in a firm, insistent movement that set her blood on fire. She moved her hips against his hand, seeking more, *needing* more. *"Please."*

"What?" he murmured huskily. "Tell me what you want, Lex."

"Your hands on me."

"But they are."

She muttered something low under her breath and he laughed softly, sliding her panties aside. "Oh, you mean like *this, cara.*" He set his thumb to her bare flesh. She was wet and slick beneath him. His quick intake of breath told her he'd noticed. His low growl told her he approved.

She thought she might die as he feathered his thumb across the taut nub of her. Began a maddening rhythm destined to drive her crazy. "More," she demanded.

He slid the tip of his thumb inside her. Held her there. Alex groaned. *"Please."*

"Because you asked so nicely…" He eased a long, elegant finger inside of her. Moved his thumb back to her center. "By the way, Elena keeps her window open."

"What?"

He brought his mouth to her ear. "Don't worry. If you scream, I'll shut you up."

Hot, he was so hot when he talked like that. She squeezed her eyes shut as he eased his finger in and out of her, kept his thumb on her center in that maddening pressure. She shifted her legs further apart, beyond caring about Elena or anything else. He slid a second finger inside her, stretching her, filling her, building her pleasure to an almost unbearable level. "Like that, angel?"

"Yes." Her body was so tight she felt as if she was going to explode. "Gabe, please I need to—"

"Come?" He dug her face out from his shoulder and tipped her chin up. "You know what I was thinking about last night in the hot tub?"

She gave him a tortured look.

"What you'd sound like when you came apart under my hands."

Her lashes came down over her eyes. His thumb worked the throbbing center of her pleasure; his fingers plunged deep, touching her in a spot that pushed her close to the edge. "God," she murmured. *"Please."*

He covered her mouth with his. Slid his tongue against hers in the same erotic rhythm as his fingers were sinking into her. She let herself drown in the heat of it, let him take her over the edge with a series of ruthless plunges that made her scream. Then moan his name into his mouth as he drew out her orgasm to impossible heights. To a hot, shimmering pleasure that radiated out from her core and seemed never ending.

"I knew you would be like that," he murmured, pulling his mouth from hers when she'd finally quieted.

"Like what?"

"All in." He lifted his fingers to trace her trembling mouth. Eased his thumb inside. The taste of herself on him made her insides pull tight. Her gaze rocketed to his. "There are so many places I want my mouth to be," he murmured.

Oh. My. God.

"We're taking this upstairs."

He scooped her up and carried her inside, using his foot to shut the door. She was hopelessly glad for the efficient mode of transportation, because she was sorely worried her legs weren't working at all. Through the dark, quiet house they went, up the stairs to Gabe's airy, masculine master bedroom at the end of the hall.

It was dark in the suite, moonlight flooding in through the windows. Gabe set her down by the big, four-poster bed and flicked on a lamp. Her legs supported her, but just barely, weak at the knees as she drank in the raw, masculine power of him—broad shoulders, muscular tanned forearms where he'd rolled his sleeves up, trim waist and powerful thighs encased in dark trousers that hugged every delectable inch of him. Her gaze shifted up to his face. There was an indomitable strength about him that underlay it all that had nothing to do with finely honed muscle. It radiated from him, a force that drew her in. As if anyone and anything he touched was protected by association. Her lashes lowered. A woman could want that. A woman could find that intoxicating if she let herself believe she could have it.

He took her jaw in his fingers. "What?"

She shook her head, disabusing herself of that silly notion. *One night, Alex. Savor it for what it is. Nothing is forever.* Hadn't she learned that from the past?

She set her fingers to the top button of his shirt. "You have too many clothes on."

"Liar," he said softly. "What were you thinking about?"

"That." She slipped the first button from its hole and started on the second. Wondered why taking a man's shirt off seemed like the most intimate activity of all. He let her take control. She finished the buttons, slipped the smooth material off his shoulders and pushed it to the floor. Her stomach tightened at the beauty of him. His torso was a work of art—bronzed by long hours in the sun, with a set of abs that made the drool pool in her mouth. She put her lips to all that smooth, delicious muscle, trailing her tongue across his nipples in a game of fair turnabout. His indrawn breath made her smile. "One of your erogenous zones?"

"I have many."

She took hold of his belt and slipped the leather from its loop. Yanked on the buckle so it worked free. Her fingers brushed against the aroused length of him as she pulled down the zipper and everything inside her went tight. He felt big and hard and the magnitude of what she was about to do slammed into her with the force of hurricane winds.

Focus, she told herself. She slid the pants down his long legs and he obliged her by stepping out of them. The beauty of him wrapped itself around her, stealing her breath. His calves and thighs were lean, perfectly hewn muscle. Her gaze slid upward. And as for his…gear, enclosed in tight white boxers that showcased it to perfection, she'd been right. She most definitely wasn't going to be disappointed.

He curved a hand around her waist and pulled her to him. Laid a kiss on her that turned every bone in her body to mush. *Lord, this man could kiss.*

"That's your secret weapon, isn't it?" she murmured when he dragged his mouth from hers and turned her around.

"What?" She heard the rasp of her zipper.

"The kisses."

The dress hit the floor in a whisper of silk. "You like them?" he asked, pressing one against her shoulder blade.

She arched into his mouth. "I like them."

He worked his way down her back, paying homage to every inch of her skin. Alex had never thought of her back as a particularly sensual thing, but the way he worshipped her, she couldn't imagine anything hotter. He went for her shoes next. He was good with feet, she remembered, and he didn't let her down, sliding her foot out of the first and pressing a kiss to the arch. *Oh.* She lifted her other foot to let him take that shoe off, too.

He stood. She pushed a hand against his chest and sent him back into the bed, his knees hitting the edge. She pushed again and he sat down. The expression on his face as he took her in, clad only in tiny panties, made her light-headed.

"You are every man's fantasy, Alexandra Anderson."

Her chest tightened with an emotion she didn't want to identify. "Fantasies aren't reality."

He reached for her, lifted her up and wrapped her legs

around him. "This one is," he murmured softly, teasing the corner of her mouth with his lips. "No place to hide here, Lex. Only the truth."

No need to tell him she never told anyone the complete truth. Not about herself. This was just sex. But then he brushed his mouth over hers in another of those soul-baring kisses and suddenly this didn't seem like sex at all. It felt like the plundering of her psyche.

It would have been easy to reach for terror. She reached for him instead. Wrapped her legs tighter around his hips and met him kiss for kiss until they were both breathing hard and she could feel his thick, hard length pulsing insistently against her.

"Alex," he forced out hoarsely. "Do I need a condom?"

"I'm on the pill," she murmured. "Although we may need to take this slow. I'm a little out of practice."

He flipped her on her back and stripped off his boxers. Her mouth went dry at the sight of his powerful, jutting masculinity. "Allow me," he murmured, kissing his way down her body.

"It's okay," she protested when it became clear exactly *where* he was going. "I can't do that again. And—I can't do it at all during…intercourse."

He raised himself up on his elbows, level with her belly, an amused smile playing about his mouth. *"Intercourse?"*

Her cheeks burned. "What else would you call it?"

"Not *that*." He gave her a considering look. "You mean you've never had an orgasm that way?"

"I can't. Lots of women can't," she added defensively.

He pressed his lips to the curve of her belly. "Let's mark it as TBD."

She could have told him it wasn't going to happen. But arguing about it would be even more embarrassing. So she let him shift her thighs apart with his big hands, part her wet, aroused flesh and set his mouth to her. Her body clenched hard at the first slide of his tongue against her. Gentle, thorough, it washed over her like a heat wave. Again and again he lapped her, licked her, brought her flesh flaming back to life. She buried her hands in the soft bedding beneath her and conceded with a groan that maybe, just maybe she was capable of more.

Then he stopped.

Shock must have been written across her face, because he laughed low in his throat as he pulled her on top of him. "You didn't think this was just about you, did you, Lex?"

Well, no, she'd told— *Oh.* She closed her eyes as the aroused length of him brushed against her slickness. Her insides contracted with the heated desire to go in a different direction—to have his thick length inside of her. To experience what it was like to make love with Gabe.

"Open your eyes, angel."

She did. His gaze was heavy lidded and shot through with want. He guided the wide tip of him against her, cradled her hips in his hands and brought her down slowly on the thick length of him. Her gasp split the air. *"Lentamente,"* he murmured. "Slowly." She sank down on him inch by inch until she had finally taken him to the hilt, and almost groaned with the fullness of it.

"I see why you make the lists," she murmured, breathing in deep.

He gave her a half tortured, half amused look. *"This* is not always on offer."

"Lucky me, then." She started to move in slow, deliberate circles, shallower, then deeper, then shallower again. When she was looser, more comfortable with him, she slipped off him, then took him deep again. Gabe groaned and muttered something in Italian. Closed his eyes. Let her ride him until his breath came faster. His control shorter.

Then his hands clamped around her waist and he put her on her back again and used his mouth on her, his tongue a maddening torture. Quick, insistent, then slower, feasting on her. Bringing her back to where he wanted her—incoherent and desperate for him, *her* breath ragged. When she sank her fingers into his hair and begged him to let her come, he flipped onto his back and pulled her on top of him again. "Like this."

She could have screamed her frustration. But he felt so good stroking up inside of her, his hands guiding her hips, her body aroused to a fever pitch that she could do nothing but feel. Stroke by stroke he massaged her until every nerve ending in her body was centered on the connection they shared. "Lean forward," he encouraged roughly. "Use the friction. Use the angle."

She did. Slanted her lips over the sensuous fullness of his because she couldn't resist anything about him and let the sensations hit her exactly where she needed them to.

Her orgasm rolled over her like a tidal wave, deeper, stronger, more shattering than anything she'd ever experienced. A guttural moan left Gabe's throat as her body clenched around his and drew his own release.

It was the sexiest thing she'd ever heard.

She rode him, drew out his orgasm until his big body was damp and spent beneath her. Without one more drop of energy left in her, she collapsed against his chest, smiling at the thunderous beat of his heart. And sighed.

"That sure as hell better not be disappointment," he rasped.

"Oh, yes, very disappointing," she murmured, dragging herself off his chest to look at him. "All two shattering orgasms' worth."

His low laughter filled the air. "Give me five minutes and I can supply more."

It never happened. Not for a long time, anyway. She woke, groggy, wondering where she was and realized she had passed out on top of Gabe. He sank his teeth into her shoulder, rolled her to her side and took her in a slow, heated lovemaking that proved his exceptional stamina.

When she woke, light was streaming through the windows and six feet three inches of warm, hard male was plastered against the length of her body like a furnace. Apparently he was the touchy-feely type, something she had precious little experience with, since she never let a guy stay overnight. No muss. No fuss. They were just…gone.

It was a reminder how *many* rules she'd broken last night. She'd slept in a man's bed. She'd slept with her client. And perhaps best of all, she'd slept with Gabe, the man she'd vowed never to cross the line with because he was dangerous to her. *And guess what, Alex? You were right on the money with that one.*

Images from the night before flashed through her head, too numerous, too blindingly hot to fully process. How Gabe had feasted on her, how they had feasted on each other in what would surely go down as the best night of sex of her life. She pressed her palm to her face and felt the heat. She was never, *ever* going to be able to look at him the same way again.

Had the sex been worth it? Worth the awkwardness of asking him to pass the salt at family meals and having *that* run through her head? Yes, she decided, breathing his masculine scent in. A woman should have that once in her life. It was only fair. However, in the cold light of day, the best course of action seemed to be getting out of this bed *now* and calling it a *fait accompli*.

She eased her body away from his. Jumped when his arm tightened around her waist in a lightning-fast reflex.

"Stay." His husky, sleep-roughened voice sent butterflies swooping through her stomach. A woman could love to hear that first thing every morning.

"I'm thirsty."

He loosened his arm. "Come back."

She contemplated running. The fact that Gabe was a rich, powerful, sexy hunk of a man who was exactly the type she'd made a big, fat fool out of herself over before demanded it. And this one had the power to hurt her even more than Jordan had.

She stumbled into the washroom. Poured herself a glass of water and gathered her willpower. Then she wrapped a towel around herself and marched back out into the bedroom. "I really need to get going."

Dreamy eyes of the lushest forest-green blinked back at her. "Where?"

"The caterers will be here soon."

He glanced at the clock. "It's eight a.m. on a Sunday, Lex. Are they coming this early?"

"I need to get a shower."

His lips tilted. "Come here."

She found for some bizarre reason she couldn't resist. Perching herself on the side of the bed, she looked down at him. "So—" His arm snaked out, nabbed her around the waist and rolled her beneath him. She swallowed as he propped himself up on his elbows and kept her pinned there with the weight of his body. "Gabe," she murmured, trying to ignore how all that testosterone made her insides melt. "I'm not very good at the next-morning-recap stuff."

A sexy smile twisted his lips. "You are at the night-before stuff, so I'll forgive you on that one."

She grimaced. "Last night was fun. It was hot, actually. We satisfied our curiosity. Let's end it cleanly."

He let his body sink into hers, imprinting her with his potent masculinity. "Does *this* feel like we're done?"

She pushed at his chest. "We *should* be done."

He studied her face. "Why so uncomfortable?"

She pressed her lips together. "I realize this might be the first time a female has ever requested to leave your bed, but anomalies do happen. We said one night, Gabe. I need to go."

He sat back so he was straddling her with his thighs. "You can go if you answer a question."

She looked at him suspiciously. "What?"

"Tell me why you get those nightmares."

"No."

He crossed his arms over his chest. "Then you stay."

"Goddammit, Gabe," she glared up at him angrily, "Let me go."

"After you tell me."

"It's *nothing*. It's ancient history."

"Then why do you still have nightmares about it? Why were you sleepwalking?"

She shook her head. "This was sex. One night. Your call. My call says it's over."

His jaw hardened, an emotion she couldn't read flashing in his eyes. "The way you were, it's been haunting me, Lex. I need to know what happened to you."

The urge to run was stronger. "It's not something I talk about," she said flatly. "Forget about it."

"I *can't* forget about it," he said grimly. "That's the point."

The self-destructive side of her that seemed to be alive and well urged her to just say it, *say it*. Tell him how messed up she was and surely he'd go running and they could just end this. "Let me up," she muttered, pushing against his legs. This time he did, rolling off her and into a sitting position beside her. She reclaimed some personal distance and wrapped her arms around her knees.

"I'm sure Lilly has told you I was the black sheep of the family."

His expression didn't alter. "She mentioned it."

"My parents' farm, it's never done well and most of our lives we lived in poverty. When I say poverty, I mean there were times when we had no money for new clothes and we'd have to go to the charity depot to get them. My parents' marriage was a mess both because of who they were and because of the financial strain of the farm. My dad had an affair with the farmer's wife down the road, my mother left us about three times...life was just a general disaster. Lilly dealt with it by starving herself and being Miss Perfect. I dealt with it by going over to the dark side. I drank, smoked, hung out with the bad crowd, anything to get the attention I was craving."

"Lilly said your parents are extremely distant. I can see why."

"Yes, but I took it too far. I stole clothes from the department store for our prom because I was so bitter at having nothing and got busted for it. I started staying out at night, sometimes not coming home until the next day. And then I met Damon, the head of a biker gang, and we started dating." Her mouth curved as his jaw dropped. "He was hot, powerful and he satisfied my rebellious side perfectly."

"You dated the head of a *biker gang?*"

She nodded.

"Your father must have lost his mind."

"He did. He forbade me to see him. Grounded me. But I loved egging him on. I loved finally having his attention."

"I would have tied you to the bed," Gabe said darkly.

Her mouth twisted. "I'm sure he would have done that, too, if he'd thought it'd work. He kicked me out instead, and I went to live with Damon."

He looked at her as though she'd just descended from Mars.

She sighed. "It was nuts. He was involved in illegal activity, I knew it, but he kept me well away from it. He had some legitimate businesses. I was only sixteen. What did I know?"

His breath hissed through his teeth. "Sixteen?"

She nodded. Stared down at her glittering champagne-colored nails. She'd thought she was so grown up with Damon—thought she'd known exactly what she was doing—but she'd been in way over her head. "Damon and I went out one night to a movie. He was doing a drop that night. I never knew and didn't suspect anything because he never did that with me around. The cops must have known, though, because they picked us up almost as soon as we left the house and searched us." She looked up at Gabe. "They found a kilogram of heroin in the saddlebags."

"Did you ever do drugs?" he asked quietly.

"No. That might have been the only smart decision I made." She took a deep breath, but her lungs felt constricted. "They threw us in jail. It was Damon they wanted, but they tried to use me to get to him. Said they would implicate me, too, if I didn't give them what they wanted." She hugged her knees tighter to her chest. "I—I was by myself in a separate holding room. The guy—the sheriff's deputy who questioned me—was the same deputy who'd answered my shoplifting call. I could tell he thought I was trash. He made me feel like I was two inches tall. But—" she sank her teeth into her lower lip "—I could also tell that he liked me."

Gabe put his hand on her knee, his expression dark and intent as a storm cloud. She realized she was rocking back and forth. "That was the guy who put his hands on you."

She nodded. "I was crying, scared. I begged him to let me call my father, but he kept coming back to question me, again and again, and he didn't let me call home. I think they were intent on breaking Damon that night."

A muscle jumped in his jaw. "That's against the law not to let you call."

She made a face. "This is Mission Hill we're talking about. Nothing is above the law."

She rocked forward—she couldn't help it when that

miserable, dirty beige room they'd interrogated her in that night was so vivid in her mind it was as if it had happened yesterday. "They were relentless," she said harshly. "Damon kept telling them I knew nothing about the drugs, but they wouldn't stop. It was late—the middle of the night—when the deputy finally gave up. I asked him again to let me call my father." Her gaze lifted to his, her lips trembling. "He told me he would if I was nice to him."

Gabe's fingers tightened around her knee. A dark thundercloud moved over his face. "I refused. I fought him when he tried to touch me. I screamed and screamed until he got scared someone would come and he let me go." Tears burned the back of her eyes and she blinked them furiously away. She did not cry about this. She never cried. "I called my father. They hadn't heard from me in weeks. He was so angry. So mad at me he just yelled. I asked him to come get me." She looked down at her hands, her knuckles white they were twisted so tightly together. "He told me I could damn well wait until the morning. That he needed his sleep."

There was a long pause. "He told a *sixteen-year-old girl* that?"

She inclined her head. "I expect I deserved it."

"*Cristo,* Alex, of course you didn't." He took her by the shoulders, his fingers biting into her flesh. "Maybe you deserved to be taught a lesson, but you did *not* deserve to be left alone with a law enforcement official who couldn't keep his hands off you."

She dropped her gaze to his chest. "I pushed him too far."

"*It doesn't matter.* You are his child. You deserved his protection. You did not deserve to be left alone in a jail cell overnight." He cursed and gathered her to him. "Thank God you were a fighter, Lex."

She stiffened. "I don't need your pity, Gabe. I reaped what I sowed."

"You were a baby," he bit out tautly.

"You don't understand." She pulled herself out of his arms. "I made it *impossible* for them to love me. They were so tired of me by then they wanted me to disappear. And I don't blame them."

His gaze softened. "I think you wanted to be loved. Your parents don't sound like they're capable of it."

"*I'm* not capable of love. I've been destructive in every relationship I've ever had. It's a pattern, Gabe."

"Not with your sisters," he pointed out. "They worship the ground you walk on."

"That's different. They have no choice but to put up with me."

"They love you. That's the difference, Lex. People who love you reciprocate. People who love you protect you."

The ache in her throat grew to gargantuan proportions, the urge to run almost incapacitating. "It's very kind of you to try and convince me I'm not as messed up as I am, Gabe, but I'm fully aware of it. I'm actually okay with it. It works for me."

His gaze sharpened on her face. "*Sì*, because you like to use it as an excuse. Just like you always make those comments about how you can't trust men. Or how you say you're a bad girl. You'd rather paint yourself like that, convince yourself you're incapable of a healthy relationship rather than face the reality of being in one."

Heat consumed her, so blindingly hot she thought she might implode. "Do *not* tell me what I'm capable of, Gabe De Campo. You have no idea what it's been like to live my reality."

His eyes darkened, a forbidding, severe green now. "I'm just saying what all of us have seen for years but everyone's afraid to say. You're so busy perfecting your prickly Alex act to keep people from getting too close that you don't know how to live. You're a fighter, Lex, in everything but your personal life."

She dragged in a breath, her gaze trained on his. "I've been through therapy. I know what my issues are. But what about you, Gabe? You're the top bachelor who can't get off the list because you're looking for perfection. For the one woman who can live up to those impossible standards of yours. Well, news flash," she bit out, glaring at him. "She doesn't exist."

"I am *not* looking for perfection."

She scrambled for the side of the bed and set her feet on the floor. "You know what's rich about this? *You* are the one who made this about sex. You're the one who suggested a one-night stand. So don't lecture me about my relationship skills or who or what I am when that's all this was supposed to be."

She ran then. She didn't care that it made her look out of control, didn't care that her emotions were plastered across her face. Getting away was paramount.

She didn't hear Gabe's softly spoken words as the door slammed shut behind her. "You're not so difficult to know, Lex. The question is, will you ever let anyone in?"

CHAPTER TEN

GABE WAS IN the winery with Pedro late that afternoon, far away from Hurricane Alex, when Elena arrived with coffee and a package.

"It just came," she said, setting the box on the counter. "I thought you might need it."

Gabe opened it. The wooden box inside the packaging contained a bottle of wine. The label bore the blue and yellow design of a Vintage Corp. premium blend. Jordan Lane's wine. His gaze sharpened on the name done in an elegant black scroll. *Black Cellar Select—A Premium Cabernet-Merlot Blend.*

He froze. Took in the beautifully packaged bottle. *This was it.* This was Lane's Devil's Peak. Pedro had not been able to get a sample of it. No one had. Now Lane had hand delivered a bottle to him to throw it in his face. *The day after his launch, when he was riding high.*

His chest felt weighted. It was difficult to breathe. Pedro peered over his shoulder and Gabe heard his indrawn breath. "This is it," he exclaimed. "The *bastardo* sent it to us."

Gabe noticed a card tucked into the box. He took it out and slipped the note from the envelope. "'Congratulations on what I've heard was a hugely successful launch, De Campo. Nice to know Black Cellar Select will be in good company.'"

Following the words were Lane's signature and a list of a dozen of the country's top restaurants that would be featuring Black Cellar Select as their wine of the month.

His blood ran cold. "Give me a corkscrew."

Pedro pulled one out of a drawer. Gabe slammed two glasses on the counter and opened the wine. The first taste of the blend on his tongue made his stomach roll. If Lane had taken The Devil's Peak and matched it scientifically, trait by trait, it couldn't have been closer.

A two-million-dollar party, a ten-million-dollar ad campaign—spent on a wine which was now one of *two*. One of *Dio* knew how many, if he knew Lane. He felt the room sway around him as everything he'd worked for over the past eight years came tumbling down around him. The board needed to see a significant profit this year. The Devil's Peak had to sell like wildfire. Now he had a competitor. A competitor who had the potential to blow him out of the water.

What was he supposed to do now?

Pedro put his glass down. His shocked gaze met Gabe's. "It's the same wine. How is that possible?"

Gabe put a hand on the bar to steady himself, to stop the roiling turmoil in his head. "It has to be one of our winemakers. Someone in the lab. It's too exact a copy."

"But there is no one—"

"There is *someone*," Gabe growled. There had to be.

Pedro took another sip of the wine. Shook his head as a slow frown crossed his wrinkled brow. "You have no choice now."

Gabe pulled in a breath, feeling as though he was breathing fire. He exhaled slowly. "You think we should launch the Angel's Share?"

The other man nodded. "The wine is *magnifico*, Gabriele. You could bottle it tomorrow and it would score a ninety-seven."

Gabe levered himself away from the counter and shoved his hands in his pockets. "The question is, is the market *ready* for it?"

Pedro raised a thick gray brow. "You made your choice on this one two years ago, *mio figlio*. Now is not the time to second-guess yourself."

No, it wasn't, he realized. Pedro had taught him not just about wine, he'd taught him about vision. About seizing the moment. His mentor had not hesitated when Gabe had asked him to come to America with him to pursue this dream. It was Pedro's as much as it was Gabe's. If Pedro thought the wine was ready, it was ready.

Gabe's mouth tightened. "Antonio will fight us every step of the way."

Pedro rested his unflinching gaze on him. "Then make him see the light."

Gabe looked at the expensively packaged bottle in front of him. It sounded so simple. Fly to New York this week for the quarterly De Campo board meeting, explain to his father and brother their star wine had been stolen by their chief competitor and secure their approval to bet the bank on a varietal that didn't even represent a 5-percent share of the Californian mix.

He grimaced. It was either madness or a stroke of genius. He wasn't sure which.

He looked at Pedro. "Can we be ready in a month?"

The old man smiled. "*Sì*. On the scale of The Devil's Peak?"

"*Sì*."

"Consider it done."

Pedro clapped him on the back and went off to make things happen. Gabe took another sip of the wine and felt it burn his soul. He would bury Jordan Lane if it was the last thing he did. Someday, at some point, there was going to be a moment when he took a nail and hammered it into

Vintage Corp.'s coffin. And he was going to relish every minute of it.

He abandoned his coffee and headed back up to the house to tackle his other problem. Alex had been wrapping things up with suppliers all afternoon, stomping around with fire in her eyes. He wanted to tell her she'd been absolutely right—it *had* been his idea to have a one-night stand. She hadn't asked for the grand inquisition he'd given her. He wasn't even sure *why* he'd done it, he'd just had to know. And now that he knew the depth of the baggage she was dragging around, his predominant thought was to agree with her and cut it off now.

She'd dated the head of a biker gang, for *Cristo's* sake! The guy she ended up with, *if* she ever ended up with anyone, was going to have to be okay with having a keg of dynamite in his backyard at all times. Not something the vice president of one of the world's biggest companies needed anywhere near him...

He walked down the hill toward the house, noting the absence of trucks in the parking lot. Good. He could get this over with without delay. Best for everyone. Because Alex had most definitely gotten under his skin. She was like a fever that way. Something that got in your system and fried your brain. And if there was one thing he didn't need, it was a fried brain when everything depended on him being clearheaded and deadly methodical about what happened next.

Elena looked up from the stove as he walked into the kitchen.

"Alex around?"

"She left for the airport an hour ago. Said to tell you there's an issue with Zambia and she's caught a flight back to take care of it."

He blinked, sure he hadn't heard right. If there was a venue issue with De Campo's SoHo wine bar, Zambia, where the New York event was to be held, surely some-one in *New York* could have dealt with it.

"She didn't want to bother you working," Elena contin-ued, turning back to the stove. "She said she'd call later to update you."

She had run. Walked out on him. Fury raged like an untamed beast, roaring to life inside of him. He should be happy she was out of his hair. Instead he wanted to strangle her.

"She said she has her mobile if we need her," Elena murmured. "Call her."

His hands clenched by his sides. Oh, no. No—he wasn't going to call her. He was going to find her when he landed in a couple of days and treat her to a rude surprise.

His fists uncurled as he flexed his fingers. It was then that he realized he and Alexandra Anderson were cate-gorically *not* done.

CHAPTER ELEVEN

IT WAS EASIER this way.

Alex slid onto a stool at the bar of the trendy Manhattan trattoria where Lilly was to join her for dinner and signaled the bartender. Parachuting out of Napa three days ago to take care of the venue issue at Zambia meant Gabe hadn't had to pretend any interest in her after her true-confession experiment, and she hadn't had to pretend it didn't bother her.

The way she saw it, she had another forty-eight hours to insulate herself against Gabe before she walked him through the venue in anticipation of this weekend's event. Forty-eight hours to convince herself what had happened between them was forgettable, one-night-stand material instead of an event she was sure was going to be burned into her memory forever.

The bartender ambled over in his oh-so-cool hipster way. She ordered a glass of Argentinean red and tapped her glossy nails on the bar, her foolishness reverberating in her head. The one-night-stand part she could almost be okay with. The truth-serum part, not so much. What had gotten into her? Sex was one thing. Opening herself up to Gabe, the amateur psychologist, was another.

The bartender slid the wine across the bar to her. She picked the glass up and started to sniff the bouquet, then slammed it back down. *Damn him.* He was everywhere, destroying her peace of mind.

She pulled her phone out to go through some emails. Saw Georges Abel's story had run. She scanned through it. The word *rift* and Antonio and Gabe's names in the same sentence made her grimace. However, he also raved about the wines and gave them a big thumbs-up. She could live with that.

She took a sip of her wine, sans bouquet. Spun the glass around on its stem in a desperate attempt to distract herself. To avoid Gabe's disturbing conclusions that kept running through her head, taunting her. *You're a fighter in every part of your life except your relationships. You'd rather paint yourself as bad, convince yourself you're incapable of a healthy relationship rather than face the reality of being in one.*

Ugh. She growled low in her throat. Had he really had the gall to say that? It wasn't in her DNA to be in a relationship. Hadn't been since Jordan.

She stared into the rich, ruby-red liquid in her glass. How was she supposed to have a normal relationship with a man? The very man who was supposed to bring her up, to nurture her, had turned his back on her when she'd needed him most. A law enforcement official, the very person she was supposed to trust, had assaulted her belief that she could trust anyone. And when she had tried, really tried with Jordan, thrown herself into her relationship with him with a blind faith that maybe her past was not the way it had to be, he had discarded her as though she was defective, worthy only of a cheap affair. And wasn't that always what men wanted from her? Her body for the short period of time it took to slake their thirst?

Her fingers tightened around the stem of her glass and drew it to her. She didn't want to be a loner. Sometimes she desperately wanted someone to lean on—to catch her when she fell so she didn't always have to be the last line of defense. But that was the way it was. She chose *not* to engage because she wasn't *capable* of a relationship. Not because she didn't want one.

Gabe was wrong.

"Lex."

Lilly's excited voice came from behind her. She turned, ready to gather her sister into a huge hug and spill her guts, then saw who was with her. All three De Campo brothers, dressed to kill in designer suits and designer smiles. All except Gabe, that was.

Oh, God. Not tonight.

"Look who I brought with me," Lilly buzzed. "Matty wanted to see you."

Alex's gaze bounced from Gabe to Riccardo to Matty back to Gabe, whose expressionless, I'm-not-angry look meant he was very, very angry.

She kicked herself out of her stupor, slid off the stool and gave Matty a hug. "Where is your gymnast? I heard you were dating an Olympian or something."

"Finito." He spread his hands with a rueful smile. "You want to help me lick my wounds?"

She detected a darkness behind his usual charming smile and would have called him on it if she hadn't been so intent on the scowling De Campo across from her. "There are about a million women who'd be happy to do that," she declined with a smile. "And you know that's not my strong suit."

"I live in hope."

She gave Lilly's hard-as-nails husband a kiss on both cheeks. The only thing soft about him was the indulgent smile he regularly lavished on his wife.

"Gabe," she murmured last, moving on to brush a very cursory greeting to his cheek, lest the whole situation look as awkward as it felt. The current of awareness that ran through her as her lips made contact with his hard, tense flesh rocked her back on her heels. "I thought I wouldn't see you until Friday."

"Surprise." The sarcasm in his tone was bested by the dark storminess of his gaze. She dragged hers away for fear of being singed. Caught Lilly staring at them.

"All the brothers together," she murmured caustically. "Should we request a sign for the table indicating who's married and who's single so all the women have the groundwork laid out for them?"

Riccardo and Matty seemed to find that amusing. Gabe didn't crack a smile.

"I'll go tell the maître d' we're five now." She grabbed Lilly's arm. "Come with?"

Lilly gave her a sideways look as she dragged her to the reception stand. "What is *wrong* with you? What is wrong with Gabe, for that matter?"

"I would have told you if you hadn't brought the whole De Campo clan along," Alex hissed. "This was supposed to be us catching up."

Her sister gave her one of those doe-eyed looks that would stop a serial killer in midstride. "Aww, Lex, I'm so sorry. I didn't realize." She curved her fingers around Alex's arm. "We can talk after, okay?"

Alex sighed. "It's fine. I just really needed to talk to you."

"After, I promise."

They were seated immediately once she threw the De Campo name around. Alex buried her attention in the menu, finding not one single item appealed to her. Why, oh, why hadn't Lilly just left it the two of them? She could at least be venting instead of having to pretend she didn't care.

"So tell us about the party." Lilly asked. "I heard Jared Stone was there with that pop singer."

"With Briana Bergen, yes. I sort of played with that match."

Gabe shot her an icy glare. "You messed with one of the matches?"

She made a face. "It was worth a hundred photos. And it was just the one."

"Do *not* do that in New York. It's unethical."

She spun her wineglass around and flashed him a recalcitrant look.

"Yes, well, the rest of the event looked great," Lilly babbled, never one to tolerate a silence well. "The wine is receiving rave reviews. Congratulations, Gabe."

"Grazie." His stiff expression stayed firmly in place.

"Somehow I have a hard time picturing you two as roommates." Lilly attempted a joke. "How did that go?"

The bread Alex was chewing lodged halfway down her throat. She swallowed hard and reached for her water.

"Alex is a moving target," Gabe said evenly. "There one minute, gone the next."

She ignored that. Looked up gratefully as the waiter came to take their order. Then excused herself to use the washroom once she was done. She took her time composing herself, applying lip gloss, anything to keep her away from *that table*. When she couldn't avoid it any longer, she picked up her purse and walked out the door. Gabe stood lounging against the wall.

"Oh, no," she murmured, squaring her shoulders. "We are not doing this again."

He caught her by the arm, eyes blazing, mouth set. "Why not, when it was so much fun the last time?"

She yanked her arm loose and stood toe to toe with him. "Why so angry? What have I done now?"

"Why did you run?"

She lifted her shoulders. "You know why. I sent you a full update."

"Someone here could have taken care of it. You ran, Lex. Why?"

"I didn't trust anyone but me to fix the problem." She pressed her hands to her hips and stared up at him. "It was one night, Gabe. We *screwed*. That's all."

A dangerous light went on in his eyes. She pulled in a breath as it slashed across her face. "I was *worried* about you. The way we left things— I wanted to know you were all right."

"I'm fine," she said harshly. "Don't try and paint me as the wounded woman-child, Gabe. I'm far from that."

"I'm surprised at you," he said stonily. "The woman who takes on the world but won't take on her feelings."

"With you?" she whipped at him. "Why would I want to do that? Can you honestly say I would ever fit into your life as more than a night of good sex?"

Hot color slashed his cheekbones. His silence sliced through her heart like a knife.

"Exactly," she murmured. "That's the way it goes."

A frown furrowed his brow. "What do you mean, 'that's the way it goes'?"

"It doesn't matter," she muttered. "What did you want me to do, Gabe? Be a girl and want to talk about it afterward? Tell you how hot you are in bed? Fall for that De Campo charm when I sure as hell know it isn't going any further?"

"Lex—"

He reached for her but she backed away and held up a hand. "I am asking you to drop this right now."

"Why?" he asked challengingly.

"Because you and I both know Saturday night wasn't as simple as we'd like to make it out to be. The fact that you're standing here glaring at me proves it." She pushed her hair out of her face and took a deep breath. "Feelings are involved. *My* feelings are involved. And if you don't want to hurt me, you'll stay away."

His gaze was hooded as it rested on her. She seized the opportunity, his brief moment of indecision, to turn on her heel and walk back toward the tables.

Alex and Gabe had been gone for close to fifteen minutes when Lilly blurted out the obvious. "Something's going on between them."

Her husband and Matty exchanged glances. "What?" she demanded.

Riccardo arched a brow at her. "They're sleeping together."

She set her glass down with a thud. "They are *not*. She would have told me."

Matty nodded. "A hundred percent they are."

"Oh my God." That's why her sister had been acting so weird. *And Gabe.*

"You think they're having sex in the bathroom?" Matty mused.

Riccardo tipped his glass at him. "Good call. Would be good for him, actually."

Lilly gave them a horrified look. "They are *not* having sex in the bathroom."

"They're doing something back there," Riccardo stated evenly.

Alex got back to the table a couple of minutes later, quieter than Lilly had ever seen her. Gabe came back shortly after that. Their clothes were intact. But the two of them were not. One look at their faces told her Riccardo was right.

That suspicion was confirmed when Alex pleaded exhaustion after dinner and suggested coffee the next day. They dropped her off at her apartment.

Lilly looked at Riccardo after the door shut behind her sister. "This is either going to be really good or really bad."

Riccardo inclined his head. "The only sure thing is it's going to be entertaining to watch."

Her cozy little apartment on the Upper East Side was not lending its usual Zen to her upended senses. Alex pulled the ultrasoft steel-blue throw over herself and pretended the matching pillow was a potent voodoo doll with Gabe's face on it. She gave it a mental stab with her eyes. Exactly when had she given him the power to bring her world crumbling down with one look from his arrogant, beautiful face?

She took a deep breath and exhaled slowly. *That* look, the one he'd had on his face when she'd put him on the spot about his intentions, took her back to that night in Jordan's apartment. To the resigned, relieved expression he'd worn. That said she was good enough for an affair, unacceptable for anything else.

She sank her fingers into the pillow and sent it flying across the room, landing against the closet with a vicious thud. Where was the rational, deliberate Alex who would not have done something so stupid as to sleep with Gabe when the outcome had always been so clearly destined to be *this*. The Alex who knew who she was and where she was going and that it didn't involve a man.

Her tirade was interrupted by the peal of the doorbell. *Gabe.* She didn't need to have aced her IQ test in school to know it was him. The tone came again, long, insistent. *Damn him.* She did not want to talk to him.

"Alex." He pounded on the door. "I know you're in there. Let me in."

He was going to wake up her neighbors! Lips pressed together, she slid off the sofa, stalked to the door and flung it open. Tall, dark, lean fighting male stood there, hand on the doorjamb. Ready for battle.

She scowled at him. "I told you to leave me alone."

"You have no idea what the hell you want or need." He shouldered his way in and shut the door.

She watched his shoes come off. "What *are* you doing?"

"You gave me two days to stew," he muttered, reaching for her. "What do you think I'm doing?"

She sucked in a breath as he yanked her against him, his hard body making full contact with hers. "You think I don't care about you, Lex? Jordan Lane just ripped off my wine. Sent me a bottle so similar to The Devil's Peak they could pass for each other in a blind taste test. And what am I doing? Instead of prepping for my meeting tomorrow, I'm chasing across the city after *you*."

Her mouth dropped open, shock momentarily muting the lust coursing through her.. "I don't understand…how could Jordan copy your wine?"

His mouth flattened. "He has a mole in the winery. Someone passing our secrets to him."

Her stomach dropped. "What about the Angel's Share?"

"It's been a top-secret team. It's fine."

Thank God. She brought her hands up to push against his chest, but all she found was impenetrable, rock-hard muscle. "Gabe—let me go. This is crazy."

He slid his hands into her hair and cradled the back of her head, his gaze branding her with a confusion that mirrored her own. "This is about more than sex," he admitted roughly. "I don't know what it is, but I know it's about more than me wanting you."

Her heart missed a beat. "Your silence said it all in the restaurant. Spare us both and let's not drag this out."

"*Dannazione,* you are prickly." His mouth twisted. "Spilling my guts in a public place is not my style."

She closed her mouth, mutinously staring back at him.

His gaze darkened. "I won't make promises I can't keep. And *Dio* knows this is new territory for me, Lex, but this thing between you and me? What you said back at the restaurant about your feelings being involved? So are mine. And I think it's time we faced them."

"What if I don't want to?" she retorted childishly. "What if I'm just fine with the status quo?"

His jaw hardened. "You want to be a coward for the rest of your life?"

"Maybe I do."

"No, you don't, angel," he countered softly. "You're just terrified."

She was. Because what would be left when this was all over?

She bit hard into her lip. "Let me go."

He shook his head. "I'm not letting you run."

"I want to," she admitted, heart pounding, every cell in her body screaming for escape. "I want to run as far and as fast as I can because I'm so scared I could scream."

"Then let me give you something better to scream about." He backed her up against the living room wall. Dipped his hands under her skirt and dragged it up. She wanted them on her so badly it hurt.

"Gabe—"

"No more talking." He found the curve of her neck with his lips as his hands sought the soft skin of her upper thighs and his knee nudged in between to spread them apart.

She sucked in a breath as he cupped the heated warmth of her. Found her damp and ready. Then he hooked his fingers in her panties and stripped them from her, the deliberateness of his movement making the breath whoosh from her lungs. "This isn't going to be long and drawn out, is it?"

He straightened, his leg sliding back in between hers. "No. It isn't."

Her knees felt weak, her limbs like molten chocolate

as he slid his hands up the backs of her thighs and urged them further apart. They threatened to give way when he dipped his fingers into the slick wetness of her and made a tortured sound at the back of his throat. "*Dio,* you are so turned on."

She arched into his hand as he established a slow, deep rhythm. "That happens when a hot man pounds his way into my apartment and pins me against a wall."

"You think I'm hot?" he murmured, pressing a kiss to the corner of her mouth.

"Insanely, compulsively hot," she admitted huskily. Her body clenched around his fingers as he pleasured her, remembering the heights he could take her to. He cursed and shifted his hands to her buttocks to take the weight of her, brace her against the wall and wrap her legs around him. She arched against him, dying to have his hard, delicious length inside of her again. "And this part," she murmured, pressing against him. "I'm a big fan of this part."

His gaze darkened as she worked her hands between them and went for the button of his pants. "Feel free," he muttered thickly as she yanked his zipper down, "to put it to good use."

She sought him out, wrapped her fingers around his silken length. Absorbed the pulsing, rock-hard readiness of him. Then she slid him against her slick flesh, smiling at the shudder that went through him. It made her feel powerful, sexy, that she could do this to him. He muttered a plea, some dark, erotic Italian word that sounded delicious. She obliged, took him inside of her. The sensation of his big body filling hers made her feel complete in a way she didn't want to examine.

"I think you can take over now," she murmured, desperate for his possession. He took more of her weight in his hands, bent his knees and stroked into her with a force that made her gasp. Hard and primal, this was nothing like the last time. It was just this side of rough, exciting in the extreme. The wall behind her did little to cushion her spine. His breathing was harsh and fast in her ear, his voice as he told her how much he loved being inside of her edged with desperation. And she loved it, loved that she'd been right. Gabe De Campo *could* lose control.

Right now, he was far, far gone.

She curved her fingers around his jaw and kissed him deep. Trusted him with her body. Begged him for more. Gasped as he shifted position, angling his hips so she felt him in a different place. *Everywhere.* Right where she needed him. "Come with me," he demanded raggedly against her mouth. And with one last hard drive inside of her, he made her body fall apart, splintering into a million pieces of delicious, mind-bending pleasure.

Her hoarse cry of release filled the air. He groaned and joined her, spilled into her with a hot wet heat that enveloped her, overwhelmed her. She buried her mouth in his sweaty, salty skin and clung to him. Held on as his biceps shook and her position against the wall became increasingly precarious.

"You drop me, you die."

His rough laughter filled the air. "Show me where."

She took that to mean her bedroom, where few men had been admitted and none had stayed. "That way," she pointed, tightening her legs around him as he carried her. He paused to let her flick on the light, blinked at the mayhem he saw there. "I'm not usually this messy," she murmured, mortified. "It's the traveling."

He set her down on the floor, keeping his hands around her waist as her legs adjusted to life back on the ground. Her gaze lifted to his. "You thinking of staying?"

His mouth quirked. "I wasn't thinking of driving all the way back across town, no."

And there it was. The offer she wasn't supposed to refuse. If a woman had ever denied Gabe De Campo her bed, she was pretty sure she had to have been deaf, dumb and blind. But for her, allowing a man to stay over was like bungee jumping off Victoria Falls.

"I have to be at a meeting at eight," she warned. "Up at six-thirty...I am a big-time hogger of covers and I don't apologize for it. And the only breakfast item I stock is cream for coffee."

His mouth curved. "I handled the cover issue just fine in Napa. Any other deal breakers?"

"You can't leave your car on the street."

"I parked a few side streets over."

She bit her lip. She had nothing left. "I *do* have a spare toothbrush."

"Grazie." He dropped a kiss on her nose and showered with a ruthless efficiency in her tiny bathroom that made two an impossibility. When she came out fifteen minutes later, a towel wrapped around her, he was sprawled across her rose-colored bedspread watching the news. She dragged in a breath. Told herself people did this all the time. But it felt as though she'd just conceded control of something she desperately wanted back.

He pulled his gaze away from the television screen. Narrowed it on her face. "Stop freaking out, Lex. We're getting some sleep, that's all."

She rubbed her hands against her temples. "It's just— I don't—"

"You've never had a guy sleep over before."

She shook her head.

"If I put down the remote, will that make it better?"

She smiled weakly. "Possibly."

He held out his hand instead. "Get over here."

She chewed on her lip. "We're keeping this between us right? You're not going to announce this to the other De Campos tomorrow?"

His jaw hardened. "I wasn't planning on it, no. It's no one's business but ours."

"Fine." *One day at a time, Lex.*

His gaze moved down over the towel. "You have that sexy silk thing around? Or are you coming like that?"

She dropped the towel and pulled on her nightie with a jerky, self-conscious movement that surely telegraphed her nerves. Her heart did a little pitter-patter as he reached out and hauled her against him. Sleeping with Gabe felt right in a way that terrified the hell out of her. She closed her eyes and forced herself to relax into his warm, hard heat.

When she finally fell into a deep, heavy slumber, it was full of a million dreams. Dreams she had no business having. Like wanting to be the kind of woman Gabe shared his life with.

CHAPTER TWELVE

AT SEVEN A.M. on a steamy day in Manhattan scheduled to climb into the nineties, Gabe stood on Alex's doorstep in his wrinkled suit, distracting himself with how sexily she did the tousled, sleepy look. She was one of those rare women who looked even better without makeup, a trait his brothers would say instantly put her into top-tier status.

He would have taken advantage of just how good she looked and allowed himself to be a half an hour late if it had been any morning but this one. Today he had to tell the other De Campos their much-anticipated big bet was dead and the way forward was the Angel's Share.

Biggest day of his life.

He took the thermos of coffee Alex handed him. She lifted her fingers and brushed the hair out of his face. "You've got this," she murmured. "You know that."

He nodded. It touched something inside of him, the strength of this woman. He'd known it for a long time, but as he climbed further and further inside her head and saw the vulnerable side of her—the side that the improper possession of a remote control could bring tumbling down—he found he wanted her even more. Wanted to protect her.

"I'll let you know what happens." He leaned down and brushed his mouth over hers in a kiss meant to get him out the door. Her soft, eager response sent a shaft of desire through him. *Dio,* this woman got to him. "That was a goodbye kiss, not a hello kiss," he reprimanded huskily, pulling away with effort.

"So sorry," she returned. "I'm not so good at telling the difference."

"*Sì*. You are." He headed out into the steamy morning, a wry smile curving his mouth. Went home, changed and made it into the office before the others arrived. The family, still the controlling force of De Campo, made a habit of meeting themselves before the main board meeting to discuss key matters of interest. He settled in the boardroom and flicked through his presentation slides. They were burned into his brain.

He had clashed with Antonio many times over the years, but never before had he believed in his vision as strongly as he did at this moment.

Riccardo walked into the conference room, followed by Matty and Antonio. His elder brother's gaze swept over him. "Tried to call you last night. You seemed to be occupied."

"I was sleeping," he returned evenly. "The jet lag kills me every time."

His brother let it go. Antonio sat down and cut straight to the chase. "Word is Jordan Lane's Black Cellar Select *is* The Devil's Peak."

His tie suddenly felt too tight. He tugged at it, a gesture his titan of a father's hawk eyes did not miss. "He has a mole in our organization feeding him information."

"Tell me you know who it is," Riccardo said tightly.

His stomach clenched. "I'm working on it."

Antonio's dark eyes flashed. "Eight years down the drain and all you have to say is you're working on it?"

"What would you have me say?" Gabe's voice vibrated with emotion. "The man is a criminal. I have a P.I. on it. We'll find the person. Meanwhile," he said, swallowing hard, "I have a backup plan."

Riccardo leaned forward and rested his forearms on the table. "Let's hear it."

"The Devil's Peak is still a brilliant wine. It's going to do well for us regardless of Black Cellar Select. I say we leave it in the fall ad campaign, but launch and lead with the Angel's Share instead."

Riccardo gave him a wary look. "The Malbec you've been working on?"

"Yes." He got to his feet and walked over to the sideboard. "This," he said, setting the bottle on the conference table, "is the wine that will make De Campo's Napa vintages famous in this country."

Antonio's face was so red he looked as though he was going to blow a fuse. "A *Malbec?*" his father rasped. "You think a Malbec is going to be our star De Campo wine?"

Gabe rolled his shoulders back and stayed focused. "It was always the plan to have The Devil's Peak lay the groundwork first, then have the Angel's Share put us over the top." He woke up his laptop screen and projected his presentation onto the wall. "Napa winemakers have been exploring Malbecs for the last few years—some more than others. They're working beautifully with the California soil. I think they're the future."

He went through the stats on the nascent market for the varietal, how it had flourished in other geographies. "See how exponentially popular it's been in Argentina and Australia."

"It's not a real grape," Antonio derided. "You want me to bet the future of our Napa vineyard on *that?*"

Gabe held his patience with effort. "If we are to lead, we need to take a risk that will break us out of the pack. The Devil's Peak is no longer that wine. But the Angel's Share is. Pedro thinks it will score a ninety-seven."

Matty rubbed his hand over his chin. "I like Malbecs.

Lots of buzz around them. But what about Syrah? Some say they're the next to rule in California."

Gabe nodded. "They're coming. But I would bet on the Malbecs."

Riccardo gave him a long look. "Pedro thinks it's ready?"

He nodded.

"Could Lane have a line on this one, too? How far do you think he's penetrated us?"

"Only Pedro, Donovan and myself have been involved with the Angel's Share. He can't know about it."

Antonio shot to his feet. "We are not making our flag-ship wine a—a second-class wine," he sputtered. "You are out of your mind, Gabriele."

Riccardo pointed at the bottle. "I'd like to taste it."

"So would I," said Matty.

He felt hope take flight in his chest. He picked up three glasses from the sideboard and poured for them all. Held his breath as they tasted. Riccardo's expression was guarded. Matty's open and curious. Antonio's outraged.

Riccardo set his glass down first. Turned to Antonio in deference to the old man.

His father pushed his glass away with a disdainful look. "I don't like it."

Gabe froze. A white-hot anger sparked inside of him. "What about it don't you like?"

The old man shrugged. "It doesn't speak to me."

"It doesn't speak to you?" Gabe stalked over and pushed the glass toward his father. "This is one of the most brilliant wines we've ever created. Tell me," he yelled, "what you don't like about it."

Antonio swiped the glass away. "This wine is not being made our marquee wine. We'll use the Devil's Peak instead."

"This is *not* old-world Italy." The pressure in Gabe's

head built to an explosive level. "We need new wines that are going to resonate with the North American market and *this* grape, *this* wine is going to be huge."

His father stood up and faced him. "Do not disrespect me, Gabriele," he boomed.

"*Me* disrespect you?" Gabe looked at him in disbelief. "You've done nothing but disrespect me ever since I joined this company. You passed me over when you chose Riccardo without even giving me a fighting chance and you've never given me credit for what I've done in Napa. So *do not* speak of respect to me."

His father's face went deathly white. "*È ingrato—*"

"*Basta.*" Riccardo stepped between them. "I think the Malbec is magnificent. It is Gabe's job to direct the wine operations of this company, and if he believes this is the direction we should follow, we will."

Antonio gave his eldest son a scorchingly furious look. "*I* am the head of this family."

"And *I* run De Campo," Riccardo said evenly. "Try and ease gracefully into your silver years, Antonio. You've earned them."

His father stood there, visibly shaking, then spun on his heel and left. Gabe's heart thundered in his ears. He paced to the window and braced his hands on the sill. And felt the world right itself. Finally. In that moment, Riccardo had annihilated any distance there had been between them because of Antonio's choice.

He turned to his elder brother. "*Grazie,*" he said quietly.

Riccardo nodded. "It was the right thing to do."

Matty refilled his glass and tasted again. He had an innate sense of wine like Gabe did, his knowledge of the market exhaustive as De Campo's head of international sales and marketing.

"Be honest," Gabe said harshly. "You, I trust."

Matty put the glass down and smiled his devil-may-care rake's smile. "I may not have tasted a better wine in my life."

Alex met Lilly at their favorite coffee shop on Broadway, both of them going for java even though it was hot enough to fry an egg on the pavement. Gabe's meeting was hot on her mind, and she found herself flicking regular glances at her watch while trying to follow Lilly's convoluted recap of a funny conversation she'd had with Marco last night.

Lilly finished, took a sip of her latte and gave Alex's watch a pointed look. "That's at least the fifth time you've checked it. Event stuff?"

She nodded. "Whatever happens in the De Campo meeting will have a big impact on our event."

Lilly put down her coffee. "You're sleeping with Gabe."

She felt the color drain from her face. "Yes."

Her sister sat back in her chair and folded her hands in front of her. "So what was last night all about, then? You two looked like you wanted to kill each other."

"We've worked it out."

"Does he know you're in love with him?"

Alex recoiled. "I am *not* in love with Gabe De Campo."

"Oh, come on," Lilly muttered, making a face at her. "You may not wear your emotions on your sleeve like I do, Lex, more like a foot under, but any idiot could see it. You have this glow on your face and despite the scowl, there's just something about you this morning."

"I do not fall in love with men," she reminded her sister. "Jordan was enough to sour me forever."

"That was five years ago." Lilly lifted her chin at a determined angle. "Honestly, Lex, I never thought I'd say this to you, but I know you'd say it to me, so I will. You need to stop using Jordan as an excuse. What he did to you was awful and damaging and I can see why you don't trust easily. But Gabe is not Jordan."

"No, he isn't," Alex agreed. "Gabe has dozens of women chomping at the bit to snare him. What would your choice be if you were him? One with issues or a society wife?"

"Aha." Lilly pointed a finger at her. "You're talking wife."

"Oh, come on." Alex took a sip of her bitter Kenyan brew. "You know I'm right."

Lilly frowned. "Gabe doesn't need doors opened for him. He's a De Campo."

"He doesn't need a scandal, either. I dated Damon Harding, Lilly. I had a relationship with the head of a biker gang, then an affair with a married man. How is that De Campo material?"

"You didn't know he was married. You were the victim there, Lex. But I'd really prefer you not be in victim mode right now." Lilly crossed her arms over her chest. "Does Gabe know about Damon and Jordan?"

"He knows about Damon."

"So tell him about Jordan. Get it over with. I think you'll find Gabe is a reasonable man."

Alex pushed her mug away. "Hell, Lilly, I'm not what he's looking for. You *know* the type of woman Gabe's looking for, and it's not me."

"I know he couldn't take his eyes off you last night even though he was mad as hell," her sister said softly. "I think you should ask *him* what he's looking for."

She set her mouth in an obstinate gesture. Sure, Gabe had said he cared about her last night. That what he felt was more than wanting. But how far could that go? How far could she let *this* go without getting her heart broken? And should she ask the question to get a level set?

Did she dare?

"So?" Lilly waved a hand at her. "You going to?"

"I'm thinking about it."

"You *should* tell him about Jordan, Lex. Darya Theriault walked out on Gabe to marry a senior partner at her law firm she was having an affair with. He needs to hear it from you."

A strange, buzzing sound filled her ears. "*That's* why he and Darya broke up?"

Lilly nodded. "Apparently Darya had second thoughts a couple of years ago and called Gabe up, but he didn't want any part of her."

Her blood ran cold, a chilled decisiveness stealing over her. Gabe's ex-lover had cheated on him and she was supposed to tell him about Jordan? Not happening. Never happening.

Lilly leaned over and squeezed her arm. "If you have a guy like Gabe De Campo in the palm of your hand, Lex, you don't wonder why. You don't question yourself and you don't act like Miss I Can Do It All Myself. You grab hold of him and secure him before someone else does."

Okay, maybe that part she agreed with.

A brutally long fourteen-hour workday later, Alex sat on the leather sofa in Gabe's very beautiful, very masculine living room in his very expensive penthouse trying to work up the nerve to ask *that* question Lilly had inserted in her head. She was also trying to ignore the lure of his steam shower long enough to get the question out. She'd forced a laugh when Gabe had showed it to her, intent gleaming in his eyes. "We have to work," she'd said, poking him in the chest. "Later."

They'd spent the next three hours revamping the event plan to include the Angel's Share, written some messaging for it and consumed an entire pepperoni pizza. "So what are you going to say when the press asks you how much

Antonio had to do with the Angel's Share?" she tested him, setting down her clipboard.

"His presence is felt everywhere and we are a great blend of the old and the new." Gabe scowled at the politically correct answer. "We are done now, *sì?*" he asked, pulling her into his lap. "I would like it to be *later.*"

She smiled, maybe less brightly than she normally would have. "We are. That was perfect. You know I'm only doing this for your own good."

"And I am listening," he murmured, setting his lips to her temple. "See? I can learn."

She reached for her glass of wine with a jerky movement. He lifted a brow. "You never talk about your mother," she said. "Where was she when Antonio was acting the overbearing patriarch?"

"Conspicuously absent." He started unbuttoning her shirt and Alex's body hummed to life. "My parents' marriage was a business merger of two influential families. My mother did her part and bore us, three boys, exactly what my father wanted, then left us most of the time to do her charity work, which is the legacy of the Lombardi women."

"So neither of us had great examples of marriages to work with."

He undid the last button of her shirt. "Some would say my parents are very happy. They're both doing their own thing."

"What do you think?"

He slid his fingers under her jaw. "I'm wondering where this conversation is going."

Her stomach twisted. Was that a warning not to get serious on him? She lifted her shoulders. "I'm curious, that's all."

He drew his brows together. "I don't know. I think relationships are complex."

"Are you still in love with Darya?"

His gaze narrowed. "No, I am not still in love with Darya. I haven't been since she walked out on me. But I *like* that you are jealous."

"She's still in love with you," she murmured. "I saw her face at the party."

"Her problem." He brushed his thumb over her lace-covered nipple, sending liquid heat to her core. "What do you really want to ask me, Lex?"

She swallowed hard. "I am not Darya Theriault, Gabe. And I am definitely not Samantha Parker. I'm a dirt-poor girl from Iowa who managed to make something of herself."

"Who I have a great deal of respect for."

That wasn't enough. "I saw the look on your face that night in the restaurant, Gabe. You say I caught you off guard, but you have to admit, you have *never, ever* considered me long-term material. You avoided me *because* of it."

His eyes flickered with an emotion she couldn't identify. "That's because I didn't know you."

"You know me now. I get that you can't make promises you can't keep and I respect that. But I have enough skeletons in my past to sink a ship. Bad things that could hurt you."

He shook his head slowly. "Your past isn't so bad, Lex. So you were a rebellious teenager. Stop trying to push me away before I can invest anything in you."

She should tell him. She knew she should.

He reached around and unhooked her bra. Stripped it from her and tossed it to the floor. "Baby steps," he murmured, locking his gaze with hers. "That's all I'm asking, Lex. Just small little steps."

Her desire to trust him fully warred with her desire never to expose her biggest shame. Her blood pounded in her veins, felt as though it didn't have enough room to move. *Goddamn Jordan Lane.* How was she supposed to open up, knowing Gabe's ability to destroy her was far more powerful than Jordan's had ever been?

How dare he take away her ability to dream?

She felt as though she was drowning with no way to surface. Caught in a riptide of wanting to believe that anything was possible. Furious she couldn't make the jump. Not once in her life had she ever let herself want anything as much as she wanted what was in front of her right now. Not with Jordan. Not ever.

She did *not* want to lose Gabe.

Burying her rational mind in a hope that somehow this could work, she kissed him. Trusted him with her heart. And prayed he wouldn't break it like every other man in her life had.

She undid the buttons of his shirt with unsteady hands. Yanked it free from his pants and went for his belt. "Alex," he muttered hoarsely, as if to slow her down, but she shook him off, freed him from his jeans and sank down in front of him. She wanted him as blinded as she was. As out of control. Then there was only the sound of his labored breathing, the feel of his velvet hardness beneath her fingers, his thighs shaking under her, his guttural groan of approval as she sent him over the edge and took back the power she needed.

When a calm stillness had settled over the room, he scooped her up off the floor and carried her to the big shower. If he noticed she was trembling under his hands, coming apart at the seams, he didn't say anything. He stripped her of her clothes, picked her up and sat down with her on the bench under the spray. She felt exposed, as mentally naked as she was physically as he washed her. When he was done, he kept her there until the connection between them and the heat of the water calmed her, and when she was quiet in his arms he wrapped her legs around him and took her with a slow, soulful possession that healed a part of her she hadn't even known was broken.

In that moment, her face buried in his shoulder, she knew she was deeply, irrevocably in love with Gabe De Campo.

CHAPTER THIRTEEN

FLASHBULBS BOUNCED OFF the step-and-repeat banner at Zambia, De Campo's hot new SoHo wine bar, as celebrity after celebrity arrived on a still-scorching summer night predicted to break heat records in the city. Alex had outdoor coolers blowing, but not even the heat could dampen the guests' enthusiasm for De Campo's big night. The buzz from Napa had trickled east and the inside scoop said the Devil's Peak launch was not to be missed.

Lilly had pulled in some of her big-name athletes, Riccardo had tapped the racing crowd and, as luck would have it, there was an A-list Hollywood couple filming in town. Alex watched them work the cameras in front of the big De Campo logos and smiled to herself. The rumors that Davina Cole and David Murray's on-screen romance was only half as tempestuous as their offscreen one looked to be true. Sparks were flying and high drama was in the air.

Matty helped Davina off the raised platform while David played to the cameras. Alex frowned. Did they know each other? How could she have missed that? Or maybe they didn't and Matty was just being his usual flirtatious self. If there was a man in this world who could charm a Hollywood diva off a dais, date or no date, it was Matty.

She made a note of it as a future problem and disappeared inside. It would be at least an hour before *that* exploded and with most of the guests arrived, it was time to do the welcome toast.

Zambia was a modern dark-wood-and-exposed-brick masterpiece inside, designed by one of the city's top architects. Thousands of bottles of wine lined the walls, highlighted by a massive glass jug-and-rope chandelier that cast a muted glow across the room. The perfect backdrop for the rich, beautiful vintages they were unveiling tonight.

She paused on the edge of the packed room. She liked to think the excessively alive, vibrant energy pulsing through her veins was due to the fantastic evening it was shaping up to be, but she was fairly certain it had more to do with the tall, dark hunk in a tux greeting guests near the entrance. Being with Gabe had added a whole new set of sensory perceptions to her toolbox. Everything felt richer, more layered when she was with him. It wasn't just that he made a mean espresso in the morning; it was that it *tasted* better when she drank it with him.

Which she'd been doing a lot lately, she conceded. As in the last three mornings straight. And if that set off a panicky feeling that she had no idea what she was doing, that was to be expected. This was a whole new state of being she was experiencing—this complex set of stimuli Gabe engendered in her. One she was doing her best to master.

If she was honest—she never wanted it to end.

He must have felt her stare, because he looked up from his conversation and returned it. Electricity ratcheted through her as though she'd stuck her finger in a socket. Innate, all consuming, their connection had never been in question. But now it was more the kind of feel-it-down-to-your-toes, inescapable plunge that at times felt too intense to handle. She'd let him break her down. She had no choice but to go along for the ride.

Dipping her head, she wound her way through the

crowd toward him. He ditched his conversation as she approached.

"You need to package that up and put it away for later," he murmured, trailing his gaze over her.

"I'm not sure what you mean," she came back innocently. "Just enjoying the scenery."

"I like how you enjoyed it this morning."

His smooth-as-silk, lightly accented words slid over her like a caress. "You can like it again tonight," she purred. "*If* I'm still standing."

"You most definitely don't need to be standing, *cara.*"

An allover body flush crept across her skin. She turned to him and lifted a brow. "I don't do blushing, Gabriele. *You* need to package that up and keep it for later."

His eyes glinted at her use of his full name, which she used when she wanted to make a point. "I'm flying back to San Francisco tomorrow."

Her hand froze halfway to her face. She'd known this was coming. Knew she lived in New York and he lived in Napa and he had two wines to get out the door. So why did she feel so distinctly off balance? "You changed your flight?"

"The ad agency wants to run some concepts by me tomorrow." His gaze settled on her face with a single-minded intensity. "Come with me. Hang out by the pool. You deserve a break after all this."

His offer soothed the tiny fissure he'd opened up inside of her, but she shook her head because it was impossible. "I've been on the West Coast for weeks. I have a million things to wrap up from the event and three new business proposals sitting on my desk."

"Emily can handle the event stuff. Bring the proposals with you."

She bristled at his imperious tone. "We live on opposite coasts, Gabe. We're going to have to negotiate."

His eyes turned a stormy, ready-for-battle sea-green. "I'm all for negotiating, angel. How about one a.m., my place, in my—"

"Gabe." She slid a wary glance around them. "We are so not talking about this now. Can you round up Riccardo and Antonio? It's time to do the toast."

He gave her a look that said they would definitely pick this conversation up later and turned to find them.

"Oh," she added. "Tell Matty to keep his hands off Davina Cole, will you?"

He turned around. "He had them *on* her?"

"Yes. Tell him to take them off. There's enough sparks flying without adding him into the fray."

Lilly joined her by the bar as the De Campos made their opening remarks. "Is there ever a non-intense moment between you two?" she murmured.

Alex surveyed the man who was systematically destroying her defenses one by one and pursed her lips. "Few and far between. What's up with Matty, by the way? He's distinctly *not* Matty."

Lilly shook her head. "Nobody knows. It's the big mystery. He won't talk about it."

"It's a woman," Alex concluded. Preferably the gymnast or some other female who was not Davina Cole.

She focused on Antonio, always a loose cannon at the best of times, as he began his speech. Surprisingly, he seemed to be on his best behavior, lavishing praise on Gabe and the Napa operations. She studied him, trying to figure out whether he'd had a change of heart or was just acting for the crowd, but he appeared genuine. Her gaze flicked to Gabe. He looked as wary as she was. But the crowd was loving Antonio's theatrics, eating it up. He might be a cranky old bastard, she acknowledged, but he could weave a spell when he wanted to.

Gabe spoke, and the party shifted into full swing. The city's most influential embraced their chemistry matches with a good-natured enthusiasm that eased the tension in her shoulders, freeing Alex up to man a jam-packed schedule of media and blogger interviews with all three De Campo men. By the time she'd done the bulk of them, she knew the Angel's Share was a hit. The wine columnists and bloggers tasted it in their exclusive cellar appointments, scratched their heads, tasted it again and almost unanimously declared it spectacular. Where it fit into the current market, they couldn't say. But they had a smile on their face as they delivered the punch line.

It occurred to Alex as she led her second-to-last interview up the cellar stairs that maybe she *could* work from Napa this week. Yes, she had three new business proposals on her desk, but one was from Jordan, which she didn't intend to accept, despite its multimillion-dollar value, and the other two were relatively straightforward. Ones she could do in her sleep. Which led to the thought of how feasible it would be to work bicoastal on a regular basis. Deciding *that* was descending into crazy talk, she snuffed it out of her head and shook the blogger's hand.

"Ready for my last one," she told Emily. "Please say it's my last one."

"It's your last one. Marc Levine. Wine importer. Does a blog on the side. Attracts a hundred thousand visitors a month."

"Impressive," Alex murmured. "Who does he want?"

"Gabe."

The blogger sounded familiar. Emily pointed him out—a tall, hook-nosed, blond-haired man standing at the far bar with a striking redheaded companion. She was far more attractive than him and younger, and for this reason Alex's gaze lingered a bit longer than usual. She was lovely, dis— The thought jammed in her head. *She was*

Cassandra Lane—Jordan's ex-wife. The woman who had arrived home from France to find Alex and her husband in bed together.

How had she not remembered Cassandra was married to a wine guy?

She turned her back on the couple, her breath coming in short, staccato bursts, but not before the redheaded woman's eyes flashed with a recognition Alex had dearly hoped to avoid. *Dammit.*

"Take this one," she muttered to Emily, who gave her a confused look, but trotted off toward the couple. Alex walked straight into the kitchen and leaned against a wall, her knees trembling as she ignored the curious looks of the catering staff. Five years had passed since that night Cassandra had walked in on her and Jordan, but it felt like five minutes.

I didn't know, she wanted to go out there and cry to Cassandra Lane. *I never knew.* But what good would it do now?

She emerged from the kitchen ten minutes later, as composed as she could make herself and intent on avoiding Cassandra at all costs. She was on her way to get another case of wine from the cellar when the redhead stepped away from the wall and into her path.

"Alex."

The other woman wore a perfectly composed look, but she could sense the raw emotion pulsing beneath her alabaster skin. Her gaze moved over Alex as though she were studying a piece of art. "He always said you were nothing, but I have a feeling you were way more than that. I think he was in love with you."

Alex felt the ground give way beneath her feet. The room whirled around her in a film strip of dark shadows that threatened to engulf her and never let her go. *She could not go back there. She could never go back there.*

Shrieking laughter jerked her head back. A woman to the left of them had had too much to drink. "Jordan told me you were divorced," she said harshly. "I am so sorry."

"How could you not know?" the other woman demanded. "How could you not know the man had a whole other life going on?"

"You were in France. Jordan and I both worked twenty-four-seven. It was—" she waved her hand in the air "—all over the place."

"It was in our *apartment*," Cassandra hissed. "Nothing clued you in? Not the fact he didn't introduce you to his friends? To his children? That he didn't bring you to the house in Long Island?"

The questions slammed into her, one after another, vicious blows to the solar plexus. It was the one thing she couldn't get past. How had she not seen *those* signs? How, in six months, had she never experienced any of that? She pulled in a breath, but it was hard to draw in air. Maybe she *hadn't* wanted to know. Maybe she'd been so happy to be loved she'd disregarded anything that didn't fit.

"I should go," she murmured. "Nothing good is going to come of this."

"You're damn right," the other woman broke out, her voice rising. "I hope you were worth the thirty-million-dollar divorce settlement, Alex. I really do."

"I'm sure I wasn't." She swung around and started through the crowd. The feeling that the past was chasing her chilled her skin, made her shoulder her way through the tightly packed collection of bodies at a half run. But she would never be able to run fast enough to escape the past. Her haunted gaze found Marc Levine and Gabe in front of her, returning from their interview. The fact that Cassandra could convince Marc to trash Gabe's wine sent a wave of panic through her. If someone had created her worst nightmare, this would have been it.

"Grazie," Gabe murmured to Marc, his gaze on Alex's face. "Let me know if there's anything else we can get you."

They shook hands. The other man strode off into the crowd. Gabe moved to her side. "What's wrong?"

"I need to talk to you." Before she could back out of it, before she could convince herself she could bury it yet again. "In private."

His gaze narrowed. "The cellar?"

She nodded. The cooler temperatures of the carved mahogany cellar made Alex's already-frozen limbs tremble. Gabe stood, feet spread apart in front of her, arms crossed over his chest, a wary look on his face. "If this is about our conversation from earlier, I—"

"It's not." The stilted nature of her response sharpened his gaze. She pressed her palms against her thighs and stared down at them. Where to start? How to make him understand? "Jordan Lane was my client—you know that. Cassandra Levine, the wife of the blogger you just met, is his former wife."

He lifted a brow. "I didn't know that."

She took a deep breath. "I was twenty-two when we took Jordan's business on, extremely junior. He was very hands-on, wanted to be involved on all levels. His business was worth a small fortune to our firm, so when he asked for me to work on his account, they said yes even though I was far too inexperienced."

"He wanted you," Gabe said flatly.

She wrapped her arms around herself. How clear it was looking at it from the outside. "Yes."

"I really don't like where this is going, Lex." The banked hostility she saw rise in his eyes made her insides tighten. She lifted a shaky hand and pushed her hair out of her eyes. "He was thirteen years my senior. Brilliant. We started spending a ton of time together working, and one night he asked me to meet him in his hotel suite." She sank her teeth into her bottom lip. "We—"

"Tell me you didn't sleep with him."

She cringed. "I did."

"While he was married?"

"I didn't know," she said forcefully. "He'd told me he was divorced. That his ex-wife was off working in France."

"Maledizione, Alex." He threw up his hands. "You know my history on this."

"I know." She took a step toward him. "That's why I'm telling you. This wasn't anything like it was with Darya, Gabe, I didn't *know* he was married."

"His wife being upstairs didn't spur this little episode of honesty?"

She steeled herself against the panic that climbed her throat. "I wanted to tell you. I did. But when Lilly told me what Darya did, I didn't think you'd understand."

"I don't understand." His big body radiated fury. "All this week when I've been struggling with how to deal with Lane, you were keeping this from me?"

She pressed her hands to her temples. "I was scared."

"You should have told me," he bellowed, making her heart pound. "He stole my wine, Alex. He's trying to destroy me. How do I know you aren't a part of this? *You* came after me. *You* wanted this job."

Her pounding heart stopped in midbeat. "You don't mean that."

He clenched his hands by his sides, nostrils flaring. "All I asked from you was honesty, Lex. The rest of your baggage I could deal with. But you couldn't even give me that."

"You don't understand." She begged him with her eyes to listen. "I almost lost my job over this. I was part of a thirty-million-dollar divorce settlement. My agency told me to keep my mouth shut and never speak a word of it."

"You don't work for them *now.*"

"Reputation is still everything in my business." Frustration and despair edged her voice. "No one would hire me if I was associated with a scandal like that. My business wouldn't survive. Dammit, Gabe, I was a stupid young girl who made a big mistake. I should never have gotten involved with a client, regardless of whether or not he was a married man."

His jaw tightened. "Yet here you are again."

Her mouth went dry. "You *know* this is different."

"How do I know anything? You've been lying to me all along."

"I have *not* been lying to you."

"That's right. You are an expert at the sin of omission." He spun away and paced to the other side of the cellar, his broad shoulders ramrod straight. "Is there anything else you haven't told me? Criminal records? Affairs with high-ranking politicians?"

Her breath caught in her throat. "You did *not* just say that."

Silence stretched, chilling in its stillness. His voice, when it came, was dangerously quiet. "We were supposed to be a team, Lex. I trusted you with my livelihood. With the most important moment of my career."

"You did," she agreed fiercely. "And I've given you everything. *Everything.* I haven't slept in a month to make this night a success for you."

"I'm surprised he didn't keep you instead." He turned around, his rich voice so devoid of emotion, the look on his face so shuttered, she knew right then and there they were done. "You're far more beautiful than his wife."

Her heart splintered into a million pieces. "I didn't *want* him. Dammit, Gabe, I was just as much the injured party as Jordan's wife. I was in love with him. I thought I had a *future* with him. When I found out he'd lied, I hated him for it. *I* had been living a lie."

His gaze hardened. "Blame isn't the issue here. The issue is you didn't tell me."

She nodded. "I should have. I absolutely should have. But please don't judge me based on emotion. Think about what you're doing."

He walked back to her, staring down at her, proud and fierce, everything she'd ever wanted. "I wanted to be there for you, Lex. I wanted to be the one to make you believe. I wanted to make *myself* believe that what we had was the real thing. But you were never going to let me in, were you?"

"I was," she whispered. "I was letting you in."

"Too little, too late," he gritted. "My appetite for taking on your issues has passed."

"Gabe—"

He held up a hand. "I need to get back upstairs."

She could have called him back. Could have tried to say more to make him understand. But the look on his face stopped her—the finality of it. The judgment. Whatever she said, it wasn't going to be enough.

The party was still in full swing when she went upstairs, the lights and loud voices stinging her senses. She put on the mask she wore so well when it was time to survive—to just get through it. She'd done it so many times it felt like putting herself on automatic pilot.

Lilly looked exhausted, so she sent her and Riccardo home. It was just about time to do the big reveal, so she prepped the staff and went in search of the fireworks crew. Then she found Gabe, refused to let his icy demeanor tear her apart and coordinated the toast on the outdoor patio.

Fireworks shot up into the air. In Napa, they had been a brilliant cascade of light against a black country sky. Tonight they were muted, overwhelmed by the lights of Manhattan. Just one more addition to a landscape already overloaded with flash. The excitement in the air grew.

The reception for the wines seemed universally positive. It made her skin hurt to hear it. She left Gabe in a throng of people waiting to congratulate him and went inside, a good proportion of the crowd still indoors. She noticed the commotion near the bar immediately.

Emily appeared by her side. *"They are going at it."*

"Who?"

"Davina and David."

Great. It had taken them longer than she'd thought. Setting her jaw, she elbowed through the crowd and took stock of the situation. David looked drunk and furious. Davina, triumphant. Matty, as she'd suspected, was in the thick of it.

"What is wrong with you," she hissed, taking him by the sleeve. He gave her an innocent Matty broad-shouldered shrug.

She pointed to the patio. "Go. Whatever this is, it is not your night to take Davina to bed."

The youngest De Campo unfolded himself from the bar, gave Davina one last look and left. Alex leaned down and gave David her most reasonable smile. "Might not want the paparazzi snapping you like this, my friend. How about we get your car?"

David started to issue a drunken protest. The look on her face must have stopped him. *Not tonight.* She dumped him in his car, minus his girlfriend. Gabe left with Matty an hour later. Minus her.

She told herself that was not her heart breaking. That that wasn't her future walking out the door. Sure, she had made a massive mistake not telling Gabe about Jordan. But she'd made a bigger one fooling herself that this one might be different.

CHAPTER FOURTEEN

"Um, Alex? You've been pacing for a half hour."

Emily flashed her a tentative smile from the doorway of her office. "Anything I can do?"

Alex stopped in front of her desk and gestured toward the coffee cup on it. "Could you tell the street vendor his coffee *sucks?*"

Her junior executive gave her an uncertain look. "You want me to get you another?"

A guilty flash went through her along with an extended growl from her stomach. Someday God was going to punish her for her smart mouth. "Sugar," she muttered. "I need sugar. Whatever empty-calorie carb you can find that will put me in a diabetic haze, I'm there."

"Got it." Emily wisely backed out while the going was good. Alex eased her hip onto her desk and breathed. Big, full breaths like Lilly's yoga instructor had counseled, only that wasn't helping either. Nothing was helping. She was apparently going through the five stages of grief her disturbingly sensible, designer shoe-loving therapist had counseled her about. Stage one—denial—she had a firm grasp on that, it seemed. She'd knocked off two of the three new business proposals this week, sent them off and begun a punishing army-boot-camp regime at six every weekday morning where the instructor did an excellent impression of the sadistic drill sergeants from the movies. And now she couldn't move. *Even better.*

Oh, and let's not forget the unrehearsed conversation with her father this morning to give him an earful about her childhood. Needless to say, that hadn't gone overly well. Perhaps par for the course when it had started, "Why weren't you ever there for me?" and ended with her father's bewildered acknowledgement that yes, he shouldn't have left her in jail overnight.

The only thing that *would* help, it seemed, was a bone-meltingly good kiss from a sexy Italian who knew his way around a woman. That was, if she could get over stage two of the grieving process—the anger part—which seemed to be burning her up faster than an oxygen-aided fire in a decrepit old building.

She braced her hand on the desk and took another of those big breaths before she had a coronary. Had what they'd shared meant *nothing?*

It wasn't fair. She picked up her stress ball and threw it across the room. The way Gabe had totally dismissed all the progress she'd made. How much she *had* trusted him. The fact she'd told him things she'd never told anyone else. Because of one bad decision he'd written her off? It had been a big one, she conceded. But you didn't just jump on a bike and fly down a hill, did you? You put the training wheels on and hoped for the best.

Clearly, it had not been enough. The De Campo–branded envelope sitting on her desk with the massive check in it said that loud and clear. Full payment for the events had arrived this morning, early and unexpected, even though she hadn't had a chance to round up all the supplier invoices and costs yet. But it had been more than enough. As if Gabe had wanted to sever all ties.

Evidently, that kiss wasn't coming any time soon. As in ever.

She stood up and shoved the check in a drawer so she wouldn't have to see it. But her throat and chest still ached as if it was staring her in the face. She missed him. She missed his damn espressos and she missed having his arms around her making her feel as though no matter what happened, she had an anchor. Someone who was willing to take a chance on her. Someone who made this whole crazy world make sense.

But it wasn't going to happen. She got up with a jerky movement and walked to the windows, staring down at the hundreds of worker bees scurrying back and forth to their offices on the bright summer day. There had been radio silence from Gabe. Not a phone call, not an email. If he'd walked into her office and announced in that smooth, rich tone of his they were over, he couldn't have done it more effectively.

When Jordan had sent her the flowers with the "we're done" note after six months together, she hadn't eaten for a week. This time, with Gabe, she wasn't sure she ever wanted to eat again. At the risk of using a corny phrase she'd said she never would, there wasn't a question in her mind that he was the love of her life.

She had broken every rule for him. She would have broken more if he'd let her.

And still it hadn't been enough.

So now she had to move on. Mop herself up with big-girl acceptance and let go of the past. Step five. And frankly, she couldn't stand here doing nothing anymore. It was making her crazy.

Three phone calls and a half an hour later, she stepped out of her building into the sunshine. She was about to flag a cab when she turned around, walked back to the street vendor she had idle chitchat with every morning and lifted her chin. "Your coffee sucks. Every morning I buy your coffee and it sucks."

He gave her a dumbfounded look. "Buy the coffee or don't buy the coffee, lady. That's what I serve."

She nodded. "I'm buying an espresso machine. I just thought you deserved my honest opinion."

She stalked to the curb, flagged a cab and called Lilly from it. "I heard about your phone call home," her sister said dryly. "Too much caffeine this morning?"

"Not enough." Alex grimaced. "I'm in a cab to the airport. In case the plane goes down and they're identifying bodies, thought you should know. Back tomorrow."

"You said you didn't have to travel for a while."

"Jordan Lane is holding credentials presentations this week."

"Alex. Gabe will lose his you-know-what if you take that job."

"What does it matter?" she asked calmly. "He's done with me."

"You don't know that. Gabe isn't a knee-jerk kind of guy. He probably needs time to think this over. Give him—"

"Remember that movie where the two women get in all that trouble and decide to drive off the cliff in the end?"

"Alex."

"I'm not driving off any cliffs. I'm done with that. But I am going to clear the decks along the way."

She heard her sister swallow. "Alex, you get out of that cab. Take a Valium—do whatever you need to do, but do not get on that plane."

"No can do," she replied cheerfully. "Oh, look. My phone's dying. Catch you on the other side."

It should have been a great moment. Gabe watched the first bottle of the Angel's Share roll off the line with a tightness in his chest that defied description. It was done. The biggest gamble of his life was in motion. And if the reaction on Saturday night, if the reaction from every wine columnist and blogger in the country was any indication, he'd made the right choice.

It didn't hurt that the sommelier of the biggest chain of hotels in the world had taken one sip of the Angel's Share and agreed to carry it. Or that all his distributors and suppliers seemed to be coming around to the idea of a pure Malbec from Napa. It would be October before the first bottle hit store shelves and they would really know the wine's fate, the most crucial selling period for a wine-maker. Between now and then, it was all about filling the supply chain and keeping the faith.

He sorely wished he could do that with his personal life. He was so angry at Alex, he'd had permanent smoke coming out of his ears. It was bad enough she'd had an affair. Even if he did believe her that it had been unknowing—which he did because he knew Alex by now—the fact that it had been Jordan Lane had sealed it for him. Along with the fact she'd kept it from him.

Inexcusable. Violated the biggest code of honor he had—absolute honesty. Darya had made that essential.

It made him sick to think of her with Lane. With the man who wanted to bury him. He was sick at the thought of having a mole in his winery. Sick of it all.

The bottles came off the line, one after another, their proud dark blue De Campo logos gleaming in the light. The Angel's Share. Alex's wine. It was impossible for him to think of it as anything else. She had named it. She had created all the buzz around it. They had been a team.

And she had let him down. Just like Darya had.

He gripped the railing that overlooked the production line, his knuckles straining white. Okay, not like Darya. Alex had other issues. But he'd wanted her to prove him wrong. That he'd been wrong to want a business partner-ship when he could have what he had with her. A woman he wanted as much out of bed as in it. A woman with a fighting spirit that refused to quit.

In hindsight, he knew deep down Alex had had nothing to do with Lane or the mole. She *had* put her heart and soul into those events. But honesty was non-negotiable. He could not live without it.

Pedro waved him down. He pressed his hands into fists and pushed away from the railing, descended the steps to the production level. His mentor handed him a bottle, a proud gleam in his eye. "*Numero uno. You should have it.*"

Gabe looked the bottle over, checked the label, verified the addition he'd requested to the back fine print was there. Too little, too late.

The wine felt right. His big bet felt right. Too bad he didn't.

"*Grazie,*" he murmured. "I should get back to work."

Alex arrived at the restaurant at Fisherman's Wharf at precisely six in the evening West Coast time. She was immaculately attired. Not one detail about her remotely resembled the naive twenty-two-year-old she'd once been. In fact, she'd just added another row of cynicism to her belt. *Perfect. Exactly what she needed.*

Her warning antennae went up as the tall, thin maître d' led her to a table at the far end of the lavishly appointed seafood restaurant. This didn't look like the type of place to have a business meeting. She spotted Jordan ahead of her. *At a table for two.* The warning signals went off the chart. Where the hell was her competition?

"I don't understand," she murmured quietly as he got up to greet her with a kiss on both cheeks. "Where is everyone?"

He gestured toward the chair opposite him. "I thought we needed to talk first."

She stood there, every cell in her body telling her to run. "About what?"

"Sit down, Alex."

She sat down. "Are the rest coming later, then?"

His brilliant blue eyes met hers. "They aren't coming."

She stood up with a jerky movement. How could she have been so stupid as to think this could be about business? That Jordan might want her for her brain?

"Let me explain." His gaze was hard, unwavering. "Sit down. You're making a scene."

She glanced around her. Noted the curious looks of the other patrons. And sat. "Do you have no shame?" she murmured. "Isn't what you did five years ago enough?"

His blue eyes darkened. "I asked you here tonight because I wanted to apologize. I'm so sorry, Alex."

"For what? For almost destroying my life?" She slammed her palms down on the white damask, anger at herself singeing her nerve endings. "I can't believe I thought my professional credentials were what brought me here."

"They are. I've told the committee they should pick you."

"Then what's *this?*" She waved her hand at the table. "This is not business, Jordan."

"But it is." He poured her wine she didn't want with a smooth movement. "I need to know you're not sleeping with Gabe De Campo."

Gabe. The man who was worth ten of him. The man he was trying to destroy. "I don't think I want your contract."

"You need my contract. Get over your personal feelings, accept my apology and move on, Alex."

That was what she was supposed to be doing today. Moving on. If Gabe didn't love her, she needed to bury herself in work. "I have no relationship with Gabe," she said tightly.

He studied her face with that ice cool gaze. Then nodded. "Fine. Shall I walk you through the RFP?"

She pulled her copy out of her briefcase, her survival patterns telling her just to do it. She forced herself to focus. But every time Jordan talked about his Black Cellar Select, it made her stomach churn. It was Gabe's wine. And yet here he was talking about it as if it was the product of his blood, sweat and tears.

She loved Gabe. The words blurred in front of her. She realized now she had been infatuated with Jordan's worldliness, with the way a powerful man like him would want someone like her. But she *loved* Gabe with a depth that was so much more. She loved his passion. She was not ready to give him up.

If she took this job, she would.

Jordan took a call, then excused himself to go to the washroom. She sipped her wine, her fingers trembling. Then picked up the RFP and ripped it in half. She could stop the vicious cycle now. Gabe might not take her back, but at least she would have tried.

She was done running.

Her gaze flickered over Jordan's phone as she waited for him to return. It was still unlocked. Before she had any idea what she was doing, it was in her hands and she was pressing through the home screen to his contacts. Her heart pounded like a high-speed train as she scrolled through the hundreds of names. She wasn't sure exactly what she was searching for and was starting to think she was looking for a needle in a haystack when a name popped glaringly out at her. Sam Withers. *Sam Withers.* One of Gabe's winemakers. *Why was he in Jordan's contact list?* She clicked on his name. He'd made multiple calls to Jordan this week.

Oh, my God. She cleared the screen and set it down with a thump. Was Sam Withers the mole?

Jordan came back. Surveyed the ripped RFP with a raised brow.

She stood up. "I can't work for you."

His eyes flashed. "You wanted me, Alex."

She shook her head. "I wanted a mirage. It never existed."

She picked up her briefcase and walked out of the restaurant, head held high. She'd put her last ghost to rest.

CHAPTER FIFTEEN

Dusk was settling over the Napa hills when Alex parked her car at the De Campo vineyard, ushering in an intimate stillness that made her heart sound even louder in her chest. She sat for a moment, gathering her nerve. If her phone call to her father had been unrehearsed, this visit was positively fly-by-the-seat-of-her-pants nerve-racking. She had no idea what she was doing, no idea what she was going to say. She just knew she had to try.

Filling her lungs with a deep breath of the fragrant, sweet-smelling air, she swung her legs out of the car and stood up. Burnt-orange light silhouetted the hills, the staccato chirp of the infamous Napa crickets dancing on the still night air.

She walked unsteadily up the front porch steps. She didn't even know if Gabe was home. *No time for second thoughts,* she told herself, forcing her feet to move. *Only forward, Alex.*

The front door was open. She called out and found Elena in the kitchen. The Spanish woman gave her a surprised but delighted look and a big hug.

"Is he home?" Alex asked, pulling back.

Elena jerked her head toward the terrace. "You'd think he'd be in a good mood. They bottled the first of the Angel's Share today. But that is one dark man."

Her heart jumped at the thought that maybe Gabe was

as miserable as she was. She quickly stomped that thought out. No communication meant no desire to communicate.

Elena gave her a long look, then set the cloth she was cleaning the counters with down. "I think I'm going to go to bed."

Alex made her way toward the French doors that led to the terrace, the flock of butterflies in her stomach so frantic she pressed a hand to her tummy. The problem with winging it was you had no idea what was coming. She turned the knob and stepped out onto the terrace. Gabe stood with his back to her, leaning on the railing that overlooked the vineyard.

"I hear you corked the first bottle of the Angel's Share today."

He spun around, his gaze narrowing, as if he was confirming it was actually her. Then he frowned. "What are you doing here?"

She dug her nails into her palms. Not promising. "I've had a bit of a date with the past today."

He gave her a wary look. "I expect you're going to elaborate."

"Yes." She forced herself to walk toward him, holding the shattered pieces of her heart together with a bandage she'd somehow managed to fashion. It wasn't strong, definitely makeshift. And when she stopped in front of him and tipped her head back to look up at him, she questioned whether it would hold. His eyes blazed a conflicted green in the fading light, his hard jaw set tight under a six o'clock shadow. But it was the sensuous, spectacular line of his mouth that affected her the most. The way she needed it on her.

She cleared her throat, rolled her shoulders back. "So I started the day with a phone call to my father. He listened while I reamed him out for not being there for me and I apologized for causing him so much anguish. Then," she continued, "I called Jordan Lane and told him I would fly down for his RFP meetings today."

He stiffened, a menacingly dark look crossing his face. "I got your check," she said evenly. "I got the message."

"So you walked straight to *him?*"

"He asked me to a dinner to review the RFP tonight. Fool that I am, I thought it was a business dinner."

His lips compressed. "You didn't have a problem working for a *thief?*"

A stab of pain lanced through her. "I was hurt. You broke my heart on Saturday, Gabe."

An emotion she couldn't identify flickered in his eyes. "So you've come to tell me you're working for Jordan Lane?"

She shook her head. "I realized tonight I couldn't work for him. I couldn't work for someone who is deliberately trying to destroy the man I love."

His jaw clenched. "Alex—"

She held up a hand. "Before I told him I couldn't work for him, Jordan went to the washroom and I went through the contacts on his phone. Sam Withers was in his contact list, Gabe. They've made multiple calls to each other over the past week."

His head jerked back. "Withers?"

She nodded. "You said you weren't sure about him."

"Yes, but—" He muttered an oath. "Let me get this straight. You went to dinner with Lane tonight intending on taking a job with him, decided you couldn't and went through his phone to find my mole?"

"Yes."

"*Maledizione,* Lex. Have you lost your mind?"

"Quite possibly."

A shadow crossed his face. "Why would Withers do that? I've given him every opportunity—everything he's asked for."

"I expect Lane is paying him a lot of money."

He rubbed a hand over that dark shadow she was aching to touch. "What did you just say to me?"

She gave him a confused look. "About Lane?"

"You said you were in love with me, Lex."

"Oh, that." She took a deep breath. "That's true."

There was a silence, a long, tense silence that raked over her nerves like nails on a chalkboard. Emotions slid in and out of those watchful eyes of his until she had to say something, *anything*. "You told me once I was afraid to be in a real relationship. So I gave myself to you. You told me all I do is run." She lifted her trembling chin. "Well, here I am. Fighting for what I want."

Emotion clogged her throat, choking her, but she swallowed and pushed determinedly on. "I want you to get down off that self-righteous high horse of yours, Gabe, and give me another chance. You owe it to me."

Fire lit his beautiful eyes. "You think so?"

"Yes." She stepped toward him, every ounce of the frustration zigzagging through her directed at him. *"You* made me open up to you, Gabe. *You* told me baby steps. *You* promised me that was enough. And then you walked away."

"I have trust issues, Lex." He moved closer, the heat of his big body vibrating into hers. "You had an affair with the man who is trying to ruin me. The *one man* I could not tolerate, and you didn't tell me."

Frustration turned to rage, surging through her with an uncontrollable force that made her whole body shake. "That's it, isn't it? You hate me because it was Jordan. You hate me because Darya left you. But none of that is my fault, Gabe. It's the past. And I'm through taking the blame for it. Jordan Lane *used* me."

He stood there, feet planted apart, the hard lines of his face so forbidding she felt as if she was battling a brick wall. Her shoulders sagged, her stomach dropped as the fight went out of her. "I've told you every secret, every last dark thing about me because I trusted you. Because I love you. But trust is a two-way street, Gabe, and I can see you don't have it for me."

She found the strength to turn her back on him and start walking. Then she stopped and swung around. "You told me that when someone loves you, you can give your heart to them and they'll protect it. I believed you. I guess I was a fool."

She went then, her steps a half run before the warmth gathering in her eyes fled down her cheeks.

"You think I don't love you, Lex?" His voice froze her in her tracks. "You think this last week hasn't been hell for me, too?"

Her legs were shaking so much she couldn't move. His footsteps echoed across the concrete, then his hands settled on her shoulders and spun her to face him.

"You're right," he said grimly. "I hate the fact that it was Jordan you were with, and I hate the fact that you had an affair." She stiffened and would have pulled away, but his fingers dug into her shoulders and held her tight. "I *know* you couldn't have known he was married, Lex. I know you. But when Darya left, she ripped my heart out."

"I can't change the past," she whispered. "I wish I could. So many people were hurt."

She saw something shift in him then, a softening in his eyes, in the hard set of his jaw. It made hope flutter in her chest. He reached up and swiped the tears from her cheeks with his thumbs. "I need you, Lex. I've spent the past week trying to convince myself you can't be trusted because the way I feel for you scares the hell out of me. Has always scared the hell out of me. But every time I tried to write you off, to tell myself I couldn't be with you, there was this voice inside of me saying you're the one."

Her heart stopped in her chest. "You have to trust me," she whispered. "I will make more mistakes, Gabe. It's what I do. But I will never lie to you."

"I know." He lifted his hands to cup her face. "I've spent the whole day trying to look at the wine I've invested two bloody years developing and couldn't because of *you*. It's *your* wine, Lex."

She shook her head. "It's your wine. *You* are brilliant."

"It's *ours*. You named it, *tesoro*. Every newspaper and blogger in this country is talking about it because of you."

She smiled. "We're a good team, aren't we?"

"Sì." He bent his head and kissed her. "We are."

Her heart seemed to lift somewhere up into the stratosphere. She kissed him with all the pent-up frustration and misery from the past week and decided she might never let him go. But she wanted to hear him say it again first. "You need to clearly articulate what you said before," she murmured, pulling back and drinking her fill of him. "Say it again."

"That I love you?" A slow smile curved his lips. "I love you, Lex. And I promise if you give me your heart, I *will* protect it."

Oh. She felt herself slither into a pile of boneless mush.

"And your body," he murmured, heat filling his gaze as he pressed his palm to her back and brought her closer. "Definitely your body. We are spectacularly hot in bed together, *cara*, and mine has been very, very cold this past week."

"I think we should go fix that right now," she murmured, his hard, sexy body turning hers to liquid.

"Did you leave a bathing suit in your stuff upstairs?"

She blinked. Nodded.

"Go put it on."

"Does that mean I'm staying?" she asked archly.

His gaze softened. "How about forever?"

Oh. He did the sappy, romantic thing so well. "I was thinking," she ventured carefully, "that maybe I could have a bicoastal office."

His gaze glittered. "How about we discuss that in the hot tub?"

She slanted a look at him. "If that's where we're going, we're not discussing living arrangements. I have experienced your technique."

A smile curved his lips. "Go."

She tripped on her way *up* the stairs, she was so eager to get there with her boot-camp-sore body, but nothing could wipe the smile off her face—it *might* be there permanently. Pulling on her bikini with eager fingers, she joined Gabe on the terrace. He was wearing those drool-inducing low-slung navy trunks that drove her to distraction.

"Come," he said, holding his hand out. But he didn't take her to the hot tub, choosing the path to the winery instead. Alex dug in her heels when he started down into the cellar.

"Forget about that. *She's* down there."

He made her go anyway, the stone floors echoing under their feet. Alex clung tightly to his hand all the way into the tasting room, where he retrieved a bottle and two glasses. No footsteps. And there were none on the way out.

"I think you were imagining it," Gabe murmured as they walked down the hill toward the house. "Or maybe one last party put her at peace."

Alex could only hope.

She lowered herself into the hot tub, moaning her thanks to the god of the jets for his ability to soothe her aching body.

Gabe eyed her. "Is that just to turn me on, or are you sore?"

She gave him a baleful look. "I went to boot camp every morning at six this week to work off my excess anger."

He slid into the water, Alex's hands aching to touch every hard, muscular inch of him. "I have a surprise for you."

"I like surprises…"

He handed her the bottle. It was beautiful—a tall, elegantly shaped cylinder—but it was the name on the front of the label that made her breath catch in her throat. *The Angel's Share.*

"The very first bottle," Gabe murmured.

"It's stunning." She turned her gaze on him. "Excited?"

"Immeasurably so."

The lust in his gaze made her pulse sprint. "Turn the bottle around," he instructed. "Look at the bottom near the Made in Napa line."

She tore her gaze from him and scanned the fine print. There, at the bottom in an elegant scroll, were two words. *For Alex.*

Her heart went into free fall.

"You'd better love me," he said huskily, "or I'm going to have to stare at five million bottles of that, and it isn't going to be pretty."

They managed one sip of the thoroughly brilliant wine before Alex was in his arms, her legs curled around him, and this time, this time there was no unfulfilled fantasy. This time she got all of him and with him the knowledge that sometimes in life you did get everything you wanted. It just might not happen the way you thought it would.

* * * * *

THE TRUTH
ABOUT DE CAMPO

BY
JENNIFER HAYWARD

For two of my great inspirations:

My family—my anchor in this journey we call life.

And my bookclub girls who inspire me to write rum punch promises in the sand. . .and keep them!

RPP Forever.

CHAPTER ONE

UNLESS MATTEO DE CAMPO was mistaken, this conversation with his brother had all the hallmarks of a classic intervention.

It *looked* like it with Riccardo staring him down like a Spanish bullfighter with his eye on the unruly target. It *sounded* like it from his cautionary, bordering-on-aggressive tone. And it certainly *felt* like it with the De Campo CEO's displeasure licking over his skin like a flame.

If the truth be known, it had always been that way. They were like night and day, he and his brother. Where Riccardo was dark and intense and bulldozed his way through life, Matteo preferred the subtle approach. Both in business and in bed. You could catch more flies with honey. Persuade more effectively with a sophisticated argument than a head-on tackle.

Entice a woman into bed with a carefully timed observation that showed you *had* been listening to her over that bottle of Chianti.

He brought his gaze back to his brother's dark face. From the looks of it, Riccardo thought he was doing a bit *too* much of that these days.

Flicking an imaginary speck of dust off his suit, he lounged back against the floor-to-ceiling windows of his brother's Wall Street office and cocked a brow. "So what you're saying is *your* behavior was perfectly acceptable, but mine is not?"

"No," Riccardo emitted coolly. "What I'm saying is I don't know what in *Cristo's* name is wrong with you. You're treating the women of this planet like they're your own personal wrecking yard."

Matteo shrugged. "Maybe I've decided your way is the better way."

Riccardo shot him an amused look. "You forget I'm a reformed man. Happily married and loving it."

"Only because you met a goddess who's willing to put up with you," he muttered, digging his hands in his pockets and giving his head a restless shake. "Did you really ask me here to discuss my love life, Ric? Somehow I think you're much too busy for that."

"You're the vice president of sales and marketing for De Campo, Matty. Your love life *is* my business when it starts disrupting things around here."

"And *how*," Matteo drawled, "do you figure it's doing that?"

"Your antics in the tabloids are making it impossible for you or anyone else in this company to concentrate. Alex is tired of doing damage control, and frankly, I don't blame her."

Ebbene, so that stung. Matteo liked his sister-in-law. Didn't like the thought of making more work for her when she already worked far too much. But he was too irritated by his brother's rebuke not to strike back. "If I made the cover every week for the rest of the year I still wouldn't beat your record."

"*Si,* but I'm a better multitasker," Riccardo taunted.

Matteo stiffened, straightening away from the windows and eating up the distance between him and his brother with long furious strides. "I am making a *mockery* of my predecessor's numbers."

"Exactly why I want you to straighten yourself out. Think what you can do with a clear head."

Matteo could have told Riccardo he was definitely planning on doing that. That he'd sworn off women like an alcoholic swears off drink, potentially for the rest of his life given his recent spat of disastrous assignations. But he liked to yank Riccardo's chain as much as his brother liked to yank his. "What are you going to do if I don't?" he queried, leveling his gaze on his brother's angular, unforgiving face. "Punish me? Send me off to sell wine to the devout?"

Riccardo's coal-black eyes flashed. "As much as I would dearly love to have you out of the picture right now, I need you. And I think *you* need a challenge. Badly."

Matteo couldn't deny the truth of that statement. He'd almost doubled sales as head of De Campo's European operations. Was killing it in his new role. But his brother continued to handcuff him, as if he was afraid to unleash him.

He sank his fingers into the knot of his tie and yanked it loose. "You don't trust me."

"I wouldn't have given you the job if I didn't trust you."

"Then why the hand-holding?"

His brother's gaze darkened. "You've been knee-jerk in the extreme the last six months, Matty. You're like a cowboy with his guns drawn at all times."

"I'm hungry," Matteo growled. "Give me something to sink my teeth into and you will have my complete and utter focus."

"Exactly my thinking." Riccardo plucked a magazine from the surface of his immaculate desk and held it up. "Warren Davis just bought the Luxe Hotel chain."

Matteo nodded. The purchase by the world's third richest man, an investment genius revered around the world, had made headlines a few weeks back. The confirmation of a deal that had been in the works for months. "I looked into it a while ago," he told Riccardo. "Patreus has it locked up for another three years."

"Not any more they don't." Riccardo tossed the magazine on his desk. "Davis is reevaluating all suppliers."

He frowned. "How do you know that?"

"I played poker with a close friend of his on Monday night. De Campo is now in the running for marquee wine partner."

Matteo sucked in a breath. "That's a six- or seven-million-dollar contract, minimum."

"Ten." The hungry light he knew so well flared in his brother's eyes. Antonio De Campo, their father, had built De Campo into a global wine empire. Riccardo, with his endless thirst to make his mark, had driven it even higher with the restaurant division he was building. But for the core wine business, which was still all-important, this was huge. It would mean De Campo would be featured in every single one of Luxe's legendary restaurants worldwide. The coveted locations where politicians, princes and A-list celebs dined...

Merda. This was massive. "What next then?"

"Davis has put his daughter, Quinn, in charge of restaurant operations. She will be the final decision-maker on the wine contract. The Davises are doing a chemistry test with the four short-listed companies next week in Chicago. From there they'll pick the final two to pitch for the business."

"A chemistry test? What in God's name is that?"

"Warren Davis is all about the relationship aspect of business. Common ideals, common philosophies, he says, are the keys to creating a successful partnership. It's not always about what looks best on paper for him. The four short-listed companies are all great candidates. It will be the chemistry we have with Davis and his daughter that will put us in the final two."

Helpful then, that Matteo happened to be a master at persuading a female to do his bidding. "What form will this chemistry test take?"

"A cocktail party at the Davis residence."

Matteo's lip curled. "Like sharks circling one another..."

"Pretty much." Riccardo rhymed off two of the largest spirit companies in the world who had swallowed up smaller regional winemakers and a niche producer out of southern Australia.

"Silver Kangaroo?"

Riccardo nodded. "They've been winning some big awards lately."

"Yes, but *odd*. They are so niche." He gave his head a shake. "Any idea which way they're leaning?

"Quinn, apparently, has her eye on Silver Kangaroo. *We* are considered an outside shot."

Against the odds. Exhilaration tightened his body, sent his blood coursing through his veins. Just the way he liked it. When was the last time he'd felt that rush? That elemental surge of adrenaline he needed to feel alive? If Quinn Davis preferred a pure wine player they had a shot. Now all he had to do was work his magic.

"Do we have any intel on Quinn Davis?"

"Tough, smart, Harvard-educated." His brother handed him a folder. "It's all in here."

Matteo took it and lifted a shoulder. "She'll be all right, then."

Humor darkened his brother's gaze. Riccardo had gone to Harvard, Matteo to Oxford. It was a standing debate between them which was superior.

Matteo leafed through the folder. "Quinn manages some of his companies for him, doesn't she?"

"*Si*. Most recently Dairy Delight. Warren is hoping her experience in the food sector will help revive Luxe's restaurants. They've been on a slow decline for years."

"*Dairy Delight?* They sell ice cream and burgers. How's that going to help bring Michelin three-star restaurants back to life?"

Riccardo shot him a warning look. "Do not underestimate her, Matty. Apparently she's a chip off the old block."

Yes, but she was a female. He'd never met one he couldn't have. If he was on his game, she'd be in the palm of his hand before he'd finished his first cocktail. His mouth tightened. He intended to be more than on his game. *All over* his game was more like it. Which didn't mean he *would* underestimate her. Women were like sleeping bears. All soft and cuddly until you awakened their inner beast. Which was precisely why you didn't go *there*.

He closed the folder. "Who's going?"

"You are."

He did a double take. "With you and Gabe?"

"I need to be in San Francisco for the restaurant opening and Gabe is in way over his head with the harvest right now. I can't pull him away."

A surge of anticipation fired through him. *Finally* he was back in the game. The deal was his to win.

Riccardo kept his gaze steady on him. "This is the most important contract we've negotiated in the history of De Campo. We win this, we enter a different stratosphere. You need to bring it home, Matty."

"Done."

His brother's eyes flickered at the belligerently confident note in his voice. Mistrust. It was still there.

His shoulders shot to his ears, blood pumped so rapidly into his head he thought it would explode. *"Do not say it,"* he bit out. "Do *not* say it."

"What happened with Angelique Fontaine can't happen again, Matty."

The liquid fire burning in his head became an all-consuming force that blurred his vision. He swung away and sucked in a deep breath. Then another. Fisted his hands by his sides until they numbed into a lifeless mass. "How long," he demanded hoarsely, "are you going to crucify me with that?"

"Bring me Luxe," his brother said deliberately, "and we're even."

Matteo bowed his head. Flexed his frozen appendages until the blood streamed back into his fingers. When he looked up, he sought, *demanded* an honest answer from his brother. "Why me? You could make time for this, Riccardo."

His brother rested that deadly sharp gaze of his on Matteo. "Because you are the only one who can win this. Quinn Davis is a man-hater. She will detest me on sight. Gabe could do it, but you are better. Not only do you have the charm but when you're on, Matty, you light up a room. You are electric."

He exhaled the breath lodged deep inside his chest. "Luxe is ours. I promise you that."

Riccardo nodded. "Absorb what Paige has put together and let me know if you have any questions."

Matteo tucked the file under his arm and headed for the door. His brain was already formulating his approach when Riccardo's low drawl reached him. "Matty?" He turned around. "I meant what I said. You are not, under any circumstances, to sleep with Quinn Davis."

All creativity fled. A muscle jumped in his jaw, his teeth clenching down so tight he thought they might shatter. "I heard you the first time. It can't happen. It won't happen. And I'm getting a little pissed you'd think I'd even go there."

Riccardo shrugged. "You're a complete wild card lately, Matty. They could announce the next shuttle expedition to the moon and I wouldn't be surprised to see your name on the list."

His insides tightened. "You *know* what I was going through. Why that happened with Angelique…"

His brother's gaze hardened into impenetrable steel. "It was a seven-million-dollar deal, Matty."

And he had brought it down like a house of cards.

He gritted his teeth. "I will win this deal for De Campo. That's all you need to be sure about."

His brother nodded.

Matteo stalked to the door. Sure he was going to charm Quinn Davis. Riccardo wanted to win. How did he *think* he was going to win? But sleep with her? Did his brother really think he wanted another two years in purgatory?

Damn. He needed a cold beer.

His mood hadn't improved by the time he was home at his new Meatpacking District loft, a bottle of said cold beer in his hand on the patio. Kicking back in a lounge chair, he devoured the file Riccardo's PA had compiled. Paige had been her usual ridiculously thorough self. It contained everything he ever needed to know about the Davis family and more. And photos. It did not escape him why his brother had warned him off Quinn Davis. She wasn't just beautiful, she was knock-your-socks-off stunning.

The photo Paige had included, taken at a charity event, hit him right where it would any libido-endowed male. Petite, curvy in a lush "take me to bed" kind of way, she had silky, thick, long dark brown hair and the most haunting green eyes he'd ever seen.

Gorgeous. And, apparently, a man-hater. His mouth curved. He could work with that.

He took a swig of his beer. Paige's notes were a gold mine of cocktail party intelligence. Quinn Davis had worked at Warren Davis's investment firm since graduating from Harvard and had earned progressively more responsibility at a pace that would have made most people's heads spin. It was clear from the opinion pieces that although many would have liked to think nepotism had played a role in her success, she had done it on her own. One business columnist commented she had an "eerily sharp brain like her father." Another that she was an "instant study." But the description that captured his attention was the one that branded her a "gladiator in the boardroom."

This was getting more interesting by the minute.

He flicked to a profile piece on her personal life. Or lack thereof. She either didn't have one or she was the most ultraprivate person he'd ever encountered. Twenty-seven years old, resided in Chicago, divorced from Boston blue blood lawyer, Julian Edwards, after one year of marriage. *One year?* He lifted a brow. What in God's name had happened there? And a graduate-level Krav Maga? The instructors he knew had attained that level but none of his buddies had gotten past an orange belt despite years of practice.

Interesting was not the word. Fascinating was more like it. His mouth quirked. No wonder her marriage had fallen apart. Quinn Davis had probably emasculated her husband within the first three months of marriage.

He scoured the file from top to bottom, then threw it on the concrete beside him. Resting his beer on his thigh he looked up at the lone star in the Manhattan sky that never seemed to get truly black. An image of all three De Campo brothers—Riccardo, Gabriele, Matteo—walking into the boardroom of the second largest airline in Europe flashed through his head. That day in Paris had been their chance to make their mark on a company ruled for forty years by their despotic father, Antonio. It was Riccardo's first high-profile deal as CEO. They had been pumped, sky-high with adrenaline, the seven-million-dollar deal to supply the airline with its house wines firmly within their grasp.

They'd nailed the presentation. Had gone out to celebrate that night at a local bar. But after the adrenaline had worn off, Matteo's recent all-encompassing grief over the loss of his best friend, Giancarlo, had stormed back. Nothing had been enough to contain it—to make the guilt and pain go away. The effort to keep up a happy face with his brothers had been excruciating, ending with him seeking solace in the arms of a beautiful woman. Except that woman had been the daughter of Georges Fontaine, the CEO of the airline. She worked for Fontaine, had been on the executive team they'd pitched to. She'd also been throwing herself at Matteo the entire time they'd been in that boardroom.

He had reasoned Angelique Fontaine was a grown woman capable of making her own decisions. But when he'd made it clear the next morning he wasn't interested in anything long-term, Angelique had gone straight to her father. And De Campo's chance to put its wine on over half a million flights a year had gone with her.

Angelique had branded him a callous son of a bitch. Georges Fontaine had been furious. It had been the worst mistake in judgment in Matteo's thirty-two-year-old life.

He shifted on the chair, the memory of his brothers' faces when Georges Fontaine had called the deal off physically painful to remember. Burned so indelibly into his mind it was like a mental scar that never healed. Shock. Disbelief. Disappointment.

The disappointment had been the worst.

He set his beer down on the concrete with a jerky movement. He had been in pain. But Riccardo was right. It shouldn't have mattered.

Resting his head against the back of the chair, that lone star blinking at him like a beacon—like his path to redemption—he knew this was his chance to finally put his demons to rest. To move on. He would win this deal if it was with the last breath he had. Despite the odds that were stacked against him.

Unfortunately, the stakes had never been higher.

CHAPTER TWO

WARREN DAVIS'S REDBRICK Georgian Revival home in the Hyde Park neighborhood of Chicago shone with a century-old elegance in the early evening light. It had been an unusually steamy summer day, climbing into the hundreds, the haze that had blanketed the city just starting to lift. Cooler night air whispered across the tops of the tall pine trees that stood like sentinels on either side of the mansion, wafting through the window of Quinn Davis's room as she watched the heads of some of the world's biggest spirit companies arrive for the cocktail meet and greet.

The air might be cooler now, but the focused, intent look on each megapowerful man's face as he arrived promised a heated competition. Winning was all that mattered to men of this caliber. She'd lived with one her whole life—the most alpha of them all in Warren. And she couldn't deny, she was their female equivalent. Except she had to be even tougher, stronger and more focused than all of them to survive. A female warrior in a male-dominated world.

She was fascinated to see how the men would play. How the testosterone party would unfold.

Every single one of them, as they arrived in everything from custom-made suits to cowboy hats, looked up at the American flag billowing from the porch, and undoubtedly, reminded himself again of its significance. Warren Davis was a national symbol of what made America great—a billionaire philanthropist who gave away more of his money than he kept. A patriot and financial genius who advised presidents on monetary policy and led social commentary. He was the man everyone wanted to know. The man people paid three and a half million to have lunch with at his charity auction date for the homeless, in the hopes they might pick up a miniscule amount of his brilliance.

He was also, as a stroke of fate would have it, the man who had chosen, along with his Irish wife, Sile, to adopt Quinn as a baby when her young Southern parents had been unable to care for her. Warren and Sile had barely brought their new baby home when Sile had miraculously fallen pregnant after years of unsuccessful fertility treatments and given Quinn her sister and best friend, Thea.

Thea, even now still primping herself in front of the mirror, fussing over yet another choice of hairstyle. Quinn grimaced and levered herself away from the window. "Please pick one and be done."

Her sister squinted at herself and gave a dramatic sigh. "How am I supposed to choose with four of the world's most powerful men coming for cocktails? This has to be daddy's *best idea ever*. I mean, he has two single daughters right?"

Since her marriage to Julian had been a certified disaster, yes, that did put her squarely in that category. Not that she had any plans to ever repeat her mistake.

"Tonight is about getting to know potential partners," she told her veterinarian sister, who knew as much about business as she knew about changing a tire. "Not speed dating."

"Ha." Thea shot her a rebellious look. "With a cattle and wine baron in the house, not to mention delicious Matteo De Campo…. You think I'm missing out on *that* opportunity?"

Quinn smiled. She wished, sometimes, she had just a

little bit more of her younger sister's boundless enthusiasm for life. For love. But she wasn't sure she'd ever even had it to start with.

"Daniel Williams is beautiful," Quinn drawled. "I'll give you that."

Thea tossed her long blond hair over her shoulder. "I fancy living on his ranch. I can take care of the animals while he tends to his vineyard. Although—" she put a finger to her mouth in a thoughtful gesture "—I'd gladly forget all about the animals if Matteo De Campo deemed me fit to give a second look. *He* is one real-life animal I wouldn't mind taming."

Quinn gave her a look from beneath perfectly manicured brows. "Matteo De Campo is a notorious playboy who couldn't take a woman seriously if she were the only one left on the planet. And even then," she declared, her lip curling, "he'd find it difficult to get past his love affair with himself."

Thea threw out her hands. "Who *cares?* I hear a woman can't be in the same room as him without throwing her panties at him. He's *that* hot."

"He's not *that* good-looking." Unless you went for the smoldering male à la perfume commercials who looked like he'd keep you up all night.

Her sister caught the gleam in her eye. "See? Undeniable. You need to throw off that 'I was married and it sucked' baggage and move on. Live a little."

Quinn's heart clamped into the hard little ball that seemed to be its permanent state since Julian had left. No one but her knew the truth of her marriage. The public line had been irreconcilable differences. What happened behind Davis doors was never revealed.

Better the truth of her marriage not be.

She forced a wry smile to her lips. "Don't go throwing

your panties at Matteo De Campo. Not only will he break your heart, but he'll be mad when he loses the bid."

Thea drew her brows together. "Have you already decided then?"

"No, but De Campo's probably last on the list." She wanted Danny William's Silver Kangaroo. The small, award-winning Australian winery was the perfect eclectic fit for what she wanted to do with the Luxe brand.

"Daddy likes De Campo," Thea said, following her to the door. "He said their new Napa wines are brilliant."

"*Daddy* isn't making the decision."

Thea gave her a sideways look. "When are you going to stop trying to live up to this vision of perfection he expects? You could do that every day for the rest of your life and it'd still never be enough."

Possibly true. But she was a little afraid she'd die trying. This was the biggest opportunity of her career and she intended to make her mark with it.

She did have to maintain *some* objectivity, she told herself as she and Thea made their way down the winding staircase, through the massive drawing room and out the French doors that led to the gardens where the cocktails were being served. It was only fair after all, even if she knew the choice she was going to make in the end.

The terrace in the middle of the immaculately landscaped gardens was buzzing as they arrived, the two CEOs of the larger spirit companies with their wives in attendance, while Daniel Williams and Matteo De Campo had obviously elected to fly solo, to Thea's delight.

Surprising. Matteo's Hollywood ex had been moaning in the tabloids about all of her ex-lover's women, but not one was in sight tonight.

All eyes settled on her and her sister. Blonde Thea glowed with the prospect of meeting her Prince Charming while her dark-haired alter ego felt herself the instant target of four sets of male eyes. Not because she was beautiful, although she knew that she was. But because she was their ticket to massive international sales growth.

They were sizing her up. Waiting to see if she was as impressive as her track record. It sat on her shoulders with the almost oppressive weight that being Warren Davis's daughter always had. She not only had to be better than the rest, she had to be ten times better.

It was exhausting.

Thea sucked in a breath. "I really may have to forgo my ranch-living plans. *He* is just unreal."

Quinn didn't have to ask which man her sister was talking about, because Matteo De Campo's laserlike gaze was focused on her and it was like being in the path of an undeniable force of magnetism the likes of which she'd never experienced before. She'd met a lot of good-looking men. Her husband had been stunning…but he—*he* was something else. Unblinking, unashamedly approving of what he saw, his gaze took every inch of her in, right down to her toes. She swallowed hard. Shifted her weight so both designer-covered feet absorbed the impact.

"I hear he has a tattoo," Thea whispered. "Hot, right?"

Quinn couldn't help but wonder where on that tall, lean, muscular body it was. The dark suit that covered him was exquisite. The body better.

She found herself gaining a bit more respect for his legions of cast-offs as she returned his deliberate inspection. A woman might risk losing some self-respect over *that*. The photographs she'd seen of the youngest De Campo had been all about his lust for life, his freewheeling persona— the thick, unruly dark hair, the devil-may-care smile. But tonight, the hair was cropped close to his head so the sexy dark stubble that covered his square jaw showcased the perfection of his face. His expression was not the relaxed,

indolent picture the tabloids loved to print. It was as intent
as the night. Deliberate. Focused.

Damn. The "I am a sexy beast" stubble really worked
for him.

She met his gaze, the amused half smile that curved
his lips making her back stiffen. He was waiting for her
to fall flat on her face. Waiting for her to fall all over him
like every other woman did. She lifted her chin. He was
so, so wrong on that. Julian had taught her well. The last
thing any woman should trust was a pretty face in an expensive suit.

Summoning the cool, untouchable look she did so perfectly, she walked to her father's side. He made the intro-
ductions, the two spirit company CEOs first, then the two
younger men. All four were impressive, charismatic per-
sonalities who would stand out in a crowd from the pure
power they exuded like a second skin. But even Daniel
Williams, the golden-haired wine-and-cattle baron who
looked like he'd just walked out of a cigarette commercial seemed to fade into the background with Matteo De
Campo standing beside him. Silver-gray, she registered
as she shook his hand. Matteo's eyes were the exact color
of the Chicago sky before a summer storm caused all hell
to break loose.

Fitting then to feel that shiver slide up her spine.

"Quinn," he murmured, keeping his gaze locked on
hers as he folded his big, warm hand around her fingers.
"A stunning name for a stunning woman."

Her stomach did a funny roll as she retrieved her hand,
the imprint of his fingers burning into hers. *Is he for real?*

"It's a pleasure to meet you, Mr. De Campo," she murmured smoothly. "Although I feel as if I should already
know you with all the tabloid attention you've been getting lately."

He blinked, that one quick movement her only indication the gibe had landed. "Matteo, *per favore*," he invited in a smooth, whiskey-soaked tone she was sure played a large part in how he slayed women. "And surely, Ms. Davis, you know better than to believe everything you read in the tabloids."

"Where there's smoke there's usually fire, Mr. De Campo."

A wry smile curved his lips. *"A volte."*

She lifted a brow. "I'm sorry, I don't speak Italian."

"Sometimes," he drawled. "Sometimes there is, Ms. Davis."

Her father flashed her a sharp look. Her head snapped back just like it had when she was ten and being rebuked at the dinner table for talking too much when the adults were conversing. Her shoulders came up and she summoned the exquisite manners the Davis family was legendary for. "Lovely to have you with us tonight."

Matteo's eyes glimmered as he held up the bottle he was carrying. "My brother Gabriele wanted you to have this. It's the first bottle off the line of this year's Malbec."

The vintage that had the whole North American wine industry talking about it. The first bottle of the year at that. How very smooth. "I'm honored," she murmured, wrapping her fingers around the bottle. "It's a brilliant wine. Thank you."

Score one for Matteo De Campo.

"And this," he added, pulling two small silver-wrapped packages out of his jacket, "is a little taste of Tuscany for you both."

He handed the tiny packages to her and Thea. Thea nearly fell over herself thanking him. Quinn thought it was a little over the top, but the look on the other men's faces pronounced it an act of genius.

Two—nil.

Too bad she wasn't a fan of doing the predictable thing.

She took the gifts inside, then spent the evening soaking up the time with each prospective partner, doing as much reconnaissance as she could before she made her short list of two. Nothing surprised her about her conversations. In fact, she grew even more certain that Silver Kangaroo was the right choice. De Campo, in her mind, was too smug, too established a brand to fit with Luxe's new direction. But she owed Matteo her time. He was the only one she hadn't spoken to in depth, and although she'd like to tell herself she'd been too busy, she had the strange feeling she'd avoided him because he was a danger zone for her.

He was chatting with her father now, the two of them engulfed in a spirited debate about business issues. Her stern father had clearly fallen under the spell of Matteo's legendary De Campo charm. Bizarre, really, when Warren usually saw right through people.

She skirted around them and headed for the house to use the ladies' room. Her face ached from the polite smile she'd pasted on while the competitors plied her with information and assessed her comment by comment to find her hot spots, her weak spots. To see if she actually had a brain. Her feet burned in the stilettos that were her armor, as if a sharp heel could puncture the hurt she felt every time someone insinuated she'd gotten where she was because she was Warren's daughter. Her head throbbed from a fourteen-hour work day.

Sometimes being Quinn Davis was just much too much.

She sliced a wry glance at Thea flirting with Daniel Williams on the porch. She'd do her due diligence with Matteo when she came back. Then she was calling it a night. Dirty look from Warren or not.

Matteo felt his blood boil as Quinn Davis walked by him *yet again*. From her frosty reception of the presents he'd racked his brain to come up with, to her complete avoidance of his attempts to snare her time, she had been sending a loud and clear message. Either she didn't like him personally or De Campo didn't stand a chance. Neither was desirable, but he'd prefer it was a personal thing. That he could work with. A dislike of De Campo, not so much.

He stared after her, distracted by the sway of her delectable hips in the conservative summer dress that still managed to look sexy on her with that hourglass figure, despite the fact she had about as much personality as a block of ice. His fingers tightened around his glass. *Chemistry test.* What chemistry test? This was a farce.

Warren excused himself with a frown and went after Quinn. He watched them exchange words, Quinn's mouth tighten and her head incline. Then she continued on into the house. He clenched his teeth. What had he done to deserve this? That first moment they'd laid eyes on each other had been an intense, acknowledged male-female appreciation of each other's assets. Unmistakable. Man-hater Quinn might not like it, but she was attracted to him. That much he was sure of. And maybe *that* was the problem. A woman like her hated to reveal any chink in her armor.

She was going to be an even tougher nut to crack than he'd anticipated.

Good then that he'd had enough, *way more* than enough.

Daniel Williams ambled over and gave him a sympathetic look. "Still waiting? She's a piece of work, isn't she?"

He would normally have agreed but he knew enough to keep his mouth shut around the competition. He inclined his head toward Warren, instead. "That hour-long chat would have cost me three and a half million in auction. I'm not complaining."

The Australian's mouth quirked. "Touché. But Warren isn't making the decision, Quinn is."

Yes, she is. Matteo crossed his arms over his chest, antagonism heating him like a thirty-year-old scotch. "I heard

Quinn say she's been out to visit you guys. How long have you been working this?"

"Since they started negotiating for Luxe. About six months now. And she hasn't dropped the ice-queen act yet." Williams flashed a conspiratorial grin. "No surprise she's running an ice-cream company, eh?"

Matteo felt his insides combust. *Six months?* He'd been pursuing Quinn Davis's contract for *six months?* What chance did De Campo have? *Bloody chemistry test.*

He kept his temper in check. Just. "Seems like you're doing something right."

Williams leaned in, his voice dropping. "I've got that filly tied up tighter than tight, De Campo. Hate to say it 'cause I like you guys and we wine folk have to stick together. But this is pretty much a lock for us. Hate to see you waste your time."

He stiffened. "Wasting my time," he said quietly, pinning his gaze on the Australian's rough-hewn face, "would be competing in a game I can't win, Williams. And I don't see that happening."

His competitor's grin faded. "Best of luck, De Campo. I gotta tell you, you're a long, long shot. Hope you know that."

Matteo showed his teeth. "Just the way I like it."

Quinn came out of the house. "Would you excuse me?" he murmured. "My number is up."

Anger pressed ruthlessly down on him, burning brighter with every step he took toward the infuriating Quinn Davis. He could tolerate a lot of things, but people wasting his time was not one of them. Unfortunately this situation required him to be civil so he pasted a smile on his face and stopped in front of her. "Might I claim my time, do you think?"

Her long dark lashes came down to shield her expression. "Of course. I was just coming to find you. Warren said you wanted to see the koi pond."

He wanted to *dunk* her in the koi pond. He nodded instead and spread his hands out in front of him. "Please."

Quinn pressed her lips together as if this was the last thing she felt like doing and led the way. Her politely worded, disinterested questions as they made their way down the path into the rear of the gardens sent his temper to a whole new level. He pushed out his practiced spiel about De Campo's history, how the Tuscan and Napa vineyards were flourishing and why he thought their one-hundred-year-old company was the best choice for Luxe. It sounded flat even to his own ears because she so clearly didn't care. By the time they got to the koi pond, a beautiful little oasis that seemed to appear out of nowhere, he had blown a fuse.

She needed to throw him a scrap.

Quinn started spouting interesting nuggets about the pond. By the time she started telling him how they removed the tropical fish in the summer and took them inside, he'd had enough.

"I get the feeling you don't like me very much, Ms. Davis."

She blinked, then fixed him with that cool stare of hers. "It's not you I dislike, Mr. De Campo. It's your type."

The tabloid comment. Cristo, those stories. He shoved his hands in his pockets and narrowed his gaze on her lush, beautiful face. "Maybe you can elaborate on what my type is because I'm not sure I know."

"The global playboy," she supplied dryly. "The man who thinks he can manipulate everyone with his charm."

His gaze clashed with hers. "Funny thing is, I don't actually think that."

"'A stunning name for a stunning woman'? Come on, Mr. De Campo. Do you really talk like that?"

His lips stretched in a thin smile. "That wasn't a line, Ms. Davis. That was the truth."

Her small, even white teeth sank into a full bottom lip more suited to a woman who was actually a flesh-and-blood human being than an icicle. Too bad all of those just right, "take me to bed" curves were even more deadly in person. As in "take me to bed *right now*." Because Quinn Davis was the epitome of a five-letter word he didn't normally care to use.

The smile faded from his lips. "Just how *much* of an underdog is De Campo?"

"Who said you were an underdog?"

"My position on your priority list," he said roughly. "If I were to rank it, I'd say Silver Kangaroo is your first choice, followed by H Brands and Michael Collins."

The flush that darkened her cheeks told him he was dead-on. He sliced his hand upward to push his hair out of his face, remembered he'd had it all chopped off and dropped it to his side. "Why are we even here if you aren't going to give us a chance?"

"You do have a chance." Her eyes flashed a taunting emerald. "Tell me why I should choose you, Mr. De Campo. I'm all ears. *Wow me.*"

He could think of a multitude of ways to *wow* this one, most of which could never be done in a boardroom...starting with shutting up that smart mouth of hers.

He bit his tongue and used reason instead. "You're big on Silver Kangaroo. I get that they're a hot brand, winning awards, but so are we. In fact, De Campo is doing things no one else is, as you know, with the Malbecs and Syrahs in Napa. Warren is big on made in the U.S.A. There's your angle."

She lifted a delicate shoulder. "I'm more interested in choosing the *right* brand. Made in the U.S.A. is nice to have."

"Good," he agreed. "Then I'm sure you know you'll get more personal attention from us than the big brands. How much love and devotion will Michael Collins or H Brands give you?"

"A lot, they've promised."

He lifted a brow. "You can see through a lie, can't you, Ms. Davis? Ultimately, the reason you *should* choose us comes down to a partnership. We're in the restaurant business. Our restaurants are hugely profitable. We can help you. *Guide* you."

Her gaze glittered. "I *run* a national chain of restaurants. I'm sure you couldn't have missed that fact."

"Fast-food restaurants," he qualified. "It's a very different industry."

The warning in her eyes intensified. "Not so different, Mr. De Campo. But you make a good point. You're a competitor. Why should we fatten your pocketbook, open sesame on our trade secrets so you can kill us later?"

He shook his head. "De Campo isn't interested in luxury dining. Our restaurants service the trendy, hip crowd. It would be synergy, not competition."

"What's to say you won't expand? You've opened five restaurants this year."

"It's not in our plans. We know where our niche is. Allow us to partner with you, share what we've learned."

Her gaze hardened to a chilly, wintry green. "I don't want your advice, Mr. De Campo. I want your wine."

Damn, but she was a pain in the butt. "Riccardo and I had dinner in your Park Avenue restaurant this week. We wrote down a list of ten crucial mistakes you're making that would put you back in the black. You may want to hear them given our restaurants have a profit margin unheard of in the industry."

Her gaze flickered. *Bingo.* She crossed her arms over her chest. "Go on."

"Put us through to the next round and I will."

Her brows tilted. "What if you don't make it? You have an opportunity now to make your case."

"I'll take my chances."

"Ah. A gambler too."

"Always. Tell me something, Quinn. You don't like being underestimated, do you?"

"Not particularly, no."

"Thought so. Funny then that Daniel Williams thinks he has you tied up tighter than tight."

"Excuse me?"

"I think his exact words were 'I've got that filly tied up tighter than tight, De Campo.'"

"Filly?" The full force of that green gaze sank into him. "He said that?"

"Just now, in fact. Ask him. And while you're at it, you might want to find out where he's staying. I could have sworn I saw him walk out of the hotel across from yours tonight. The one with the three-word name that is not the Luxe brand."

Quinn's mouth dropped open. She stood there gaping at him, then apparently realized what she was doing and slammed it shut. Matteo flashed her a grim smile. "Appearances are deceiving, aren't they? You think I'm a playboy? You think I manipulate with my charm? Sure I do. I appreciate women. I appreciated you the moment I saw you and I know the feeling was mutual." He lifted his shoulders in a careless shrug. "But the thing is, you aren't my type, Quinn. I prefer the warm, affable ones over the ice queens. So perhaps you can tuck away your claws and play fair. Judge De Campo on our track record, not your misguided presumptions of who you think I am. Or this chemistry test is going to be a joke."

He walked after that, afraid if he said anything else he would sink De Campo's chances.

If he hadn't already.

Quinn followed him back to the others. Gut churning, he grabbed a drink from the tray of a passing waiter. What in God's name was wrong with him? Hot-headed was not an emotion he would normally have associated with himself. Reckless at times, yes. But that woman was *impossible*. And his career depended on her.

He watched her interact with the others, visibly cool with Daniel Williams now. At least he'd made her think twice. If he'd guessed right, the Silver Kangaroo CEO's arrogant words would make a woman like her crazy. And maybe it would make her do exactly the *opposite* of what she'd been planning. Backed up by the sound reasoning he'd provided.

The thought he might have once again destroyed the biggest opportunity in De Campo's history kept him awake for much of the night as the monogrammed Luxe Hotel sheets stared him in the face. Eventually he threw them aside with a curse and got out of bed for a 5:00 a.m. run before his flight.

It would be a couple of days before he learned the fallout of his actions. Quinn had said they'd be informed the beginning of next week.

The only thing he knew for sure right now, he thought, grimacing and picking up his pace into a flat-out run through the park, was that he, the master of charm, had not only failed to ace the chemistry test, it had been an adjunct failure of epic proportions. Quinn Davis might actually hate him after last night.

CHAPTER THREE

MATTEO HAD JUST stepped into his loft after his flight back
to New York when his phone buzzed in his pocket. Riccardo no doubt, looking for the full debrief.

He dropped his bag on the entryway floor, pulled out
his phone and checked the caller ID.

Quinn.

His chest tightened like a vice. Fast. *Too fast?*

"Quinn."

"Congratulations, Mr. De Campo." Her tone was brisk,
businesslike. "De Campo has made Luxe's short list of
two."

He let out his breath in a long, slow exhale. Relief mixed
with the sweet taste of victory, a heady cocktail that made
his blood surge in his veins. "No doubt it was my sparkling
personality," he offered dryly.

"No doubt."

The wry undertone in her naturally husky voice made
him smile. He leaned back against the foyer wall and ran
his palm over the stubble covering his jaw. "I am thrilled,
of course, that you picked us. *Grazie.*"

"Thank my new head sommelier for swinging the vote.
One taste of Gabriele's Malbec and she was onside."

"Remind me to thank her."

"I think the better route would be to keep you well
away from her."

He lifted a brow. "Why would you say that?"

"She isn't as jaded about men as I am. I'd prefer not to have a train wreck on my team."

"I think you overestimate my allure, Ms. Davis."

"I think I don't. Thank you for the perfume, by the way. You didn't need to do that."

"I thought a little piece of Tuscany was apt. You like jasmine then?"

"I do."

"Good. It's one of the world's great scents."

"I assume this is one of your techniques? Plying women with expensive perfume?"

"One of the more rudimentary ones, yes," he admitted. "I also know my way around a kitchen. You'd be amazed how impressed women are by a man who can cook."

"I can only imagine." There was a pause. "I have no doubt about your…capabilities in any department you choose to apply yourself in, Mr. De Campo. Would next week suit to visit your Tuscan operations? I'd like to do that first, then show you two of our Caribbean properties we're reopening in St. Lucia so you can get a feel as to where Luxe is headed before we do the pitch in early August."

"Of course. Will cowboy Jack be along for the ride to the Caribbean?"

"If you're referring to Daniel Williams, then yes, he is the other half of the final two."

"Perfetto," he drawled, sarcasm lacing his tone. He was sure he could find a way for the Australian to stick his mouth in it again. It would be his pleasure. "We can do Tuscany whenever you like. Name the time."

"How about Friday? That way I don't miss the working week."

His lips twisted. God forbid the workaholic miss a day

churning out money for Davis Investments. "Shall I send the De Campo jet for you?"

"Thank you but I'm mandated by Davis rules to fly commercial. Demonstrates good corporate governance."

He shrugged. "The offer's there."

"Thank you."

"I do have one, nonnegotiable condition to us moving forward."

A pause. "Which is?"

"You need to start calling me Matteo."

He could have sworn he heard her smile. "I want your top-ten list, *Matteo*."

The Chagall he'd recently purchased at auction drew his eye, a vivid splash of color against the cream entryway wall. "Over a bottle of Brunello in Tuscany, Quinn. Bring a sweater for the *castello*. It gets chilly at night."

"Have you forgotten?" Her low, sardonic tone dripped across the phone line. "I'm already ice-cold."

Low laughter escaped him. "Why, Quinn Davis, I think you have a sense of humor."

"Don't go imagining things.... I'll have our admins connect on the details."

She disconnected the call. He slipped his phone back into his pocket and shook his head. As far as standoffish women went, it was his theory that some were cold and uninviting at their core, while others just pretended to be so for a whole variety of reasons. The latter category had always fascinated him. Often proved the biggest challenge *and* the sweetest reward. He'd bet his Chagall Quinn was one of them.

Too bad that particular challenge was off-limits. If his vow to swear off women wasn't enough of a reason to put Quinn in that category, his ten-million-dollar one was.

He settled in and called Riccardo, an intense feeling of exhilaration moving through him. They had made it to the pitch. That's all he needed. No one could beat him in a room. *No one.*

His cold beer on the patio that night tasted very sweet indeed.

I should have taken the De Campo jet. Quinn embarked her commercial flight in Florence stiff, sleep deprived and wanting to strangle the man who'd sat beside her on the London to Italy leg, humming incessantly in her ear. She could have used the luxury of Matteo's flying spa to actually get some work done considering she was too much of a control freak to sleep on planes. Instead, she'd done an excellent impersonation of a Quinn sandwich lodged between two overweight men on the seven-hour overseas flight, unable to move and completely unproductive. Then had come the humming.

She pulled up the handle on her carry-on and wheeled it through to the arrivals area of the tiny airport. Unproductive was the sore point here with the amount of work she had on her plate. Luxe was in far worse condition than she and Warren had ever imagined. When they'd started peeling back the layers and taken a hard look at the real financials—it was clear Luxe's former parent company had been hiding a multitude of sins, including the fact that the restaurant wing of the chain was bleeding money at light speed. The rosy glow of Luxe's heyday had long since passed and things were definitely on a downward spiral.

Enter Quinn Davis. Miracle worker.

She sighed and sat down on a bench to wait for her suitcase. She could do this. One step at a time, her mother had always told her when she was a little girl, fretting over some issue or another. Even at six, Quinn had been the girl waiting for the hammer to drop. Waiting for the pin to prick the bubble of her happy existence. The only girl in her first-grade class who had refused to get a dog because it might get run over by a car like her friend Sally's had.

As if, despite all of Warren's and Sile's efforts, she'd known at the core of her she was different. That her life wasn't destined to be the gilded storybook it had been presented as.

She closed her eyes against the pressure starting to build in her head. Hadn't she proven time and time again in her short career she could do the impossible? She just needed to get this whirlwind two-day trip to Italy over with and move on to solving her real headaches. Like the handful of her restaurants that were literally falling apart because they hadn't been renovated in so long. The local strikes that were paralyzing her Mediterranean locations. Completely incompetent management in others.

Luxe had seen better days. Her dream assignment was turning into a nightmare. Fast.

The baggage belt finally coughed to life and spit out her suitcase. Pulling up the handle she wheeled it and her carry-on through the barely there customs checkpoint and out into the Tuscan sunshine. The heat of the summer day burned down on her head and shoulders. She stopped, stripped off her cardigan and wrapped it around her waist, pushed her sunglasses to the top of her head and searched for a sign with her name on it. She found Matteo instead, leaning against an atrociously expensive-looking sports car. Dressed in an Oxford University T-shirt and jeans that molded his long legs into a work of art, he looked cool, elegant and very Italian. Also scorching, singe-yourself-on-him hot.

Quinn's hand flew to her head and the French twist she hadn't straightened since…when? London? She must look a sight. Her slacks were creased, her shirt had a coffee stain on it from where one of the men from her personal sandwich had dumped it on her and she was pretty sure she'd forgotten to wipe the breakfast cream cheese off her face. She reached up and swiped a palm across her mouth. What was it about the Italians that made you feel incredibly gauche just from your pure lack of style?

She had not expected her ride to be *him*.

He strolled toward her, his relaxed, indolent stride catching the eye of about twenty women around her. Her gaze dropped to the black lettering stretching across his biceps. *The tattoo.* Damn if it didn't give the whole package some serious edge.

Exactly what it didn't need. Her husband had been a pretty boy, the Ivy League son of a high-powered lawyer Warren had admired. Not Quinn's choice. His ego had required the kind of massive stroking it was impossible for one woman to administer. Unlike Matteo De Campo. He had it all built in. She doubted he'd had an uncertain day in his entire life.

The glitter in his gray eyes as he stopped in front of her said he hadn't missed her lustful look. She yanked in a breath of the fragrant, rose-scented Tuscan air. She needed to squash the physical attraction between them like a bug. Fast.

"You didn't need to come yourself," she murmured, caught off guard when he bent and pressed his lips first to one cheek, then the other. It was like being branded by a force she had no ability to cope with.

He drew back, his mocking glance sliding across her flushed face. "You're in Italy now, Quinn. We don't shake hands. We kiss."

She stepped back, wrapping her arms around herself. "You'll have to excuse my appearance. It's been a long day. I'm a mess."

"If that's a bad day," he murmured, his lazy gaze taking her in, "most women would kill to have more of them."

Her breath jammed in her throat. "You just can't help it, can you?"

"No," he agreed, smoky eyes laughing at her. "That's what playboys do, Quinn. Play. However," he drawled, picking up her bags and tossing them into the pitifully small backseat of the car, "I will endeavor to keep it to a bare minimum, just for you."

"You are too kind."

He held his hands up in a typically Italian gesture, then opened the passenger door for her. She slid in, absorbing the butter-soft interior of the car. "Fits the bad-boy image don't you think?"

The exotic car growled as he brought it roaring to life. She had to agree as he gunned it and they sped out of the airport that yes, it was sexy and so was the tattoo, which close-up, she could now see was in Latin, the beautifully scripted symbols set in a perfectly straight line across the hard muscles of his biceps. Unfortunately the Latin was mumbo jumbo to her. She was about to ask him what it meant when she clamped her jaw shut. Deciphering Matteo De Campo's tattoo was an activity better left for those actresses and models who were happy to let themselves fall for that type of meaningless charisma. She, on the other hand, knew better.

Matteo flicked her a sideways glance. "The *castello* is about an hour's drive. Feel free to relax and nap on the way. You look tired."

She grimaced. "I don't sleep on planes."

His mouth curved. "Don't tell me, you'd prefer to be flying it?"

"However did you know?"

"Just a wild guess. If you aren't going to sleep I'll pick your brain."

Pick her brain he did during the drive along the windy *autostrada* toward Siena. Commanding the powerful car

along the highway's twists and turns with a fearless aban-
don that made her heart pound, he asked a series of excellent questions about Luxe's operations and mandate while
at the same time managing to act as tour guide. His multi-
tasking, expressive hand movements and excessive speed
had Quinn grabbing for the door handle more than once.

"Any chance you can slow down?" she muttered after
one particularly terrifying turn. "Or is that too much to
ask of your playboy persona?"

His smile flashed white against his olive skin. "Too
much. Driving in Italy is a blood sport. You'd be asking
me to emasculate myself."

Not a chance, she thought grimly. It wasn't possible.
Not with those mouthwateringly muscled thighs flexing
beside her, drawing her attention every time he shifted
gears. Or his big, beautifully tapered hands that looked
as if they'd be masterful at any activity he pursued.... He
was the type of ultradangerous male you wouldn't know
you were in trouble with until you were way, *way* gone.

She lifted her gaze to the road, to the vibrant red pop-
pies dotting a sea of green on its edge. That was enough
of that.

Quinn focused on the information Matteo was impart-
ing about Montalcino, the town where the *castello* was
located. It had a bloodthirsty history, warred over for decades by its powerful foreign neighbors and even her own
neighboring city-states back in the days before Italy had
become a nation. The *castello* was actually a fortress, he
relayed. It had played a strategic role in the struggles between the Sienese and the invading powers.

"The cellar is actually the old dungeon where the prisoners of war were held. It's quite a showpiece. We think
it gives it great atmosphere."

That was one way of putting it. "They actually locked
people up down there?"

"*Si*. Some of them died." He laughed at her horrified expression. "When my grandfather bought the *castello* and we renovated, we found two old skulls we keep on display."

She recoiled. "How very macabre."

He shrugged. "Wars happen. Have since the beginning of time."

They swept around a turn and a magnificent stone building came into view, perched on the top of a hillside, towering over the mountainous forests that surrounded it. Quinn gasped. "Is that it?"

He nodded. "The *Castello* De Campo. Dates back to the Middle Ages."

She took in the sprawling brawn of the imposing burnt-orange structure, its square turrets and tall watchtower like something out of a movie. "It's incredible."

Matteo pointed toward the terraced vineyards that extended from the top of the mountain to the bottom. "The De Campo estate is actually a constellation of vineyards. The different slopes and elevations of the mountain offer each varietal the optimum growing conditions. Some of the whites such as the Chardonnay, for instance, are planted further above sea level, where the nights are cool and the ripening season long, whereas the Brunellos, the king of our reds, thrive at a lower level."

"Margarite is obsessed with your Brunello."

"Who?"

"My head sommelier."

"So she should be," he murmured cockily. "We'll have one tonight."

She was so exhausted she might fall flat on her face if she drank anything. But Margarite would kill her if she passed up the opportunity to try the famous, lusty De Campo red.

"The scale is breathtaking," she said to him. "How many varietals do you produce?"

"Fifteen." He flicked her a glance. "Do you ride? I thought we would do the tour by horseback tomorrow."

"Not well," she admitted. She was suspicious of horses. They were big, heavy, unpredictable animals. Kind of like men. She didn't need either of them in her life.

It was impossible not to think how much more history De Campo had than Silver Kangaroo as Matteo parked the car in front of the magnificent *castello* and carried her bags inside. It was everywhere. In the century-old, mature vineyards surrounding the castle, in the family crest on the building as they came in, in the third generation of winemakers producing the glorious vintages here. Silver Kangaroo was only twenty years old. Although there was something to be said for such a young winery winning so many awards in such a short amount of time, it couldn't compare to De Campo in lineage.

Matteo led her into the magnificent tiled hallway of the west wing which was the personal residence of the De Campo family. With its cathedral ceiling and stunning frescos it was truly amazing. Like she'd walked into the home of royalty.

Matteo introduced her to Maria, the Italian housekeeper who had run the De Campo household since he was a boy, then led her up a winding staircase to a turret bedroom that took her breath away. The exposed brick walls of the *castello* extended into a double-arched stone wall that separated a sitting room with a fireplace from the bedroom and its huge canopied bed. The beautiful, rich fabrics covering the room cast everything in a golden, luxurious hue that might have been a royal princess's bedroom.

It evoked a strange feeling in Quinn. She'd spent much of her life feeling like the imposter princess. Her birth father, a factory worker in Mississippi, even now worked two jobs to make ends meet for his family. She knew because she'd hired a private detective to find them and learned the real truth about her adoption. Unlike the story she'd been fed by a well-meaning Warren and Sile, it hadn't been as simple as her mother having an affair with a married man and giving her up because of the complications of their relationship. Her mother had gone on to marry her father and they'd had another girl. Her sister.

To replace the girl they'd given away.

"Quinn?" Matteo was looking at her with a raised brow. "Everything okay?"

She blinked. "It's stunning, thank you. I can't imagine what it must have been like to grow up in a castle."

"I have stories." A wry smile tipped his mouth. "You can imagine the hiding spots three industrious boys found."

She smiled. "Some impossible to find ones, I'll bet. Will I get to meet your parents tonight?"

He shook his head. "Unfortunately, no. Antonio serves on the boards of a couple of major corporations. He's in London right now for meetings and my mother is in Florence where she prefers to stay."

Interesting arrangement. While her mother was alive, Warren would fly all night to get home to her. They hadn't spent a night apart that wasn't business. Her stomach twisted. In many ways, Sile's tragic death at a far-too-early age had turned her father into a different man. Taken the small amount of softness Warren possessed with her, his anger at her death so raw and all-consuming.

"Does seven suit for dinner?" Matteo asked. "If you sleep after that you should be able to get into the time."

"That's perfect, thank you."

"*Fino a stasera.* Until tonight…"

And why did even that sound sexy? She closed the door behind him and blamed it on the accent. Accents were always sexy on a man. His, particularly so.

She looked longingly at the bed. *Just a couple more hours,* she told herself, intending on showering first and catching up on email. But her eyelids burned from fatigue and she felt as if her body had been pummeled in a boxing match. Maybe a few minutes with her eyes closed on the high canopy bed in the beautiful, fairy-tale-ish room would refresh her enough to make it through dinner.

Help her figure out exactly how she was going to avoid the inescapable attraction she felt toward her host. Her reaction to him, she decided, curling up on the satin comforter, was probably due to the fact she hadn't looked at a man since Julian had left. Had buried herself in work lest the humiliation of it all become simply too much to bear. She hugged the pillow to her. Quinn never intended to feel that kind of humiliation ever again. From any man. So she was missing the gene that allowed her to be truly intimate with another person.... The way she'd survived in this world, the way she'd survived as a Davis was to shield her heart. To not let herself feel.

It was easier that way. To not *need* anyone. And she wasn't changing her strategy now.

Matteo knocked on the heavy wooden door of Quinn's suite just after seven, his game plan firmly in place. Ply her with an incomparable Brunello, impress her with the history and atmosphere of De Campo over dinner in the cellar and, most importantly, find out why she'd ranked them fourth on her list.

A piece of cake, as the Americans would say.

When there was no response to his knock, he rapped again, harder. Nothing. Strange. Quinn seemed like the overly punctual type. He was knocking on the two-inch-thick door a third time when it flew open and she stood before him, bleary-eyed, dark hair flowing over her shoulders in a jumbled mass of curls.

"I'm so sorry," she murmured. "I fell asleep."

He wasn't. She had the face of an angel when she wasn't

frowning. Her big green eyes had a sleepy, muted golden edge to them, an intense vulnerability he couldn't tear his gaze from. He had the feeling this was the *real* Quinn Davis. The softness behind the hard edge she liked to present to the world. Unfiltered.

His gaze drifted down over the flushed, rosy skin of her cheeks, her full, pouty lips that were the kind a man imagined wrapped around a certain part of his anatomy...

Matteo's body temperature soared. Quinn cleared her throat. The flicker of sexual awareness that replaced the vulnerability in her eyes slammed into him with the force of a hammer. *Merda.* Where had he ever gotten the impression this woman was cold? Or maybe it was just that she was a perfect combination of fire and ice?

Quinn dropped her gaze to somewhere around his shoulder and waved a hand at him. "Give me five minutes and I'll be ready."

He nodded. The click of the door brought back his sanity. Bringing Quinn Davis to her knees in that particular fashion might have been the natural order of things for him—but, regrettably, he needed to use his brain on this one, not his body.

Unfortunate. But not nearly as unfortunate as the consequences of not playing this one by the book.

Quinn emerged in a navy dress that made the most of her voluptuous curves in her usual, conservative fashion. Her ultracomposed, cool demeanor was firmly back in place.

"I hope this is okay?" She smoothed her hands over her hips. "You didn't specify."

"Perfetto." He nodded. "I'm sorry, I should have mentioned it was just the two of us dining in the cellar. Anything goes."

A wary look crossed her face. His lips curved. "I promise my best behavior, Quinn. We can recite every last statistic on De Campo over dinner. I'll even tell you what we polish the floors with."

"Ha, ha," she murmured, long lashes coming down to veil her expression. "I wasn't worried."

Si, *you were.* He wasn't the only one having a hard time handling the chemistry between them, but he instinctively knew Quinn Davis had to feel in control of a situation for him to accomplish anything tonight, so he let it go.

Fortunately, he was an expert at the slow, insidious penetration of a woman's defenses.

He took her on a tour of the west wing, showing her the centuries-old library, the opulent, chandelier-encrusted ballroom and the music room with the grand piano. When she had a suitably glazed-over look at the pure scale of things, he took her through the stone hallways to the east wing where the restaurant was just starting to fill up with locals and tourists. She was unfailingly polite and charming to his chef, making Guerino Pisani smile broadly and insist she come back after dinner to let him know how she liked it. Was it just him, the playboy, she disliked then?

His ego slightly dented, Matteo led Quinn down the dark, winding stone stairwell to the cellar. "You weren't kidding," she murmured, craning her neck to take in the two ancient skulls that sat backlit in one of the alcoves. "Do you know who they belonged to?"

"We assume someone unfit for a Christian burial. Spaniards, the French, the forces of the Holy Roman Emperor Charles V, they were all imprisoned down here. Also the Aldobrandeschi and the Guelphs of Florence—powerful families at war with the Sienese."

She followed him down the hallway to the cellar. The stone walls on either side of them were thick slabs of rock that would have made escape impossible. Collections of medieval weapons—swords, pikes, helmets and breastplates—were lit on either side of them.

"It all seems so brutal," Quinn said, giving them a long look.

"It was. It was hand-to-hand combat in its most savage form."

That feeling of brutality remained in the majestic cellar Matteo's grandfather Alfonso De Campo had built. The exposed brick walls rose thirty feet, tiny bar-encased windows the only natural light entering the room. The muted lighting hinted at a history of darkness. But it was the feeling that souls had suffered here that got into your bones. Even with all the elegant touches Alfonso had included—the dark walnut shelving that rose fifteen feet high to house De Campo's most precious vintages and the elegant, hand-turned showpiece of a bar.

"It's breathtaking," Quinn murmured, wide-eyed. "Did they *execute* prisoners down here?"

His mouth tilted. "From what I've been told, most died from existing injuries."

She didn't look so reassured by the response. He held a chair out for her at the candlelit table for two the serving staff had set in the middle of the room. Then he sat down opposite her and swept his hand toward the bottle of wine breathing in the middle of the table. "You'll have some?"

She scanned the label. The Brunello he'd chosen was the highest-ranking bottle in De Campo's one-hundred-year-old history. Apparently, its significance wasn't lost on Quinn, a wry smile curving her mouth. "Refuse the 1970 De Campo Brunello? I think not."

He poured the rich dark red, almost brown liquid into their glasses and held his own up. "To a successful partnership."

She tilted her glass in a mocking salute. "So confident."

"I don't intend to lose, Quinn."

"Then let the best candidate win." Her green gaze glittered as she lifted her glass and swirled its dark contents around the edge. She closed her eyes and breathed the wine in. He found himself hypnotized by the way she gave herself over to the full sensual experience. Quinn Davis was *definitely* scorching hot on the inside. The type who would be more than a match for any man. The question was, did she ever drop that rigid exterior and let herself go?

Stretch out like a cat and let a man pleasure her until she screamed?

She opened her eyes. Looked directly into his. He was not nearly quick enough to wipe the curiosity off his face. A rosy hue stole over her golden skin, her gaze dropping away from his.

He could work with this.

"So," she murmured huskily, after their food had been served, "give me your list."

He sat back in his chair and balanced the Brunello on his knee. "The wine list in your Park Avenue property is far too big. You're giving people too much choice. Distracting them. You need to allow your sommelier to do his job and sell the wines."

She frowned. "People like choice. I like choice. I hate it when I go to a place that tries to tell me what I want to drink."

"*Si,* but you have too much choice. The night Riccardo and I were there, a couple at the table beside us were all set to splurge on an expensive bottle, but by the time they got through your monstrosity of a list, they gave up and ordered a midend vintage they were familiar with. Your sommelier," he drawled, "never made it to their table that night."

"We're short-staffed there," she said defensively.

"It was a Tuesday night at six. There were empty tables."

She was silent. Pursed her lips. "Go on..."

"You need more beautiful women working the bar."

She lifted a brow. "So men can go ogle them and spend

their money? This is a high-end restaurant I'm running, Matteo, not a strip joint."

"Precisely. Seventy-five percent of the patrons at the bar that night were men—financial power players having a drink after work. Those types are all about the eye candy. You put a beautiful woman in front of them, they'll stay longer, drink more and I guarantee, they'll keep coming back."

"I suppose I should have them in short skirts, too?"

"Sex sells, Quinn."

She sighed and leaned back in her chair. "Sometimes I think life would be so much easier if I were a man. You are such simple creatures."

He smiled at that. "If you mean honest and straightforward about how we feel without a hundred pounds of analysis spread on top of it, then *si*, it's true."

"But in being that way, you miss many of the subtleties of life."

"Care to give an example?"

"I'd prefer you finish your list."

By the time he had and they'd eaten dinner, Quinn had the glaring feeling she'd vastly underestimated how valuable De Campo could be in helping her dig Luxe out of the mess it was in. Matteo was clearly a brilliant businessman and a marketing genius. De Campo *was* making scads of money at its übertrendy wine bar locations on the East and West Coasts. She'd done the research.

"You make some very good points," she conceded, pushing her empty plate away. "But there still remains the fact you are competition for us in the restaurant space."

He shook his head. "It's not the same clientele. Go sit in one of our wine bars. The customer is ten years younger at least. They do not have the disposable income to eat at Luxe."

Her gaze sharpened. "How would you guarantee you wouldn't compete with us in the future? Write it into the contract?"

He flinched, a slight, almost imperceptible movement. "We could talk about that."

She pressed her lips together. "It's a problem. I agree that there are synergies there. But I can't sell this to the board if we're going to be competing against each other."

"Who's to say Silver Kangaroo won't get into the restaurant business? You can't know what's going to happen in the future."

"But I can hedge my bets. Make my decisions based on the facts I have now."

He picked up the wine and poured the last of it into their glasses. It occurred to her she should probably refuse any more but the legendary Brunello was just too good to turn down.

He fixed that intense dark stare on her, the one that made her pulse jump all over the place. "Why fourth, Quinn? Why originally rank us fourth when you so clearly want a pure wine play, not a big behemoth."

Maybe the wine was loosening her tongue, but she decided he deserved to know. "In my mind, De Campo is an arrogant, self-satisfied brand. Yes, you make exceptional wine. Your lineage is impeccable. But you represent what Luxe *used* to be. Not where we're going. Silver Kangaroo is young, vibrant and fresh. A bit on the eclectic side. It fits perfectly with where I intend to take the Luxe brand."

A frown furrowed his brow. "De Campo is not an arrogant brand. A proud brand—yes. A brand with a century of heritage behind it—yes. But arrogant? You're wrong."

She tilted her head to one side. "I beg to differ."

"I have third-party brand studies that will *show* you you're wrong. That we appeal to a young, hip demographic."

"Brand studies are a self-serving exercise in making a

company feel good about itself," she countered. "It's an instinctual feeling I have, Matteo, and at the end of the day, that is how I will make my decision. Instinct."

Frustration glinted in his eyes. "You need to visit Gabriele in Napa. He is light-years ahead of Silver Kangaroo."

She nodded. "I will if time permits."

A server came to take their dishes away. "That was fantastic," she murmured, sure she could crawl into bed right now and sleep for twenty-four hours. "Maybe I should steal Guerino away from you."

He flashed a lazy smile. "Sorry. He'll never leave Italy."

"So sad." She tried to ignore how the dark stubble that covered his jaw was even more pronounced tonight as he spoke to the waiter in Italian. How it took his rakish good looks to a whole new dangerous level. But the warmth from the wine had turned her limbs into mush and her brain along with it. He had been mentally undressing her earlier, she was sure of it, and what had she done? Just let him keep on doing it. Insane, really, when this was all about business and this was Matteo they were talking about. The playboy who couldn't keep it in his pants.

Unfortunately that didn't stop her from studying his beautiful, elegant hands as he gestured to the server. It made her think of a quote she'd read in one of the tabloids while getting her hair done. One of Matteo's exes—the curator of a Manhattan art gallery—had made an incredibly blunt comment about how he'd been the best she'd ever had. Then had gone on to suggest she'd like to sample him again—all while dating the studlike quarterback of New York's pro football team.

He couldn't be that good. Could he? Or would those gorgeous hands be the perfect instrument to seduce a woman slowly, taking the time to savor her?

"Quinn?"

Her gaze flew guiltily to his. "Sorry?"

The grooves on either side of his mouth deepened. "Crème caramel or chocolate torte for dessert? Personally, I think Guerino's crème caramel is the best in Italy."

"Definitely the crème caramel." She might even manage to spoon some in her mouth before she did a face-plant in it.

Matteo relayed their choice to the server, then miraculously produced another bottle of Brunello. She held up a hand. "No more wine for me, thank you."

"I'll drink most of it," he said smoothly. "Live a little."

Her shoulders stiffened. Julian had said that to her all the time in that condescending, highbrow voice of his. *"Live a little, Quinn. Show me you can have some fun or you might drive me elsewhere."*

"Just half a glass," she said quietly.

"That was a joke, you know," he murmured, his gaze on her face. "Although you are known to be a workaholic. Just as driven as your father, insiders say."

Impossible. She'd never met a human being on this earth as driven as Warren. Her mouth twisted. "And what else did your intelligence turn up?"

"You made the top thirty under thirty business people in America this year. One of only two women. That must have made Warren proud."

Questionable. He hadn't much commented even though she'd been aching for him to. Quinn took a sip of the heady wine. Rolled it around her mouth and set the glass down. "No matter what people like to believe, there is still a glass ceiling for women. But I had advantages from the start."

"*Si*, but you've also had the disadvantage of being very beautiful. Many men don't take that seriously."

"Do you?"

His smile flashed white in the candlelight. "I've never underestimated a woman in my life, beautiful or otherwise. You would rule the world if men weren't physically stronger."

He looked genuine when he said that. Quinn had the ghastly idea she might actually like Matteo De Campo after these couple of days. Which was really, really not a good idea.

"So," she murmured, taking another sip of her wine, "what else was in your report?"

"The usual. Harvard, your rapid climb up the corporate ladder…" An amused glitter entered his eyes. "I have to say, the graduate-level Krav Maga caught me off guard. Interesting choice."

How had he found out about that? She never talked publicly about it. Went to the most discreet school in Chicago specifically to avoid that type of publicity.

She waved her hand at him, brushing it off. "It's an outlet."

"Hardly." That smoky, perceptive gaze stayed on hers. "Krav Maga is a street-fighting martial art, Quinn. The Israeli army trains its soldiers in it. It's hardly a casual outlet."

She shifted in her seat. And lied. "A girlfriend was doing it. It suits my competitive personality."

It would also make any man think twice about putting his hands on her ever again.

"Since we're trading interesting facts about one another," she said, changing the subject, "I'm intrigued by the tattoo. What does it mean?"

He touched his fingers to his biceps, as if he'd forgotten it was there. "It means 'never forget.'"

"Never forget what?" The words tumbled out of her mouth before she could stop them.

Matteo's gaze darkened to the deep slate of gunmetal. "My best friend, Giancarlo, died in a car accident recently. It was pointless. Unnecessary."

Oh. The way he said *unnecessary* sent a chill through her. The grief she saw in his eyes was something she knew all too well. *Dammit,* she castigated herself, she should not have asked that. The wine had been a bad, bad idea.

"I am so sorry," she murmured huskily, needing to say something into the heavy silence. "I lost my mother when I was ten. It makes you question everything, doesn't it?"

He nodded. "*Si.* It does."

The conversation stumbled after that. There was a darkness surrounding Matteo that contrasted strikingly with his earlier charming demeanor. When they'd finished dessert, he suggested she must be tired. She nodded and said that she was. Her head was starting to spin now. It was way past time for her jet-lagged body to be in bed.

They stopped by the kitchen where she gave Guerino her compliments, then walked over to the west wing. On the circular, steep stairwell to her turret bedroom, her head started to spin in a dizzying pattern that made the ascent in four-inch heels particularly challenging. Halfway up, her shoe caught in a rivet. She stumbled and teetered in the ridiculously high designer heels, and would have fallen if Matteo hadn't been behind her. He cursed, swept his arm under her knees and caught her up in his arms.

"Wh-what are you doing?" She dug her fingers into his muscular shoulders and held on for dear life.

"Making sure you don't break your neck," he muttered, carrying her up the last flight and down the hallway to her room. "Why you women wear those heels is beyond me."

She was too busy registering that wow, he was strong and so hot carrying her like this to pay much attention to the rebuke. He smelled delicious, too, the spicy, exotic scent of his aftershave filling her nostrils.

"I think I might have overdone the wine," she offered faintly as he set her down on the floor outside her room. He kept his hands around her waist as if scared she would keel over, his fingers burning into her skin like a brand. Quinn looked up at his gorgeous, sexy face, at the dark stubble she was dying to run her fingers over and told herself this was business.

Business. Business. Business.

The heat that arced between them like a living, breathing thing was not. It had been there from the moment she'd laid eyes on him and it was getting worse. The reluctant but oh-so-interested glitter in those smoky gray eyes wasn't helping.

"Ice-cold?" he drawled. "I think not, Quinn."

The heat pooling in her abdomen rose up to her face. For the first time since Julian had walked out on her two years ago, *she* was interested. She wanted, badly, to kiss a member of the opposite sex. And not just any member of the opposite sex. Matteo De Campo!

CHAPTER FOUR

IF IT HAD BEEN any woman other than Quinn Davis that Matteo had his hands on, if he hadn't just plied her with a bottle of Brunello and perhaps most importantly, if he hadn't promised his brother he'd keep his hands off her, Matteo would have stepped in, closed his hands firmer around her tiny waist and taken what she was so obviously offering.

Her forest-green eyes were hazy with desire and a curiosity that hit him square in the solar plexus. Her hips were soft under the span of his hands, her body primed for an exploration he was oh so ready to give her. And that perfume she was wearing, the one he'd given her, *merda,* did the spicy scent do something to him.

However, this *was* Quinn Davis standing in front of him, a tipsy Quinn Davis, and his fantasies had to stop here. He switched off the part of his brain that said to hell with it, lifted his hands from her with an exaggerated movement and stepped back. "See, Quinn?" A taunting smile curved his lips. "I can keep my hands to myself."

She planted a hand against the wall to steady herself, a defiant glitter stirring to life in her eyes. "Too much wine and a brief moment of madness. Don't flatter yourself thinking it would have gone anywhere."

He quirked a brow. "You don't think so? I may be all

kinds of arrogant, Quinn, but I know when a woman wants me to kiss her."

Her lush mouth parted, then slammed shut. At a loss for words. It might just have been the best part of the whole evening.

"Breakfast at eight tomorrow." He waved his hand in the direction of the family dining room. "We'll take it downstairs. And wear something appropriate for horseback."

She sunk her teeth into her bottom lip. "I told you I don't ride well."

"Not to worry, I have a gorgeous, even-tempered mare for you to ride. You'll love her."

She didn't look convinced.

"Good night," he murmured. "I'm at the end of the hall if you need anything."

The look she flashed him said it would be a cold day in hell before she ventured into his bedroom. Laughing inwardly, he turned on his heel and left.

If she only knew the things he could do to her.

With his brain on New York time and unable to sleep, Matteo headed down to the study, called Riccardo and told him to get working on a solution for Quinn's competitive concerns. "The board will never approve a clause in the contract," his brother dismissed. "We'll have to find another way."

"That's why they pay you the big bucks," Matteo inserted. "Find it."

His brother's husky laughter echoed in his ears. He put the phone down, pushed to his feet and paced to the window. The lights from the *castello* cast an amber glow over the surrounding hills, their peaks looming dark and endless the farther the eye traveled. The view was usually enough to bring him peace, but tonight he knew how steep his journey was about to get. He needed to convince Quinn that all this was what she should sign De Campo for. That no vineyard anywhere in the world produced vintages as fine as theirs or was as impressive. Which was what tomorrow's tour would do.

What concerned him more was Quinn's perception of De Campo as a self-satisfied, traditional brand. How was he going to dispel that if she wouldn't even look at his research? Sending her to visit Gabriele in Napa might be the only way. She was as stubborn as Matteo was. And as closed a book as he'd ever seen. You might manage to penetrate those outer layers, but she was never going to let you any further in than that.

Exhaling deeply, he pushed away from the window and climbed the stairs to his room. He needed sleep. But his mind, as he folded himself into bed, was wide-awake. The anniversary of Giancarlo's death was just days away. His role in that tragedy haunted him every waking hour of his life. Made it impossible to forget. So he focused on that utterly beddable version of Quinn standing outside her room instead. Anything not to go there.

He was now convinced Julian Edwards was a fool. That he couldn't have been man enough for his wife. Because if that'd been him, if he'd had Quinn in his bed, she wouldn't have been going anywhere.

He didn't need to know what it would be like to taste her. He'd already done it in his head.

Quinn woke with a massive headache and a severe desire to avoid snorting, four-legged beasts who could accidentally crush you with a misplaced step. Also a particular two-legged variety whose name started with Matteo and ended with De Campo.

Unfortunately avoidance was not an acceptable strategy, so two aspirin and two cups of Maria's strong black Tuscan coffee would have to do for the headache. As for the beast part? Both versions looked disgustingly fresh and beautiful in the dewy morning air, a jeans-clad Matteo in a navy T-shirt, his dark hair still damp from the shower, making a mockery of 99 percent of the world's male population in casual attire. He was holding the reins of a dark brown mare with elegant long legs, certainly of aristocratic heritage.

Quinn stood there, head throbbing, staring dubiously at them both.

"I'd really rather go on foot."

"She is irreproachably lovely," Matteo countered. "You'll be fine."

He held the stirrup out. She took a tentative step toward the horse. Jumped as the mare snorted and blew out a breath, sending a puff of steam snaking through the air. She pressed a hand to her pounding heart. Matteo's mouth curved. "You had a bad experience with a horse?"

She nodded. "One bolted on me as a child. I've been too afraid to ride since."

"Someone should have gotten you back in the saddle right away. That's the key."

"They tried. I wouldn't do it." She shifted her weight to both feet and exhaled slowly. "Really, I'd rather walk."

"Quinn." There was no mistaking the command in his voice. "You cannot miss out on this experience for the rest of your life because you're scared. I've never seen Marica bolt on someone. *Ever.*"

She sliced him the sharpest of looks. "I'm not stupid. Anything can make a horse shy and bolt. Even the nicest animal in the world, which I'm sure she is."

"And here I did not take you for a quitter," he taunted, eyes flashing. "Fine." He gathered up the reins. "I'll take the horses back to the stable and we'll take the car."

Humiliation seared through her as he started to lead the

mare away. She wasn't a quitter. She wasn't ever a quitter. *Damn him*.

"Okay, fine." He stopped and turned around. "I'll do it. But so help me God if she bolts on me I will make you pay."

His gray eyes crinkled at the corners. "How...thought provoking. You have a deal, Quinn Davis."

He led the horse back to her. The inquisitive mare cocked her ears and budged Quinn's arm with her nose. Her heart slammed into her chest. God help her. This was so not right.

Matteo held the stirrup out for her. "I'll be here beside you every step of the way."

That was not supercomforting. Not after last night. Not after she'd pretty much thrown herself at him and he'd walked away. She pressed her lips together and slid the ball of her foot into the stirrup. Hoisted herself up. Mounting a horse wasn't nearly as easy as it looked and her lack of momentum would have sent her back to the ground if Matteo hadn't planted a firm hand on her denim-clad behind and pushed her into the saddle.

Heat flooded her face as she sank her hips down into the leather. "Thank you."

"Mounting's the hardest part," he came back, deadpan.

She picked up the reins and focused on the terrifying beast rather than on Matteo's double entendres. She had no doubt he could dish them out all day and night.

He swung into the saddle of his very big, very dangerous-looking stallion with a lithe movement.

"What's his name?" she gibed. "Lucifer?"

His eyes gleamed with laughter. "Anteros, after the Italian god of love and passion. Perfect for me, don't you think?"

"Utterly."

His smile widened. "*Andiamo*. Let's go."

He went first on the big stallion, leading the way down

the narrow dirt road that wound its way through the mountain. True to his word, Marica followed quietly, picking her dainty way down the path. Quinn's heartbeat slowed as she took in the lush green hills dotted with the most exquisitely colored wildflowers. The rows upon rows of perfectly straight, perfectly groomed vines. Matteo pointed out the different crops at each elevation, detailing the ideal growing conditions for each varietal and why.

When the sun had risen high in the sky, they took a break for lunch in the winery. Matteo and his master winemaker took her through the complex techniques they used to produce some of the world's most exquisite wines. Then it was back on horseback to explore the other side of the mountain where the prize Brunellos and Chiantis were cultivated.

They finished the tour high up on the mountain as the sun was setting, a fiery red ball sinking behind the hills. Quinn pulled her mare to a halt behind Anteros, so glad she had taken the challenge and gone on horseback. The view would not have been nearly the same in a Jeep. Would not have allowed her to truly appreciate the beauty and scale of the massive historic vineyard.

She leaned over and patted the mare's silky neck, feeling rather victorious at conquering her fear. The sun and fresh air had cleared the throb in her head and chased away her jet lag.

"You really are lovely," she murmured. The mare's ears pricked up as if to say, *yes, I know.*

Matteo dismounted, tethered his horse and came to stand beside her. A smile curved his lips. "Feeling braver?"

She shrugged. "You were right. She's wonderful."

"She is."

She slid her feet out of the stirrups. Her legs felt like limp spaghetti, her butt so numb she couldn't feel it anymore. "Walking might be an issue," she murmured.

"Why do you think I'm standing here?" He held out his hands. "Come."

Why that command made her heartbeat increase by about ten beats per second was beyond her. She swung her leg over the saddle and let him lift her down. He kept his hands around her waist as he had last night to steady her, except this time she hadn't consumed a bottle of wine and she had her wits about her. Not that that seemed to help. His earthy, male scent was even more intoxicating than the aftershave he'd had on the night before. The hard strength of his arms around her equally so. Maybe it was just the general Matteo effect, she admitted, pulling in a steadying breath. Because he was more male than any man she'd met in her life. Hands down.

She stepped back and made herself busy spreading the blanket he handed her on the grass. If she didn't look at all the maleness and certainly if she didn't touch it, she could keep this under control.

Right?

Matteo took a bottle of De Campo's prizewinning champagne out of the saddlebags, along with glasses and a Swiss Army knife. Quinn gave him a wry glance as she eased her sore body down on the blanket. "Not too much for me."

"You can't enjoy this view without at least a taste." He handed her the glasses and deftly opened the bottle. "It's a tradition."

The sparkling liquid he poured into their glasses was the palest of golden yellows. The blanket seemed to shrink to miniscule proportions as he folded himself down beside her and handed her a glass. She eased toward the opposite edge in a subtle movement. The corners of Matteo's mouth lifted. "I'm hogging," she offered in an offhand tone.

"Mmm," he nodded. "You and your huge surface mass." She couldn't help her smile. She unleashed it so infrequently these days it felt good to get it out. "Thank you for today," she said, tipping her glass toward him. "I'm glad you convinced me to do it on horseback. It was amazing."

"Prego." He lifted his glass. *"Salute."*

She tipped the liquid into her mouth. The tiny bubbles exploded on her tongue like the most potent ambrosia. Wow. She wasn't normally a huge fan of champagne or any sparkling wine for that matter, but this was dry and tart and perfectly balanced.

Matteo sat back on his elbows. "So tell me about our trip to St. Lucia. What are we going to see?"

She drew her knees up to her chest and wrapped her arms around them, letting her glass dangle from her fingers. "We have two hotels on the island. They'll allow you to see the two sides of Luxe, one of our jewels, and one of our properties that needs a lot of work. Paradis Entre les Montagnes near the island's famous twin volcanoes has been ranked one of the world's top five luxury hotels. Our chef there is top-notch, the menu ready to go for the wine pairings. Le Belle Bleu, on the north end of the island, is about to reopen after an extensive renovation. It's a work in progress. The menus haven't been finalized yet. But all the more reason for you to meet with the chef and develop the pairings from the ground up."

He plied her with questions as they drank their champagne. Lifted the bottle in question when she finished her half glass.

"No...thank you," she murmured dryly. "But I am sold. On all of it." She waved her hand at the vineyard and *castello* spread out in front of them in all its magnificence. "You must be so proud to be part of such history."

He nodded. "I'm incredibly privileged to be a De Campo. Absolutely."

She heard a hesitation in his voice. "But?"

He shrugged and looked down at the *castello,* sparkling

like golden fire in the dying rays of the sun. "Being a De Campo can be a challenge."

"Your father is difficult." Which was putting Antonio De Campo's legendary reputation mildly.

His mouth twisted. "He's a titan. I'm sure you can relate."

"Ah yes. I wonder what would happen if we put Antonio and Warren in the ring together? Who would win?"

His smile deepened. "I'd be fascinated to see."

"Did you all choose the family business or was it expected of you?"

"There was no choice. We are De Campos."

Sounded familiar. "Didn't Riccardo race cars for a while?"

"*Si.*" He took a long swallow of his wine. "My father made it hell for him when he came back."

"Why *did* he come back?"

"Antonio was ill. He wanted Riccardo to take the reins."

She threw him a curious look. "What would you have been if you hadn't been a De Campo then? If you could have chosen?"

He arched a dark brow at her. "Is this an attempt to peer into my psyche? Part of your partner personality analysis?"

She smiled. "Answer the question."

"I would have been a concert pianist."

Her jaw dropped. "Seriously?"

He lifted a shoulder. "I'm not half bad. I minored in music at Oxford."

Those hands. Her gaze slid to their elegant length. She yanked it back with effort. *Oh, no, you don't, Quinn. Don't you dare start getting fascinated.*

"And you?" He waved a hand at her. "What would you have been if not a high-ranking executive?"

"I don't know," she said honestly. "I've never stopped to think about it. From the minute Warren saw me make scads of money with a lemonade stand, there was never any question of my path."

His mouth tipped up at the corner. "How did Thea end up, of all things, a veterinarian?"

"She was hopeless with numbers. It was just never going to happen. Warren gave up."

"And you filled the gap." He slid her a sideways look. "You seem very different, you two."

She lifted her shoulders. "I'm adopted. Not surprising."

"How did my intelligence miss *that?*"

"It's not something we talk about publicly. Warren and Sile adopted me when I was less than a year old."

"Do you know who your birth parents are?"

She nodded. "They live in Mississippi. They weren't able to keep me."

Something in her voice must have alerted him to the wealth of emotion beneath the surface. His gaze rested on her, but he didn't push. "You and Thea seem close despite the differences."

"We are." She smiled. "Thea is the one who believes in fairy tales. I'm the cynic always waiting for the penny to drop. We balance each other out."

"Does the penny always drop?"

She stared down at the glowing *castello*. "Sometimes it does."

He studied her for a long moment. "My brothers and I are very different too. But close as well. Riccardo likes to rule the world. Gabriele is obsessed with his wine."

"And you?"

"I'm not sure I want a label. Care to give me one?"

Undeniably sexy. Broodily magnetic? There were just so many. She shook her head. Safer that way.

"Do you play the piano for others?"

"Not usually no."

"Do you take requests to do so?"

"Are you asking?"

"Maybe." Dammit, yes she was curious, so curious to see how those beautiful hands worked a piano.

It was better than imagining them carrying out the slow and easy seduction of a woman. Something she was definitely, absolutely never going to experience.

His gaze turned an incendiary gray. "How about I play for you when De Campo wins the pitch?"

Her heart tripped over itself. "Gambling again…"

"Gambling is a miscalculation." He levered himself up off his elbows. "Like me betting on the fact that you don't want me to kiss you right now when you absolutely do."

"I don't," she whispered, her palms going sweaty as he leaned toward her.

"Liar," he murmured, cupping her jaw in his fingers, his gaze locked on hers. "You wanted me to kiss you last night and you want me to kiss you now."

"To which you did the smart thing and walked away," she protested weakly.

"Yes, but last night you'd had a bottle of wine. Tonight you're sober."

"Matteo—this is—"

"Just a kiss…" he murmured, bending his dark head toward her. She sucked in a breath, sure that wasn't going to be an adequate description. The slow, easy slide of his mouth across hers, as if he had all the time in the world, was so unlike the urgent, rough caresses Julian had always started with that it rocked her world. Then he did it again and again, until she was craving a firmer contact. Needing it. Her fingers curled into the soft jersey of his T-shirt, steadying herself, urging him on, she wasn't sure which.

He made a low sound under his breath, angled his mouth over hers and took the kiss deeper, exploring every centimeter of her lips with a sensual thoroughness that turned her into a mindless pile of flesh, his to command.

She had never known it could be like this—so deliciously intoxicating, so obviously meant to arouse and enjoy; not to dominate. Here on the top of the mountain, in a place like heaven, where nothing and no one else existed, she never wanted it to end.

"Matteo—" The word sounded so breathless and needy Quinn could hardly believe it was coming from her. He reached down, captured her hand and brought it to the back of his head. Invited her closer. The wiry coarseness of his hair beneath her fingertips was undeniably male, the teasing pressure of his tongue against the corner of her mouth tantalizing. She knew if she let him in it was going to be another mind-bending demonstration of what she'd been missing. But she did it anyway because she couldn't resist.

Big mistake. It was hot and never ending.

She never wanted it to end.

"Quinn."

The husky word pulled from Matteo's throat penetrated her consciousness with the force of a hammer. He dragged his lips across her cheek and rested his forehead against hers. "Now might be a good time to stop."

Stop? What was she doing?

She yanked her hand from around his neck and sat back, her palm covering her mouth. *Oh, my god.* She couldn't believe she'd just let him do that. That she'd participated in it. Eagerly.

Matteo's mouth flattened. "It was just a kiss, Quinn."

Just a kiss? She'd been necking with a man she could potentially award a ten-million-dollar contract to. If that wasn't a conflict of interest she wasn't sure what was!

Apparently he was starting to realize that too, because he'd whitened under that dark tan of his. "It won't happen again."

"You're damn right it won't happen again…" She jammed her palms against her temples. "We can't be kissing each other, Matteo. Despite your need to satisfy your curiosity with every woman on two legs."

He scowled. "That is not what that was."

"What was it then?"

He sighed. "A need to satisfy a curiosity specific to you, Quinn. And, a massive mistake, I agree."

She squashed the flutter that flickered to life in her stomach. Matteo rolled to his feet and held out a hand. "Your flight is early tomorrow. We should go."

She eyed the appendage warily, then took it. He pulled her up, stepping away from her as soon as she was level.

They didn't speak as they made their way down the mountain, the sky darkening into early dusk. Matteo led the way on Anteros, Marica following at a slow, steady pace. Quinn wished desperately for some of her mare's calm demeanor. Because that had not been her. She hadn't been able to let a man near her since Julian. Hadn't wanted to. Yet every time she got within five feet of Matteo De Campo she wanted his hands all over her.

Matteo De Campo. She wasn't sure if she should be thrilled she wasn't the ice queen everyone, including herself, thought she was or distraught at her incredibly bad judgment.

Her mouth compressed. Matteo was playing a game. He was playing to win. And she was acting like some silly pawn in it. She clenched her legs around Marica as they went down a steep section, her muscles crying out at the request. Crazy when she had a to-do list as long as her arm of major do-or-die issues she needed to take care of with Luxe.

She needed to get on that plane tomorrow morning with her head on straight, primed for what lay ahead.

Put temptation out of reach.

Unfortunately, her track record of late wasn't stellar.

CHAPTER FIVE

MATTEO HAD KNOWN he was going to kiss Quinn from the moment she'd gotten down off Marica, her green eyes glowing with the exhilaration of having conquered her fear. Most definitely after he'd heard the intense vulnerability in her voice when she'd said her birth parents hadn't been able to keep her. He'd taken action after one too many not-so-subtle invitations from the queen of mixed signals, and the result had been a scientific experiment gone horrifically right. A chemistry test he wished he could forget, but had been burned into his brain ever since Quinn had left Italy two days ago.

Not even the mountain of work he'd plowed through on the ten-hour flight to St. Lucia had been enough to banish the memory of an eager, passionate Quinn in his arms. The fact that she'd answered his question about what she'd be like when she totally let go hadn't put his curiosity to rest. It had made it much, much worse. Because now he knew.

His low curse was drowned out by the roar of the surf below the dramatic, open wall of his suite at Paradis Entre les Montagnes, Luxe's world-renowned luxury resort tucked between the island's famous twin volcanoes. He straightened his bow tie in the mirror and scowled. Why in God's name hadn't he just packaged up the insight he'd gained from digging into her hard-to-penetrate psyche and used it to work her angles? Why had he had to *kiss* her?

He picked his jacket up and shrugged it on with an antagonized movement. Bad judgment seemed to be his specialty. No matter how many times he told himself Angelique Fontaine had pursued him that night in Paris, had followed him to his hotel room after his drinks with his brothers and thrown herself at him, it had been *his* huge error to let her in. His shortsightedness to medicate himself with a woman intimately involved with a deal that could make De Campo's future.

His breath came out in a long hiss. Things might not always have been perfect in his family, but they were everything to each other. Family was everything. He had to find a way to rid himself of that little demon that sat on his shoulder urging him to do all the wrong things. Because the Luxe deal was his chance to rebuild his reputation with his brothers. To right his past mistakes. And he wasn't screwing it up.

A glance at the clock told him he had five minutes before he met the others. He strode out to the edge of the patio with its mind-blowing view of the volcanoes, wrapped his fingers around the iron railing and tried to find the focus that usually came so easily to him. Tucked into the mountains directly across from the spectacular peaks, Paradis Entre les Montagnes—literally translated as Paradise Between the Mountains—had proven to be as beautiful as its namesake. A lush, green haven perched above the Caribbean Sea, it disappeared into the mountainside with its tropical hardwoods, stone and tile chosen to blend in with its surroundings.

He moved his gaze over the layered blues of the Caribbean Sea that sparkled at the bottom of the cliff, over the tropical flowers of every hue and variety that bathed the resort in a jumble of color. The two mighty volcanoes loomed over it all, a vivid reminder of the power of nature. They were, apparently, still active. What would it be like if they roared back to life? Would they match the combustive feeling inside of him? Like he was ready to blow...

He shook his arms and legs out, the long flight from Italy leaving him stiff and sluggish. His head throbbed with that low, insistent pulse that had been with him all day. The three-year anniversary of Giancarlo's death was tomorrow. And as usual, nothing or no one had been able to wipe it from his mind.

Three years ago his best friend had perished because of a stupid bet. His bet.

It rested just below the surface, ready to push Matteo into inconsolability whenever he began to feel a measure of peace. Had been the driving force of every mistake he'd made since. Had driven his frenzied partying and out of control lifestyle until he'd shut it all down.

Without that oblivion, he felt like a man with enough burning lava inside of him to destroy an entire civilization.

He braced his hands against the railing and looked out over the water. A desert island would be preferable right about now. Instead, he had a manager's cocktail party to attend with Quinn and Daniel. A head chef and sommelier to win over. Perhaps a good thing since drinking himself into a stupor was no longer an option.

Something else he had banned from his life.

He clenched his hands by his sides. He would do this like he always did. By pretending to the world he didn't care. By being Matteo the Charming. Matteo who lit up a room when he walked into it. It was like switching on a lightbulb. Declaring it showtime.

The sky was transforming into a potent cocktail of pink and orange as he took the path down to the terrace that overlooked the sea. A small group of exquisitely dressed men and women chosen to enjoy cocktails with the manager sipped champagne in the sultry tropical air that still steamed from the heat of the day, a calypso band lending a distinctly West Indian flavor to the party. He stopped at the edge of the crowd and took in the scene. Daniel Williams was schmoozing the resort's manager, Thomas Golding, with that same smarmy smile he seemed to have constantly painted across his face.

Margarite, Quinn's head sommelier from New York, looked cool and elegant in a sleek royal-blue dress as she spoke with Paradis's head chef, François Marin, Quinn and a tall, distinguished-looking male in his early fifties. The gray-haired man's attention was riveted on Quinn. Matteo didn't blame him. Margarite had French chic, but Quinn looked...drool-inducing.

Gone was the conservative style of dress he was used to. In its place was a figure-hugging fuchsia sheath with a slit up the side just far enough to make a man look twice. Spaghetti straps made a mockery of the gravity required to wear the dress, because it was not the straps holding it up, it was the full-on perfection of Quinn's voluptuous curves that was doing it.

Damn. His mouth went dry. Why choose now, after that kiss, to pull out this new weapon in her arsenal? She'd even left all of that soft, silky hair down, sliding against the bare skin of her back. It took very little imagination to picture it spread across the ivory silk sheets of his suite's king-size bed. Less still to picture himself picking up where that kiss had left off, indulging the urge to explore every inch of her creamy flesh.

He shut the fantasy down in the middle of its full glory and grabbed a glass of champagne off a passing waiter's tray. *Get a goddamned handle on yourself, De Campo.* To-night was the night he was going to master the devil inside of him. Not let it loose.

Work the room. Get François Marin and Margarite Bellamy on your side. And then get out.

* * *

Quinn told herself the dress was absolutely appropriate as she watched Matteo's jaw hit the ground. She hadn't had time to shop for the sweltering St. Lucian temperatures before she'd left Chicago, so she'd turned herself over to Manon in the hotel's boutique to outfit her with a few dresses. Manon had assured her this soft, gorgeous designer dress in the finest silk was perfect for the cocktail party, but Quinn had felt it clung far too much.

She was now sure of it.

She smoothed the silky material over her hips and gave him her most professional smile. Margarite caught the nervous movement, her gaze sweeping over her. "So what's with the dress? You never wear anything like that."

"New addition to my wardrobe," she muttered.

Margarite's thin mouth quirked upward. "I heard François say it was a definite improvement."

Quinn bristled. "He did?"

"He's a French male, Quinn. By the way, he's right. You should play up your natural assets, not hide them."

Quinn wasn't sure what to do with that so she pushed her hair out of her face and directed a glance at the hottest man in the room. "I should introduce you to Matteo."

"Oh, I don't need an introduction." Her blonde, very young, very talented sommelier's blue eyes glittered. "I met him on the beach earlier. He had the whole place in an uproar. It's cruel and unusual punishment making me do business with him, Quinn."

She wasn't the only one. Quinn had the distinct feeling the sight of Matteo De Campo in swim trunks would be as impossible to eradicate from her memory as that kiss.

"He brought me a bottle of the Brunello," Margarite crowed. "Too bad I can't invite him back to my suite to share it with me."

Quinn shot her a look that told her what she thought of

that. Margarite waved a hand at her. "God, you've got to loosen up and learn how to take a joke, Quinn."

She bit down on her lip. Another of Julian's complaints about her. How dull and uninspiring a wife she'd turned out to be.

"Focus on business," she said shortly. "You wanted to be a part of this process. Make the best decision for Luxe."

Quinn started across the room toward Matteo, her sommelier trailing after her, a bemused look on her face. She knew she came across like a bitch sometimes but that's what happened when your husband verbally abused you for a year. You shut down. You just didn't care.

Whatever electricity she'd sensed between her and Matteo was nowhere in sight as he bent down to kiss her on both cheeks. He looked focused, all business, and kept his gaze on Margarite as he grilled her with questions, interspersed with enough charm that her sommelier just kept spilling the goods. Why that hurt her feelings she didn't know. She should be *glad* he seemed to be taking their agreement seriously.

Except there was a part of her that had come alive with him on that mountain. That kiss had blown her perception of herself apart—made her wonder exactly who she was. Because not once had she ever kissed her husband like that. Or wanted to for that matter.

Was she Quinn the ice queen or Quinn, a woman capable of more?

She blinked and gave her head a shake. That was all inconsequential right now. Why was she devoting even a tenth of her brain to her ill-advised attraction to a playboy she couldn't have anything to do with when she had at least two hours of paperwork to do after this cocktail party and a report to give to her father? She ought to be taking a page out of Matteo's book and not going there.

They finished their cocktails and sat down to dinner

on the outdoor terrace with François, Margarite, Daniel and Thomas Golding. There was no lack of conversation at the table of extroverts as the sun slid down behind the mountains and dusk settled over the island. Daniel was his usual smooth, conversational self, regaling them with his tall tales from the Outback; François, with his equally tall tales from the kitchens of Paris. Matteo won the chef and Margarite over with his charm and extensive knowledge of the hospitality and wine industries. But there was an edge to him tonight she couldn't put a finger on. A tension to his demeanor that took her back to that night in the cellar.

"Quinn tells me we'll get to explore the kitchens tomorrow and see the new menus you have planned," Matteo said to François. "I'm very much looking forward to it."

"*Oui,* in the morning." The chef nodded. "In the afternoon we must prepare for the celebrity chef challenge we're hosting."

"Every year we host a prestigious competition amongst all the chefs on the island to raise money for the schools here," Margarite explained. She nodded toward Matteo. "François is down a sous chef. Didn't you say you trained with Henry Thiboult in New York?"

Matteo inclined his head. "Not really formal training. I like to cook. He was kind enough to let me work in the kitchen with him a few times."

Quinn's mouth dropped open. "When in the world did you have time to do that?"

He let loose one of those flirtatious smiles she hadn't seen much of this evening. "Here and there. I told you I liked to cook."

François's sun-aged face split in a wide smile. "Anyone who has trained in Henry's kitchen is welcome in mine."

Margarite arched a brow at Matteo. "Are you up for it?"

"I'd be honored. As long as you don't mind my amateurism."

The chef beamed. *"Mais, oui.* I need you. It's all set then."

Daniel Williams looked dumbfounded. "I'd like to do it, too, then."

François looked down his nose at him. "Do you have any training?"

"Well, no, but—"

"So sorry." François waved a hand at him. "Only trained chefs in my kitchen. You'll cut off a finger and I'll lose my license."

A pout twisted Daniel's lips, if that was possible for a man. He sat and watched Matteo talk about working in Henry's kitchen, the famous Manhattan chef notorious for his culinary theatrics. François's booming laughter lit up the night. By the time dinner had stretched past the two-hour mark, Daniel Williams was distinctly red in the face.

"I hear De Campo's expanding into Chicago next year." The Silver Kangaroo CEO picked up his beer and took a sip. "Y'all are doing great. Next thing you know you'll be pushing that top-chef guy right out on his skinny behind."

"I hope so," Matteo agreed evenly. "We are focused on that very niche segment of the market."

Daniel shrugged. "You're making a lot of money in the restaurant business. Can't imagine De Campo's going to stop there."

"But we are." Matteo set down his beer, his gaze locked on his opposition. "Organizations that spread themselves too thin ultimately fail. You should know that, Williams. Your first venture collapsed, didn't it?"

Daniel flinched. "I consider that a war wound. Gotta take the hard knocks to get where you're going."

Matteo shrugged. "From what I've heard, poor management was to blame."

And the gloves were off. Quinn set down her coffee cup. "Perhaps we should call it a night. We have an early start tomorrow."

"I think I'd like an after-dinner drink," Daniel interjected, a belligerent tilt to his chin. "Care to join me, De Campo?"

Matteo started to decline, but Margarite jumped in. "We have some amazing ports at the bar. Let's have one then call it a night."

What was she doing? Quinn shot Margarite a warning look, but the other woman was already standing up, smiling at Matteo. Quinn set her mouth in a grim line. One drink and they were breaking this up.

At the bar near the cascading waterfall, she tried to slide onto the empty stool beside Matteo, intent on keeping the two men apart, but Daniel beat her to it. She took the one on the other side of the Australian while Margarite moved behind the bar and started picking out the ports.

"I might have something harder," Daniel drawled. "How about some Armagnac?"

"Sure." Margarite plucked the bottle out. "Matteo?"

"Not for me, *grazie*. The port is fine."

The rough, uneven tone of his voice drew Quinn's gaze. She stared at his face. His tanned skin had lost all its color, his gray eyes vacant.

"Oh, come on, De Campo," Williams boomed. "Be a man. Have one with me."

"I said no."

Three set of eyes gaped as Matteo stood up. "I'm going to turn in. Good night."

He was gone before Quinn had a chance to register what had happened. Margarite frowned. "Is he okay?"

No, he was not. He was far from okay. Heart pounding, Quinn stood up. "I'll go check on him. You two enjoy your drink."

* * *

In his suite, Matteo pulled off his jacket and the tie that
threatened to choke him. Yanked the top buttons of his
shirt loose. He stared at the bottles of the fully stocked bar
for a long moment, the heated rush of a hard shot calling
to him like a siren's song. Then jerked away. The keys of
the grand piano in his suite, undoubtedly Quinn's idea,
would normally have beckoned but he was too far gone
even for that.

He kicked his shoes and socks off and walked down to
the private beach. Strode through the powdery white sand
to the water's edge. Giancarlo had been drinking cognac
the night of the accident. That big smile of his on full display, his friend had slapped him on the back and gestured
for the bartender. *"Come on, De Campo, let's close it off
with the good stuff. A perfect drink to end a perfect night."*

He could have saved things right there. Instead he had
gone along with the insanity. Fed his best friend's death
wish.

The contents of his stomach rose up to the back of his
mouth. *Why didn't you stop it? You were supposed to be
the sensible one.*

Or had he had his own death wish?

"Matteo."

Quinn's voice penetrated his haze. He stayed where he
was, his back to her, because he didn't want her to see him
like this. Didn't want anyone to see him like this.

"I'm fine. Go back to the others."

"You aren't fine. You haven't been fine all night. What
happened back there?"

He turned around. "It was nothing," he said harshly.
"Go back to the others."

She crossed her arms over her chest. "I'm not leaving
until you tell me. You look like you've seen a ghost."

A harsh bark of laughter escaped him. "I have."

She stepped closer, her gaze on his face. "This is about Giancarlo."

"Dammit, Quinn. Go."

"What happened with him? You are clearly not okay, Matteo."

Frustration erupted like a spew of volcanic ash. Rose up inside him like an unstoppable force, curling his hands into fists at his sides, sending his breath flaming through his nostrils. "It's the anniversary of his death tomorrow. It's a bad night for me, that's all."

"Oh." She pushed her hair out of her face, her beautiful eyes gleaming with compassion. "I'm so sorry. How long has it been?"

"Three years," he said bleakly. Three years of hell.

She stepped closer, her fingers curving around his forearm. "Do you want to talk about it?"

"One kiss does not make a confessional," he rasped, jerking away. "The only thing that makes this better is alcohol or a woman, Quinn, and since I've sworn off the former as a source of anesthesia and we've agreed you are off-limits, you need to walk away."

She stared up at him, her hazel eyes huge. "I don't think... I don't want to leave you like this..."

"Walk, Quinn." Close to the edge and terrified of her seeing him go over it, he reached up and brushed his fingers across her cheek. "I'm doing my best to keep this strictly business. But you in that dress tonight isn't anything about business. All I can think about is stripping it off you and knocking my brain senseless because I know it would work." He ran his thumb down over her full, lush mouth. "I know you would blow my mind enough to pull me out of this. But we both know that can't happen. So leave...now."

Her mouth quivered under his thumb. She stood there and for a moment, he thought she might stay. Then she stepped back and did exactly what he'd known she would. Retreated. But her gaze remained firmly fixed on his face.

"I'm in the suite at the end of the road if you need someone to talk to. At any time, Matteo."

Then she turned and left.

He waited until she was out of earshot. Then he let out a primal yell the pounding surf swallowed up.

It was not nearly enough. It would never be enough.

CHAPTER SIX

WHEN A SLEEPLESS night had only made your brain more combustible, your balance on the high wire that was life more tenuous and your need to scream near deafening, you did whatever it took to make it through the day.

Fortunately for Matteo, working in François Marin's kitchen was an intense form of therapy that left no room for thought. A well-oiled machine, his kitchen ran with military precision, timed down to the minute, with no room for mistakes. Exactly what he needed right now on this darkest of days.

He had spent the morning touring the kitchens with François, Margarite, Daniel and Quinn, followed by an exhaustive study of the hotel's new menus. His knowledge of food and the unique wine pairings he'd suggested for François's menu had elicited an excited response from the chef. They fit perfectly with Quinn's eclectic vision and made Daniel Williams look like a neophyte in the process.

Exactly as planned. He sliced up a scallion with ruthless efficiency. After the menu review, much to Daniel William's chagrin, Matteo had joined the other sous chefs in the kitchen to prepare for tonight's chef's challenge. The guests weren't due until seven, but the preparation for this type of an event was massive. He alone had three sauces on the go and salads to plate.

Adrenaline pounded through his veins and fired his

movements as the clock ticked until he was a finely tuned cog in the machine, operating on command. He started on the hot peppers, tearing through them with a razor-sharp knife. If he moved from point A to point B to point C without deviating, he might, just might, not become unhinged.

Might forget that Quinn had seen into the deepest, darkest recesses of his mind last night. A place he'd never let anyone go.

Quinn tossed her pencil on the desk, sat back and rubbed her hands over her eyes. She'd finally gotten that report on her progress over to her father last night, but the rest of her paperwork and troubleshooting emails for the Mediterranean hotels had taken until well into the early hours. She was good at existing on six hours of sleep but anything less than that and she started to get distinctly unbalanced, her judgment skewed and unreliable.

Right now was a case in point. She should be working. Instead she couldn't get the haunted look on Matteo's face last night out of her head. The way he'd looked ready to tip over the edge. She'd had some tortured moments in her life, like the morning the private investigator had turned over that file on her parents and she'd found out the truth. That it had been her they hadn't wanted. But it hadn't come close to the look of pure agony on Matteo's face. Like he was being tortured by something beyond his control....

She frowned and steepled her fingers against the edge of the desk. Losing a best friend must be awful. She couldn't imagine losing Thea. But it had been three years since Giancarlo had died. Time enough to heal. So why was Matteo so tortured?

Picking up the pencil, Quinn pressed it against her temple. As if questioning her sanity. Because last night, even after Matteo had made it clear women were his anesthesia, that likely any woman would have done in that moment, she'd been tempted to stay. She could have said it had been her human side making a rare appearance. She was afraid it was a whole lot more than that.

She would check on him. Shoving her palms against the desk, she rolled to her feet. She'd stop by the kitchen, see how he was doing, then dress for the chef's challenge. Not that Thomas was going to need her help. Unlike his counterpart at Le Belle Bleu on the other side of the island, who apparently, from the paperwork, did not have everything running smoothly, Thomas was a genius at running a high-end establishment.

Quinn sighed. Tonight would be fun. Tomorrow, when they did their walk-through, she'd deal with Le Belle Bleu.

Taking a shortcut through the back of the hotel, she stepped into the kitchen. She'd seen grown men reduced to tears in François's pressure cooker of a production, but there was Matteo, working in a group of a half dozen sous chefs, looking like he'd spent his life there.

She watched, fascinated, as he pulled the pan half off the burner and tossed in four or five herbs. Was there anything the man couldn't do? And how had she ever pegged him a flirty playboy? He was a brilliant businessman. He also made chef's whites look outrageously good.

She stepped closer to see what the last sauce was. He gave her an even look. "Quinn."

"Just wondering what you're making," she said brightly. She pointed at the green sauce. "What's that?"

"An Indian mint sauce."

"Looks exotic."

"And I can't mess it up." He gave her a dark look. "You're not supposed to be in here."

"Just checking to see how you're doing."

He threw a couple of drops of hot sauce into the third sauce. "You're distracting me."

"How could I be distracting you? I've been here two seconds."

He gave her a deliberate once-over. "Do you really want to know?"

Heat burned a path up to her cheeks. "Not so much."

His eyes glittered. "François," he called out, pointing a finger at her. "She needs to go."

The chef quirked a finger at Quinn. "You know the rules. Out."

She gave Matteo an outraged look. "That was low, calling in the teacher."

He added the mushrooms to the hot sauce and shook the pan over the flame. "I want to win. Out."

Quinn turned around with a huff and left. He wanted to win because he wanted to make Daniel Williams look even more lackluster than he had this morning going through the menus. It had been painful to watch. He was rapidly shifting the tide and he knew it.

She got dressed and greeted the guests and judges with Thomas. The judges spanned everything from a native pop singer who'd made it big on the international music scene, to the prime minister and governor general of the island, to one of St. Lucia's most celebrated artists.

The evening went smoothly. Dinner was a gastronomic study in perfection, but it was François's main course—the lamb with Matteo's green mint sauce that stole the night. Quinn didn't even need to see a scorecard to know who had won it was so patently obvious from the looks on the judge's faces.

As the results were being tabulated, the chefs changed and came out to mingle with the crowd. She watched Matteo turn on the charm, drawing the VIPs to him like moths to a flame, including the St. Lucian pop singer, Catrina James, who was beautiful and vibrant in a fire-engine-red dress that showed off her creamy, perfect skin. Quinn had never seen such a chameleon as Matteo. He molded himself into exactly what he needed to be at any given moment. Brilliantly.

He had changed into gray pants and a white shirt, his olive skin darker, swarthier from the hot rays of the Caribbean sun. It made his startling gray eyes stand out even more. Added to the intensity surrounding him, sitting just below the surface. Made him look even more dangerously attractive. If that was possible.

He caught her gaze. She pulled hers resolutely away and sat down at the bar, ordering herself a soda water. She'd been running all night, making sure things went smoothly. Sitting for a couple of minutes and reviewing the itinerary the manager of Le Belle Bleu had sent over for their walk-through tomorrow would be a beautiful thing the way her feet ached.

Matteo slid onto the stool beside her just as the bartender delivered her soda water. The sexy scent of him drifted into her nostrils. Made it hard to concentrate.

"Would you like a drink?"

"*Si.* That kitchen was smoking hot."

Not the only smoking hot thing around here, her recalcitrant brain proclaimed. She ordered him the island beer he'd favored at dinner, and turned to him.

"You were brilliant in the kitchen. Is there anything you can't do?"

He gave her a thoughtful look. "I am hopeless under the hood of a car. Desperately bad at sudoku. And my grammar is sometimes suspect."

"Shameful."

"I wasn't blowing you off, Quinn. It was an act of self-preservation."

From what? Her stomach did a funny little jump. "How," she asked deliberately, "are you today?"

He pulled the beer the bartender set down toward him. "I'll be better tomorrow."

"Matteo—"

He held up a hand. "How about I ask you a question?"

Quinn surveyed him warily as he took a long swig of his beer. "All right."

He propped his elbow on the bar and rested his chin in his hand. "What was with the one-year marriage? Most people's exercise routines last longer than that."

She felt her face turn into fully petrified papier-mâché. "We were…incompatible."

He shook his head. "I'm not looking for the press release, Quinn. I'm looking for the truth."

"That is the truth." And a million other intricacies she couldn't even begin to get into.

Matteo looked at her for a long moment, those gunmetal-gray eyes of his seeming to look straight through her. "I think you were too strong a personality for him. He wasn't man enough to be with you."

She choked on the sip of wine she'd taken. "That's a big assumption coming from someone who doesn't know anything about it."

His eyes glittered. "I know you, Quinn. You aren't that hard to figure out."

She bit into the side of her mouth. "I think Julian would disagree," she said tightly. "He would tell you I was a boring workaholic who didn't know how to have fun."

"Then he'd be as much of a fool as I thought." His baldly stated words made her heart jump. "Any man with balls would recognize that for the lie it is. There isn't any part of you that could ever be described as boring, Quinn. As anything but full-on fascinating."

A flush of warmth swept through her. "You don't have to feed me compliments, Matteo. I have thick skin."

"Then you can take me telling you the truth." He let the

loaded statement sit on the air until he was sure he had her full attention. "If we were doing anything but negotiating a ten-million-dollar deal right now, we'd have been in bed together already. And I'd be taking apart the puzzle that is Quinn piece by piece." His gaze held hers, the intent behind it riveting. "I guarantee you I wouldn't be bored."

Her breath caught in her throat. Refused to continue on its way up to her brain where she needed it most.

"You are not a woman to be discarded," he said harshly. "He was a fool."

Quinn sat there speechless. Drowning in a new perspective that had never occurred to her before. Had Julian been intimidated by her? Had he tried to hurt her, humiliate her to make himself feel like more of a man? Because she'd been too much of one?

Her world tilted on its axis. Fractured apart as a seismic shift ripped the ground from beneath her feet and set her adrift. She'd spent the past year torturing herself with ways she could have saved her marriage. Ways she could have changed to keep her husband from straying. Allowed her self-confidence to be completely ripped apart when he'd found her wanting every time. When in reality, maybe her marriage had been destined for failure from the start. Because of the man Julian was. Who they both were.

One of the chefs came over and grabbed Matteo for the winner's announcement. Quinn sat there, head buzzing as she watched him walk away. She had always believed that at the heart of her, she was somehow defective. Her disastrous marriage had only underscored it. *What if it wasn't true*? What if her inability to please her husband in bed had been more about him than her?

With her belief about her biggest failure turned upside down, she stood at Thomas Golding's side as they announced the winner of the chef's challenge. Paradis, to no one's surprise, won, François's lamb dish and outrageously eclectic-green banana pie outclassing the competition by a landslide.

Catrina James presented François with the winner's trophy and gave each of the chefs a kiss on the cheek as she posed with them for photographs. Her one for Matteo was extra enthusiastic. *Of course.*

Champagne bottles were popped and the night dissolved into a big party. It was impossible not to get caught up in the exuberant celebrations, but as she watched, as the clock slipped closer to midnight, Matteo's easy smile faded. His face shuttered and the darkness descended. It was like watching a curtain fall and she knew he'd been hiding his pain under that charming, devil-may-care demeanor.

Tonight was the anniversary of Giancarlo's death.

It did not surprise her to turn around sometime after midnight to find Catrina James attached to another male and Matteo gone. She stood at Thomas Golding's side, the ground feeling unsteady under her feet. She should go back to her room and work. She had enough of it for an army.

Matteo was a conflict of interest in the most important assignment of her career. She should be running in the opposite direction. But some things in life were more important than work. Funny how she'd realized that now of all moments.

Quinn looked down at the golden shimmer of the Riesling in her glass, the sparkling liquid reflecting the light of the moon. *I know you would blow my mind enough to pull me out of this....*

Her heartbeat picked up into an insistent rhythm that made the blood whish in her ears. How could any deal matter when a person was in agony? She could not leave Matteo alone. She would not.

She could not spend another minute of her life wondering about the truth of herself.

"Excuse me," she murmured to Thomas. "I have some work to do."

Crossing the terrace, she took the path to the upper level of luxury suites. Saw the light burning in Matteo's living room. She climbed the steps to the door and was about to rap on it when she heard music. A haunting piano score played so beautifully it froze her in her tracks.

Matteo.

Her heart pounded so loud in her chest she thought it might break through. She knew she was invading his privacy. Knew she should walk away. But the melody reached out and wrapped itself around her heart. The blackness of it.

Quinn walked around to the back of the suite and took the stairs up to the patio. Leaned back against the wall in the shadows and listened to every heartrending note. She did not recognize the piece, but there was no doubt in her mind Matteo had written it for Giancarlo. It was poignant, stunning and full of grief.

Her knees shook, her eyes burned. She was not someone made of emotion. But this was breaking her heart.

She wasn't sure how long she stood there, pressed against the wall, listening to him play. When he finally stopped, she took a deep breath, steadied herself and stepped into the light. He sat at the piano staring at the keys. He looked up as she appeared, as if he wasn't at all surprised to find her there. His bloodshot eyes were nearly her undoing.

"I told you last night you can't help." His voice was gritty, broken. "This is my personal forty-eight hours of hell, Quinn. Leave me to it."

She shook her head. "Whatever this is, whatever happened to Giancarlo, you have to let it go. You can't keep doing this to yourself."

He looked down at the keys, his back ramrod straight. "You should go."

Her stomach convulsed in a long pull. She looked down at the threshold that divided the patio from the inside space. Made her choice.

He looked up as she walked into the room. "Quinn—"

She sat down on the stool beside him and took his face in her hands. "You have to make it stop," she told him huskily. "I know what it's like to keep your demons inside. To let them torture you. You will destroy yourself."

He pulled her hands away, the desperate, hopeless look in his eyes of a man who'd suffered too much. "I can't. Dammit, I can't."

She sank her palms into the hard line of his jaw. "Then help me chase our demons away together."

He went completely still, his gaze holding hers. "What are you saying?"

She swallowed hard, fighting the part of her that wanted to run because that was what she always did. "I need to know what you said to me earlier is true. That Julian was wrong about me."

The color seemed to leech from his skin. "You must know it's true."

"I don't," she said quietly. "I don't know anything. You said the other night that I could knock you out of this. Then use me. And let me prove him wrong about me."

Matteo shook his head, a desperate glitter in his eyes. "This is way over the line."

"I know. I just walked over it."

He rubbed his hands over his face. "The deal… I…"

"The deal doesn't exist tonight," she said harshly. "I am here and I am not leaving you."

He squeezed his eyes shut. "*Cristo*. Quinn…"

She sat there, heart slamming against her chest, terrified that he would reject her, that once again she would be deemed unacceptable. The silence hung between them like a loaded missile. When he opened his eyes, the anguish she saw there made her draw in a breath.

"I told you last night this is about numbing my mind. You have to know that."

She wanted someone to numb hers. To make her forget she was Quinn Davis for just a few minutes. Make her feel alive again like she had on that mountainside.

His big body tensed beneath her hands, his breathing changed and became rough, fractured. "You're sure?"

She nodded. "One night. One night to make it go away for both of us."

Something shifted in his expression. A dark wildness moved within him. She drew in a breath as he slid a hand against her nape and brought his mouth down on hers. Her softness met his hardness in a caress that blew her mind right from the very first second. But unlike his kiss on the mountain, this one was hotter, all-consuming. Devouring and needy, it quickly descended into an urgent quest to pull her into the fire with him. Her fingers fisted against his chest in an involuntary reaction to a dominant male exerting his power over her. She flexed them against him. Forced herself to relax. *Dammit, Julian. You are not doing this to me. Not anymore.*

Matteo's scorching, openmouthed kisses drove the past from Quinn's head. He tasted her, licked into her until she could do nothing but focus on the heat they were generating. She pushed closer, met him kiss for kiss. And when that wasn't enough, he sank his hands into her waist, lifted her up and wrapped her legs around him, her bare skin sliding against the rough material of his trousers. The feel of his hard flesh beneath her made her heart slam against her chest. He was already aroused. Potently, highly aroused.

She wasn't sure she knew how to handle him.

Matteo pushed her back so he could look at her. Ran his

fingertips up her bare arms to her shoulders, his heated gaze sending goose bumps to every inch of her skin. Got her so caught up in him that was all she could think about. "You are the most beautiful woman I have ever seen," he murmured, sinking his teeth into her shoulder. "If you knew how close I was to breaking all the rules that night at the *castello*..."

She sucked in a breath. "You walked away..."

"I was one step away, Quinn. One."

She watched, hypnotized, as he slid his fingers under the straps of her dress and pulled them down. His muttered oath told her he appreciated the fact she'd had to lose her bra. His gaze as he cupped her hot, ultrasensitive flesh was reverent. "I'm a chest man," he murmured. "And yours..." he said, sliding his callused fingertips against the tips of her breasts, "is magnificent."

He held her gaze as his thumbs covered her nipples, circled them into erect, aching points. Her soft moan of pleasure made him take her mouth again in approval. "Talk to me, Quinn. Tell me what you like."

"More," she muttered. "Just...more."

He turned her around, pressed her back against the piano. The hard wood dug into her back, made her arch against it, but when he lowered his head and took her nipple into the heat of his mouth, she stopped caring. She dug her fingernails into his biceps and let out another low moan. He tugged, sucked and laved her until she was half-crazy with the pleasure of it. Feeling it deep down inside of her.

"You like that?"

"Yes."

He cupped her other breast in his hand and lavished the same treatment on it, tortured her with his swirling tongue until her insides collapsed and everything went liquid. She had never felt so needy, so desperate. So lost in something.

In him. Too shy to put it into words, she clamped her legs harder around him and begged with her body for more.

"Slow down," he murmured, pulling back. "We should take this to the bedroom."

She froze. "No bedrooms."

"No bedrooms?" He frowned down at her. "Why?"

"Here," she insisted. Moved her fingers to the buttons of his shirt. "I want you here."

A dark fire lit his gaze. He let her unbutton the shirt. Let her uncover his drop-dead gorgeous six-pack of a chest that was every bit as amazing as that of her ultrabuff Krav Maga instructor. Then he captured her hands at her sides. "I wasn't finished."

Her throat went dry. She was pretty sure she wanted him to finish. Positive actually.... He held her gaze as he spread her thighs wider, pushed her back firmer against the wood so that she was exposed to him. Vulnerable. Then he pushed the hem of her dress up her thighs in a deliberate motion that made her breath seize in her throat. His palms skimmed across her bare skin, branding her. "I thought you might have lost the panties too," he murmured, pressing the heel of his palm against the heat of her. "Not that I'm complaining. They're very sexy."

She sucked in a breath as he worked her with the heel of his hand. Her pleasure had never been of any consequence to Julian, it had been all about him. But Matteo was so focused, intent in the way he touched her. "You want more?" he asked, setting his mouth to the sensitive spot between her neck and shoulder.

"Yes." She moved her hips against him in an instinctive plea.

"Good," he murmured, sinking his hands into her waist and lifting her so her hips rested on the piano keys. "Because this is one fantasy I'm not denying myself."

He slid his hands under her dress, hooked his fingers

into the sides of her panties and made her lift her hips so he could strip them off. A bolt of excruciating self-consciousness sliced through her at the way she was displayed in front of him. Like an instrument for him to play.... But her heart was racing, the blood in her veins thrumming. The air sat heavy and humid around them, fragranced with a million exotic flowers. The only sound in the whisper-still night was the crash of the waves on the shore below. And it calmed her....

He kissed his way from the inside of her knees to the hot, pulsing core of her, taking her dress with him as he went. When she thought she might actually go mad for his touch, he worked his hands under her hips and lifted her to him. She jammed her hands into the keys on either side of her, the jarring sound of two opposite notes filling the air. It was raw and it was outrageous, but when he bent and put his mouth to her, she had never felt more perfectly connected to a person in her entire life. Like she was made for him to touch her like this.

Leisurely, exquisitely, he savored her, traced every nerve ending in a practiced seduction that drove her slowly, inexorably mad.

Her body tightened, her eyes flew wide. It had been impossible for her to orgasm with Julian. To perform on command. She had no idea what it felt like to experience it. But right now she felt as if her whole body was about to take flight. To soar into a place she'd never been before.

He flicked his tongue over the hard nub of her, took her there, then yanked her back. Again and again. She threw her head to the side. "God, please, I need—"

"Not yet," he rasped against her skin. "You can take more."

No, she couldn't. Not anymore. Then he slid a finger inside her and took her higher. Stroked her until he reached a spot that sent white-hot pleasure ratcheting through her.

Oh, my God. She jammed her palms into the keys. Sent another crazy symphony of sound bouncing off the walls. She was burning alive....

"Now," he ordered. "Now, Quinn."

He played the throbbing center of her with his tongue, expertly, urgently, his finger curving up inside her until the blinding heat made the blood roar in her ears. Then he took her over the edge, her scream of pleasure as he brought her to shuddering completion reverberated throughout the room.

On and on the pleasure coursed through her as he kept his mouth on her, drew out her orgasm, made her take it until her shaking body could handle no more and she pleaded for him to stop.

She was half-delirious when he picked her up and started toward the bedroom.

"Not there—"

He stared down at her. "What in *Dio's* name is wrong with a bedroom?"

She buried her face in his chest. "I just can't."

"What did he do to you, Quinn?" His voice was a low growl.

She shook her head and burrowed closer. "I don't want to talk about him."

He carried her to the silk embroidered sofa with the incomparable view of the Pitons and sat with her cradled against him. Lifted her chin with his fingers. "I knew it would be like that."

Her face burned. She had screamed, literally screamed for him.

His gaze was direct, steady. "You weren't like that with him."

"No."

She was acutely aware of his arousal, hard and unfulfilled beneath her. But her absolute inability to enjoy the sexual act in the past froze her in a purgatory of indecision. She wanted to give him as much pleasure as he'd given her. Wipe away the demons still blazing in his eyes.

But there were other ways to do it. And he made her feel beautiful and empowered enough to try. She sat up in his lap, framed his face with her hands and kissed him, the taste of herself on him so erotic it made her toes curl. His instant, heated response made her blood surge in her veins. "I'm not an expert at this," she whispered against his mouth. "So you need to tell me how I'm doing."

"Tell me," Matteo returned, his lips clinging to hers, "exactly what is it you're doing?"

She pressed her mouth to his hot, hard flesh as she worked her way down. "This."

Quinn took her time exploring him, learning him. It was so different to want to touch. To want to make him utter those soft sounds that told her she was doing it just right. To know she was doing it right. She sat back in his arms and brought her lips to his perfectly cut abs. Traced the dips and curves of his salty skin as she worshipped at the altar that was Matteo. When she reached the taut muscles of his abdomen, he tensed so completely she wondered if he was still breathing.

"You okay?"

His tortured *"eccellente"* made her smile.

"You want more?"

"You have no idea."

She slid the smooth leather free of his belt loop and undid it. Made swift work of his trouser button and zipper. He lifted his hips, helped her as she dragged his pants down over his long legs. Then there was nothing but a very virile, very aroused Matteo in black boxers staring her in the face. And her very, very dry mouth.

He was big. Bigger than Julian had been. The most perfectly put-together male she had ever seen. She wanted to touch him so badly her self-consciousness vaporized on a wave of lust.

His olive skin took on a ruddy hue as she sank to the floor in front of him, his gray eyes darkening to a sultry, mesmerizing slate. "This could have been another of my fantasies," he muttered as she lowered her mouth to the taut muscle just above the band of his briefs. Dragged her lips across the elastic band. "I'm going to give you the thumbs-up on that," he encouraged hoarsely, his big body stiffening beneath her, "but ask that you pick up the pace."

She slid her fingers into his boxers and sought him out. He was velvet soft over hard steel, so very masculine her breath caught in her throat. She wanted to learn this part of him too. To worship him as he'd worshipped her. To make him feel as desirable as she had.

She moved her hands over him, stroked him, explored him until he arched his hips toward her, his eyes tortured.

"Dammit, Quinn—more."

She lowered her head and took him into her mouth. Heard his guttural growl of approval. It was heady, empowering to be in control when she had never been in the past. Slowly at first, then faster she took him until he was covered in perspiration, until he was shaking beneath her, as out of control as she'd been. Until he couldn't be thinking about anything but what she was doing to him—just as she had. And the demons were banished.

Then she didn't hold back. His breathing fractured. His hands reached for her, tangled in her hair. "I want you with me."

Her stomach twisted, too many memories, too many humiliations filling her head. She pushed his hands away and took him deeper in her mouth. Increased her rhythm. His low curse filled the air. His hips jerked into her hands, his big body ready to explode.

"*Maledizione,* Quinn."

She lifted her head and watched as he caught himself with his hands and came with an explosive force that made her heart pound like a jackhammer.

Primal, erotic, beautiful. She was spellbound.

The room was silent except for the harsh force of his breathing. The weight of his gaze sat on her. Probing.

"I need to clean up," he muttered, rolling to his feet. "Do not move."

He came back in another pair of black boxers and drew her into his arms on the sofa. Set his lips to her hair. "When I said I wanted you to knock me senseless I didn't expect you to take it literally."

She laid her head against his chest. "I wanted it that way."

"I have condoms, you know."

"It wasn't about that."

He sighed. "You don't want to talk about it."

She shook her head and closed her eyes. For the first time in so long, she felt at peace. As if there wasn't a fractured part of her ready to disintegrate at any moment. She wanted to hold on to it. Savor it. Because it couldn't last. This had been one night. One night to get Matteo through the fire and one night to make her feel whole again. That's all it could be.

Minutes, hours passed. When she woke, Matteo's chest was moving slowly up and down beneath her cheek. The sky outside was pitch-dark, not a sound in the air.

She eased herself off him, looked down at his beautiful, hard-edged face. Shadows were painted beneath his eyes, making her wonder when the last time he'd slept well had been. But his jaw was relaxed, his body slack. He was peaceful now and she thought he would sleep for a long time.

Quinn walked silently to the piano, picked up her underwear and made herself walk out the door.

* * *

Matteo woke to flickering shadows. He blinked and sat up. Struggled to get his bearings. He was alone, the suite dark, the sky over the volcanoes just beginning to lighten.

Quinn's perfume lingered in the air. Her taste, her smell was all over him. Pieces of the night before stormed back, came together like puzzle parts. His near desperation. His struggle to rid himself of it at the piano. Quinn's appearance. The mind-blowing intimacies they'd shared...

The fact that he'd broken the one promise he'd made to his brother...

His stomach lurched. Yes, Quinn had needed this as much as he did; she'd had her own demons to slay. But it still didn't make it right. Nothing made it right.

A sheen of perspiration covered his body. Drove him to the fridge for water. He snatched out a bottle, twisted off the cap and tipped it into his mouth, the icy liquid chilling his throat like the most horrific of wake-up calls. He had slept with Quinn Davis. It would be impossible for him to believe he'd done it if she wasn't all over him. If the image of it wasn't so graphically implanted on his brain.

One night, she'd said. This has nothing to do with the deal.... Yet wasn't that exactly what Angelique Fontaine had promised just before she had destroyed him crying out her sorrows to her father?

His stomach dropped. What if Quinn couldn't handle what she'd done? What if she chose Silver Kangaroo because it was the only unbiased thing to do?

It occurred to him he might actually have a death wish. With a muffled curse he strode out onto the terrace. But the filtered light of early day only made his sins more blatantly clear. He raised his eyes to the rising sun and let it brand him with the truth. He had put his relationship with his family in jeopardy again over his inability to forget the past. To forgive himself for his trangressions.

He pressed his palms to his cheeks. Was it ever going to go away? Was he ever going to feel as if he deserved a place on this planet again when Giancarlo would never get to live out the best years of his life? Exactly how long was he going to punish himself? Destroy those around him?

Was there even any hope he ever would?

He thought about the trust Riccardo had put in him. Prayed his instincts were right and Quinn would not betray him. His chest tightened until it felt impossible to pull in air and everything went a hazy white.

He did not consciously register himself striding inside and pulling on swim trunks. Taking the stairs to the beach, walking straight into the water and setting out toward the volcanoes with powerful strokes.

Quinn had saved his soul last night. Now he had taken himself straight to hell.

CHAPTER SEVEN

"Say, was that De Campo I saw swimming across to the Pitons this morning?" Daniel Williams slopped half a cow's worth of milk into his coffee and looked across the breakfast table at Quinn. "I'm all off with my time zones and I sure as heck could have been seeing something, but I could swear I saw him out there and holy crow, that has to be some swim."

Quinn's spoon fell to her saucer with a clatter. "That can't be right." That swim was miles.

Daniel shrugged. "Like I said, I could be wrong but I thought I recognized him."

Her stomach tightened. Lord knew what state of mind Matteo had woken up in this morning. Sharks weren't a common worry in the waters here, but that was a bloody long swim. Even for a good athlete. He was supposed to have met them for breakfast a half hour ago before their trip to Le Belle Bleu...

She stood up abruptly. "I'm going to go see if he misunderstood the breakfast invitation. I'll meet you in the lobby in ten minutes."

She walked straight into Matteo as she exited the restaurant. Her heartbeat slowed to a more manageable rhythm as she took in his navy trousers, pale yellow shirt and the grim look he wore like a badge. At least he was in one piece....

"Daniel said you'd swum across to the Pitons.... I told him he must have been mistaken."

"I did."

She stared at him. "That was exceedingly stupid."

"A skill I seem to be perfecting of late."

"Matteo—"

"Later, Quinn." His sharp tone stopped her in her tracks. "We need privacy for this discussion."

She bit into her lip. Or they could avoid it all together....

He waved a hand toward the restaurant. "I need coffee. I'll get one to take with us."

Matteo strode into the dining room, leaving Quinn standing there watching him go. She spent the windy drive around the coast to Le Belle Bleu trying to ignore the fact she'd just slept with the man behind her. Engaged in no-holds-barred raw sex with a man who had proven that far from her being the frigid, unfeeling creature Julian had made her out to be, she was capable of losing herself in the moment. As in screaming losing herself in the moment.

Images from the night before flashed through her head like a real-time movie she'd played a starring role in. Her spread across the piano keys...Matteo feasting on her willing body...

An allover flush consumed her. She wanted to feel regret. And she did. Sleeping with the bidder of an open contract likely wasn't spelled out in the Davis Investments ethics manual because they'd probably figured no one would ever go there. But if the board or Daniel Williams ever found out, there'd be hell to pay. Her judgment would be called into question and her reputation compromised.

Her head throbbed in her skull. The problem was she'd never felt so alive. Never knew she could. She had pulled Matteo back from the fire last night. And in a bizarre way, she had reinstated herself among the living too.

One night, one lapse of sanity might be acceptable. She

could still make a decision on this contract with a clear head. If it never happened again. If she wiped it from her brain…

The irony of it all made her shake her head as the marina came into view, sleek, expensive sailboats bobbing in their moorings. The one man who did it for her was the one man she couldn't have.

Le Belle Bleu was no Paradis.

Located on the northern tip of St. Lucia, on a peninsula that boasted the island's best beaches, Matteo could see why it had once been described as "one of the most dramatic resorts in the Caribbean" by a famous luxury hotel magazine. "A mermaid's paradise…" Surrounded on three sides by water, each suite boasting a million-dollar ocean view with a private plunge pool that connected to the sea, its world-class restaurants weren't just set on the water, they were *in* the water with glass floors, walls and ceilings immersing patrons deep into the sea with the most incredibly colored tropical fish as dining partners. And then there was the spa which was undeniably impressive with its renowned organic sea treatments favored by the globe's elite.

As far as Matteo was concerned, that's where the travel brochure ended and reality began. Five minutes into their walk-through with the hotel's manager, Raymond Bernard, it had become clear the property's ten-million-dollar face-lift was more of a disaster than a fix. If the shoddy renovations didn't bring the kitchen falling down around Quinn's head, the questionable wiring would. There was no way this hotel was going to be ready for its opening in two weeks. And from the scowl on Quinn's face, she'd figured that out too.

He asked another pointed question of Raymond since Quinn seemed to be too busy fuming. No doubt wondering how she was going to host every VIP in the Caribbean in this mess in two weeks for the relaunch of a hotel that was considered a national treasure.

Raymond gave a completely inadequate answer to his question. Quinn rolled her eyes. She appeared to have exactly zero patience for the manager who was obviously struggling in his role and wasn't trying to hide it.

They followed Raymond through the glitzy, opulent lobby. His ill-advised swim this morning had managed to knock some sense into his brain. What he'd done last night had been the height of stupidity. There were no excuses for it. But what he could do now was make sure it never happened again. Give Quinn no reason to think what had happened between them should have any bearing on her decision. He was going to prove beyond a shadow of a doubt that De Campo was the right partner for Luxe. And Le Belle Bleu provided the perfect opportunity for him to do that. He'd been through restaurant construction with De Campo's properties. Knew what to look for. Quinn's ice cream and hamburger franchises were built on an identical blueprint that had nothing to do with this type of scale. Complexity. Right now, she looked as out of depth as he had been this morning in water way over his head, unidentifiable sea creatures lapping at his feet.

Raymond stopped in front of the new kitchens and started detailing their attributes with as much enthusiasm as a tortoise sunning himself on a rock. "So," he summed up in that all-the-time-in-the-world West Indies drawl of his. "Impressive, isn't it?"

Quinn stuck her hands on her hips. "Not at the moment, no," she said sharply. "But it will be."

Raymond paled. "I thought you would be pleased with what we've done."

"I'm not exactly sure which part of this disaster you're referring to," she responded curtly. "We'll deal with it later. Right now let's review the menus so we can discuss them over lunch. That's what Matteo and Daniel really need to see."

They sat on the poolside terrace while Le Belle Bleu's head chef took them through the new menus he'd designed. By the end of his presentation, Matteo was convinced the lineup showed such an abject lack of creativity it wasn't even appropriate for a three-star hotel, let alone Luxe.

"Where is the seafood?" Quinn asked, jamming a hand on the table as if to physically restrain herself. "St. Lucia is a Caribbean island. People expect seafood."

The chef pointed to the entrées. "There are two fish dishes here."

"Two out of twelve?"

"W-we thought it was sufficient…. We have an international clientele."

"Who don't eat appetizers?"

"Well, there is some crab in this one…"

Quinn dropped her head in her hands.

"Quinn?" Raymond's placid tone was filled with apprehension. "Any other comments?"

"Yes," she snapped. "But since it's way past time for lunch, let's do it over that."

She sliced a look at Matteo and Daniel. "Consider this a work in progress."

They ate by the sea. When Quinn attempted to sit on the other side of the table from him, Matteo deftly presented the chair beside him with a gallant flourish.

"The view is much better here."

"I thought," she stated evenly, "I would save it for you and Daniel since I'll have more of a chance to enjoy it than you will."

"Oh, no," Daniel said hastily, clearly recognizing he was running this race a few too many steps behind, "the lady should have the best view, always."

Matteo's lips twisted as Quinn sat down. "I'm not sure 'lady' is the best description for you today," he murmured in her ear as he pushed her chair in.

She gave him a glare that would have felled a lesser man. "You're not giving the man a chance to breathe," he counseled quietly, sitting down beside her. "I would have thought Warren taught you allies make better bedfellows."

Her shoulders dropped. "He won't last long enough to become an ally," she muttered icily.

Matteo's return glance was reproving. "You need to take a deep breath."

She did. Lord knew she did. But she didn't need to hear that coming from him right now. "Don't think," she said in a deadly quiet voice, pretending to point out a particularly good bread in the basket for the other's benefit, "that last night gives you the right to cross the line with me."

He took a piece of cornbread. "Oh, I wouldn't dream of it," he murmured. "But we do have to talk about it. Have a drink with me before dinner."

She stared mutinously at him. The last thing she wanted to do, given her mood, was talk about last night. But she was pretty sure it couldn't be avoided.

She nodded. "One drink."

Matteo was waiting for her in the cliffside bar when she arrived, seated at a table near the sheer drop to the sea. Cool and elegant in black pants and a lavender shirt that only a man with the highest degree of self-confidence would wear, he made drool pool in her mouth.

He stood and held out her chair. "I ordered you a glass of the Riesling."

Her favorite in the heat. His powers of observation were incomparable. As they had been this afternoon, noticing everything she had not. Like some superhero with X-ray vision.

"Thank you," she murmured, sliding into the leather seat. "We're due to meet the others in a half hour."

He lowered himself gracefully into the seat opposite her. "I'll get straight to the point then."

Her head throbbed anew, despite the two painkillers she'd ingested. "Last night was an aberration," she pronounced sharply. "A one-time thing. Never to be repeated. Can we leave it at that?"

"We should." His mouth flattened into a straight line. "It would be disastrous for both of us for this to go anywhere."

She let out a sigh of relief. So good they agreed on that.

"I wanted to say thank you, however."

His huskily issued words made her heart skip a beat. "For what?"

He raked a hand through his close-cropped hair, and lifted his gaze to hers. "I'm not sure what I would have done if you hadn't come to me last night. I was in a dark, dark place."

The vulnerable gleam in his eyes, the tense set of his big body made the urge to slide her hand over his monumental. But she kept it glued to the table because this could not go there. It couldn't.

She swallowed hard. "I needed to exorcise my own demons."

"He's a jackass, Quinn." His harshly issued words caught her off guard. "I don't know what your husband did to you. I don't know what he said to make you feel like any less of the woman you are. But a man who would walk away from the woman I held in my arms last night is crazy."

Her heart went into free fall. "It's complicated."

"It's a travesty."

They sat there in silence because to say any more

would be going to a place neither of them could venture. Matteo took a long pull of his beer, set it down and gave her a steady look. "Le Belle Bleu will never pass its inspection, Quinn. You have a seriously big problem on your hands."

She exhaled deeply. "I know. But I'm not sure what to do. Raymond swears he has the best contractor on the island."

"And today convinced you of that?"

What alternatives were there? Warren had asked her to handle it, but she was no construction expert. And she didn't know the local business climate.

Matteo reached into his pants pocket, pulled out a business card and slid it across the table to her. "We've used this company to build some of our American restaurants. They have an impeccable track record and a presence here. I made a phone call this afternoon to them and they're willing to come take a look."

"In the next hundred years?" She pressed her hands to her temples. "I have an opening in two weeks. We need to at least have the kitchen in some sort of safe, working order. The rest we can do in phases."

"If they agree to take on the job, they would do the urgent items right away. *If* they agree to take it on," he underscored. "Because of De Campo's relationship with them, I think we have some leverage. They've offered to come look at the hotel next week."

"Really?"

He nodded. "If you like, I will stay and do the walkthrough with you."

Her lips formed the words *yes, please*. She needed his contact because no one else was calling her back. She was terrified Le Belle Bleu wasn't going to open on time. But she was also clear on why Matteo was doing this.

The closer he inserted himself into Luxe's operations, the harder it would be for her not to choose De Campo.

It was also so not her style to accept help and Lord knew, the Quinn of last night was a terrifying, alien creature not helped by Matteo's continued presence on this island. However, the panic raking its way up her throat was all-consuming. The hotel was a disaster.

"They will not screw you over, Quinn." Matteo gave her an even look. "I know these guys. If anyone can fix this, they can."

"All right." She nodded. "But you need to understand, this will in no way help you in the bid process."

He nodded and stood abruptly, his expression hardening into one that was all business. "Let me see if I can get them before dinner."

Matteo strode off in the direction of his suite. Quinn wondered why her heart was now somewhere in the vicinity of her toes.

He was going to help her, wasn't he? Help her drag Le Belle Bleu out of the mess it was in before her hotel chain's reputation went into the toilet? This was no time to pine for him to acknowledge how amazing their night together had been.

Her grip around her wineglass tightened. *Oh, my God.* That's exactly what she'd wanted him to do. She'd been expecting him to rehash last night, when all he'd wanted to do was help her relaunch her hotel, and, in doing so, ingratiate himself even more to Davis Investments.

Where in all this had she become *that* creature?

And if a man was crazy to walk away from her, then how had he just done it so easily?

Quinn, the queen of business, the queen of logic, suddenly had to swallow a very bitter pill. Last night might have been explosive. A once-in-a-lifetime chemistry. But she wasn't worth a ten-million-dollar deal.

It was that simple.

She stood up with a squeal of her chair that made the couple at the next table stare. It's not as if she should be surprised. When it came to Quinn Davis, there was always a reason to leave.

CHAPTER EIGHT

THINGS ALWAYS GOT worse before they got better.

Wasn't that the saying?

Matteo sat at the lobby bar of Le Belle Bleu knocking back a local beer as the last of the contractors beat a hasty retreat before Quinn could catch them and ask for just one more thing to be done. They were wary of her perfectionism, working like dogs to get the last cosmetic fixes done to the restaurant and bar before the hotel was unveiled to everyone who mattered in five days. But at some point they had to sleep. Not that Quinn seemed to have noticed. Or needed to herself...

When the scale of the work to be done had become clear, he'd offered to stay and help manage the contractors. Quinn couldn't do it all on her own and his familiarity with the contractors went a long way. He had to be back in New York right after the reopening for a board meeting and then in Chicago for the pitch, but at least he could help her get the doors open. Make the hotel shine for its debut.

He'd worked side by side, day and night with her and François to get the menus fixed and the human machinery of the bar and restaurant functioning as a five-star hotel should. Now it was just a question of execution. Could the chefs perfect the dishes? Could the bartenders master the complex cocktail list they'd created? Could the staff come together like the well-oiled machine they needed to be to impress a crowd that would be discerning to a fault?

He reached up and massaged the back of his neck. He was beat. Exhausted. But it was worth it. Daniel Williams had boarded a flight back to the outback looking utterly disgruntled at leaving the competition behind. Quinn was relying more on Matteo every day. It was exactly where he wanted to be. But funnily enough, this hadn't been all about his endgame. Quinn was struggling. She'd taken on a task no human being could do by themselves and refused to admit she was in over her head. She'd plowed ahead against the odds with a mind so patently brilliant he could see why she'd gotten where she had at such a young age.

They might, just might, pull this off.

His mouth quirked. Her management style could use an overhaul. Her passion for what she did meant she came on a bit strong. But everyone, right down to the busboys and bartenders, respected her work ethic. Even Raymond Bernard, presently making his way across the lobby with Quinn, seemed to be catching the fever. He might even keep his job at this rate.

The pair pulled to a halt in front of him. Matteo studied the dark circles under Quinn's eyes. She needed help. More than he could give her. She looked longingly at his beer. "Our sommelier's flight was canceled. He'll be here first thing in the morning instead."

"So we come back then?"

"We have a big storm rolling in." Raymond gestured toward the darkening sky. "I don't advise you driving back to Paradis under those conditions, not on these roads."

Quinn gave the sky an uncertain look. "It won't be that bad, do you think?"

The manager lifted his shoulders. "It's going to be a proper tropical storm. I wouldn't chance it."

Her brow furrowed. "Are they finished with the floors on any of the suites?"

"The Dolphin Suite, yes. I had them finish it in case you wanted to stay."

"That's it?"

He nodded. "Everything else is still being polished. That one has three bedrooms in it though."

Quinn caught her lip between her teeth. Matteo could have saved them all the breath and suggested that, no, staying here in a suite with Quinn with the electricity that raged between them was a distinctly bad idea. However, even he, a lover of windy roads and tricky driving, didn't relish the thought of traversing the narrow, hair-raising St. Lucian highways in a tropical downpour.

Quinn glanced at him. "Okay if we stay?"

"Of course." He could make it through one night with a single wall between them. Couldn't he? He'd managed to get through an entire week without putting his hands on her. Had kept things straight as a board between them. *This* was definitely doable.

"All right then, thank you," Quinn accepted. "We'll stay."

They raided the hotel boutique for a change of clothes while Raymond got them a key. Quinn held up a tangerine-colored bikini. "I need a swim," she said with a grimace. "Get yourself some trunks."

He stared at the curtain of the changing room as it flapped shut behind her. Was she crazy? What planet was she on? Sharing a hotel suite was bad enough. Getting naked with her was insanity.

Not happening.

Except he was severely hot and tired. He needed to unwind from the pressure cooker that was Quinn, and a beer in the plunge pool or hot tub was an irresistible siren's call. Mouth tightening, he grabbed a pair of trunks, an extra

shirt and a pair of khakis. He could swim while she was
working. God knew she did it 24/7.

Showered and changed into casual pants and a polo shirt,
Matteo emerged from his bedroom into the main living
area of the luxury oceanfront suite destined to house heads
of state and rock stars, to find Quinn pacing the space,
phone pressed to her ear, her gait agitated, voice sharp.

Not something he needed to be present for, he decided,
walking out onto the terrace. He took in the forbiddingly
dark sky, its ominous gray-black clouds that seemed to
hang suspended over the island. Raymond had been right.
It was going to be a proper tropical storm, hard and heavy,
any minute now. There was nothing like an island rain-
storm to relieve the tension and humidity in the air, and
right now they both needed it. Badly.

He fought the urge to strip down and dive into the ocean
and stay there. No swimming allowed until Quinn, in that
sapphire-blue dress of hers, which made the most of her
voluptuous figure, was safely immersed in work and the
sweats he now knew she preferred to do it in.

Focus. Get the job done, Matteo.

Quinn's voice floated out onto the terrace, hard, determined. "No, Warren, I do not need you to fly down here.
It's coming together."

A pause. "You don't trust me."

Another pause. "I'm fine. Focus on the U.S. hotels. The
reopening will go off without a hitch, I promise you."

If everything fell into place. He winced as he thought
about how much there was still left to do in five short days.

The rest of the conversation was short, abrupt. The ping-
pong back-and-forth of two intensely driven, strong wills
ended in a defiant silence. It was a good five minutes before Quinn joined him on the terrace, her green eyes glimmering with frustration, full mouth drooping with fatigue.

"Where is the wine?"

He poured her a glass of the sparkling white chilling in the ice bucket. "When," he asked quietly, handing it to her, "are you going to admit you're human like the rest of us?"

The tigerlike fierceness he'd come to know so well sparked in her eyes. "It's not that," she growled, taking the glass from him. "He never fully trusts me with anything. He says he does, then he undercuts me. He has to put his stamp on everything. Point out where I'm lacking..."

Matteo shrugged. "It sounded to me like he was offering help."

Her mouth twisted. "He only offers it when he thinks you're about to screw up."

"Maybe you're looking at it the wrong way," he suggested. "The most successful people in the world don't do it on their own. They surround themselves with good people."

She lifted her chin as if she hadn't even heard him. "Once, just once, I'd like to do it on my own. Prove that I am not successful just because I am Warren's daughter, but because of my damned impressive abilities."

"I don't think anyone's doubting that."

"Yes, they do. All the time the other vice presidents take shots at me. I've heard them behind my back."

He took a sip of his wine. "So you're going to spend the rest of your career worrying about what everyone else thinks?"

She pointed her glass at him, antagonism darkening her eyes. "Do you know that after I made the top thirty under thirty list, Warren did not say a word of congratulations to me? Not a word. He said, and I quote, 'It's too bad you weren't the first woman on it.'"

Matteo blinked. "Perhaps it's not his thing to give compliments then, but I'm sure he was proud of you. He had to have been. That list is brutally hard to get on to."

"I wouldn't be so sure about that," Quinn came back bitterly. "Warren's standards are so high you can't be human. You have to be a machine."

"How's that going for you?" he asked softly. "You seem to be doing a pretty good impersonation of one and it's still not making you or him happy."

She squeezed her eyes shut. "I just need to do better."

"No, you don't." He took a step closer. "Dammit, Quinn, you need to believe in yourself. You are working miracles here but you need help."

"I just need to get through the next few weeks and I'll be fine."

He sighed. "There are too many issues with too many properties."

"I will manage."

"You will self-destruct."

She looked him dead in the eye. "I didn't ask for your commentary."

He hissed in a breath. She could be a cold bitch sometimes. He'd been busting his butt for a week trying to help her and this was what he got? But even as he thought it, he knew better. Knew the puzzle that was Quinn had grown a hard shell to protect herself from getting hurt.

Let it go, Matteo. The voice of sanity echoed in his head. *Drop it now before you get more emotionally involved with a woman who is mortally off-limits to you.*

They ate at the candlelit table for two that overlooked the ocean, protected by a canopy as a crackling thunderstorm descended. It lit up the night with outrageously beautiful white light that arced across the sky and stole their breath. The small talk made him crazy. The need to hold her made his hands curl at his sides. He gritted his teeth and went through the key points to review with the sommelier in the morning. Forced the salmon down his throat. Did not acknowledge how she bit her lip against the electricity that raged between them every time their gazes collided, just as strong as the storm around them.

One more taste of her, he knew, and he was a dead man.

Matteo did not do relationships with women. Didn't even know if he was capable of one with his checkered past. With his parents' business merger as his prime example of what one could encompass. Quinn needed someone she could believe in. Someone who could restore her faith in men. Not him.

She offered him a liqueur after dinner. Coffee. He turned them both down flat. Watched the disappointment slacken her lower lip. "I have work to do," he murmured, getting to his feet and throwing his napkin on the table. "Thank you for dinner."

Then he escaped to his room.

Quinn poured herself another glass of wine and paced. She was out of control with her stress, no doubt about it. Matteo did not deserve her ire, not when he'd just spent the entire week bailing her behind out of an impossible situation they might actually pull off if they were very, very lucky.

It's just that he was so damn perfect sometimes. So calm and in control and able to see the big picture. Her fingers curled around her wineglass, absorbing its icy chill. That was, when he wasn't falling apart over a death he wouldn't talk about....

She stopped in front of the incomparable view of the sparkling sea that stretched for miles in front of her. And admitted it. Wasn't the real problem what a good job he was doing ignoring her?

She wanted to kill him. How rational was that?

Quinn stalked inside and changed into the bikini she'd raided from the boutique. Who cared if the sides were cut so high you could see her butt? Or if the triangles of fabric on the top didn't do a great a job of covering her chest?

Matteo had damn well walked away from her again. Without a backward glance. Which was absolutely their deal. It was. She just didn't know how he could so completely turn off his feelings. Forget how unbelievable that night they'd shared had been. Because she'd tried. She'd really tried. And it wasn't working.

She went back outside and sat on the edge of the plunge pool. The storm had moved off, silvery moonlight slanting across the smooth surface of the water, reflecting her confusion back at her. One night was supposed to have been all it was, yet she felt changed somehow. Matteo's hands on her skin, his passion for her, had replaced the fear and inadequacy Julian had implanted in her with the alternate reality that she was beautiful and desirable. Worthy of being treasured.

It had shattered a perception of herself carved over a roller-coaster year of marriage. She wasn't home enough, Julian had said. She wasn't warm enough to the wives of his business associates. Which had degenerated into the fact she wasn't warm enough in general. She didn't treat him like the man of the house.

She downed another gulp of the wine with a jerky movement. Her inexperience in bed had been a major disappointment to Julian. But now that that night with Matteo had proven she wasn't a cold fish, now that she'd sampled her ability to feel, to want, she was struck by the disturbing thought that she would never experience it again. That no man would ever know her as instinctively as Matteo did. Had from day one.

She sank her toes into the water. Lifted them out and watched the droplets fall like big fat tears from her skin. Hot moisture gathered at the corners of her eyes. She didn't want to be that person anymore. The woman who had written off a part of herself as unrecoverable. Who had never believed herself capable of more. A lump formed in her throat, swift and hard. Julian had taken away her desire to feel. Matteo had given it back to her. But he was just a playboy doing his thing. He would move on now, win this deal. Focus on what was important to him. And Quinn would be left with the empty shell of who she'd always been.

The tears slid silently down her cheeks, shocking and unbidden. She hadn't cried like this since Sile had died. When she had finally lost the fight she had so valiantly waged against the cancer that had been too strong even for her adopted mother, who had been the most courageous woman she'd known. Now it felt like a fissure had opened up inside her and exposed everything. Every part of her. Made it painful to breathe.

The silvery moon dipped behind the clouds. Everything became blindingly clear in that moment. So blindingly clear that she didn't care anymore. She wanted more. She wanted her life to be more. The problem was, she thought, swiping the tears away from her cheeks with the back of her hand, she didn't know any other way to be. This was all she'd ever been. Quinn, who got the job done.

She blinked hard as the tears flew faster down her face. Matteo was damn right she didn't want to be human. Being human sucked.

Sometime around midnight Matteo, hot and unable to sleep, emerged from his bedroom and headed for the pool. The rhythmical song of the tree frogs filled the otherwise silent air with a deafening symphony he was surprised anyone could sleep through, yet he had slept through it these past couple of weeks, finding it exceptionally soothing white noise.

But not tonight. He'd emptied his email in-box, read every last report and talked to Gabe who was presently wildly excited over a new wine. And he was still wide-awake with no sign his head wanted to join his body in its state of complete exhaustion.

He grabbed a towel from the rack and turned toward the pool. Then he froze as he saw Quinn sitting with her legs dangling in the water. Her gaze was fixed on the dark mass of the Caribbean Sea, her profile so exquisitely drawn he couldn't tear his eyes from it. He had never met a woman whose beauty was so all-encompassing—so layered. Just when you thought you'd reached the end of it, she revealed more of herself that made you fall deeper under her spell.

If he had continued on with his sensible behavior of late, he would have turned on his heel and gone back inside. Instead he focused on the spare amount of material in the tangerine-colored bikini that did little to cover her mouthwatering curves. Her upswept ponytail revealed the long, graceful curve of her neck that he wanted to sink his teeth into. Dammit. He should never have shared this space with her.

She sensed his presence as if a whisper of air had carried him to her. Looked up at him, the bright glimmer in her eyes wrapping itself around his heart and tugging. She'd been crying. Quinn, who took everything on the chin like a prizefighter and just kept on going, had finally showed a chink in her armor.

Run, a voice inside him warned. *Run before this all comes falling down around you.* Except he didn't. He stepped closer, lowered himself down beside her and dunked his feet in the bathtub-warm water.

"Couldn't sleep?"

She shook her head.

"What's wrong?"

She pressed her lips together. "I don't know."

He pushed a wayward chunk of her hair behind her ear so he could see her face. "You're too hard on yourself. You need to back off and accept help before you break."

"It's not that."

Just as Quinn had crossed the threshold into his room that night, Matteo knew what he was about to ask was the verbal equivalent of doing the same. But the words tumbled out of his mouth anyway. "Then tell me what it is."

She looked down at her hands. Twisted them together in her lap. "You made me feel alive the night we were together. Like for the first time in my life I could feel like everyone else. That I wasn't a machine programmed to churn out profit numbers…"

His heart stalled. "You aren't unfeeling, Quinn. You just don't know how to express yourself."

"I'm scared to." She lifted her gaze to his. "Being like this," she said, waving a hand at herself, "is the only way I know how to be."

"You can do it," he growled. "I've watched you command a room of fifty workmen with your pinky, Quinn. A little self-honesty is not that hard."

"All right then." She turned to face him, amber fire burning in her eyes. "You want me to face my feelings? Speak my mind? You said a man would have to be crazy to walk away from me and yet you've had no problem doing that…. Actions speak louder than words, Matteo."

"You know why I walked away from you," he said harshly. "You know why we both walked away."

She balled her hands into fists. "And so now you move on. You go your merry way, chalk me up as another of Matteo De Campo's conquests while I—" She stared down at her fists. "I am…conflicted."

Matteo felt as if someone should read him his rights. Tell him anything he said could or would be used in a court of law against him. Except his particular court of law was a ten-million-dollar deal that had become his personal hell.

"You see?" She sliced a hand through the air at him. "It's easy for you. You probably have a dozen names in your smartphone you're just dying to call when you get home."

"That is ridiculous," he muttered. "We are negotiating a deal that will make the front page of *The Wall Street Journal,* Quinn. This is not about our hormones."

"I know that." She slammed her mouth shut, wrapped her arms around her chest and did an impression of a statue. Saliva pooled in his mouth at the sight of her plush flesh fighting for freedom over her bikini top. God, he wanted to touch her.

Her eyes grew brighter, the delicate muscles of her throat convulsing. "Tell me what's really bothering you," he said roughly. "Despite what women think, we men are actually not mind readers."

"I'm afraid," she threw at him, aggravation lacing her tone. "I am scared that I'm never going to feel what I felt for you the other night for anyone else. That what we had was some one-night aberration and I'm going to go back to being cold old Quinn who can't have an orgasm because she can't let go long enough to let it happen."

His heart plummeted to somewhere beneath the concrete. "That's crazy. Of course you will."

She shook her head, lips trembling. "I'm scared I'm never going to feel that alive again, Matteo. It terrifies me."

"You will," he said hoarsely. "You just need to find the right man."

"The right man?" She looked at him as if he had cotton batting for a brain. "Am I the only one who thought what we shared the other night was inordinately special? Please tell me I'm not that big a fool."

He pressed his lips shut.

"Goddamn you, Matteo." She planted her hands on the ground to roll to her feet. "You could at least tell me the truth."

His hand clamped around her wrist. "You want the

truth?" She gasped as he yanked her back down, her thighs landing hard on his, her hand against his chest to steady herself. Blood pumped through his veins, filled his head with such pressure he was blinded to common sense. His gaze locked on hers like a heat-seeking missile. "The truth is I've spent the last week trying desperately not to make a mistake that will damn both of us. And if you think," he ground out harshly, "that there has been one minute I haven't thought about us together, then you can think again."

Her eyes were big pools of forest-green laced with gold, her breath unsteady as her fingers bit into his hot, tense flesh. A trickle of sweat made its way down his nape. "You were not a placeholder that night, Quinn. You were the only woman who could have saved me from myself. The only woman I wanted so blindingly much I could have lost myself on that night of all nights."

The hitch in her breath was deafeningly loud in his ear. He ran his thumb across the flushed skin of her cheek. "You know this would be a total disaster."

She arched into his touch like a feline craving his possession. "I don't care. I'm done caring. I will recuse myself from the committee. But if I'm just a deal to you, Matteo, you should walk now."

His heart pounded like an out-of-control freight train. "Quinn—"

She pressed her lips to his forehead. Kept them there. "I need to be with you tonight. I need to know I'm capable of more."

Perspiration slid down his chest, rivulets that pooled at the waistband of his trunks. He flexed his fingers against her soft skin, struggling for control. But this was bigger than both of them, this need for each other. It operated on a whole other level from anything he'd experienced before.

His hands came up to frame her face as he dragged his

mouth up to hers. "If we're doing this, if we're jumping, it has to be all-embracing, Quinn. I'll make love to you, but I won't have sex with you."

"What's the difference?" she whispered against his lips.

"Try it and find out."

His hands absorbed her still-damp, silky-soft skin. His mouth found the sweetness of hers, claiming it in a long, slow kiss that telegraphed just how this would be. She tasted like honey, like something he never wanted to leave. And he decided in that moment, if he was going to hell, he was going to enjoy every single minute of it.

"Matteo…" She breathed the word into his mouth, the edge of anticipation to it setting his blood on fire. His fingers sought out the knot of her bikini top at the nape of her neck and pulled it free, her soft ripe curves spilling into his palms. Her sigh of pleasure was like the most heady of aphrodisiacs. He pulled back so he could see her, drink in the rose-tipped perfection of her breasts.

"You knew this bikini was going to send me over the edge."

"Maybe."

He smiled, dipped his head and brought her nipples to firm, pink erectness with insistent sweeps of his thumbs and tongue. He waited until she was fully aroused and moaning softly for him before he slid his hand down over her stomach and eased his fingers under the elastic of her bikini bottoms. She was hot, wet and felt like velvet. Responsive to his every stroke. He wanted to taste her again, feast on her as he had before, but he wanted to sink his hard, aching flesh inside her more. To make her writhe beneath him until she begged for him to get her off.

He would. Eventually…

She arched under his hand as he stroked a finger into her. Took it deep. "God, that feels so good."

"I can make it better," he promised. He added another

finger, curved them against her in an insistent caress he knew would take her higher. She moaned and ground her hips against his hand. He smiled with satisfaction and brought his mouth to her ear. "This time we're taking it to the bedroom, Quinn."

She stiffened against him. "I said no bedrooms."

"Then you don't get any more." He pulled out of her, held her away from him so he could see her face. He struggled to control the beast inside of him that wanted to find Julian Edwards and extinguish him. "I don't know what he did to you, Quinn. What he did to make you so frightened. But I promise you, I will never hurt you."

He watched her waver. Saw the uncertainty flicker in her eyes. He rested his forehead against hers. "You have to trust me."

A tremor went through her. Her hands curled into his shoulders as if she were waging a war with herself. Then she burrowed into him. "Yes."

Matteo scooped her up off the concrete. Carried her across the terrace inside to his bedroom. When he set her down on the tile, he could feel the tension in her hips. See it etched in excruciating detail across the delicate lines of her face. He raked her hair back and let it fall down her spine, tangling his fingers in the smooth, satiny richness of it. "You say stop, I stop. No questions asked."

She lifted her chin. Put her palm to his pounding heart as if to steady herself, to feel the connection between them. He lowered his head and kissed her. Took her lush mouth again and again until she swayed against him, her hands circling his waist. "You make me crazy," he murmured, nipping at her lower lip until she bit back, sending his pulse into overdrive as her sharp little teeth sank into his sensitive flesh. "If you knew how many X-rated dreams I've had about that performance of yours on your knees... It was the hottest experience of my life, bar none."

Quinn pressed her lips against the throbbing pulse at the base of his neck. Dropped her hand to slide her palm against the rigid hardness of him. He went willingly to his knees. Slid his fingers under the almost nonexistent sides of her bikini bottoms and yanked them off. The musky, aroused scent of her hit him like a brick to the head.

"God, Quinn."

He put his mouth to her, drank in her essence until he was so crazy with want he thought he might lose it. Palms pressed against her buttocks, he held her to him, dragged his tongue across her, inside her. Made her cry out and dig her hands into his hair. She murmured unintelligible things, begged him to slide his fingers deeper into her in a caress he now knew made her crazy.

"Dammit, Matteo—"

He lifted his mouth from her. Pushed to his feet and brought her hands to the waistband of his trunks. "Take them off," he growled.

She shoved her fingers into them and ran them down his long legs. When she straightened and came back to him her face was pinched, expectant. He lowered his mouth to hers, sucked her bottom lip into his and kissed her until she was pliant beneath his hands. "Relax, *bella*. You say stop, we stop."

She rested her forehead against his and nodded. He picked her up and set her down on the massive king-size bed, her dark hair fanning out against the white silk sheets. She was creamy-skinned perfection, had the most exquisite hourglass figure he'd ever seen. Somehow he had the presence of mind to rummage up a condom and slide it on before he returned to her and smoothed his hand down over the curve of her hip, between the juncture of her thighs. Where he wanted to be.

Her eyes went huge. He straddled her, holding her gaze

the entire time. "Touch me," he rasped. "I need your hands on me."

She leaned forward and curved her fingers around the heated, throbbing length of him. He was sure he'd never been this hard, this aroused in his life. She was just that beautiful to him.

Her lips parted, the focus she devoted to his pulsing erection just about doing him in. He reached down, cupped her buttock in his hand and brought her thigh around his waist. "Take me inside of you," he urged. "I need to be inside of you so badly, Quinn."

She closed her fingers around him and guided him to her slick, hot flesh with that same intense concentration. He sank his palms into the mattress on either side of her and forced himself to wait. "More?"

"Yes."

He sank into her just enough to find his place. She arched her hips against him. "Please—"

He gave it to her, excruciatingly slowly, an inch at a time, waiting for her body to adjust to his. Waiting for her to relax—fully trust him. Deeper and deeper she took him, flexing beneath him until he was buried to the hilt. The shocked, dazed pleasure in her eyes had him whispering mindless pleas in Italian for control. He had never felt anything so good in his life as she clenched her tight muscles around him.

He let out a husky groan. If this was hell, he never wanted it to end.

Quinn wrapped her leg tighter around him, brought him closer. "Tell me," he said softly. "Tell me what you want."

She lifted her hips. "More."

He shook his head. "No. Tell me. I want to know what you like. What you need."

She began with soft, breathy requests that were half shy, half eager. He gave it to her, easy, leisurely, leashing the hard demand of his body to give her the buildup she needed. She caught her lip between her teeth. Her cheeks turned rosy. He urged her on with husky commands, goading her, making her tell him more. Making himself half-crazy in the process. Her demands became more insistent, more graphic. He hooked her leg higher around his waist and stroked even deeper inside her.

Deeper, harder until he was shaking with the effort it took to hold back. She flung a hard, raw demand at him that was the end of him. He swore under his breath and set his thumb to her center.

"Come, *sei bella,* Quinn," he murmured, dropping his mouth to hers. "Come for me."

She moaned and closed her eyes, pushed up harder against his thumb. Something inside her was still holding back, unable to let go. He held his screaming body in check and took her apart with one firm rotation of his thumb against her clitoris. Her hot contractions around him set him off like fireworks.

He kissed her, hungry, wild, his hoarse cry spilling into her mouth. And then there was only the long, sweet road back, his body cradled in hers, their connection so complete, so inviolate, he knew he'd never experienced anything like it.

Neither of them dared say anything. It was that heavy in the air. He rolled onto his side, took her with him, loath to break the bond. Her hot tears dampened his cheeks. He brushed them away, murmuring soft endearments in his native language until she fell asleep in his arms.

Moonlight poured into the room from the skylight, bathing them in an otherworldly glow. He stared up at it, his arms tucked securely around Quinn. He was definitely going to hell. He'd definitely passed Go. He'd definitely collected the girl.

It was a done deal.

CHAPTER NINE

QUINN WOKE WITH the birds, their boisterous song nudging her from a restless sleep that had seen her toss and turn most of the night. She wasn't used to sleeping with anyone. She and Julian had occupied separate beds for the last few months of their marriage when things had become intolerable, and Matteo's warm body wrapped around hers, his arm keeping her anchored securely against him was as alien as it was wonderful. She felt claustrophobic, secure and cherished all at the same time.

Light filtered through the skylight, sliding across the bronzed sinewy strength of Matteo's forearm. Her stomach did a slow roll, her fingers twisting in the whisper-soft silk sheets. Last night had been incredible...unforgettable. But had her need to be human been worth the fallout that was sure to follow? Because she had to recuse herself from the committee now. There was no other option.

Which meant telling her father she had developed a personal relationship with Matteo De Campo.

A wave of perspiration blanketed her skin. Throwing off the sheet, she slid her legs over the side of the bed and slipped quietly to the floor. Pulled on her bikini and padded out onto the patio where the first signs of dawn were tracing a hazy pattern across the sky. It was warm already but she knew the slightly feverish sensation heating her skin was the thought of disappointing her father yet again.

Watching the disapproval stain his blue-green eyes until she thought it would be easier just to turn around and take it all back. She pressed a hand to her stomach as her muscles tightened in a full-on revolt. Warren would not understand her letting her personal feelings get in the way of an assignment as big as this. He would be furious—questioning his decision to give it to her.

Standing there, watching the waves roll into shore, the surf rougher this morning after last night's storm, remembering how slowly, how exquisitely Matteo had made love to her, using his body as an instrument of pleasure, not punishment as Julian had done, she knew she had the answer to her question. She would do it a million times over. She felt as if she had truly honored her feelings for the first time in her life.

Quinn raked her hair away from her face with an unsteady movement. It wasn't as if she was ignoring the fact that she'd just made the career-limiting move of all career-limiting moves. It's just that the emptiness wasn't enough anymore. She'd had enough of it for a lifetime.

More troublesome, really, was who she'd just shared her soul with. Matteo De Campo, whose attention span with a female lasted about as long as his perusal of the morning paper.

She squeezed her eyes shut and breathed in the fragrance of frangipani, gardenia and magnolia. Matteo had said he wouldn't have sex with her, he would only make love to her. But he didn't love her. He lusted after her. And therein lay the real foolishness of last night's actions.

If you were smart, you didn't wait until Matteo ended an affair with you. You got out first before you were burned. Made a timely exit so the memories were good and the heart was intact.

The humid blanket of air bore down on her. She looked

longingly at the clear, turquoise water. Maybe a swim would cool her overheated brain.

Matteo woke to an empty bed and an urge for a woman that would have been disconcerting if he hadn't been wondering where in God's name she was. Followed closely by the even more disturbing reality that he had well and truly crossed the line this time and there was no going back.

A throbbing pressure filled his head. Expanded in his skull until it drove him from the bed and onto the cool tile to look for Quinn. It was like déjà vu, her being gone like this again, except this time everything was different. This time he hadn't slept with Quinn Davis in a self-medicating, over-the-edge fashion. He had made a conscious decision to be with her. To honor his emotions for her which ran so deep into uncharted territory he didn't care to contemplate them at the moment.

He pulled on his boxers and strode out onto the terrace, but it, too, was empty. Where would she have gone at just after six in the morning? Was she coming down from the high of last night and realizing what she'd done?

He winced as his head throbbed. There were consequences for both of them. Extreme consequences. He was going to have to tell Riccardo what he'd done, and it wasn't going to be pretty. But he couldn't do it until Quinn told the board, he knew the lay of the land and he had all his ducks in order. His brother would not see it as the complex situation it was. He would see it as history repeating itself in the worst, most reckless fashion possible. Matteo playing with another multimillion-dollar deal that could make De Campo's decade.

His low groan split the air. His brother was going to lose his mind.

Matteo paced to the other end of the patio, looking out over the water. He was a different man than he'd been three years ago. He had been laser-focused on this deal, had laid all the groundwork in a brilliant, understated fashion that would win it for them. He had done his job. Differently than Riccardo would have done, but strategically, it was perfect. Riccardo would crucify him anyway. He didn't get him. Never had.

He lifted his gaze to the sun slipping up from the line of the horizon. It struck him he should be taking the advice he'd given Quinn. He needed to stop trying to live up to everyone's expectations of him and do what he knew was right. Being with Quinn had been right. He knew it in his bones. He needed to convince Riccardo to believe in him. That he would win this deal regardless. That he had always had his eye on the prize.

He was about to go back inside and shower when he saw a lithe figure slicing through the ocean toward their suite. Quinn. He sat down on the edge of the pool while she swam the last hundred meters. She hit the edge, reached up to grip the concrete and blinked the water out of her eyes as she looked up at him, wet dark hair floating behind her like a mermaid come to visit.

He cocked a brow. "You like 5:00 a.m. swims too?"

She reached back and squeezed the water out of her hair, a rueful smile curving her mouth. "Only when I've had earth-shatteringly good sex with a man I'm supposed to be doing business with and I'm trying to process. Other than that I'm usually an end-of-the-day, sneak-out-of-the-office-for-a-class kind of girl."

"Earth-shatteringly good," he repeated, liking the taste of that on his tongue. "That's when you're supposed to stay in bed for more of the same."

"Did you hear me say process?"

"Processing is overrated." He leaned down, took hold of her hands and hauled her up onto the concrete. "Regrets, Quinn?"

She settled herself down beside him, water dripping from her wickedly good curves. "I think," she said with a wry twist of her mouth, "I've processed that right out of me."

"Good." He captured her chin in his fingers and lowered his mouth to hers for a long, lingering kiss. Her lips were soft and salty, capable of endless exploration. There was something so right about being with Quinn that he couldn't see the wrong in it. Even when there were ten million reasons why he should.

Her breathing was choppy when the kiss ended. "Maybe," she said unsteadily, "you should convince me some more."

He set her away from him with reluctant hands. "Maybe you should talk to me about Julian first."

She blinked. "Julian?"

"I want to know."

Her emerald eyes clouded, her gaze falling away from his. "There isn't much to say. Our marriage was a disaster on all fronts. Julian married me because I was Warren's daughter. Because I was the ultimate networking opportunity. He didn't love me and he couldn't cope with the wife he got in return."

He frowned. "What do you mean, 'couldn't cope'?"

"He wanted a wife who'd rather host dinner parties than work. Someone who was content to stroke his ego 24/7."

"Did the man not know you at all? That isn't you, Quinn."

"He thought I'd want to give it all up at some point. That he should be enough."

"Did you love him?"

She hugged her knees to her chest. "I was infatuated with him. He was good-looking, successful, everything I should have wanted in a husband. The catch of the cen-

tury if the prebilling was to be believed. But then I learned
who he really was."

A man who had hurt her so badly she didn't want to go
near a bedroom... He ground his teeth together. "So what
happened? I know he hurt you and I know the fact that
you took up Krav Maga isn't an accident."

She looked out over the sparkling water. "I was inexperienced sexually when I married him. I'd had a couple of
relationships, none of them great. Julian didn't like that.
The more I disappointed him as a wife, the more I disappointed him out of bed, the more frustrated he was with
me in it. The more he wanted to punish me." She pushed
her hair out of her face in a movement he now recognized
as a nervous tick. "The more angry he got, the more I retreated. I couldn't seem to please him. In the end, I was
afraid of him. It became Julian asserting his dominance
over me in the only way he could."

His body went tight. "He assaulted you?"

She shook her head. "I never refused him. I thought that
would just make things worse."

Flames licked at his skin. "So what would you call it
then?"

She chewed on the corner of her lip. "Like I said, he
was rough."

He closed his eyes. "Quinn, why didn't you leave him?"

"Because he was Warren's choice. Because I knew the
dissolution of my marriage would be my father's biggest
disappointment." Her mouth turned down. "And it was. I
don't think he's ever forgiven me for it."

His face darkened. "Please tell me your father didn't
know."

She turned a scathing glance on him. "How would I
tell my father that? Daddy, the man you wanted me to
marry has verbally abused me every day of our marriage...

has been borderline abusive. Cheated on me with other women…"

The heat flaming through Matteo threatened to fry his brain alive. "He was unfaithful to you?"

She nodded. "At the end. But honestly by then I would have begged him to use someone other than me."

He pressed his fists against the concrete, the desire to use them on Julian Edwards immense. "You should have left. You should never have been with him, your father's choice or not. Warren would have lost his mind had he known what was going on."

"But you see that's not what we do." A haunted smile curved her lips. "We Davises specialize in making things work. No matter what. A merger, a marriage. You do not give up. You make it a success."

"That's an insane statement. What if he had escalated things? Started hitting you?"

She paled. "He wouldn't have done that. Control was his power. If he had that he was satisfied."

"You think that. That's how it starts, Quinn. It doesn't usually end that way."

She was silent for a moment. Lifted her gaze to the horizon. "He's gone now. That's all that matters."

He studied her defiant profile, her upturned delicate chin. "Didn't you ever think you deserved more?"

She shook her head. "I saw my marriage as my failure. I didn't want to admit I was incapable of a relationship."

"That marriage was not any kind of an assessment of you," he scowled. "Your husband was a monster. He should have been stopped."

She looked at him, the vulnerability shining in her beautiful eyes making his heart hurt. "I was hopeless at letting him in. I know in the beginning it was equally as much my fault as it was Julian's. I can be a supreme bitch when I want to be. I shut people out."

"Yes," he agreed. "But you can also be an insightful, compassionate, sexy, warm woman if you dig deep enough to find out." He ran a finger down her cheek. "And you aren't pushing me away right now."

Her gaze softened. "You," she said wryly, "are another matter entirely."

"Si," he agreed, reaching for her. "Story of my life, *bella*. But I know you like it, in fact, I know you *love* it."

Quinn was attempting to choke out a reply when he sank his hands into her waist, deposited her in his lap and pulled her wet limbs around him. "Sometimes the penny doesn't drop," he murmured, tipping her heart-shaped face up to his. "Sometimes things are exactly as you see them."

He watched that overactive mind of hers try and process that. Then she reached up and ran her finger over his bottom lip, a sultry glitter in her eyes. "What am I supposed to be seeing right now then?"

Matteo captured her finger in his mouth. Ran his tongue over the soft underside of it. Watched her pupils dilate. "You. On top of me. Now."

A dull rosy glow stained her cheeks. He released her finger. Bent his mouth to her ear, a raspy edge to his voice. "Up on your knees, *cara*."

She did it. Set her knees down on the concrete on either side of him. And he knew from the sparks in her eyes she was just as turned on as him. Needed more as much as he did.

He ran his hand down her trembling stomach, inside her briefs and explored her soft, yielding flesh with teasing strokes that made her body moisten and ready for him. He hardened so quickly he had to bite back a groan. Then she pressed her lips to his stubble-covered jaw, her breathing jagged, uneven, and he did it anyway. She was so sexy when she let herself go.

"Condom," he croaked, stumbling inside in an Olympicworthy performance. When he returned, she straddled him, released him and slid the condom on. He reached down and pulled her bathing suit aside. *"Portami dentro di te tesoro,"* he murmured. "Take me inside of you, sweetheart."

She reached down and grasped the thick, highly aroused length of him. This time his groan split the air in a fractured moan. Quinn brushed him against her core. Teased him. When he thought he might die, she took him inside her. Slowly, torturously, her gasp filling his ears. It made him feel proud, intensely male that he could do that to her and he swelled even larger inside her. Forced himself to stay completely still as she sank down on him. More, more, until he was buried completely in her.

She trembled in his arms. Dug her nails into his shoulders. He pushed her back, held her hair away from her face so he could see her. "You are the most beautiful, responsive woman I have ever had," he said huskily. "Never ever doubt your ability to feel, Quinn."

Her chin quivered, her fingers curling around his shoulders in a fierce grip that telegraphed her struggle. Then she brought her mouth to his and kissed him blindly. Soulfully. Until their union was taken to another level completely.

He dug his hands into her hips and lifted her. Brought her back down on him in a rhythm so slow and deliriously good he closed his eyes and savored it. The sound of them filled the air, the raw push and pull of their bodies heartstoppingly erotic. Quinn buried her head in his shoulder and whispered encouragement. Faster. Harder.

Her body tightened around him. Brought him torturously close to the boiling point. She begged him to make her come, needed his guidance. And he did, pulling her hips hard against him, placing a hand against her bottom and grinding them together. "Like that," he told her. "Use me."

She leaned forward and rubbed her flesh against him

with every stroke. His body tightened, ready to explode, and he cursed and told himself to hang on. Hold on for ten more seconds so that she could get there. Be with him.

Her soft cry shattered the air. She shook wildly beneath his hands as the orgasm tore through her and caused his. He arched his hips and let loose a guttural, primal grunt of satisfaction that might have traveled to Pluto it rocked him so furiously. They stayed like that, aftershocks ricocheting through their bodies, until he picked her up and carried her to the shower. Sensuously, reverently, he washed her beautiful body all over until he couldn't help but want her again and took her against the wall.

It occurred to him he might never stop wanting her.

CHAPTER TEN

ON THE LAST LEG of what seemed like an impossible journey to reopen Le Belle Bleu, things were finally falling into place. The night before the reopening, Quinn could almost see the light, although she wouldn't dare say it aloud for fear some other disastrous calamity might occur. But she was smiling for the first time in a week.

Optimistic enough that she had agreed to a stir-crazy Matteo's plan to take an hour's break to go for roti at the shack on the beach, legendary with the locals for its version of the piquant Caribbean specialty.

They both needed a break. Needed to let off some steam. A walk on the beach might do it. She pulled on shorts and a T-shirt in the bedroom she and Matteo were sharing in the suite at Le Belle Bleu in the hectic lead up to the relaunch, his clothes left in the other bedroom for optics, and pulled her hair into a ponytail as he showered. She hummed to herself while she slicked on some lip gloss, the glimmer of Matteo's sleek gold watch catching her eye on the dresser. She picked it up and tested the weight in her palm. It was an exquisite timepiece with diamonds marking the hours and an understatedly elegant black pearlescent background. A collector's edition, likely.

She turned it over to examine the back. Saw there was a finely drawn inscription laced across the matte gold surface. It was in Italian. And although she knew she shouldn't do it, that it was private to Matteo, she sat down and typed it into her computer to translate.

You meant everything to my son. Take him with you always. Affonso.

Her heart stuttered in her chest. The watch was Giancarlo's.

She replaced it on the dresser. Stood looking at it. Matteo's darkness had receded since that night at Paradis, but it still had him in its grip. She saw it in those unguarded moments, when his mask slipped and the haunted look returned. As if it never really went away.

She frowned. He called her a closed book. If she was a closed book, then he was a buried story. Pretending to be open to the world when he was anything but.

The sun was setting as they walked along the beach to the restaurant, if you could call the ten-foot-by-ten-foot brightly painted slatted wooden structure that. She kept the conversation light while they shared their rotis on the sand in front of the rolling waves, a cold beer beside each of them.

Matteo lifted his beer to his mouth and took a long swallow. "Have you heard from Warren yet?"

She shook her head. "I rarely hear from him while he's in Asia with the time difference. He may not get back to me until he returns to Chicago."

"He needs to know," Matteo said sharply.

"And he will." She slid him a sideways look. She didn't understand why he seemed so anxious about her telling Warren and the board about them. It was she who should be stressed. It was she that was severely curtailing her career with this decision. Her father and the board would ultimately make the right choice. The fair choice.

"He's back tomorrow regardless."

He nodded. Looked out at the ocean. "Have you talked to Thea today? How's the foot?"

Quinn grimaced. A fifteen-hundred-pound stallion had stepped on her sister's left foot yesterday while she was conducting an examination, shattering the bones in multiple places. "She's at home twiddling her thumbs, cursing that damn horse. You see," she pointed out, "I was right all along."

That won her a smile. "That was just bad luck."

Quinn pushed her roti aside and decided the only way to get him to talk might be to start talking herself. "I'm thinking while I'm making all these radical decisions I might like to get to know my sister in Mississippi."

"Have you had any contact with your birth family?"

"No." The hollow feeling that invaded her every time she thought about the parents who had given her away made her chest ache. "I don't really have anything to say to them. They chose not to keep me. They had another girl. End of story. But my sister—it wasn't her fault. I just feel like I should know her at some point. Even if we aren't ever close."

He lifted a brow. "You don't think there might be more to your parents' decision than that?"

She brought her beer to her lips and took a deliberate sip. "They gave me away and had my sister a couple of years later, Matteo. How else can you interpret it?"

He swiveled to face her. "Like maybe they weren't ready when they had you. Like maybe there are complexities involved you know nothing about. Life isn't black and white, Quinn, as much as you'd like to think it is. There are a lot of gray areas."

Gray areas. That's what you called giving your child up, never to see them again? Marking her defective in the process? "I wouldn't expect you to understand."

"Why don't you try?" he challenged. "There are no prizes for being an island, Quinn."

She turned to face him, latching on to the opening. "I don't know about that, Matteo, you are. You pretend to be everyone's man, but you're no one's man really."

His mouth flattened. "What's that supposed to mean?"

"Exactly what I said. You talk, but you don't really talk."

He sliced her an even look. "How about we finish with you before we move on to me? How is it you think I cannot understand what you're going through?"

"Because you have a family who loves you. Who are yours. Your flesh and blood. How could you possibly understand what it's like to not be wanted? To have Warren and Sile so desperate for a child they adopt me, then months later get everything they ever wanted in Thea? To not be good enough for my old family, and not be needed by my new one?" She blinked against the fire burning the back of her eyes. "It was heartbreaking, Matteo. Heartbreaking to grow up knowing that."

"And finally we get somewhere…" He pushed his dinner aside, sat back and wrapped his arms around his knees. "You know what I know, Quinn? I saw how much Thea adores you that night at the cocktail party. I heard how much your father respects you when he talked about you. Do you have any idea what I would do to have that same level of acceptance from my father? My family? I have spent my life fighting for it."

She pushed her beer into the sand, thrown again by another of Matteo's perspectives that upended her own. Was her frame of reference really so totally off when it came to her family? Was she so colored by the past it distorted all else?

"You live in a family of gladiators," she finally offered when the silence had stretched taut between them. "Isn't that what you do? Fight to be the best?"

He gave her a long, gray-eyed stare. "Perhaps."

She clasped her hands between her legs and looked over at him. "Giancarlo's father gave you his watch. Why?"

His shoulders stiffened. "I'm sorry," she murmured, "I was admiring how beautiful it was and I saw the inscription."

A shutter came down over his eyes. "There is nothing to be gained by talking about Giancarlo. He's gone. There's nothing I can do about it."

"Oh, for God's sake." She waved a hand at him. "You accuse me of being an island. You're so far out there you aren't even a speck in the ocean."

His eyes flashed with that lightning-storm intensity that signaled a clash of the elements was on its way. "I was responsible for his death, Quinn. I caused it. Is that what you want to hear me say? Giancarlo's father gave me that watch so I wouldn't feel guilty about what I did. Because he knew I would every day for the rest of my life."

Her mouth dropped open. "I'm sure that can't be true."

Matteo stared out at the horizon, his back ramrod straight. He was silent for so long she thought she'd pushed him too far. Then he dropped his hands between his knees. "Giancarlo was everything to me. My brothers, we're close, but I've never had the bond with them Giancarlo and I had. We grew up in Montalcino together, both of us groomed to be powerful men with the accompanying responsibility. Giancarlo became the CEO of one of Europe's largest car companies, a star of the corporate world, and I was running De Campo's European operations. We had power, money and youth. We were on top of the world. Drunk on our success…"

"Power can be an intoxicating thing."

He turned to look at her. "Giancarlo didn't handle it well. He drank too much, drove too fast, partied too hard. Maybe it was in his blood, I don't know. He had an alcoholic father with a high-flying job who managed to bury his issue under his success for years. It was not a good example. G told himself he could handle it, but he couldn't stop. Couldn't recognize his limits like the rest of us."

A chill settled over her. "Was he drinking the night of the accident?"

"Si." His hands curled into fists between his knees, a dark glitter entering his eyes. "I was annoyed with Riccardo for always handcuffing me, for holding me back from the things I wanted to do with the company. He didn't think I was ready and I knew that I was. So to spite him, to blow off some steam, I went on a tear with Giancarlo in Monte Carlo. We partied hard, won a lot of money, had more than a few women hanging off us willing to divest us of it. But at some point, my rational brain kicked in and I suggested we leave. G insisted we have one more drink to finish the night off…"

Her stomach rolled, pitched in a sickening twist. "That's why you reacted like that when Daniel pushed the drink on you."

His olive skin took on a white sheen. "Cognac was G's drink of choice…or perhaps I should say his weapon of choice." He shook his head. "I should have shut him down. I should have known it would put him over the edge. Instead I got caught up in the competitive thing we always had going on, had the drink and suggested a race back to our hotel."

"After drinking like that?" She couldn't keep the horror out of her voice.

He nodded jerkily. "I was out of control. *We* were out of control. We left—took different routes back to the hotel, and when I got there, G wasn't there." The blank expression on his face made her blood go cold. "I knew. I knew right away."

She put a hand to her mouth. "He'd crashed."

Matteo nodded. "I backtracked. He'd taken a one-way street the wrong way and wrapped his car around a tree. When I found him, the police were there, but there was nothing we could do to save him. He died in front of me while we waited for the ambulance."

Quinn's heart contracted. "Oh, God, Matteo—"

"He wasn't paying attention to any of the women that night." He went on, tonelessly. "He told me he was in love with his girlfriend, Zara. That he wanted to marry her and settle down and become a father because he knew this life we were leading was crazy. And he wanted better than what he'd had." His gaze moved to hers, a flash of agony darkening the emptiness. "A few weeks ago, I saw Zara's engagement announcement. That she's marrying someone else."

Quinn's throat swelled, thickened, until it was physically hard to get the words out. "You were both out of control, Matteo. You cannot blame yourself for what happened."

"I was the stronger one." He lifted his chin, the brief glimpse of pain she'd seen dissipating into cold, hard steel. "I should have known better. I could have saved him."

She took his jaw in her fingers, her eyes burning. "You can't save other people. We have to fight our own demons."

His jaw twitched under her fingers. "I should have done better. I *will* do better from now on. It will be my legacy to him."

A tear slid down her face. "You're a good man, Matteo. You have to believe that. I'm sure if Giancarlo could see you now, he would be so proud of you."

He was silent, the dying rays of the sun lighting the hard contours of his face. "Why should I get to be vibrant and enjoy the best years of my life when he is gone? I don't know if I can ever accept that."

She shifted closer to him, swung her leg over his, straddled him and brought his face to hers, the tears streaming down her face now. "Because somewhere up there he wants you to. Because the only tragedy worse than what's happened already would be for you to spend your life grieving for him instead of honoring him."

"But how?" he asked hoarsely, resting his forehead against hers. "How do I do it?"

"One day at a time," she murmured, absorbing the warmth of his skin. "My mother Sile once said it's not the mistakes we make that define us, it's what we choose to do with them. Choose your path, Matteo. Be better than your mistakes. And know, as G's father said, you were everything to him."

She sat there holding him, absorbing his pain, until his body seemed to give beneath her hands. Until she thought maybe, just maybe, what she'd said had gotten through to him.

They were silent as they walked back to the hotel, ankle deep in the sea, hand in hand. She had chosen her path, was starting to make pivotal decisions which would define her future. She just wished she knew they were right. Hoped they would carry her where she was going. Because she no longer knew where that was. She only knew she couldn't stand still any longer.

CHAPTER ELEVEN

IT WAS QUITE literally a miracle when Le Belle Bleu opened on August 5 with a VIP party that was next to flawless.

Italian marble shone in the opulent lobby, the cracks it had sustained during installation filled and polished to perfection. The connected series of fountains and pools which hadn't been close to finished when Quinn had arrived in St. Lucia were miraculously complete and bubbling with a magical shimmer that made them flow like liquid silver. And the hors d'oeuvres from the new menu being passed out by white-coated serving staff were spectacular—decadent and full of local flavor.

Quinn stood at the edge of the crowd on the torchlit patio by the sea as the evening shifted into the later hours and took it all in. She drew in a deep lungful of air and exhaled slowly, feeling her equilibrium right itself. It was the perfect debut for the legendary hotel. The blood, sweat and tears had all been worth it.

Bar staff moved seamlessly between the groups of guests who had decamped to the fire pits scattered around the patio. A reggae band played for the dancers. The shadowed profiles of every important personality in the Caribbean gleamed in the firelight, joined by their first round of guests and the global travel press. Her mouth curved. The staff hadn't missed a beat, polished to their own version of perfection by a newly inspired Raymond Bernard.

She might even keep him.

Lifting her glass to her lips, she took a long sip of champagne. Matteo had been right about giving Raymond a second chance. Right about a lot of things. He had brushed aside her mounting panic this past week and brought her back to earth, teaching her to take one day at a time. That with the right groundwork, everything would work out as it should.

Faith. It was all about faith, he'd told her. Not a trait she had a whole lot of experience with. But he'd inspired her to look deeper. To find it in herself. And in doing so, she had become a different person.

She sought him out in the crowd. He was talking to François and a government official, looking like the force of nature he was in a dark gray suit with an expensive sheen to it. The kind of handsome that made her heart race in her chest. Although she and Matteo had been unfailingly discreet during the day, given her inability to get hold of her father and recuse herself from the committee, every night they had come together in an insatiable melding of mind and body that had rocked her world.

It was crazy, dangerous, being with him like this but she couldn't seem to stop her headlong plunge back into the living. Being with Matteo was like ingesting high-octane fuel when she'd spent her life running on regular. And not even her promise to end it first was penetrating the rosy glow surrounding her.

He appeared at her side as if summoned by the pull of her thoughts, magnetic, lethal, far too disconcerting. "Stop looking for things to fix," he murmured. "The penny isn't dropping tonight, Quinn."

But it would eventually, wouldn't it?

"I can't thank you enough," she threw into the silence between them. "I couldn't have done this without you."

He lifted his broad shoulders. "We make a good team."

They did. He softened her hard edges. She made him tighten up on process when his creativity ran amuck. Their combined skills had made this night happen. One piece could not have existed without the other. And she couldn't help but wonder what it would be like to always have him by her side. To always have him.

Her lashes fluttered down. That was dangerous, silly thinking. Matteo De Campo did not do permanent. And neither did she.

He gave her a long look. "Dance with me."

She eyed him. "Not here, Matteo."

"A dance between business partners," he murmured, sliding an arm around her waist and ushering her through the crowd. She let him propel her through the guests, sure she wasn't a good enough actress for this. And when he took one hand and slid the other around her waist and started moving to the sensual rhythm of the reggae, she was sure she wasn't.

"I can't move my hips like that," she complained. "Can we do this later?"

He bent his head to her ear. "Let go, you little control freak. Let me lead."

She tried. Tried to match her undeniably stiff steps to his sinuous, smooth ones, but she kept stepping on his feet and stumbling to catch up. He wrapped his fingers tighter around hers and brought her closer to his body so he could force her steps into line with his. "It's a good thing there are times when you do know how to follow or a man wouldn't know what to do with you," he said roughly in her ear.

Heat filled her cheeks. "Matteo."

"What? No one can hear us."

She could hear her heart pounding in her chest, its insistent drumbeat reverberating in her ears. The burn of his thighs against hers was primal. The way he made her want to throw caution to the wind disconcerting in the extreme. She pulled in a breath and pushed back to put some distance between them. It wasn't just that he was the most charismatic man she'd ever met. He was also kind. Insightful.

She was a better person around him. Happy.

And tomorrow he would fly back to New York and she would fly back to Chicago and it would be over.

She stumbled. He tightened his hold on her waist and drew her back to him, those all-seeing eyes drilling into hers. "What's wrong?"

She was madly in love with him, that's what was wrong. Although she had no experience with the feeling, the inescapable, glaring truth hit her like a slap in the face.

She swallowed hard. "Nothing."

He studied her face. "Your lying skills have not improved."

"This has to end, Matteo. You know it and I know it."

His eyes deepened to that stormy hue that telegraphed a fight. "When did you happen to come to this conclusion?"

"You…I…" She shook her head. "We're flying back to the States tomorrow. To two separate cities. To two separate lives."

"So? This is the jet plane age, Quinn. Soon to have regular space travel."

Yes, but soon he wouldn't want her and she couldn't go through being left again.

He read her thoughts as effortlessly as he always did. "Oh, no, you don't," he growled, his hand tightening around hers. "We started this and we're seeing it through. I want you in my life, Quinn."

The crowd around them grew louder, buzzed in her ears. What did that mean, he wanted her in his life? For a month? Six? Until he lost interest and ended it, his contract intact? Until she went the way of all his other women, with a broken heart and a bar set so high no man could ever live up to it?

Her insides curled in on themselves. Julian hadn't even come home to pack his things. Instead he'd sent movers on a Saturday morning when she was still in her pajamas, barely awake and on her first coffee. She'd stared dumbfounded at them, wondering what they were doing there. Called Julian in Boston where he was supposed to be watching a ball game with his brother, only to discover he was with his lover of three months. And he was leaving Quinn.

The movers, he'd said, were the civilized way to end things.

After the movers had left, she'd closed the door, leaned against it, and slid to the floor. And hadn't been sure whether her tears were ones of relief or humiliation. Failure. All she'd been able to think of was what was she going to tell Warren. How she was going to explain his perfect match had been a failure before it had even begun.

"Quinn?" Matteo squeezed her arm, his gaze impatient. "Are you listening to me?"

She lifted her chin. "What's the longest you've ever been with a woman?"

His dark brows came together. "What does that have to do with us?"

"Answer the question."

"I was with my last girlfriend for six months. I cared for her, Quinn."

Six months. She, the failure at relationships and he, the man most likely never to commit were going to make this work?

"I think we should call it quits while we're ahead." She kept her gaze level, her tone even. "I'm about to put a major dent in my career aspirations when I tell my father about us. Perhaps that's enough for now?"

His gaze darkened. "Not when the only reason you're doing it is because you're afraid of failure."

Her blood fired in her veins, mixing with confusion to form a deadly cocktail. "What exactly are you offering, Matteo, beyond a hot affair with an Italian stud? What does having me in your life entail?"

His eyes flashed. "You had best take that back right now, Quinn."

Her gaze bounced away from his. "You know what I mean."

"Somehow I don't. Perhaps you'd like to explain."

"Your track record makes it very clear where this will end."

"This isn't about the past." A muscle jumped in his jaw, a heated fury building in his eyes as he captured her jaw in his fingers and forced her gaze back to his. "This is about the future. Our future. And you're trying to end this before it's even begun."

She pulled out of his grasp. "It's an act of self-preservation, Matteo. I have more brains than the rest."

His stormy gaze sliced over her. "You really are spoiling for a fight."

"That would be you, not me." She felt a set of eyes burn into them, fueled undoubtedly by Matteo's caveman tactics and turned her head to find the source. A photographer sat with a camera at the bar watching them intently.

"This is not the place to be having this conversation."

"You're right." He nodded tersely. "But you are not going to withdraw from me, Quinn. Get that through your head. It might have been an insane idea on both our parts to get involved, but it's done. Now, later, we are going to see this through. I promise you."

The music ended. She stepped out of his arms, relief flashing through her. "I should go talk to the governor general before he leaves."

His gaze followed her as she walked across the terrace with quick steps toward the governor. No way was she doing this now. No way was she making life-altering decisions when her head was clearly not on straight. Because agreeing to be with Matteo De Campo would have a ricochet effect on her life she couldn't contemplate right now.

It was the early hours of the morning before the party started to wind down and Matteo joined François at the bar for a drink, content in the knowledge that the evening had been an unqualified success. The tourism press and the VIPs had raved about the hotel's return to its former glory. The contractors would stay on to help Quinn finish the outstanding issues.

His work here was done. He and Quinn were not.

"Where's Quinn?" he asked François.

"She went to find a bottle of port for a guest. She said she'd join us after."

His mouth tightened. She'd been avoiding him ever since their conversation earlier. Deliberately. Unapologetically. He'd watched her shell come down around her as the minutes had ticked by. Shutting him out.

François handed him a shot of the ten-year-old rum he'd promised and babbled on about the night, his hands moving expressively through the air. Matteo lifted the glass to his lips.

This has to end. You know it and I know it.

Quinn's rash preemptive strike was festering like a gigantic sore. He didn't know it. In fact, he'd been avoiding the whole subject entirely until she'd said it. And as soon as she had, he'd realized he didn't want it to end. He wasn't ready to give her up. Might never be. But she was doubting what they had. Her history was kicking in and he didn't like it—not one bit.

Not when they'd both risked everything to be together.

He set his glass down with a thud. "I'll be right back."

Matteo's long strides carried him into the empty restaurant and down to the massive, ornate cellar. He found Quinn in the perfectly climate-controlled showpiece of a space, staring bemused at the rows of ports.

She looked up at him, hand on her hip. "Another request?"

"No. Which port are you looking for?"

She named it. He scanned the rows, yanked out a couple and found it. Setting it on the shelf, he caged her against the racks with his hands on either side of her.

"I'd like to know what's going on in your goddamned head."

Her eyes went round. "I thought we were going to talk about this later."

"Now. Why are you withdrawing? Why do I feel like we've regressed a week in a few hours?"

The delicate muscles of her throat convulsed. "Matteo, not now. I need to get someone a drink."

"And I need to know what's going on in your head."

She pressed a hand to her throat. Was silent for a good two or three seconds. "I'm panicking."

"About what?"

"I don't know, it's just all too much right now and I—I—"

"Spit it out, Quinn."

She glared at him like a cornered animal that wanted out, her emerald eyes sparking. "I am falling for you. I know it's stupid and I don't want to be but—"

He cut her off with a kiss. It might have been relief because it flooded through him like a life-infusing force. Or it might have been the need to put his mouth on hers and feel her sweet lips beneath his and know that it wasn't over between them. Because it couldn't be. She had wormed her way inside his heart, had become his weakness. And he couldn't resist her.

She sighed into his mouth as if she'd lost a battle and brought her hands up to frame his face. He wedged his knee in between hers and hauled her closer. Took the kiss deeper until he was sure he had branded her irrevocably his.

"You have to believe in us, Quinn," he murmured against her mouth. "This is real. We are real. And we are going to figure this out together."

"That's a nice cutline for the photo."

The amused voice came from behind them at the same time a bright light exploded. He jerked his hands from Quinn and spun around as another flash went off. *A photographer.*

The shorter, slighter man turned and ran. Matteo lunged for him but he was too quick. He fled up the stairs, Matteo in hot pursuit. Through the restaurant, out the doors to the terrace they ran. The photographer must have cased the place and knew exactly where he was headed, because Matteo lost him in the crowd. He stood there, breathing hard, his arms dropping by his sides. Damn.

He grabbed a security guard. The guard alerted his co-workers and they scoured the grounds. To no avail. The photographer was long gone.

Matteo sought out Raymond Bernard and demanded to see the press credentials. A white-faced Quinn joined him as the manager went off in search of them. She flicked him a glance. "I saw him watching us earlier while we danced."

"I don't understand." Matteo ran a hand over his head. "The door to the cellar locks automatically. You need a code to get down there."

"There's a ten-second delay before it locks again," Quinn said numbly. "If he was watching us and saw you go down he could have slipped in."

Matteo wanted to kick himself for being so indiscreet.

Like a cowboy with your gun drawn at all times, Riccardo had said. Was that what he was?

Well, he was paying for it now.

"It was a *Whispers and Tales* photographer," Raymond said, returning with a sheet of paper. He handed it to Matteo, a frown on his face. "Why would he be shooting in the cellar? It was not included in the permissions."

Quinn looked as if she wanted to throw up. Matteo studied the photographer's picture. It was definitely him.

He left a voice mail with Alex to put pressure on the magazine not to use the photograph. Threaten them with legal action. But it was 2:00 a.m. Chances were, the photograph would be making the rounds before she even had a chance to speak to his editor.

Quinn pressed her hands to her temples. "That's not going to make any difference, is it? They're going to use it."

"Probably."

They closed things off for the night, then headed back to the suite. It was nearly two-thirty in the morning by the time Quinn paced the floor of the living room, steam coming out of her ears. "With your notoriety, that photograph's going to be everywhere by tomorrow morning."

"Likely."

"We need a game plan."

"We've done what we can do for tonight." He kept his voice level, but his stomach was churning. The sense that he was on a one-way ticket to Hades binding its way around his brain. "It was a great night for Le Belle Bleu, Quinn. You did a superb job. Get some sleep and we'll figure the rest out tomorrow after I talk to Alex."

"I am not you." She went from agitated to Mount Vesuvius in under a second. "You might be used to having graphic photos strewn across the internet, but I am not."

He gritted his teeth. "I am generally very discreet about my relationships. This is not a usual occurrence for me."

"Yes, well, I have a reputation to protect. This is a disaster."

He took a step toward her, his blood heating at the gibe. "It's done. We can't take it back. There's no use being melodramatic."

"Melodramatic? You won't feel that way when my father hits the roof. When the board realizes how ethically wrong we've both been. Goddammit, Matteo. I was going to recuse myself. Now what is everyone going to think?"

"We will deal with it," he said firmly. "Together. It will be fine."

"You don't think Daniel Williams is going to see this and not cry bloody murder?" Her voice rose another octave. "I have breached an open bidding process with completely unethical behavior. It is not going to be fine. It's going to be awful."

"Quinn—"

She started pacing again. "Why couldn't you have just listened to me? Kept your hands to yourself until that party was over?"

"You want to discuss who hasn't been able to keep their hands to themselves?" He gave her a dangerous look. "Because you started this."

Color flared in her high cheekbones. She turned and walked to the open French doors and leaned against the frame, looking out at the sea. "It's not just about me, Matteo. De Campo could lose the contract over this."

He was well aware of that. Well aware of the nausea forcing its way up his throat, threatening to choke him.

"Panicking isn't going to help," he said grimly.

"My whole career is hanging in the balance." Quinn turned around, her face paler than he'd ever seen it. "What else would you suggest I do? I've spent the last seven years killing myself to get where I am. To prove myself. People are finally starting to respect me for who I am. And then I do this. For *what?* For me to satisfy my need to *sleep with you?*"

He went to her then, wrapped his fingers around her upper arms and pulled her to him. "Do not start tearing us apart because you're afraid. I told you I won't let you do that."

"Why not? You haven't even said—"

"What?" He slid his fingers under her chin and brought her gaze up to his.

"Nothing." She shook her head. "I don't even know who I am anymore."

It hit him then. She wanted him to say he was falling in love with her....

The words jammed in his throat. He cared about Quinn. He really did. But he wasn't sure he even knew what love was. How could he say it?

He might never be ready to say it.

He swallowed hard. "I care about you," he said gruffly. "I told you earlier I want you in my life."

She looked up at him, her pupils dilating like those of a wounded animal. "Really it was my fault wasn't it? Falling for a playboy? Because what does that really mean? You want me in your life until you eventually tire of me?"

"Quinn—"

She held up a hand. "I've had enough for one night. Like you say, let's see what the morning brings."

She marched toward the bedrooms. He watched her go, chest tight, the injured look on her face almost making him go after her. But what would he say? He'd forced her to open up and now he didn't know what to do with the information he'd unearthed.

His mouth tightened. He jammed his hands in his pockets to restrain himself. It was a better idea to let them both cool off and focus on the fact they'd just put a ten-million-dollar deal in jeopardy. His own career, his relationship with his family was hanging in the balance if he didn't figure a way out of this.

He needed an action plan and he needed it fast. Now was a time for logic. Not emotion. Because, undoubtedly, all hell was about to break loose.

CHAPTER TWELVE

IT WAS WORSE than he'd envisioned.

Matteo sat at his computer the next morning, a half-drunk cup of coffee by his side, the *Whispers and Tales* photo emblazoned across his screen. The placement of his hands made him wince. The cutline made him think selling wine to the devout might actually be a viable occupation.

He read it again to make sure it was as bad as he thought.

A Merger Made in Heaven?
After cutting a swath through the globe's most eligible women, all eyes have been on devastating Matteo De Campo to see which leading lady he'd end up with next. Seems the much-sought-after bachelor might have his sights set on a very lucrative merger between the De Campo and Davis clans. De Campo, seen here engaged in a passionate clinch with Luxe Hotels vice president, Quinn Davis, during the reopening of the chain's legendary property, Le Belle Bleu, in St. Lucia, seems to be having no trouble melting the heart (or other parts) of the "ice princess." We give this particular merger a hearty thumbs-up.

Damn. He sat back and pressed his palms to his temples. If he was Daniel Williams, he'd be out of his mind.

Questioning the integrity of all of it. The board, Warren—who knew how they'd handle it? And then there was Riccardo. He'd wanted to have all the facts, know who the new decision-makers would be so he could assure his brother he had things under control.

Not happening now.

Quinn came out of her bedroom, dressed and bleary-eyed. "It's up," he said grimly. She sat down beside him and scanned the cutline. Her skin paled. His chest tightened. "Quinn—"

She stood up. "I need to head Warren off at the pass. My flight doesn't get in until eight. Can you take me in the jet and drop me off first?"

"Si." He stood up. "Do you want me to come with you?"

Her eyes flashed with an icy brilliance. "I run multimillion-dollar companies, Matteo. The last thing I need is to be babysat by you."

"I was offering to support you, not babysit you."

"I need neither, thank you." She headed toward the bedroom. "I'll be ready in thirty minutes."

He glanced at his watch. Heard a beep as a text came in. Riccardo.

Meet me at the house when you get in.

He sat down, a feeling of such intense déjà vu rolling over him it was hard to breathe. *"Mi deludi,"* Riccardo had said that night after the airline pitch. *You disappoint me.*

It had been the second-worst moment of his life. Seeing G's car wrapped around that tree the absolute lowest.

Alex called. Asked him point-blank if he was having an affair with Quinn. He confirmed it, wincing as she swore in his ear. "Do not say a word to anyone, not even the goddamned air hostess, Matteo," she warned him, and arranged to meet him at Riccardo and Lilly's to discuss damage control.

They did the flight up the East Coast in silence. When they landed at O'Hare, Matteo helped Quinn off the jet, his pilot anxious to keep their stop short and move on to New York. His mind trained on his upcoming confrontation with his brother, he gave her a quick, hard kiss. "I'll call you." Then he stepped back on the plane, the pilot went through his preflight takeoff checklist and they were back in the air.

He leaned his head back against the leather seat. His plan consisted of one strategy and one strategy only. He had to hope that Warren Davis was a reasonable man, that the board allowed De Campo to pitch and he won it so outright that no one would ever question his relationship with Quinn.

There was no backup plan. There was nowhere to hide. This was it.

Two and a half hours later, he stood on the back terrace of Riccardo and Lilly's Upper East Side Manhattan town house. His brother's jerky, barely controlled movements as he poured each of them a scotch sent Matteo's shoulders to his ears. "You need to let me explain," he started in a preemptive strike. "I care about her, Riccardo."

His brother whipped around, eyes blazing, a half-filled glass in his hand. "You care about her? I told you to keep your hands off her, Matty. Once, just once, I asked you to do something for the betterment of this company. And you're telling me, with all the women on this planet who would beg for you to *screw* them, you care about Quinn Davis so much you had to *do* her?"

Matteo took a step toward him. "Watch your mouth."

His brother slammed the glass on the bar, his legs

spread wide in a fighting stance. "Right now I'd like to take your head off, Matty. I swear to God…"

He swallowed hard. "I think I'm in love with her."

"I don't care if you think she's the future mother of your children. You cannot have her."

"Well, that's unfortunate," he said quietly. "Because I intend to."

Riccardo's ebony eyes bored into him. His nostrils flared, his fists balled tight by his sides. For a single, heart-stopping moment Matteo thought his brother would finally hit him. Let loose the aggression that had been pulsing between them for years. He stood his ground, his body tense with adrenaline. But it was like a crystal clear clarity had come over him. He *could* see Quinn as the mother of his children. For the first time in his life, he saw that potential with a woman. And he wasn't giving her up.

Riccardo let out an oath, picked up a glass and shoved it at him. Then he retrieved his own, filled it the rest of the way and took a long swig. "I have tried to be patient. I have tried to give you the benefit of the doubt time and time again, Matty, but I am very afraid you have inherited Giancarlo's death wish and I no longer know what to do with you."

Matteo felt the blood drain from his face. "I admit for the last couple of years I have been out of control. I had lost my way. But I am back. I have spent the last two weeks laying some brilliant groundwork to win this deal. Luxe will choose us."

"*If* Warren Davis does not eliminate us from the process after he finds out you have been screwing his daughter. *If* Daniel Williams doesn't make such a stink Luxe can't help but eliminate us."

His jaw hardened. "Quinn will not let that happen. She knows the right choice."

"She is compromised."

"She is going to recuse herself. And she will make her thoughts known. I know her."

"That doesn't mean the committee will go her way."

"I will convince them when I'm in that room."

Riccardo's lip curled. "Do you really think I should let you walk into that pitch given everything that's happened? If I were a smart man I would end this and do it myself."

Matteo's jaw tightened. "If you are a smart man you'll keep with the plan. I know the company. The players... I will win this."

His brother shook his head. "I must be mad."

"You need to trust me."

Riccardo paced to the other side of the terrace and stood looking out at the glasslike surface of the pool. When he turned back, his face was grim. "So help me God, Matty, it will not be just our business relationship that's in jeopardy if you let this family down."

A potent surge of anger raged through Matteo. He strode forward until he was toe-to-toe with his brother. "You always think I care less, Riccardo. That everyone cares less than you do. Well, you'd be surprised if you dug deep. Because I care. I care more than almost any damn person in this company." He pointed a finger at him. "I will win this for you, but on my own terms. Quinn Davis is nonnegotiable. Take it or leave it. That's my offer."

A long moment passed as Riccardo's hard gaze rested on his face.

"Do it then."

CHAPTER THIRTEEN

SUMMER IN CHICAGO got just about as hot as anywhere.

Quinn nudged the café door open with her hip, keeping her two iced coffees tucked to her chest as a wall of heat greeted her. The roiling, hundred-degree temperatures that had blanketed the city all weekend had stayed with them for the start of the workweek. She'd had a trickle of sweat rolling down her back not two minutes down the sidewalk.

She longed for the cooling breezes of the Caribbean. For the peace she'd found there.... Yes, they'd worked like dogs getting Le Belle Bleu up and running, but being with Matteo had made her feel settled in a way she'd never experienced before. They had been in their own private bubble, sheltered from the world. And maybe that was the problem. As soon as reality had hit, it had felt as if everything was falling apart.

She wound her way around a group of tourists, and headed for the gold facade of the Davis offices. The minute she'd taken one step into the O'Hare airport, Matteo's distant "I'll call you" ringing in her ears, the familiar anxiety had surfaced. The need to be someone she didn't want to be anymore. The uncertainty of who she wanted to be.

Then she'd faced off against her father. He'd been furious, as expected, questioning her commitment to the job with no regard for her personal feelings which had, in turn, prompted her anger and the devolution of their conversation into a whole lot of issues that had nothing to do with the deal. But she'd convinced him and the board to keep De Campo in the final two. Her father had appointed Walter Driscoll, Luxe's Chief Operating Officer, to take her place as the head of the committee, smoothed Daniel Williams's feathers, and her fall from grace had been cemented.

Now she could focus on doing her job. Except, she thought, lips compressing as she pushed her way through the revolving doors of the Davis building, everyone she worked with seemed to be reveling in the controversy, whispering behind her back. The tabloids had been having a field day, and worst of all, she missed Matteo like crazy.

She'd responded to his texts and calls to see if she was all right with polite if brief responses, as if her self-preservation was finally kicking in. Because if she'd had reservations before of things working out with a playboy like Matteo, the media coverage over the weekend had persuaded her she could never live in a fishbowl like this.

She exited the elevator on the executive floors, stopped at her PA's desk to drop off her coffee and pick up her messages, and shook her head as Kathryn held up a newspaper. "No more. I can't take it. Let it be a mystery to me."

"Perhaps you might prefer the life-size version lounging in your office," her PA purred.

Her heart jumped—raced in her chest like a jackhammer. She pressed the sheaf of papers against it. "Matteo is in my office?"

Kathryn nodded with a sly smile. "I didn't think he needed an appointment."

The prevailing attitude from everyone here all day. An intense, persistent interest in her personal life. Quinn the ice queen demystified as a human after all.

She stood there torn by how much she missed him and the desire to be her smart, rational self.

Kathryn flashed her an amused look. "Are you just going to leave him in there?"

She pursued her lips. "I'm trying to decide how the new Quinn would do this."

"I would start by closing the door," her PA said archly. "I like the new Quinn, by the way."

So did she. Although she was scary as hell and none too certain about the transformation.

Minimalist, fern-endowed and done in creamy, soft colors, her office was the perfect backdrop for a sensational-looking Matteo, draped across her desk, immersed in his smartphone. Dressed in dark pants and a light gray shirt with a contrasting darker charcoal tie, he looked like a cool, elegant drink of water.

She stopped inside the door and stuck her hands on her hips. "The pitch is not until Friday, you know."

He looked up and smiled that slow, easy grin that made her already excited heart go pitter-patter. "I'm here to see you."

She swallowed. "You trying to stir up more gossip and speculation parking yourself in my office like this?"

He gave her an even look. "I'd prefer to pursue the real story."

Which is?

"Shut the door, Quinn."

She stepped backward and pushed it closed, if only to prevent even more gossip.

He tilted his head to one side. "When you've taken my calls you've been annoyingly brief. Same with your texts. How am I supposed to know how you are if you won't talk?"

She shook her head, trying desperately not to fall into the trap that was Matteo because therein lay disaster. "Hasn't any of this craziness convinced you I was right in St. Lucia? This has to end?"

"Was *I* not clear enough we are going to work through this together?"

She sank her teeth into her bottom lip. Tucked the papers under her chin.

"Come here." He held out a hand and dammit if her feet didn't obey as if she was a trained animal. He smelled like spice and Matteo and when he tucked her between his legs and pushed her hair out of her face, it was the most right place on earth.

"First of all," he murmured, holding her gaze, "thank you again for ensuring De Campo's position in the pitch."

"It was the right thing to do."

"Secondly," he drawled, "I know you wanted me to say I was falling in love with you the night of the party. But I need to do things in my own time, Quinn. I have baggage too."

Her stomach did a loop-the-loop, ending up somewhere in the base of her abdomen. "I don't know how to play this game," she said huskily. "I need more, Matteo, to hang in here with you because right now this is all too much for me."

His eyes flashed. "What do you need me to say?"

She shook her head. She didn't even know.

"This isn't about the deal, Quinn," he said harshly. "I could pull De Campo out of it but it still wouldn't help with your trust issues."

"*Earned* trust issues."

He sighed. Lifted his hands to cradle her jaw, his smoky eyes holding hers. "I'm crazy about you, Quinn. I'm falling so hard it terrifies me. But this is a place I've never been before. You have to cut me some slack."

She felt her insides liquefy. "How are two commitment-phobes supposed to make this work?"

"Because it's you and me," he said softly. "And we are perfect together."

If anyone could have expected her to hold up after that, they were sadly mistaken. She rose on tiptoe, set her mouth to his and let her kiss show him how much she'd missed him. It was about two seconds before it burst into full-on flames. Matteo made a sound low in his throat and set her away from him. "If you want a decrease on the gossip you'd better cut back on that." He rubbed a hand across his jaw. "Please tell me you don't have plans for tonight."

"I do," she said with a nod. "With my bathtub. I could possibly amend it to include you."

The slow smile that stretched his lips pulled her insides tight. "I will make it worth your while, *cara*."

The new Quinn was fully in evidence as they left the office just after five. They stopped at a local grocery store, bought some cheese Matteo knew far more about than she did and a bottle of wine and took them back to her penthouse apartment in the Loop.

Far more than she needed with three bedrooms and an impossibly gorgeous view of the skyline, it had been an investment. Matteo walked to the edge of the lushly landscaped terrace and took in the view as she worked the cork out of the Pinot Noir he'd chosen.

"So how did your conversation with your father really go?"

She'd given Matteo the glossed over version of her no-holds-barred confrontation with Warren. "He thinks my judgment is way off." She poured the wine and walked over to hand him a glass. "He thinks you're using me to get the contract."

He winced. "Quinn—"

She held up a hand. "I know it's not true and I told him that. I also told him I needed him to be more of a father than mentor sometimes. That the tough love can be too much."

"And what did he say to that?"

Her mouth twisted in a wry smile. "I think he was flabbergasted. He thinks I'm as tough as him which clearly I am not." She shrugged. "He also pointed out I am not the best of communicators."

Matteo's face softened. "We'll call that an understatement."

"I also told him about Julian."

"Did he have any idea?"

"I think he didn't want to have any idea. He was horrified. But I think maybe it made him understand me a bit more. Understand why I've been the way I've been. Done the things I have."

He stepped forward, slid a hand behind her neck and pulled her into him. "You see? It wasn't that hard."

His heat, his strength enveloped her, swept over her like an elemental necessity of life she couldn't do without. She reached up and cupped his jaw in her hand. "I can't do another Julian, Matteo. If you leave now, nobody gets hurt."

He shook his head. "Getting hurt is part of life. But I am not going anywhere and neither are you. We are going to do this together. *Capisci?*"

Tears stung her eyes. "Yes."

He swept her up into his arms and carried her inside. She guided him to the master bedroom with soft, husky instructions. Peeled the clothes from his taut, muscular body with hands that shook with emotion. She wanted, needed him to possess her, to fill the void inside so badly it hurt.

He divested her of her clothes in a haphazard, completely un-Matteo-like fashion. His urgency should have frightened her, set off the old alarm bells. Instead she urged him on with husky commands. Told him how much she wanted him. Needed to know he could possess her completely, that she could give herself to him without reservation.

That she had the power of surrender.

He sensed it. Pushed her further. Set his hand to the small of her back and held her firmly against the mattress while his other hand slipped between her legs and brought her to hot, wet readiness.

"Matteo," she groaned, wild for him. "I need you."

The sound of foil ripping filled the air. He came back to her, slid a hand under her stomach, lifted her so he could bring the thick, insistent pressure of him against her pulsing core.

"You want me to take you," he rasped.

She gasped as he brushed the wide tip of his erection back and forth along her aching flesh. "Yes, now, please…"

He took her with a powerful thrust that stole the breath from her lungs. He was dominant, fully in control, using her body for his pleasure. His palm on her back held her secure, made her take all of him, but it was her pleasure, too. She felt him everywhere, stroking into her. Wildly excited, she pushed her hips up, meeting him stroke for stroke, murmuring her appreciation as he took her higher, gave her more.

When she couldn't take it, when she begged him in broken pleas to make her come, he flipped over on his back, his arm banded around her waist so she came with him. He was still buried deep inside her and brought his thumb to her clitoris. Maddeningly, insistently, he rotated against her pulsing flesh until she screamed, hurtling into the most intense orgasm he'd ever given her.

His big body pulsed inside of her, his hands clamped down on her flesh as he groaned and came. Made her his from the inside out.

They fell into a hot bath, had their wine and cheese on the bed. Then he wrapped her in his arms and held her. It was perfect, so perfect Quinn stayed awake long after Matteo's raspy snore sounded in her ear.

Maybe it was the lingering effect of always waiting for

the penny to drop—maybe it was because her father had pretty much said she and Matteo wouldn't last. But she couldn't help but wish he'd offered to walk away from the pitch. Had made his feelings for her that clear.

But he was right. She had to learn to deal with her trust issues. She needed to have faith in him. The problem was, she was still very, very new at this faith thing.

CHAPTER FOURTEEN

MATTEO WAS ADDING some last-minute statistics to his pitch presentation over coffee on Quinn's terrace when his mobile pealed, wrecking his concentration. He glanced at the screen. It was Gabriele.

"This better be good," he barked into the phone. "As you know my future with the De Campo family rests on me nailing this presentation tomorrow."

"No pressure there," his perfectly controlled, sanguine brother came back, rich amusement flavoring his tone. "Win and De Campo moves to another level entirely, lose and you are the permanent black sheep."

Matteo scowled. "You called for a reason?"

"I need you down here for a meeting today. I finally nailed an audience with the liquor board. The director had a last-minute cancellation."

Matteo pulled the phone away from his ear and stared at it. "You want me to fly to California *today* for a meeting?"

"A late afternoon meeting and dinner. You can head back first thing in the morning in plenty of time for the pitch in the afternoon. Rehearse on the jet."

He brought the phone back to his ear. "No way, *fratello*."

"I need you there, Matty. The director is a woman, apparently she knows you."

Matteo stood up and paced to the edge of the terrace. "I've stopped renting myself out as a stud, Gabe."

"Her name is Katlyn Jones. Remember her?"

Ah. He did. She'd been at a couple of parties he'd attended with his Hollywood ex.

"You're killing me, Gabe."

"Two years, Matty. Two years I've been waiting for this. To get them listening about the Malbecs."

"Two years I've been in purgatory, *fratello mio*."

"So we'll both win. Be here for two. I promise I'll get you back in time."

The line went dead. He dialed their pilot with a low curse, then his PA and went inside to change. Texted Quinn his whereabouts from the cab to the airport. And thought about the doubts he still saw in her eyes every time the contract came up. Since he was now sure he was fully, irrevocably in love with her, perhaps he needed to do something to demonstrate exactly how serious he was.

Quinn let herself in the penthouse, juggling an armful of groceries, her heart thumping in that ridiculous way it did any time she was about to see Matteo. She had taken the rather risky step of attempting to cook dinner for him given he'd been working until all hours getting ready for the pitch and as far as she could see, not eating very much. Risky when it happened she couldn't cook at all. But being with Matteo these past few weeks had inspired her to try a lot of new things. To push beyond who she'd thought she was.

She deposited the groceries on the counter and headed out to the terrace where Matteo preferred to work. They'd agreed he would stay with her until the pitch was over and take it from there. Figure out their schedules. But the door to the outdoor space was locked and there was no sign of him.

Figuring he'd gone for a run after the heat of the day, she slipped on an apron in the kitchen and started the water boiling. How hard could pasta be? Boil the water and put the pasta in. Throw it against the wall, apparently. But dicing? That was a foreign language. She took a wild guess and started chopping the vegetables into bite-size pieces. Thought how quiet, how lacking in life the apartment was without Matteo in it. How much she wanted him to come home so she could tell him about the insane step she'd taken of contacting the adoption agency to get in touch with her birth parents. Who knew where it was all going to end, but at least she might get some closure.

Butterflies swooped through her stomach. She shooed them determinedly away. Baby steps, that's how she was going to do this. With Matteo too. The scariest part was how easily she could see him fitting into her life. Last night he'd started talking about how he'd love a house in Lincoln Park, and it had not been a stretch to picture herself living there with him. Which wasn't baby steps at all. It was a huge, monstrous step that should have made her run, terrified. Except she hadn't.

She reached for the prosciutto rather than address the adrenaline surging through her. She loved him. She finally understood what it was that had been missing with Julian. How your heart could feel so empty with one person and so full with another. How when it was right, it was just right.

When the pasta sauce was done and "reducing" in the pan, she went into the bedroom to change. The clock on the bedside table read 8:00 p.m., which made her frown because surely Matteo should be back from a run by now? She reached for her Harvard sweats hanging over a chair. Noticed Matteo's overnight bag that had been lying in the corner was gone.

Her stomach seized. She strode into the bathroom. His toiletries were missing from the counter. She went into the living room and checked the table where he kept his laptop. Gone.

He was gone.

A buzzing sound filled her ears. Julian had walked out the door that day to Boston as if it was a run-of-the-mill trip to see his brother. And he'd never come back. Bile rose in the back of her throat. Had Matteo left her?

She gave her head a violent shake. That wasn't him. He wouldn't do that to her. She picked up her mobile and called him. Got his voice mail. Checked her email and texts to make sure she hadn't missed anything.

Nothing.

She thought about calling his PA but it was late and it didn't seem appropriate at this time of night, so she showered, turned the stove off and sat down to wait with a glass of wine. Ten o'clock passed. Eleven. She tried him again and got his voice mail. Surely if there had been some sort of emergency he would have called?

Eyes burning, head throbbing, she went into the kitchen, dumped dinner into the garbage and brushed her teeth. Told herself to stay calm, that there must be some explanation for this. People didn't just walk out on you.

When she came out of the bathroom, her phone was beeping. She snatched it up and pulled up the text message. It was from Matteo.

Saw you called. Can't talk now. I need to talk to you before the pitch tomorrow. I'll pick you up for a coffee before?

She stared at the message. For a good two or three minutes she just stared at it. Then it hit her. He was dumping her. He was about to accomplish his goal of winning the Luxe contract, so why keep her around any longer? It was just like it had been with Julian. Once she'd outlived her usefulness to him, once he'd forged the contacts he'd needed to with the Davis elite, he'd left.

But why now? Why hadn't he just waited until the pitch was over? Had the guilt gotten to him?

She turned off the lights and slipped into bed. Tears slid down her face—hot, silent. She didn't understand any of it. Didn't understand how her emotions, her instincts could be so wrong.

But she would not let another man break her. She was stronger than that. It's just that she should have known. She really should have known.

CHAPTER FIFTEEN

LIGHT FILTERED THROUGH the floor-to-ceiling windows of Quinn's bedroom, ushering in a new day. Head throbbing, she swiped at her alarm, rolled out of bed and stumbled to the bathroom for a shower. The thought of walking into that pitch room made her feel ill. The coffee with Matteo more so. If he dumped her today, she wasn't sure she was ever going to trust herself again. She had been so sure he was the one.

She pushed shampoo through her hair. Tried to jolt her brain out of the fog it was in. But all she could do was wonder why. What part of her was so deeply bruised, so inherently defective that everyone always left? Her birth parents. Julian. Now Matteo. What was it about her that made them change their minds?

She rinsed her hair, dried herself off and walked into the bedroom, stumbling over the clothes she'd kicked off last night. Her brain on automatic pilot, she stopped in front of the dresser and reached for underwear. Froze at the glint of metal on the top of the dresser.

Matteo's watch. Her heart jumped. *He would never leave something with such sentimental value anywhere unless he intended on coming back.*

Her mind whirling, she turned to the closet and pulled out a blouse. Stopped dead in her tracks when she saw Matteo's favorite suit hanging at the end of the row of her clothes. His lucky suit. The suit he'd been going to wear to the pitch.

Something like hope sprang to life inside her.

I am not going anywhere and neither are you. We are going to do this together. Capisce?

She'd believed him when he'd said it. She'd promised to believe in him. So what was she doing? What if she was wrong? What if he hadn't left?

I need to talk to you before the pitch tomorrow... What did that mean?

What if her past was eating her alive?

Wasn't it time she started believing in something?

Matteo entered the boardroom on the fifty-fifth floor of Davis Investments ten minutes late from a delayed landing, with the tense stance of a man ready to do battle. He was poised to annihilate the past. To right everything that had been wrong and secure his future with Quinn.

He had gone through the presentation with Gabe. It was perfect. He had spent the flight back imprinting every detail on his brain so he could focus on selling it. If this didn't win it for De Campo, nothing would.

Adrenaline firing through him, determination tightening every muscle with purpose, he greeted Walter Driscoll, Luxe's COO and the new head of the decision committee. Shook hands with the others, including Margarite and Warren Davis. It wasn't until he stopped to press a kiss to Quinn's cheek that he noticed she was all wrong. There were big dark bags under her eyes, they were puffy as if she'd been crying and her gaze was so packed full of emotion, he didn't know which one to choose.

"What's wrong?"

Her gaze fell away from his. "Daniel Williams is right after you. You should get started."

He stepped closer. "Quinn, what's wrong?"

She shook her head. Stepped back. "You should start."

He walked to the front of the room, pushed a button on his laptop to project his presentation on to the screen and tried to ignore how the woman he was now convinced he loved beyond a shadow of a doubt looked as if she might cave in at any minute.

Walter Driscoll nodded for him to start. He began, training his gaze on the first slide. Channeling the mood he wanted to create. Focusing on the presentation he could not lose. Heads were nodding, eyes flashing with the recognition of what De Campo could bring to the table as he worked through it—the wines, the restaurant experience, the revolutionary work Gabe was doing in Napa. But the further he got into the presentation, the farther Quinn slid down into her chair, as if it were physically painful for her to be sitting there.

Something inside him snapped. He clicked to the next section of the PowerPoint and set the remote down. "Would you mind," he asked Walter, "if I borrowed Quinn for a moment?"

Walter frowned. "You have fifteen minutes left to make your case, Mr. De Campo. Use them as you will."

Matteo inclined his head toward Quinn whose eyes were as big as saucers. "Join me in the hallway for a moment?"

She started to protest, then a quick glance around the room at the undivided attention the two of them were generating brought her scrambling to her feet. "What are you doing?" she hissed as they walked out into the hallway and he shut the door. "You have at least a third of your presentation left."

He braced his palm against the wall. "Tell me what's wrong."

"Matteo, you need to get back in there and—"

"Not until you tell me why you look like crap."

"Where were you?"

His gaze sharpened. "In California with Gabe like my text said."

She stared at him. "The only text I got was the one that said we needed to talk."

He frowned. "I sent one in the morning before I left. Told you I'd be back today in time for the pitch."

"I never got it."

His mind whirled in a race against time. "Where did you think I was?"

"I thought you'd left."

"Left?"

She squeezed her eyes shut and leaned back against the wall. "The first I knew my marriage had ended was when Julian sent movers on a Saturday morning when he was supposed to be in Boston watching a ball game."

His jaw dropped. "You think I would have walked out like that? Dammit, Quinn, has this week not convinced you of how I feel? I was talking about buying houses with you, for God's sake."

She pressed her palms to her face. "I came home so excited to cook a meal for you. I was so hurt when you weren't there. I didn't get that text. I wasn't thinking rationally. All your things were gone. Then I saw Giancarlo's watch this morning, and your suit, and I told myself I needed to trust you. That for once I needed to have faith in someone." She locked her gaze on his. "Because if it isn't you, Matteo, I won't ever have it."

His heart contracted into a tight fist in his chest. "Do you think a confirmed bachelor starts making plans to buy a house with a woman he isn't crazy about?"

"You were very casual about it."

"I was fishing. Seeing what you thought."

"Oh." A tiny smile curved her lips. "Sometimes I'm not so good at the subtle."

"You don't say." He shook his head. "You operate with all the subtlety of an 18-wheeler."

The vulnerability staining her green eyes tore at his heart. He uttered a low curse. "You are killing me right now, Quinn. I have a very beautiful, very *you* rock in my pocket I was going to give to you in a very romantic proposal after this presentation to prove I love you no matter what happens with this deal. Do *not* make me do this now."

Her eyes rounded. "You have a ring in your pocket?"

"Yes." He put her away from him with a grimace. "Now if you could please wipe the thought from your head, preferably until tonight when I can do it right, I will go and try to secure our future with the ten minutes I have left."

"I'm not sure I can do that," she whispered.

"Work it out," he came back grimly.

She followed him back into the room. Heart racing, he tore ruthlessly through the rest of the presentation in just enough time to get to the last slide, take five minutes of questions and look around the room. All the committee members were smiling except for the cagey Luxe head chef. He exhaled deeply. He'd done all he could. And when it came down to it that's all a man could do. Lay down your best and hope it was enough.

Walter Driscoll thanked him and said he'd be in touch within the week. Matteo shook hands with the others, gathered his things and gave Quinn a pointed look. "Time for a coffee?"

Quinn tried not to think about the ring as she dropped her things off in her office and rode the elevator to the ground floor with Matteo. But she was walking on air and dammit, the man she was crazy about had a ring in his pocket. How was she supposed to pretend it didn't exist?

Her heels clicked on the pavement as they walked outside, her love for this man bigger than all of it. Bigger than the vibrant city that pulsed around them. Bigger than the sunshine beating down on their shoulders, gilding everything in a warm golden glow.

Bigger than the pain of the past.

She tugged on his hand as he dragged her toward the coffee shop on the corner and dug in her heels.

"I can't."

He eyed her. "Can't what?"

She pulled in a breath. "I can't go for a coffee with you when I know you have a ring in your pocket. It is physically impossible."

He lifted a brow. "And what would you have me do? Give it to you now?"

Her lips curved. "Yes."

"You really want to ruin the proposal I had planned?"

"Yes." *Definitively yes.*

All the blood seemed to rush from her head as he reached into his jacket pocket and pulled out a box. And there on Michigan Avenue, one of Chicago's busiest streets, with people streaming by in all directions, he got down on one knee.

A woman walked by, openly ogling the beautiful, charismatic man at her feet, and yes, he was that; yes, he was gorgeous and one of the world's most notorious playboys, but he was so much more than that. He was brilliant in so many different ways he made Quinn's head spin. He was also deep, a philosopher beyond his years and he'd shown her who she truly was.

She was not Quinn the ice queen. She was a woman capable of loving this man with everything she had.

Her heart tattooed itself across her chest, beating a frantic dance as he opened the box to reveal a jaw-droppingly beautiful square-cut emerald surrounded by a band of sparkling white diamonds.

"Your eyes," he said simply. "When they're spitting fire at me, they're the most gorgeous thing I've ever seen."

A little old lady and her husband started to skirt around them. Then she pulled to a halt, her eyes widening. "Look, he's proposing."

Her husband tugged on her arm. "So let him. They don't need an audience."

"They're standing on Michigan Avenue, aren't they?" The blue-haired old lady stood to the side and crossed her arms over her chest. "You just keep going." She nodded to Matteo. "Don't mind us."

Matteo grimaced up at Quinn. "Nice idea of yours, this one."

"Just spit it out," she returned, a smile stretching her lips. "You're used to an audience aren't you?"

"You," he murmured meaningfully, as more people stopped and joined the old couple, "will pay for that later."

Her smile grew even bigger. He took her hand in his. Her eyes widened. Mr. Cool and Collected, who had just put in a rock solid performance under immense pressure the likes of which most men would have buckled underneath, was nervous. The tremor in his strong hand holding hers was enough to make her want to melt to the pavement.

His gaze held hers. "I had no idea what I was looking for until I met you," he said quietly. "I was so lost I didn't know how to find my way back. And you—you have given me clarity in a way I never thought possible, Quinn Davis. You've made me see the man I want to be. How the mistakes I've made have shaped me into who I am." His fingers tightened around hers. "So no matter what happens with this pitch, I have already won the biggest prize."

Her need for air came out as a sob.

"Marry me," he murmured. "Marry me so we can spend the rest of our lives together."

Another sob filled the air, this time from an anonymous woman burying her head in a hankie.

Quinn focused on Matteo. "You make me believe I can do anything. That anything is possible. You make me so much better than I am."

"That's impossible," he said softly, "because you are perfect to me."

A lone tear blazed a trail of fire down her cheek. "I love you."

His gray eyes darkened. "Me, too, *tesoro*. Now give me an answer before this turns into any more of a public spectacle."

"Yes." The word came out more as a croak than an answer, but he got the message and slid the ring on her finger.

"You see," the old lady murmured, "that's how it's done."

The crowd broke out into applause, whistling their approval as Matteo stood and pulled her into his arms.

"I suppose she wants a Hollywood-style kiss," he murmured.

"Undoubtedly." Quinn shot a sideways look at the local news photographer who'd arrived just in time to capture the action. "But after this you're announcing your official magazine-cover retirement."

"I'm good with that." He took her mouth in a kiss that was front-page-worthy and then some. Then he whisked her off on the De Campo jet for the champagne celebration Lilly had planned in New York—the one part of his proposal Quinn hadn't managed to upend.

Lilly and Alex whisked Quinn off when they arrived in the garden, lit with lanterns on a sultry New York summer evening. Riccardo poured the men a scotch. "You know I hate this stuff," Matteo muttered, wrapping his fingers around the glass.

"Be a man," Riccardo taunted. "Walter Driscoll just called. Said he'd been trying to reach you."

Matteo froze. "Have they made a choice?"

"Si." His elder brother swirled the amber liquid around the base of the crystal tumbler. "Want to know?"

His heart stalled in his chest. "Dammit. Do not play with me, Riccardo."

A wide smile split his elder brother's harshly carved face. "You did it, *fratello*. The Luxe contract is ours."

He felt the ground sway under his feet. Three years he had worked to put the past behind him. And just like that, it was done.

"Driscoll said you were brilliant." Something like pride glittered in Riccardo's eyes. "That you made it impossible for them to choose anyone else."

Matteo's heart jump started again. "So we're even then?"

His brother inclined his head. "You were right. I should have let you do it your way." He paused. "Maybe that's the way I should have played it from the start."

"And upset your idea of how the world should be?" Matteo lifted a brow. "Surely not, oh, powerful one."

Riccardo smiled and nodded toward Quinn. "You didn't waste any time putting a ring on her finger. She must be good in bed."

Matteo's fist was cocked and ready to strike when his brother held his up his hand, laughing. "Mine was, too. She was also a hell of a lot more than that. Really, Matty, when are you going to learn I'm just pulling your strings?"

Matteo lowered his fist and scowled. "Maybe if you chose your moments with a bit more finesse…"

"What fun would that be?"

Matteo went off to join his fiancée rather than spar with Riccardo. "Where is buffer brother?" he asked Alex. "He's needed. Badly."

"Getting us something to drink." She jabbed him in the ribs. "Nice work on the photo. It was drop-dead fantastically romantic, Matty. Phone's been ringing off the hook."

They could all wait. He drank his fill of his ridiculously beautiful soon-to-be wife in the cherry-red cocktail dress she wore. It fit perfectly with the third part of his proposal plan that included Quinn alone in his rose-strewn loft Lilly and Alex had done up, with her wearing the ring and nothing else.

Quinn flushed, as if she knew exactly where his head was. "He has a way with words. I think the little old lady watching would have dumped her husband for him."

Gabe came outside, a bottle in his hand. "Congratulations," he murmured, giving Matteo a hug. "I heard the news."

Silence fell over the group. Lilly gave Gabe an expectant look. "I think we should do the toast."

Gabe handed Matteo the bottle. He felt the blood drain from his face as he read the label. *Bianco Frizzante Giancarlo.*

"You finished it," he said slowly, his fingers caressing the elegant slim cylinder.

Gabe nodded. "It's magnificent."

Matteo blinked back the moisture that stung his eyes, his heart feeling too big for his chest. "I need a moment."

He walked to the side of the terrace and looked out over Lilly's wildflower garden. The wine had been his and Gabe's tribute to Giancarlo. They had created it together. But to open it meant acknowledging his friend was gone. To finally let him go.

He wasn't sure he could do it.

Quinn appeared at his side. Took his hand in hers, pried his fingers open and wrapped hers around them. "You loved him, Matteo. This is such a beautiful thing you and Gabe have done for him. Open it and let him go."

His fingers tightened around hers. She was right. It was time. And he could let go, he realized, because Quinn was his future.

They walked back to the others. Gabe uncorked the wine and poured them all a glass. Matteo lifted his. "To my past, to my brother, Giancarlo, who will always be with me." He swallowed past the thickness in his throat. "This one is for you."

The wine tasted fruity and life-affirming on his tongue. *Perfetto.*

He shifted his gaze to the woman at his side. "And to my future. The woman I want to spend the rest of my life with. *Tu sei il mio cuore.*" He leaned down to kiss her. "You are my heart, Quinn Davis."

She gave him a misty-eyed smile. "Really, Matteo De Campo. You are much too silver-tongued."

But she kissed him anyway, her lips clinging to his in a promise of forever. Because for him and Quinn, the journey was just beginning.

* * * * *

MILLS & BOON®
By Request

RELIVE THE ROMANCE WITH THE BEST OF THE BEST

A sneak peek at next month's titles...

In stores from 7th September 2017:

- **His Sweet Revenge** – Miranda Lee, Lucy Monroe & Maya Blake
- **The Duchess Diaries** – Merline Lovelace

In stores from 5th October 2017:

- **Irresistibly Exotic Men** – Paula Roe, Anne Fraser & Laura Iding
- **Bombshell Baby** – Rebecca Winters, Marie Ferrarella & Caroline Anderson

Just can't wait?
Buy our books online before they hit the shops!
www.millsandboon.co.uk

Also available as eBooks.